"You said bodies. What bodies?" Rog "You fool," Novara answered. hands did not pull Roger into a walk but stood on his toes, his back pinned agair Our prey was cornered, nowhere to go with the fire escape above it. And you come stumbling out and land on top of the beast. I should have let it kill you. The loss would have been worth the sacrifice to end the hunt."

"What are you talking about?"

"I saved the one, I think. The other, may God have mercy on her soul. But the beast just kept talking, taunting me…"

"What are you talking about? What was taunting you?"

Roger never saw the hand. All he knew was one moment he was standing up trying to understand what Novara was saying and the next he was on the ground, his cheek numb and eye throbbing.

"Do not get in my way again, priest, or I will let it kill you. Is that what you want, to die along with your friend? If you can't do this, I will hunt alone."

Roger watched Novara stomp away, wondering if he had served enough penance for whatever sin caused God to assign him this task.

Copyright © 2015 by Kirk Dougal
Cover Design by David Dodd
ISBN 978-1-946025-59-3
All rights reserved. No part of this book may be used or reproduced in any manner whatsoever without written permission except in the case of brief quotations embodied in critical articles and reviews.
For information address Crossroad Press at 141 Brayden Dr., Hertford, NC 27944
A Mystique Press Production - Mystique Press is an imprint of Crossroad Press.
www.crossroadpress.com

Crossroad Press Trade Edition

DREAMS OF IVORY & GOLD

BOOK 1 OF THE FALLEN ANGELS TRILOGY

BY KIRK DOUGAL

PROLOGUE

*P*ain.
The hunger rips at me. The gnawing pulls from side to side, following its own will, forcing me to trail behind. It rakes bloody chunks from my body until every moment is agony. I need to feed.

Pain.

I am blind. The light that once warmed me now scars my eyes, searing them and driving me away to cower in never-ending darkness. The part of me that ached for the light is dead, shrinking in the distance as I travel farther from it with each passing moment. Now my memories of the light hold no pleasure, no contentment, no comfort. I curse the light.

Pain.

I touch nothing. My fingers long for the feel of skin, the brush against a smooth cheek, the caress of hair cascading across my hands. I grope unfulfilled in the darkness.

Pain.

I remember the taste of her. The memory whips me faster after the urges, the void in my heart crying out for what I need to survive. A cruel twist of the light, holding out the chance to do its bidding and then casting me aside like a forgotten thought. All the more spiteful because what I now need to live is what caused the light to shun me. I gnash my teeth and bite only the darkness.

Pain is my new master. I embrace the agony and live within its walls, feeding in its wake, breeding with it until we are one and misery is our child. It spreads through me. I am the channel it uses—touching all it can grasp, seeing all within light and dark, and feeding on those that wish to spread life. In my dreams, I release pain and it causes the light to flicker, fluttering faster on the breeze until it is snuffed out, never to ignite again. And when all that was once dear to the Deceiver is destroyed, then he will remember what he has done to me, remember the one who once bowed to his wishes on willing knees.

He will remember me.

I am pain.

CHAPTER 1

NEW YORK, THURSDAY AFTERNOON

The TSA officer sat straighter on her stool as the passengers rounded the turn of the jet bridge and walked up the incline towards her station. The humidity of a New York City early summer swam through the hallway with the group, encircling them like fog rolling over the water, and pushed the air conditioner to its limit. The air hit her in the face and left the memory of a damp washcloth on her cheeks. She glanced down at her flight schedule and noticed the arrival was an international flight, originating out of London, and could contain passengers from anywhere in the world. Time to be serious.

"Good afternoon, ladies and gentlemen. Please have your passports in hand as you step through the scanner. You can help shorten any delays by having your paperwork ready before moving on to customs." She flashed her best smile in hopes that once, just once, she could process a group of passengers without half of them complaining about the wait.

The situation immediately went to hell-in-a-hand-basket as her grandmama liked to say. The first couple in line stopped on the threshold of the rectangular metal screener, the man patting his pockets while the woman searched through a purse the size of a small gym bag. Frantic whispers of "I gave them to you" followed by "No, you didn't" quickly led to the zipping open of the carry-on bags strapped over their shoulders. Meanwhile, the line behind them slowed and finally ground to a halt, the heat of anger and frustration adding to the rising temperature. The officer, on the verge of asking the couple to step to one side, stopped when the man let the jacket slung over his arm fall to the floor. Two passports slid out onto the worn carpet and lay there, harsh fluorescent lights glinting off the gold print in accusation. The woman huffed in victory and walked through the security gate while the man picked them up, a red bloom touching his cheeks.

"Sorry," he said, attempting a little boy grin. "It was a long flight home."

The security woman typed the couple's name in the computer and it came back clean. *Not that they wouldn't.* The woman smiled and handed back the passports. The system only held 3,500 names out of 30,000 suspected terrorists so the idea she might find someone at the gate using their real name bordered on the absurd. Oh well, the pay was decent and the government benefits were great.

She quickly settled into her routine—smiling, typing, smiling, and moving on. TSA and Homeland Security did not dictate a quota, per se, on the number of passengers from each flight she needed to ask to step behind her and meet her three burly co-workers for a more thorough inspection, but a higher count helped her appear vigilant for her personnel evaluation. Two men were easy calls: one whose trip started in Kuwait and another with the skin color and hair of someone born in the Middle East. Her grandmama, who still told plenty of stories about Alabama back before the Civil Rights marches and Miss Rosa, would have been appalled at the blatant profiling but the security guard knew the facts of life. And those facts said there were not a lot of blond-haired, blue-eyed Caucasians on the terrorist computer list.

The line dwindled until only one passenger remained to step through the detector. He hesitated for a moment, appearing to wait until he had her attention before walking forward. The light on top of the machine immediately flashed and the warning siren blared out into the narrow room, echoing back in waves. One of the other security guards behind her would now be on the telephone, describing everything that happened to someone in a room with a whole wall of monitors elsewhere in the terminal until the all-clear sign was given.

"Please forgive me," the man said while placing his passport and a small metal carrying case on the table in front of the security guard. His accent was noticeably Italian but not so thick she fought to understand him. "I haven't been to New York for a long time and I'm not sure if I came to the right gate."

The security woman felt at least one of the other guards walk up behind her and probably pose in some macho idea of protective menace, but she could not have cared less at the moment. The passenger's olive-colored skin perfectly complimented his black hair with just a hint of gray at the temples. Yet, it was his eyes she could not rip her gaze away from, held in place by the caramel depths only a couple of feet away, even though he did not look directly into hers. She found herself hoping the man would need to have enhanced search techniques used behind the screen and she was more than willing to volunteer for the duty. The guard behind her cleared his throat before she felt his elbow in her back. *Damn. They're going to jump my butt about this one in the break room.*

"Ah, yes, ah, hmm," she stammered. "Please leave the case and walk back through the detector."

The man's smile never wavered as he reached into his sport coat pocket and pulled out a key. Only then did she notice, with a little warmth rising in her cheeks, the handcuff and chain attached to the man's wrist.

The man left the case and key on the table and walked back and forth through the opening with the other security guard paralleling his movements, this time without the alarm tripping. The passenger returned to stand in front of her, but it took another elbow in the kidneys before she remembered to ask some questions. "Passport, please."

The heat rushed into her cheeks again when she realized the document was already in her hand. She flipped open the cover and noted the man's place of origin, Barcelona, with a large amount of travel stamps covering the other pages. *Greg Novara*. The issuing body for the passport threw cold water on her private thoughts, however.

"I'm sorry, Father Novara. This says you have diplomatic privileges through the Vatican. You should have come straight to the front of the line rather than waiting."

"Mister will be fine, Miss Jackson. I am not a priest. Besides, I did not want to cause a problem and since your 9/11 tragedy, I thought it might be best to wait my turn at the gate."

Jackson held back a giggle at hearing him read her name off the lapel tag on her uniform. She also wondered what her mama and grandmama would say if she converted from Southern Baptist to Catholicism. Religion would not be a problem; they would understand as soon as they saw those eyes. It seemed odd, though, that he never quite made eye contact with her, always looking just slightly above or to the side.

"Well then, Mr. Novara. I'll need to see what you have in your case and you can be on your way. I'm surprised someone from the embassy is not here to meet you. They usually prepare us for special arrivals. I can phone the office and ask if your escort has been delayed."

"No, there is no one to greet me. My trip was planned at the last moment, I'm afraid."

Then the man sighed, not a bored self-important sound, but one of resignation, as if what lay in the box was something he did not want to see himself. He touched a numbered keypad on the top of the case, spun the metal carrier around on the tabletop, and flipped open the lid.

Officer Jackson blinked and the guard behind her sucked in a breath as light glared back off the blade of a knife. No jewels bedecked the plain wrap around the hilt. Nor did any etchings decorate the curved, white blade. Her weapons identification training flashed through her thoughts and told her this was no ordinary knife. She sensed the blade had drunk deeply in blood, sucked the life from victims, and left the world cold in its wake. Dark stains on the leather told her she was right. A chill traveled down Jackson's back as she stared at the weapon, wondering how pain and sorrow could live in an inanimate object.

"What is it?" she asked, her voice barely above a whisper.

"A holy relic of the Church," Novara said, closing the lid with a snap. He breathed out as he spoke, pent-up force behind each word. Jackson studied the man, gazing into his face, searching for more of an answer. For the first time, she noticed the age written there, the tale of many years in each of the furrows in his forehead, the tiny wrinkles on his temples. The eyes appeared different now, still holding the unreachable depths she had wanted to swim in before, but now also reflecting the pain of the knife, an echo of the blade's soul-numbing sadness. She wanted to jump over the counter and cry on his shoulder but she did not know why.

"Makes my damn skin crawl." Officer Jackson recognized the deep bass of Jake's voice behind her. "What's it for?"

"The knife is a disturbing piece," Novara said. "Over a thousand years ago, it was used to sacrifice women in an effort to save their souls. It was found in a horde from Emperor Constantine, but most certainly from the Carthags originally." He shrugged as he spoke and a smile touched his lips again. But Jackson thought the humor had fled, leaving behind only the shadow of a grin. "The whole idea is odd when you think about it: A person must be killed in order to be saved."

"Why are you bringing it to the U.S.?" Jackson asked.

"The Pope recently raised Archbishop Atchison to the position of Cardinal. He is well known throughout the Church as a noted historian and his Eminence thought a private viewing would be a nice gesture of congratulations."

"Thank you for understanding, Mr. Novara. We will need a few minutes to fill out some paperwork and you can be on your way. I hope your stay in New York is a pleasant one."

"I hope so, too, Miss Jackson. I hope so, too."

CHAPTER 2

NOVARA, ITALY, 1408

Father Vittolo leaned back in his chair, the blanket draped over the slats as much a concession to his age as to the night's weather. His gaze followed the candle light playing across the manuscript on the table in front of him. A sigh escaped his lips and gnarled hands rose up to rub tired eyes before pulling the blanket against his shoulders again, a Sisyphean attempt to keep the chill from seeping deeper into his body. His eyes closed and he lost himself for a while in the rhythm of the rain on the roof.

Boom. Boom, boom. Boom, boom.

A cough wracked his body and the priest sat up, sleep clearing from his mind when he moved. Rain beat harder and thunder grew louder as the power of God played out in nature's music. The night demanded a roaring fire and thick blankets and Vittolo decided he had denied himself both for too long. He stood and turned toward the inviting bed.

Boom, boom, boom.

This time the priest realized the sound was not thunder rumbling in the distance. He shook his head even as cold feet took him down the hallway toward the door. *What kind of fool would dare the night in this storm?* He prayed he did not open the door for a madman.

Boom.

"Per favore! Per favore…"

The last cry finally added speed to his step. The plea rode on a female voice trailing off on such a note of despair, Vittolo wondered how any soul could feel so helpless. He flung open the door.

The night withdrew only a little from the candle he held in his hand, trying to suck the light from the wick and plunge the priest into its black grasp. Lightning flew across the sky, laughing at the dark in its fury, and exposed the world for a moment with the power of the sun.

And there she stood.

The girl hunched over with her arms wrapped around her stomach, water running from black hair flung forward over her face and revealing only a dirt-smudged chin. Mud clung to her skirt in such quantities Vittolo could not have guessed the color of the material if the material was not brown. That was all he had time to notice before the lightning passed and the night regained control. Before the rumble of thunder followed, however, he heard the girl whimper in pain.

"Come in, my child! Come in!" He braved the elements long enough to stick one arm out into the storm and pull her into the shelter of his home, only to be rewarded with half a drenched robe.

The girl staggered through the door and threatened to fall to her knees before the priest grabbed her by the elbows.

"Thank you, Father," she said, straightening up with his help. "I get tired so easily these days. And the pains…"

Vittolo did not listen to the young girl prattle on about how she felt. She wore the face of a girl—no, barely more than a child—yet beneath the mask of innocence sat the belly of a woman full of child.

"… and then it became so dark…"

"Child. Child!" The priest needed to raise his voice before the girl finally stopped her rambling. "Child, where is your husband?" He hoped his voice did not carry the doubt of the answer he dreaded.

"I have no husband, Father," she said, biting her lip until a line of red formed.

"My hands are tied then," Vittolo said, releasing the girl's arms and holding his hands away from his body. He hated the vision of Pilate springing into his thoughts, ceremoniously washing his hands of Christ's fate when he knew he could have stopped the crucifixion. "If the boy who did this to you will not accept the responsibility…"

"Aieee!" The girl doubled over as another contraction sent pain shooting through her body. "No boy," she panted once the worst of it abated. "No boy. There has been no man. Aieee!"

Father Vittolo did not move quickly enough to catch her as she fell to the floor in agony.

Vittolo stood in the corner of his bedroom, rainwater running from his hair and mixing with the sweat on his face. A fire roared in the hearth now, his pangs of guilt at keeping himself comfortable quashed by the girl's needs. Another scream echoed off the walls, bare except for the crucifix hanging in silent vigil above the bed. He sneezed in reply.

A woman stood up from the end of the bed and waddled across the room, sweat shining on her face from the heat. On the way she grabbed the nightshirt Vittolo had been about to put on before the girl arrived and the blanket off the chair.

"Father, please, go to the other room and change. You must stay warm or you'll become sick and then I'll have two people to watch over instead of one."

Vittolo accepted the bundle before tilting his head in the direction of the bed.

"How is the girl, Signora Francesca?"

The midwife turned to look at the bed as well. Her daughter sat on the edge, holding the pregnant girl's hand and whispering words of encouragement through a smile. The grin disappeared, however, when she glanced up at her mother and the priest.

"She's so young, Father. Out traveling on a night like this, in her condition... I'll do everything I can for her, but I'm afraid we'll need your help before the end of the night." The woman turned to look Vittolo in the eye as she raised a finger toward heaven. Another scream of pain called her attention back to the bed. "I hope you can do that, Father. I mean, no husband here with her..."

Vittolo knew the midwife was fishing for information and anything he told her would travel around their tiny village three times by the end of breakfast. A virgin birth! More than likely the girl had found herself in a bad situation, another sinner in need of redemption. Yet, on the slimmest of chances she told the truth... the possibilities! But, steps needed to be taken, processes the Church must fulfill, questions searching for answers—he must have time. Time he would not have if the midwife spread word of his taking in the mother of a bastard child. His gaze rose to the crucifix. God would need to forgive his buying that time.

"The husband is not with us, Signora Francesca," Vittolo said, almost grinning at the turned phrase keeping his words from an outright lie, no matter which way the answers fell. "That's about all I was able to get from her before I ran to bring you back. I don't even know her name."

"Ah," the woman said with a knowing wince. "The Black Death. Probably trying to return to her home in the country after her man died. I'll spread the word tomorrow to the nearby villages and see if someone knows who she is." The girl screamed again. "Now, go on, Father, and let me see to the poor thing."

"Father. Father."

Vittolo felt himself drawn from sleep for the second time on this storm-ridden night, a dark and soundless path when compared to the visions marching through his thoughts. That he had been able to doze at all showed just how tired he had been.

"Father. Wake up, Father."

Now a hand on his shoulder helped pull him along faster, reminded him of the aches in his joints and the pain in his back where the chair dug into him.

"Yes, Signora Francesca. Is it over?" He sat up before noticing the bundle wrapped in the midwife's arms.

"Yes. He's a fine boy, as strong and healthy as any mother could pray for and as beautiful as the sunrise."

Vittolo could not help but notice the sadness in her voice.

"And the mother?"

"She's gone, Father. I've never seen anything like it before. The closer he came, the farther she fell until it seemed her last breath was his first. It's not right he should've lost both mother and father before he ever knew them."

The two of them stared at the baby for a few moments, both caught up in his sleeping face.

"Who shall look after him now, Father Vittolo? My daughter and I can…"

"No, Signora. The Church will raise him." He had answered impulsively, realizing the many questions needing asked, but the words felt right in his mouth as he said them.

Disappointment fell over the woman's face but she did not argue the decision.

"He will need a name."

This time Vittolo did not answer as quickly. He weighed the good with the bad and wondered which way the scales would fall. They finally tipped in his mind.

"We'll name him after his Eminence. His name shall be Gregor."

CHAPTER 3

NEW YORK, THURSDAY AFTERNOON

"I still think it was a trick question."

Two of the other priests laughed while the fourth leaned back quietly in his chair, a grin spreading across his lips.

"Of course it was a trick question, Ron," said one of the laughing priests. "Otherwise it wouldn't be a game."

"The question was: Who was the first *American* saint? It said nothing about the person needing to be from North America," said the second. "Tell him, Roger."

"Ian's right. That's why the correct answer is St. Rose of Lima," said the smiling priest. He stood up and began pacing back and forth with quick little steps, his hands gesturing in the air or brushing back his dark blond hair with excitement.

"Your answer, St. Frances Cabrini, the patron saint of immigrants, was the first U.S. citizen canonized for the works she performed during the Irish immigration rush… you know the orphanage she was sent to take care of didn't even exist when she arrived," Roger continued. "Anyway, the priests told Cabrini to go back to Italy but she stayed and helped thousands. Ah, but St. Rose of Lima fought her parents for years to join the Church. They wanted her to marry but she refused, spending almost ten years isolated in their house, helping anyone who would come to her. After she was finally allowed to join the order of St. Dominic, she began wearing a metal crown with barbs on the inside that cut into her scalp. She even slept on a bed made from stones and bits of broken glass. And she performed all of those works before she died at the age of thirty-one.

"The wording I chose was to prove the point our congregation is the whole world. Remember the Great Commission—'Go ye among all the peoples.' We aren't just shepherds to the flocks in Manhattan or New York or the United States. The world is our pulpit."

"And you wanted to win the game," Ron said, holding his hands up in surrender.

"Yes," Roger said over the laughter of the other priests, "and I wanted to win the game."

"That's the true lesson to be learned here," Ian said as he stabbed his finger playfully on the tabletop. "It's just not fun for us to play Church trivia games with you when Cardinal Atchison isn't here. We don't stand a chance without his help."

"Father Greene?"

Roger turned to look at one of the cathedral secretaries standing in the library doorway.

"Yes, Mrs. Branson?"

"I'm sorry to disturb you, Father, but the mother of one of the boys in your catechism class is on the phone. Should I take a message?"

"No, thanks. I'll follow you back to the office and take the call. We're done here."

The other three priests stood and the four of them left the library together. Roger slowed his pace so he could walk beside the youngest of the group.

"How are the preparations for your first service going, Ian?"

"I'm still really nervous about speaking in front of so many people, but I think I'm ready. The ideas you gave me on the scripture to use helped a lot. Thanks, Roger."

Father Greene gave a dismissive wave.

"Cardinal Atchison told me how much he's looking forward to Sunday before he left. He said he'll be back to see you no matter what happens at the conference. Just remember you have us, the Church, the Vatican, and his Eminence all behind you."

"Oh, I don't feel nervous at all now."

The two men laughed again as they rounded the corner of the hall.

Morgan glanced around the room for what she hoped was the last time and grimaced at the colors—again. She decided if old pastel paint sets were elephants, this room would be the hidden jungle valley where they all wandered to die. Blues, greens, and yellows—even some pinks—decorated the walls in a kaleidoscope of washed-out tints, one palette blending softly into the next so she could never be quite sure where one ended and the next began.

The color scheme continued down to the man seated across the desk from her, his light blue and white sweater vest nearly blending into the polo shirt beneath it. He did not need to stand up for her to know he wore a pair of khaki pants above a pair of well-polished penny loafers. She smiled at the thought he might actually put a penny in the tongue slot.

Her hands picked at lint on her skirt and jacket, tilting her head so the walls were no longer in sight. She also purposely kept her gaze off the clichéd couch underneath the window and instead turned her attention to the row of books prominently displayed on the corner of the desk. The doctor had written three of them and the others were by authors, "friends," he had met at various conferences.

Red flashed by the corner of her eye and she hooked the stray hairs back over her ear again. In an act of desperation for change during her time off, she had let her hair grow out from its normal short cut. She had tied the mass back into a pony tail before the meeting but already strands threatened to break loose and run wild, a rampaging red cascade flying in a thousand directions. The hue matched the color of the freckles marching across her cheeks and nose, marks she hated as a teenager, loathed as a twenty-something, and now hoped made her look younger than her thirty-six years.

"Morgan," the man said, drawing her attention. She stared at his bald head, tufts of black on the sides attempting to cover his scalp in a horrible three-fingered comb-over and losing the battle. He finally glanced up from the manila folder in his hands. "It's been six months since the shooting?"

"Six months next week, Doc."

He nodded and wrote something down in her file before tossing the folder up on his desk. "So how are we feeling?"

I imagine you're feeling pretty damn good, Doc. You get to go to work every day. "Good. Anxious to get back out on the job."

"I imagine so. But what I meant was: Is anything in particular bothering you right now? People? Situations?"

Morgan laughed. "I'm a divorced cop in my thirties with no children. My mother bothers me about my situation every day."

The psychiatrist shared a laugh with her. "Nothing unusual

about that." He never paused, his smile never slipping. "How're you sleeping?"

Morgan wondered briefly how he would have done interrogating a suspect. Keep prodding and use humor to keep them off balance. She decided he would do fine.

"Better. Good." She adjusted her seat and changed her crossed legs. "I mean, I haven't had trouble falling asleep for several weeks."

"But you're still not sleeping the whole night, are you? Did you try the sleeping pills I prescribed?"

Not on your life. I'd rather wake up screaming than be stuck in a drug-induced nightmare. "No, I haven't needed them. Besides, you know I don't like to take anything stronger than aspirin."

The psychiatrist leaned forward and glanced at his notes. "Ah, yes. Your brother and his hockey injury. Well, that's understandable." He flipped through four or five pages before closing the folder again and leaning back in his chair. "Well, policy says I should release you back to active duty but…"

Morgan felt the ache in her lungs and realized she had not taken a breath for quite a while. Her heart pounded in her chest with bone-rattling intensity. Suddenly she knew if she had to spend one more afternoon at home watching some mindless, surgery-enhanced bimbo on another nameless talk show, she really would need to talk to someone like the psychiatrist.

"… I just have this feeling you haven't been completely open with me during your sessions. I believe we still have some unresolved issues with your family dynamic and the circumstances surrounding the shooting." He sighed and leaned forward on his elbows. "Promise me you will talk with someone you trust—your family, a friend, your priest, anyone—if you begin to have problems again. And of course, you can always come to me."

For the first time since her lieutenant had ordered the counseling, Morgan felt ashamed at holding back from the psychiatrist. The concern for her well-being lay in his eyes like two still pools, untouched by ripples of accusation.

"I will, Doc. I promise."

They both rose and shook hands, the smile returning to his face.

"All right. Go on then, Detective Kelly," the psychiatrist said. "Go catch some bad guys."

CHAPTER 4

NEW YORK, THURSDAY AFTERNOON

Novara waited patiently to one side of the luggage carousel, his gaze dancing over the variety of different suitcases passing by his spot. His attention was drawn away for a moment when he noticed an older lady reach forward, her gray hair peeking out from underneath an old-fashioned pillbox hat, and try to pull off a large bag. She lost her balance and nearly stumbled onto the moving belt. Before he could step up and give her a hand, the man who had held up the line at the metal detector quickly retrieved the woman's case and sat the luggage down on its wheeled base beside her.

Novara found himself surprised at the act. The clichéd stereotype the world, and he himself, held of most New Yorkers was one of pushy, self-absorbed, money-driven Americans. The type was all he had ever seen of the tourists he had run into around the globe. Yet here was an act of kindness he had not expected, absent any reward except for a quick pat on the back and smile from his wife. Perhaps at least part of his stay would not be as bad as he had feared.

His garment bag swung into sight on the luggage merry-go-round with the matching soft leather suitcase only a few feet behind. He walked forward, settling his overnighter strap more firmly on his shoulder and gripping the metal briefcase tighter before grabbing the handles of the two bags.

"My, what lovely luggage," the woman said as she let go of her husband's arm and stretched out a tentative hand, letting her fingers delicately caress the garment bag. "Does the leather hold up well to the baggage handlers?"

"Yes, madam," Novara replied. A smile quickly leaped to his lips at this reinforcement of part of his previous view of Americans but he made sure not to make direct eye contact with her.

"Gary," the woman continued, pulling her husband around so he could see the bags as well. "With all our traveling, don't you think this is what we need?"

The man eyed the bags for a moment, his gaze taking in the bags with a look accustomed to appraising fine items. "Looks like Italian but the design is very conservative. They are older than they appear, aren't they?"

Novara held back laughter at the irony of the question. "Yes, I've had the bags for a long time."

The other man paused while he pulled four bags off the luggage conveyor. "Well, I think you're right, Hon, a set of those would be nice to have. Is the company that made them still in business?"

Novara did laugh this time. "In a sense. The bags were hand-stitched by priests-in-training at the Vatican. They were a gift from the Pope."

The man raised an eyebrow and gave out a low whistle, the sound stopping short when he finally noticed the metal briefcase handcuffed to Novara's wrist.

"Oh, how lovely," the woman said, oblivious to her husband's amazement. "We were in Italy, as well, when the new Pope was named. It was quite spectacular when the white smoke came out of the chimney."

"Oh, not the current pope," Novara said. "Pope Pius the Eleventh." He bent over and grabbed the handle of his suitcase, noticing the man's lips moving in silent rote. "Have a pleasant day."

As he walked slowly away from the couple, Novara heard the man begin talking to his wife, his voice trembling.

"That's impossible."

"What is, Gary? That we met someone who knows the Pope? Why, Susan once met..."

"Forget about Susan! He said those bags were a gift from Pope Pius the Eleventh."

"So?"

Novara slowed his pace even more, not wanting to walk completely out of earshot before the man finished.

"Have you forgotten where I went to school? They made us memorize the list of popes. Pope Pius XI died in the late 1930s! How old was that man!?"

Novara walked on, the smile widening out to a full-fledged grin. It disappeared, however, when he wondered if this was the only fun he would have on the trip.

Novara climbed out of the cab, his gaze wandering around the spikes, lifting with vaulted arches, and drinking in the sun reflecting off stained-glass windows, all while his head tilted farther and farther back. The spires reached into the sky like twin dirks, stabbing the air with their tips, forcing everyone who looked upon them to raise their eyes to the heavens. The gothic beauty of St. Patrick's Cathedral felt even grander and more elaborate alongside the modern glass and steel surrounding the facility yet also brought a note of melancholy, a remembrance of days past when glorious workmanship was still attempted and did not reduce buildings to the cookie-cutter molds of the present.

"Yeah, she's a beaut all right," the cabbie said as he put Novara's luggage on the sidewalk beside him. "A lot of out-of-towners make this their first stop in the city. Don't get to starin' so much you forget about your suitcases though, pal, or they'll walk away from you and all you'll wear will be that suit for the rest of your stay."

"Thank you," Novara replied with a smile, handing over his fare and a generous tip. He picked up his luggage and walked through the doorway of the Cathedral, struck immediately by two worlds living in one space. A number of people sat scattered among the pews, their numbers made to feel fewer by a sanctuary capable of seating over two thousand worshippers. They sat in silence, making their own peace with God or waiting patiently for their turn in the confessionals.

The other world consisted of small groups of people wandering about the Cathedral, causing a background of white noise, a whispered buzzing as they either took tours around the architecture or led themselves around, oohing and ahhing over shafts of light penetrating the great rose window or the solid bronze baldachin over the main altar. It was an odd mixture of the secular and the religious worlds, jarring in its contrast, brought together over the beauty and function of the building.

"May I help you, sir?" a young priest asked. "You are more than welcome to wander around in the public areas of the Cathedral and take in the wonder of God's works. Or you may wait and take a guided tour."

"Thank you, Father," Novara said as he put down his luggage and pulled his Vatican credentials from his pocket. He had learned from experience the smoothest beginning was to go straight to the top. "I was hoping to have a word with Cardinal Atchison."

The denial died on the priest's lips and the blood drained from his cheeks as the recognition of the Pope's seal made his jaw drop open.

"You can't. I mean, I'm sorry, sir, Father, uh, you can't see Cardinal Atchison, I mean, he's not here right now."

"Will he be back later today? I can wait, Father."

"No, you can't. I mean, the Cardinal is out of town at the Bishops' Conference. He is not expected to return until tomorrow night at the earliest."

"Hmm, is there someone else in charge that I may speak to?"

"The Cardinal took his assistant so Father Greene has sort of been overseeing... but he is only a practicing priest, sir. I'm afraid we don't have anyone of a sufficient title to greet you."

"You let me worry about that. Is Father Greene here in the Cathedral?"

"No. Yes! Yes, he is down in the classrooms. I'll go bring him to you." The flustered priest turned and took two quick steps before Greg stopped him with his voice.

"Just a moment, Father. Why don't you just lead me to him. It will save you a trip back." *And probably a stroke.* Novara smothered a grimace at the thought.

They crossed the sanctuary and left the majority of the sightseers behind, meeting only staff and other priests once they entered the east addition. Novara slowed his steps more than once to glance at sights like the Lady Chapel or marvel at some of the shrines for the American saints. Before long they had traveled down a flight of stairs and entered an area with a more modern feel with rooms opening on both sides of the hallway. At one of these open doors, the guide stopped and Greg looked into a room with approximately twenty teenage boys seated at desks while a priest stood at the front talking.

"Prophecy. Now I can stand here in front of you young men

and tell you I prophesize the Mets will win the World Series this year and the Yankees will finish in the basement." The priest smiled while chuckles rose from the boys. "But that is really only my hope and not a God-revealed sign. Besides which, none of us really believe that prediction with the money the Yankees are willing to spend." Another round of laughs rose. "Okay, but St. Thomas did discuss real prophecy and he labeled them in three different ways. Who can tell me the three types? Kory."

A tow-headed boy of about fourteen stood up from his desk.

"Prophecy of Denunciation, Foreknowledge, and Predestination." He sat back down with a relieved look on his face.

"That's correct. Denunciation. A prophecy that reveals a future governed by secondary causes. The prediction can be stopped but it will take an act or a miracle. Can someone give me an example?"

A younger boy stood hesitantly.

"Sodom and Gomorrah?"

"Very good, Curtis. God told the cities to turn away from their sinful ways or they would be destroyed. It wasn't the orgies, and drunkenness, and other sins that caused them to burn down in one night; they were the conditions for the destruction but not the cause.

"Next, Foreknowledge. The Prophecy of Foreknowledge depends upon man's free will. If King David does that, this will happen. If Elijah says this, that will happen. The Bible is full of examples of this type.

"Lastly, Prophecy of Predestination. This is a prophecy written in stone by God himself. Nothing will stop the prediction from happening no matter what mankind does to change their ways." The priest glanced down at his watch. "One last question before we go and this is not something we have covered yet. Who can tell me the last piece of prophecy officially recognized by the Church?"

Novara watched the boys mutter amongst themselves for a few seconds before he stepped the rest of the way into the room. He knew he should just wait another couple of minutes and stay out of sight but something drew him into answering. "The Book of Revelation."

Every head in the room swiveled in unison to see who had spoken. Even the priest looked over, the disappointment of his usual stumper question being answered draining away from his face at the sight of the stranger. A smile quickly appeared, however.

"Our guest is correct. Although there have been other prophesies and prophets the Church has deemed holy since John, the final book of the Bible is the last officially recognized piece of prophesy. And who have you brought to us, Father McElroy?"

"Father Greene, this Mr. Novara. He is an emissary from the Vatican and has asked to speak to Cardinal Atchison."

"Oh, I'm very sorry, Mr. Novara, but the Cardinal is out of town. I can, of course, phone him and I'm sure he will return at once."

"No, no, please," Novara said, raising his hand in protest. "There is no need for that trouble. This was an unscheduled visit, actually unofficial, so he did not expect me. I will be staying in town for a few days, however, and I was hoping someone could help me with accommodations. But please, I can wait in the hall while you finish your class."

Father Greene glanced down at his watch. "I'm sure the young men wouldn't mind leaving five minutes early. I will see you gentlemen next Tuesday. Please read the next two chapters in your catechism text and be prepared to discuss the major prophets." The sliding of chairs and shuffling of feet filled the air and soon the three men were left standing in the wake of the escaping boys. "Father McElroy, you can return to your duties in the sanctuary," Father Greene said as he bent over and picked up Novara's suitcase, "and I'll take our guest to the parish and see what I can do about finding him a room. Perhaps I'll even quiz him on the way to see if I can find a question I can actually stump him on." A twinkle played in the corner of the priest's eye.

Novara returned the friendly smile. He had found a helper for his task.

CHAPTER 5

NEW YORK, EARLY FRIDAY MORNING

The smells of corner-cart hot dogs and liquor wafted around Novara, mixing with the odor of decaying garbage drifting out of alleyways when he walked past. Bright, pulsing lights flooded through windows and out open doors, partially blocked by hulking men standing guard over their lords' kingdoms, deigning who could and could not enter with a glance at a list or a long look at high-slit dresses and what they revealed. Music beat in rhythm with the blasts of light, rumbling bass felt as much in the quiver of his body and through the soles of his shoes as with his ears. Now he understood why New York was the city that never slept: Who could sleep with all this commotion?

He weaved his way around, and sometimes through, the crowds of late-night partiers. Mixed groups moved with couples draped over each other's shoulders, some with the familiarity of long-time lovers and others with the lust and passion fueled by new experience. All-male groups stalked down the concrete like wolves on the hunt, leering openly at any woman who happened into their line of sight. Sometimes these glances were returned, an alpha bitch accepting the challenge and the packs melded together, circling off into the night. Novara was on the receiving end of his share of these looks, these unspoken offers to answer his baser needs but he offered nothing in reply. Though he felt the pull on his body, he was on a hunt of his own and it did not include the dance between man and woman.

Novara looked up at a clock hanging above a nearby shop. *3:35 a.m.* No wonder he felt every step in the back of his legs, every turn of his neck with a dull ache. With the flight from London this morning and then getting settled into the parish, he had been on the go for more hours in a row than he cared to think about at his age. Yet, even with the jet lag and lack of sleep, he had snuck away before midnight on the barest of feelings in his stomach, a stirring whisper in the back of his thoughts, pulled by the urge that here in the late-night clubs of Manhattan was a good place to start his search. A handful of times over the hours he thought he had felt a tickle of the presence for which he hunted but every time the feeling eluded him, fading away into the night between the music and the light, leaving him like the little boy trying to catch the fog in a jar to show his mother. He shuddered to think this time was starting like the hunt in Paris, or God forbid, London all over again. Novara stumbled at the thought, driving the memories away with all the power his tired mind could muster. He must have closed his eyes in concentration because he suddenly felt his shoulder pushed hard from the side.

"Hey! Watch where the hell you're walkin', buddy."

"Yeah, a little too late for you out here, old man? Doin' a little sleepwalking?"

Novara looked at the four young men standing around him, two with dates draped over their arms. "Please, forgive me," he said. "I was not watching where I was walking. It was entirely my fault."

"God, Bobby, listen to that accent. He sounds like my Grandpa and the old man barely speaks English through all that Italian. This guy must be straight off the boat."

"Yeah, you're right, Vin. Go on, old man. Go back to the old country and watch where you're going from now on."

"I will. Thank you." And then Novara made his mistake.

He smiled.

A gasp escaped from the girl on Bobby's arm, a pretty black-haired girl with olive skin and one or four drinks too many. Novara looked into her eyes and he knew the situation was about to grow worse. The girl lurched for him, both hands extended, reaching for his face, trying to grasp whatever pleasure she saw in his eyes.

"Yo, Gina, what the hell!?" Bobby stood there for a moment, the confusion of what was happening playing out on his face. Needing to make a choice of whom to blame, he took the easy way out.

"Yo, buddy!" he said as he reached out and pushed Novara on the shoulder. "You movin' on my girl? That takes a lot of balls with me standin' right here with my boys." He glanced around, looking for confirmation, the barking dog searching for the pack at his back. A smile rose to his face when the other young men moved in a step, closing the circle tighter.

Novara felt the weight of the knife in his belt, the rigidity of the haft running up his lower back. The blade cried out to his thoughts, urging him to let the edge drink these bullies' blood, sucking the heat from their bodies until they were cold shells rotting on the sidewalk. He ignored the pleas. This was his fault and he would not let the night end in blood.

"Please, gentlemen, I meant nothing. I merely smiled at your joke…"

"Oh, so now you think I'm some kinda clown? That I'm fuckin' funny? Is that it, old man? Well laugh at this!"

Novara saw the punch coming and tried to roll with the blow. He was brought up short by one of the men behind him, however, and the knuckles made solid contact beneath his right eye. Bright stars exploded in his sight. He realized he only had one more chance before this situation really did get out of hand.

His eyes lost focus and he felt a click in his mind, the latch raised on a seldom-used door in a dusty hallway. The calls for blood grew louder from the knife, rising in volume until they echoed in an eternal round. Novara's hands stayed clenched by his sides, however. Instead, he exhaled, a slow breath passing through his lips with the whisper of spring. He felt the air reach out for the group around him, encircling them, drawing them down into his calm.

"Yo, Bobby," Vin said, not even trying to stifle the huge yawn suddenly splitting his face. "I'm too tired to spend the rest of the night talkin' to the cops about this bastard. Let's go home and sleep." The man on Novara's left nodded in agreement, his own yawn adding emphasis. "Look, man, Gina's already asleep."

Novara watched the young man glance over at his girlfriend being held on her feet, barely, by the other girl whose eyes kept slamming shut before fighting back open. Only then did a yawn finally escape Bobby's mouth. It was all Novara could do to hold back a sigh of relief.

"My boys are right, old man. It's too damn late to be mixin' up now. Don't ever let me catch you eye my girl again, though, or it won't matter what time it is. Let's go fellas."

Roger wrapped the robe more tightly around his body as he walked down the hallway, his slippers slapping in rhythm with the young priest's footsteps beside him. A glance out a window as they walked by revealed just the barest hint of pink rising in the east around the surrounding buildings. With the Cardinal flying home on an early flight from the conference because of their visitor, today promised to be very long.

"I'm sorry I had to wake you, Roger," the younger priest said again, "but with the police with him and wanting someone to vouch for who he was…"

"It's okay, Ian. There's no reason for both of us to lose sleep. You can go on back to bed and I'll see to the problem." Roger smiled as he waved his fellow priest away. "But you'd better make sure I don't take a nap in my breakfast."

Roger rounded the last corner of the hallway and was greeted by the sight of two uniformed policemen standing by the doorway with the emissary positioned between them. He did not know which to worry about more: How the visitor would accept this situation or what in the world the man had been doing outside the parish in the wee hours of the morning.

"Gentlemen, my name is Father Greene. While the Cardinal is out of town, I suppose you could consider me in charge. What's happened?"

"Father, we found this man wandering around outside the building and he claims to be a guest. The only identification he had on him was an Italian passport."

Roger watched his visitor turn and face him, only then noticing the swollen eye and small cut where dried blood left a burgundy path down one cheek.

"Mr. Novara, you've been hurt!"

"I'm quite alright, Father Greene. With the time difference between here and London, I was not able to sleep so I went for a walk where I bumped into a couple of not-so-friendly young men. When I came back to the parish, I was in the process of trying to find an unlocked door when the constables found me."

"So, he is a guest here, Father?" the police officer asked.

"Yes. Mr. Novara is an emissary sent by the Vatican to meet with Cardinal Atchison and he just arrived today, uh, yesterday."

The other policeman stepped forward. "In that case, do you want to file a report against the punks who clubbed you, mister?"

"At the very least, allow me to take you to the hospital to have that cut looked at," Roger said.

"No, gentlemen, please. I don't require medical attention and officers, you and I both know you will never find those boys. I'm more embarrassed about the situation than hurt." Novara smiled but Roger thought it was only a reflex of his mouth, no humor making it as high as his eyes. "Now if you don't mind, I believe I've had enough excitement this evening to be able to sleep now."

With that, Roger watched the emissary walk down the hallway toward his room, leaving the priest to shake his head in bewilderment.

CHAPTER 6

It is time to feed.

Every day, I long for the night's hunt. The sweet smell of skin, the salty sweat on my tongue after a lick, the glorious blanket of silence wrapping itself around me—my world revolves around each victory, each kill.

The night is my friend, my only companion. It hides me in its dark embrace, shielding me from unseeing eyes until it is too late. We hunt in pairs. It coaxes our prey out, convincing them the blackness means safety. Their belief is their death.

The night has been there for me since…since the new beginning. When I must go away to sleep, it awaits my return, never forsaking me to the agony of the light. It has been that way for as long as I can remember.

Or at least as long as I want to remember.

It is time to feed.

CHAPTER 7

NEW YORK, EARLY FRIDAY MORNING

Morgan sat up, her hand flying toward the gun lying on the table beside her bed. She grabbed the grip but it slipped in her hand, sweat lining her palm to match what matted her hair to her forehead. Her breath rasped against her throat, tongue dry despite the slick wet of the rest of her body.

Who was here? Someone was just here.

She kept still now that her weapon was ready, letting her breathing slow so she could hear the sounds of someone in her apartment. But nothing reached her ears.

"I wish nothing but the best for youuuuu," belted out Adele's voice.

Morgan nearly squeezed off a round at the sound of her ringtone and instantly offered a prayer of thanks when she did not. That kind of incident would put her back in the shrink's office for at least another month.

"Hello."

"Detective Kelly? This is Frank… Detective Mason. I'm sorry I had to wake you."

Frank Mason was Morgan's new partner now that she was back on active duty. A good solid cop who had started walking a beat over thirty years earlier, he was within six months of retirement and probably what her lieutenant considered a safe way to ease her back into full duty—a by-the-book detective whose ego did not keep him from calling for backup.

"Damn it, Frank. Can't you just call me Morgan like my other partners did?"

"No, Miss. That would be disrespectful."

"Oh, good God! You're killing me, Frank." She stifled a yawn.

"Okay, what's up?"

"We've got a body down in an alley off the late-night scene. I'm on my way to your apartment right now and will be there in about ten minutes. I thought you might want to meet me in the lobby so your neighbors wouldn't see a strange man come to your door at this late hour."

Holy shit. He's more worried about my reputation than my mother. "That's okay, Frank. I'll be ready when you get here."

Red and blue lights flashed off the buildings and gave the concrete a moving paint job. Morgan hopped out of the car almost before the wheels stopped, half afraid Frank would try to run around and open the door for her if she waited. He had tried at her apartment.

Together they walked around the medical examiner's van and nodded to the two men waiting to take the body back to their lab. One of them may have grunted in reply. A uniformed policeman waved the two detectives under the crime scene tape once he noticed their badges, Frank's flopping out of his suit jacket pocket and Morgan's dangling from a chain around her neck. They grabbed cloth booties and pulled them over their shoes before putting on purple surgical gloves as well. She watched Frank out of the corner of her eye as he struggled to take off his wedding ring and slip it into his pocket.

At least I don't have to worry about that anymore.

When Frank finished shoving the sausages he called fingers into his gloves, they looked at each other and nodded. Only a few more steps and they stood in the opening to the alley.

Morgan felt alive.

She had not realized until this moment just how much she had missed her job, although deep down, she thought she had known all along. The horror at what people could do to each other, the tedium of searching through all the irrelevant items for the one clue that would break the case, the frustration when the piece of evidence did not appear, and the thrill of nailing the suspect—this was the life she had chosen. Police work had demanded the trade off of a normal life but now, as she smelled the garbage and looked at the other cops standing in the bright glare of the mobile lights, she knew every sacrifice was worth the effort. A uniformed officer walked over and handed her an evidence bag with a dainty purse inside.

"Detectives. The victim's name was Kirsten Janey, twenty-two. We found an NYU student card in her purse and a driver's license. She still had about fifteen bucks and a credit card so it doesn't look like a purse snatch unless it went really bad."

"How'd we find her?" Morgan asked "The friendly anonymous tip?"

"Nope. Plain, dumb luck. A patrol unit was driving by and one of them saw a dog or cat or some kind of shadow out of the corner of his eye. They shined the patrol light down the alley and saw her leg. We're still going door to door but most of these buildings are businesses, not apartments. The guy picked a nice quiet spot, that's for sure."

"Did they get a good look at him?"

"Nope, neither one. But one of them thought he saw something big fly away. Must have been time for shift change. It was probably just an owl or a bat."

The policeman returned to searching the alley with the other officers.

"Okay, Overholt. What have we got here?" Frank already had his notebook out as he stood over the crime lab tech.

"What we have here is what is commonly referred to as a fuckin' mess, detective." The man snapped off a couple more pictures before standing. "This is going to take some sorting out on the slab, but whoever did this is a piece of work."

Morgan walked around to where she could see the victim and barely held back the gasp that leaped to her mouth. What was left of a pretty brunette lay in a thickening pool of blood, the congealed liquid soaking in the light and reflecting back the night. Her dress was a shredded memory but still clung to her shoulders in defiance of what had happened to the rest of her body. From the ribs down to her hips, the victim was essentially gutted, organs spilling out of the skin in chunks. Morgan was glad she had not had time to eat breakfast.

"Raped?" she managed to ask.

"No. I'll do a kit to be sure, but I don't think so. There's no tearing or signs of force in the pubic region. She had sex tonight, though." He held up what was left of the victim's skirt to show her panties were missing.

"What kind of weapon are we looking for?" asked Frank.

The man hesitated and sighed, then looked up at the two detectives.

"A knife, obviously, but there's more to it than that. Look here." The man gestured with his hands. "Here and here. The weapon went deep to make these cuts but there is no sign of ripping or jerking to get the blade through. It needed to be pretty damn sharp to make those wounds. The lab'll know more, but my first impression is the blade was curved to make those kinds of slashes."

"Are we talking about medical tools? Surgical knives?" Morgan asked.

"Possibly. Also, you might be looking for more than one person or someone who is ambidextrous. This is a right-handed cut and this one here was delivered from a left hand. This is going to be an interesting case. I'll tell you what, I'll bump her up on my list and try to have a preliminary report for you after lunch. Just come on down to the lab."

"Thanks. One more thing. Time of death?"

"Call it two hours ago. About three o'clock."

Morgan continued to stare at the girl, something refusing to let her attention be drawn away. She looked at the pale skin silhouetted by the dirt and blood on the concrete beneath her, thin arms acting as roads of white down to smooth hands. Her brown hair floated against the backdrop while her cheeks and forehead remained clear with only a splash or two of blood around the smile…

"There are no defensive marks on her hands. She might have known her attacker." Morgan's comment stopped the conversation of the other two men.

"That's right, detective, there are no defensive wounds, but that doesn't mean she knew her attacker," agreed Overholt. "I'll run a full tox screen. She might have been drugged."

Morgan shook her head before gesturing down at the girl's face. "Stop looking at the naked body long enough to look at her face, boys. She's smiling like she's just waking up from a great dream."

CHAPTER 8

NEW YORK, FRIDAY NOON

Morgan swore under her breath and moved the manila folders like a little kid shuffling a deck of cards, both hands sliding in circles to reveal what lay underneath. Somewhere below the collection of loose papers and files was the top of her desk but no passerby could tell with just a glance. Only a couple of days back on the job and her area looked like a Gulf Coast hurricane had taken a turn north. After a few more seconds of frustrated search-and-rescue, she gave up.

"Frank," she asked, "have you seen my interview notebook?"

Her partner leaned across his desk. He rested his weight on his knuckles sitting between the three neat stacks of reports on a monthly planner, every notation written in clear print on each day. A line of demarcation split the two desks like the demilitarized zone between two warring countries, Morgan's clutter ending at the line where his pristine area began. A smile finally creased his lips—the smile of a grandfather laughing at the foolish behavior of his grandchildren. "It's on top of your computer, Detective Kelly," he said. "Up where it's safe."

Morgan shook her head in disgust while she grabbed the notebook and flipped through the pages looking for the information she needed to complete the initial report on the murdered coed. "Tread lightly, Frank. I've seen your hunt-and-peck style on the keyboard so I'm only typing this report so we can get back out into the field sometime before your retirement."

What passed for a chuckle rumbled through the burly detective's chest. "Yes, ma'am. How soon do you want to knock off for lunch?"

Morgan leaned back and glanced up at the clock hanging on the wall behind Frank. "Ten after twelve. I tell you what. It'll take me about another twenty minutes to finish this report and then we can grab a bite at McCluskey's before going down to the lab. How's that sound?"

"I never argue about good corned beef, Miss." He stood up and downed the last of the coffee in his over-sized Yankees mug. "Can I get you some coffee while I'm up?"

"My God, Frank. How big is your bladder? You must've drank two pots by yourself this morning." She rummaged around in her top drawer until she found her old chipped cup, the red Rutgers University letters stamped on the side faded to a deep pink. A glance inside revealed a black stain circling the bottom which meant it was anyone's guess the last time the mug was cleaned. "A good spoonful of sugar," she said as she handed it to her partner. "None of that blue packet crap."

She watched Frank shake his head as he walked away, eyeing the inside of her cup. Glad he was starting to loosen up a little around her, at least in the precinct house where other cops were around, she turned back to her computer and the elusive notebook and quickly typed away.

The steady noise of the station washed around Morgan with the effect of a gentle breeze against a granite wall. Other officers walking past, telephones ringing, and voices rising and falling in chaotic rhythm—nothing broke her concentration until Frank's extension rang. On the third ring she looked up and noticed he was nowhere in sight. A glance at the clock revealed almost fifteen minutes had passed since he left to bring back coffee so she reached across and grabbed his phone while throwing a puzzled look toward the break room. "Detective Mason's desk. This is Detective Kelly."

"Detective, I was afraid I'd missed you. This is Tech Overholt down in the lab. I finished the report on the girl from the alley last night and I think you and your partner better come down here as soon as you get a chance."

"Okay," Morgan said, already reaching for her jacket and shoving her notebook in the pocket. "I'll grab Mason and we'll be right down." She hung up the receiver and walked to the break room door.

"Come on, Frank, the lab..." She stopped in mid-sentence, her mouth hanging open in surprise. Her partner stood at the sink, scrubbing her mug with a wash pad. "What are you doing?"

"It looked like your cup hadn't been washed in a while and that's not healthy, Miss." He shrugged his shoulders. "I'm having some trouble getting the stain out, though." He grabbed a towel and started drying off the mug while he turned to face her. "Did you say the lab called?"

"Yeah. Yeah, the tech called and said he wants us to come down ASAP on the Janey girl. He found something he wants us to see."

Frank took a last look inside the cup and shook his head before tossing the mug to Morgan. "Looks like the corned beef and coffee will have to wait. Let me get my coat."

"Tech Overholt is in Autopsy Room 4. End of the hall, hang a left, numbers above the doors."

Morgan nodded to the clerk and wrote her name on the sign-in sheet before following Frank through the doors into the lab area, her nose wrinkling at the first sniff. She had seen enough blood in her professional life to drown a horse and too many corpses to put names to all the bodies, but the smell of the lab—the tang of chemicals mixed with hospital antiseptics and an undertone of rotten meat—left her with a cold lump in her stomach.

Give her a gory crime scene anytime; the lab was the smell of death.

Overholt glanced up from the folder he was reading as the two detectives entered the room. On the table was the body of a boy in his early teens, his left arm revealing the half-healed scars of a garage-colored gang tattoo. Morgan looked away but not before noticing the two bullet holes in his chest.

"The parents were down earlier this morning and ID'ed the body. They're expecting a visit from you later," Overholt said as he set down one folder and picked up another, waving it at them. "Detectives, this is a first-class bad one."

"Tell us about it," Frank said. "We saw her this morning."

"Just give us the overview," Morgan chimed in, keeping her gaze fixed to the tech's face. She might be able to forget about the dead boy if she did not look at him again.

"Okay." He flipped through a couple of pages before looking up again. "Young Miss Janey had sex but it was not rape, no tearing or bleeding, and no semen or pubic hairs left behind."

"So it was consensual?" Frank asked.

"Probably, but it does not rule out your killer."

Morgan nodded her head. "She wasn't going to walk around town without her underwear in a short skirt after having sex so it more than likely all happened right there in the alley."

Overholt glanced down at the file again. "This morning I told you the weapon was curved. I still stand by that." He referred to his notes. "Only two to three inches long by the penetration but as sharp as a surgical knife." Overholt closed the file and walked over to a refrigeration unit, opened the door, and slid the murdered coed out into the open. He pulled back the plastic bag covering her and started gesturing with his hands. "As you can see here, these slashes were made with a left-handed attack and these over here by a right."

"So there might be two attackers. You told us all this before," Frank said. "What did you find that was so important we had to run down here before lunch?"

"It's what I didn't find that was so disturbing."

The words hung in the air between them, clinging to the fog rolling out of the refrigeration unit. Morgan felt the icy touch and wondered if her shiver was from the cold air or the fact she now had to stare over the body of the dead boy to face Overholt.

"What was missing that you expected to find?" she asked.

"Footprints."

"Footprints?"

"Yes. There should have been plenty of them, even if they were unusable smears. There was blood everywhere. I was booted up and some of it still made it through to my shoes. The murderer couldn't have been close enough to slice her up and not leave bloody tracks. I've checked the scene photos twice and... nothing."

Morgan blinked in surprise, remembering the initial officer report which said something large had flown away. She glanced at Frank and received a nod before she spoke again. "Anything else?"

"Well, metal fragments, for another. There were nicks on her ribs and pelvic bones as well as all the way through to her spine. No matter how expensive or nice the knife, it should have left bits of metal behind. I couldn't find any."

"What about one of those plastic cooking knives they're always advertising on the television late at night?" asked Frank.

"I thought about that," Overholt answered, shaking his head to add emphasis. "The fragments would be harder to find but some of those ceramic knives, the cheaper ones, are more brittle than metal. I would've expected to find broken shards in some of the cuts. Regardless, all I found in the cavity was bone chips." The silence fell over the three of them again.

"That can't be all," Morgan finally said after a few seconds.

"Excuse me?" Overholt asked.

"You still haven't told us the real reason you wanted us to come down here right away. Everything you just said could've been put in the report notations. What really caused you to get nervous enough for an immediate face-to-face?"

Overholt waggled his finger in the air and nodded in agreement before sliding Janey's body back into the cold unit and shutting the door, the click of the latch echoing in the room. He rubbed his hands over his face as he leaned back against the metal, a tired watchman guarding over the body. When he looked up, he stared straight into Morgan's eyes.

"A uterus," he said. "When I got her cleaned up and had a chance to look over all the internal damage, I saw it had been ripped out of her body. It was not found at the scene." Now his gaze swept back and forth between Morgan and Frank.

"He took body parts. Detectives, I think you've got a certified nut case on your hands."

CHAPTER 9

NEW YORK, FRIDAY EVENING

Roger stole another peek into the mirror above the buffet and straightened his jacket again. Although he and the other priests who were assigned to St. Patrick's ate at least one meal a week with Cardinal Atchison, this was a formal dinner with an emissary from the Vatican. No matter how friendly and low key Novara had acted to this point, there was always a certain amount of pomp and circumstance to be observed, especially when the Cardinal was involved. He hoped the process would not end in a boring evening.

The priest noticed the doors to the dining room opening in the mirror and he turned in time to see the Cardinal and his secretary stride into the room. An athletic man in his youth, captain of the baseball team at Notre Dame, Atchison still exuded the confidence and posture of a man ready to tackle any situation. Only the white hair on his head and the lines around his eyes spoke of his age and experience. With a different calling, Greene could easily have imagined the man as a politician preparing to work a crowd or as a CEO in a boardroom.

"Father Greene, our guest should be here at any moment. Would you be so kind as to open some wine while I go check with the chef?"

"Yes, Cardinal." The priest picked up the bottle off the buffet and quickly had the cork pulled. In the meantime, the secretary busied himself with checking the table setting.

"It appears we will need to entertain ourselves tonight," Atchison said after returning to the dining room. "Our friend specifically said he did not want any other diners with us this evening. Perhaps I can still talk him into a formal reception before he leaves."

Roger thought for a moment.

"Maybe, sir. With his knowledge of the history of the Church, I wonder if he isn't some sort of a teacher, perhaps here only on a research trip. He seems to be a very private man, though. In fact, I don't believe he has left his room all day."

"He's probably just adjusting to the time difference," the secretary said while gathering four wine glasses. "When we arrived this afternoon and went down to speak with him, I had the impression we had roused him out of bed."

Roger merely nodded his head at the statement. He had not mentioned the late-night visit from the police to the Cardinal.

"I know I asked you earlier, Father Greene," Atchison continued, "but do you have any idea why he is here? He was rather vague this afternoon."

"A shortcoming born of too much time in my life spent traveling alone, I'm afraid," Novara said as he walked into the room, the light glistening off his silk suit. Roger noticed at once only a small scratch remained below the man's eye from the attack the previous night. The wound must have only looked worse because of the dim light in the parish foyer. "Please forgive me, Cardinal Atchison."

"No, no. It's quite all right. I'm sure you will tell me in your own time what I can do for his Eminence. You remember Father Greene, of course, and my secretary, Stephen MacGregor." Handshakes were quickly exchanged. "Would you care to join us for a glass of wine while we wait for dinner, Mr. Novara?"

"Yes, that would be fine."

By the time all four glasses were filled, the chef had appeared with salads so the men made their way to the table. Atchison spoke quietly to the cook before sitting down.

"I hope you don't mind, Mr. Novara, but when I dine with the priests in my care, we usually dispense with formality and eat family style." A big smile crossed his face. "Besides, after a week of eating rubber chicken at the Bishops Conference, I was in the mood for something a little tastier. Timothy will bring out the dinner and then leave us so we will be the only people in the residence."

Before the men had time to finish their salads, the chef returned with a cart loaded with platters of food. Roger's mouth watered at the smell of the pepper-crusted roast beef smothered in a blue cheese sauce, garlic potatoes, and spring peas with mushrooms.

Except for the sauce, the meal reminded him of Sunday lunches at home while growing up, hearty food that usually left enough meat for a sandwich to take to school on Monday. The memory also reminded him he had not telephoned his mother in three weeks.

He listened with fascination as he ate, the conversation quickly turning into a fencing match. Cardinal Atchison and MacGregor took turns prodding at their guest, never openly asking the nature of his visit, but nibbling around the edges like a moth at a wool blanket.

How was your flight? Did you have a chance to meet with any of the bishops when you were in London? Did you go to school in Rome? Are you stationed out of the Vatican? How is the Pope adjusting to the rigors of his position? Will you be staying long enough to do some sightseeing in New York?

Novara smoothly parried each thrust away, turning the questions back on the inquisitors until the Cardinal went off on a tangent about the Bishops Conference. Roger thought he saw the emissary relax a little then but something still lingered in his eyes, a hint in the glances he cast at the other men and around the room. The man's gaze never stopped moving, never stopped drinking in his surroundings. The priest thought he recognized the look. It was the wariness one saw in the eyes of a child raised in the streets, a reflection of the desperation of living from day to day, minute to minute, that kept them on edge.

Cardinal Atchison finally pushed his plate away, a sigh escaping his lips. "I don't dare eat another bite or I'll be dozing off in a few minutes. If we are all finished, and I can manage to stand up with all that wonderful food in my body, we can go into the library and continue our conversation over some brandy." He gestured toward the doors and the men made their way down a hallway leading into a large room lined with book-filled shelves.

This was Roger's favorite room in the formal residence. He had always imagined this was how a library at an English gentlemen's club would appear. Mix in a little pipe smoke and the room would be perfect.

"So, you haven't visited New York in a while, Mr. Novara," MacGregor said after sitting in an over-stuffed leather chair, still prying at their guest. "Is the city anything like you remember?"

Novara stared at the far wall for a few moments, long enough Roger thought the man had wearied enough of the questioning to ignore the secretary, but eventually he sighed and turned his gaze back on the other men. The young boy had been cornered in an alley and would not try to escape any longer.

"The only other time I've ever been to the United States," he said, "I was only in New York long enough to change ships before sailing on to New Orleans. But the skyline has certainly changed in all these years."

"Yes," the Cardinal said, emotion creeping into his voice. "There's not a day that goes by I don't look toward where the towers stood and pray for all the souls lost on 9/11. Those buildings may have left a big hole in the ground but they left an even bigger hole in our hearts."

"Yes, and the world felt your pain, believe me," Novara said. "But I was not referring to the tragedy of the World Trade Center. You see, the towers weren't built the last time I was here."

Roger searched his memory, trying to remember when the Twin Towers had been built. The Cardinal beat him to the punch.

"You must have been a boy when you visited," Atchison said with a laugh. "They started building the towers in the mid-Sixties. When was the last time you were here?"

"In 1858."

Silence hung over the room, enveloping the men with a thick embrace. After a few moments the Cardinal threw back his head and laughed, MacGregor joining in with a nervous chuckle. Roger did not even smile. Novara stared him in the eyes, holding his gaze with a grip as solid as if he had reached across the room and held him in place by force. The stare pierced his mind, reading his thoughts and dreams as easily as Roger could read any of the books lining the shelves. He had never felt so exposed, so naked, in his life.

"Oh, Mr. Novara," the Cardinal said. "Please forgive me for laughing but your English has deserted you. You meant 1958. But even then you could only have been, what?... Five? Six years old?"

Novara turned to look at the other two men and Roger slumped in his chair, released from the grip that had held him. Sweat popped out on his forehead and he struggled to fill his lungs with ragged gasps. The feeling of exposure was gone but now fear flooded his thoughts while the other two men did not appear able to see the danger.

"Yes, of course. How foolish of me. You wanted to know why I was here, Cardinal Atchison," Novara said, changing the course of the conversation. "There is evil loose in your city."

"Yes, I know. Greed, promiscuity, sexual deviancy, drugs—it is as if a plague has been called down upon God's children. Sometimes I feel like I am presiding over the second coming of Sodom and Gomorrah. The previous mayor did as much as he could to clean up the downtown with drug busts and prostitution stings but we have a long way to go."

Roger watched the visitor shake his head, a little anger now flashing in the emissary's eyes.

"No. I'm talking about true evil, not the temptations man falls prey to in his weakness. My job with the Vatican, my commission from the Pope, is to hunt down that evil wherever it goes."

"That is a commendable responsibility," MacGregor said. "But isn't that the duty of all Christians?"

Roger kept his gaze on the Cardinal who, judging by the frown touching the edges of his lips, was beginning to catch up to the deeper meaning of the words.

"Who decides what the evil is, Mr. Novara?" Atchison asked after a brief silence. "An act? A place? A..." He hesitated for another moment. "A person?"

"No people, at least not in the way you mean. And certainly not me." Roger noticed he was not the only one in the room who sucked in a breath at the statement. "I'm not the herald of a new Inquisition."

The emissary rubbed his hand over the armrest of his chair. It was a casual flick of his wrist but everything else in his manner spoke of seriousness. Roger thought the man was gathering himself for a storm, hunkering down to weather a blast of wind only he could sense. The young priest suddenly did not want to know what it took to frighten this man.

"We are talking about evil, pure evil, Cardinal Atchison. Evil manifested of the sin of lust and forced to survive on the nourishment of that drive. It has been my duty for many years to hunt it down and kill it." Novara leaned back in his chair.

Roger stole a look at the Cardinal and the secretary. Sweat dotted MacGregor's chin and he appeared on the verge of throwing up his dinner. Atchison, however, leaned forward on the edge of his seat, his legs pulled back so some of his weight rested on the balls of his feet. The priest realized then the man had made himself into a spring, ready to be released at the first sign of movement from their guest.

"Mr. Novara..." The Cardinal cleared his throat and started again. "Mr. Novara, please do not take this the wrong way but, have you been feeling all right? Perhaps the change in time zones has affected you more than you think."

The sigh that escaped from the emissary almost drew tears from Roger's eyes. The release was the sound of exhaustion combined with despair, the dying whimper of a soul without hope. His voice, however, was full of steel.

"Cardinal Atchison," Novara said, each word clipped. "You are the leader of the Catholic Church in your country and a member of his Eminence's extended circle. You have pledged your life as a soldier of Christ and his Church, yet deep inside you disbelieve of his teachings of heaven and hell, good and evil. Are you the type of priest who rationalizes away miracles and sainthoods with excuses of embellishment by the Bible's writers and ignorance on the part of the people who saw them?"

"Now wait a minute!" MacGregor exclaimed. "You can't just traipse in here..."

Atchison laid a calming hand on his secretary's arm, silencing the man with his touch. Despite the tension in the Cardinal's body, his voice carried only soothing reassurances. "Mr. Novara, my beliefs are between God, the Pope and myself. But now, I believe it is time for you to leave before we call the police. And if you will accept a piece of advice, you should seek help—mental help—as soon as possible."

Novara looked back and forth between the two men, his demeanor never changing from its emotionless appearance. Roger was glad the gaze never strayed to his face but he found his exclusion odd after the earlier intensity, an afterthought on the far side looking through the gate.

"Well, that settles the situation," Novara said, raising his hands in a surrendering gesture. "I don't wish to walk out of here tonight. Would you allow me to call for a cab?"

The Cardinal shrugged and waved his hand at the telephone. As soon as the other man walked away, however, he leaned forward and began whispering. "This man is obviously unbalanced. Killing evil? Dear God, he thinks he's judge, jury, and executioner. Father Greene, if he tries anything, you and I will need to hold him while Stephen phones for help. He looks like he's in pretty good shape, so be ready for him to be stronger than you think." He stopped and shook his head. "He's probably stolen the passport from the real Novara. We will need to call the Vatican as soon as this is over and report it, Stephen. Hopefully this situation was just a robbery and nothing more serious."

He glanced over his shoulder but Novara was still talking quietly into the telephone. "Remember, this man is sick, so we don't know how he will react to what we do or say. Be prepared for anything." Atchison stopped talking when he heard the man hang up the receiver.

Novara walked back to the group and sat down in his chair. "It will only be a few minutes," he said. Awkward silence fell over the four men, MacGregor fidgeting in his seat the only sign of life from any of them. After a couple of minutes, Novara turned and looked at Roger. "You are an avid scholar of Church history, are you not, Father?"

"Yes… ahem… yes, I am. The history classes were always my favorites in school."

"You were teaching the young men about the history of the Church and prophecies yesterday when we met."

"Yes, that's correct." The young priest noticed the man's entire attention was once again directed at him. Where before he had been as noticed as an additional book on a high shelf, now it was the Cardinal and his secretary who were ignored. "It is a part of their catechism classes."

"So if I was to say the words 'nabi' or 'nabi'ah' you would know what I was talking about?"

"Roughly speaking, they are the ancient male and female terms for prophets." Roger did not know why but suddenly he felt a calming wave wash through his body and he knew, down to the foundation of his soul, everything was fine in the room and nothing tragic would happen. The soothing focus of the other man's eyes told him they were just talking, a pleasant conversation between two men about a subject they both cared about.

"Actually, the more accurate translation is 'mouthpiece of God,'" Atchison said, injecting himself into the conversation, irritation at being cut out, clipping each word. Novara and Roger looked his way despite the distraction.

The telephone rang.

"Well, Mr. Novara," the Cardinal continued, "that will be the cab company."

"Actually, sir, the call is on your private line," said MacGregor.

"Answer it then, Stephen. Take a message unless it is an emergency."

The secretary stood up and walked over to the desk. He returned a minute later, his face pale and voice trembling when he spoke.

"Excuse me. Cardinal Atchison, it's the Vatican calling. The office of Camerlengo Nowaski."

Atchison's head snapped around and his eyes opened wide. Novara's gaze never left Roger as he spoke.

"I wouldn't keep him waiting, Cardinal. Lolek can be a real stickler for protocol and will probably keep you on hold for twice the amount of time you make him wait." A tired smile rose to his lips when Atchison jumped up and ran to the telephone.

"The Camerlengo," Roger said.

"Yes, his Eminence's right-hand man and the favorite student of Pope John Paul II from his days of teaching in Poland. Everyone knows the Pope sets the rules for the Church, the guidelines of how the priests are to act. But this is the man who sees the rules are followed, the disciplinarian." Novara hesitated, finally looking away and breaking the stare with Roger. "He's also my capo. My boss."

Roger and MacGregor watched the Cardinal on the telephone while Novara stared at his hands. The Cardinal listened more than he spoke, even absentmindedly nodding yes though there was no way he could be seen on the other end of the phone call. After ten minutes, he gently set the receiver back down on the cradle and leaned against the desk for a moment, apparently drawing strength from the feel of solid wood beneath his hands. Roger had never seen the Cardinal look as frail as he did at that moment. After several deep breaths, Atchison walked over to the other men.

"Stephen, you must call the airport and book us on the first available flight to Rome tomorrow. You and I have been ordered to report to the Vatican immediately. We are to give our report on the Bishops Conference in person and our accounting of all finances for the past year has been moved up. I also must meet…" At this point he stopped and turned his stare on Novara but only Greene noticed. "… with a council of other Cardinals to discuss my beliefs in the Church. The Camerlengo said the Pope may have a few questions for me on the subject as well." Atchison swallowed hard. "Father Greene, you are to be the emissary's aide during his stay here in New York. All of your other duties are suspended until Mr. Novara leaves. The Camerlengo said if you do everything he says, when he says it—no matter how bizarre the instructions—you might live to receive your own parish. He also wanted me to deliver a message to you, Mr. Novara."

"He usually does, Cardinal."

"Camerlengo Nowaski said you should check in more often. They worry about you when so long a time passes between calls. He also said you should come back to the Vatican after you are through here. His Eminence has been asking about you a lot lately and wants to finish the last discussion you started because… because he still has hope for you. He said he believes the two of you owe it to your mutual friend."

Roger noticed the moisture gathering in the emissary's eyes.

"He never gave up on anybody," Novara said, his voice barely above a whisper. "No matter how far down the wrong path they may have strayed, Karol always held out hope for the sinner's soul."

"Well," Atchison said, visibly stunned by the familiar mention of Pope John Paul II's real first name. "I will leave you to see to our guest, Father Greene. Stephen and I must plan our trip." He hesitated before sticking his hand out toward his guest. "I apologize, Mr. Novara. It appears I will need to re-evaluate some of my thoughts on the flight overseas."

Novara jumped to his feet at the gesture and shook the offered hand. "We all have things we need to think over at some point in our lives, Cardinal. Believe it or not, before this is all over you will probably thank me that you were gone for the rest of my visit."

The two men walked out of the library, leaving Roger and Novara alone. After a minute or two of silence, the priest finally burst out with the first question that popped into his thoughts. "Mr. Novara, why didn't you have the Camerlengo call before now and announce your mission? It would have saved the Cardinal embarrassment and you the hassle of proving who you are."

Another gut-wrenching sigh. "Just once it would be nice to have my words taken at face value, to be believed without needing to have the stamp of the Church on everything I say or do." His gaze wandered away towards the shelves of books. "Do you know what the Camerlengo's other main responsibility is as well as being the disciplinarian, Father?"

Roger thought for a moment before answering. "In addition to what you said earlier, he is in charge of the treasury for the Vatican and the entire Catholic Church."

"Partially. He is the administrator for all Church funds and property. And he is my capo." He turned to stare at the priest again. "I am nothing more than a piece of property to the Church, Father. I might as well be this chair." He slapped his hand on the leather but a smile quickly crossed his face. "And you report to me. So where does that place you in the hierarchy? Hmm, Father?"

Greene tried to come to grips with the bitterness tainting the statement. "So what do we do now?"

Novara smiled. "I hope you received plenty of sleep last night, my young priest, because tonight, we hunt."

CHAPTER 10

FRANCE, 1602

Gregor stepped down from the stirrup and glanced at the sun setting beyond the western edge of the village. Though his face hid his true feelings, the shake of his head spoke of disgust. He wished he could swear at their bad luck but his vows denied the release.

"Are you sure this is a good idea, Brother Gregor?" the priest on the carriage's seat asked. "Shouldn't we try to press on?" Though he remained silent, the third clergy in their group nodded in agreement from the back of his horse.

"Do you want to meet her… friend… out on the road in the dark, Brother Vinceni?" Gregor's voice fell to a hissed whisper. "How about you, Brother Michel? Do you want to meet him without four walls and your Brothers around you?" His gaze swept over the local people walking by but none of them gave him a second look, probably because they had spoken in Latin and not French.

The other two clerics looked away from Gregor. Even though his face showed the smooth skin of a boy only now turning into a man, it was their faces covered with sweat despite an autumn breeze drifting down the street. He knew neither of them liked the idea of spending a night outside a monastery's walls but they had no choice if they were to perform their task.

"Vinceni, you stay with the coach while Michel and I go inside and ask if they have rooms for us." Gregor managed to raise a weak smile. "Try chanting while I'm gone. I think it will help you."

The two men stopped at the inn door and slapped road dust from their cloaks in small puffs. The cleaning was all for show, however, a moment's hesitation to give Gregor a chance to gather his thoughts. A great religious fervor was sweeping through southern France and there were pockets where violence had broken out. The fighting should not cause them any problems this close to the border, but even so, he was not sure what to expect in a strange inn.

A murmuring of noise drifted out as he stepped into the building, the normal ebb and flow of conversations coming from the half-filled common room with only the occasional word spoken loudly enough to understand. Gregor looked into the room, his gaze stopping on each of the score of men, taking in their dress and expression before moving on to the next. Only after assuring himself everyone appeared to be part of the local village did he allow his breath to escape.

A man in a faded but clean apron leaned over the half-wall separating the foyer and hallway from the common room and eyed the two newcomers.

"A traveler's welcome to you, stranger," he finally said to Michel. "I'm Innkeeper Croisille, owner of the King's Men. Can I help you with a fine hot meal this evening, lodging, or both?"

Gregor decided to take a chance with the man and threw the cloak back over his shoulders, revealing the gold embroidered cross on the front of his shirt.

"I will need meals for four and two rooms if you have them, Master Innman."

Croisille looked confused for a few moments, obviously struck by Gregor taking charge over the much-older-appearing Michel. He adapted to the odd situation, however, quickly ducking his head.

"Please forgive my familiar greeting, Brother. Your cloak covered your station." A practiced eye took in the dust remaining on Gregor's cloak and the sweat stains on the shirt. "Did you have trouble on the road today, Master Priest?"

"Yes. A harness strap broke and by the time we mended it, a half a day was lost and kept us from reaching the monastery."

"Well then, I will keep you no longer." The innkeeper scratched his chin before speaking again. "I'm not all that pressed for rooms tonight. I've two on the east side of the inn that will show you the morning sun and help start your day early."

Rousing laughter burst from the men in the common room. From the sounds of their slurred speech, the men must have been drinking for some time.

"Everyone seems to be in a fine mood this evening."

"Yes, your holiness. We burnt two of those Christ killers that were traveling through the village earlier today. Had a whole wagon full of booty they probably stole from good, God-fearing men. Would you be kind enough to say a prayer on the men for their good deeds?"

So the killing of Jews had reached this portion of France as well. "I will be happy to do God's work and give them a blessing once we have settled in our rooms," Gregor said, forcing his friendliest smile. "May the light of our Lord always shine on your house's roof."

The stairway creaked beneath the weight of four sets of feet. Gregor was glad to know no one would sneak up on them from this direction. The relief evaporated when he thought of all the other openings that could be used, however.

He turned at the top of the stairs, allowing a glance back at the short figure walking between him and the two priests at the rear of the procession. The overly large cloak was pulled tight around the body, closed by fists clenching the material into balls. The hood flopped forward over the person's head and shrouded the face in shadows the lamp light could not breach. Man or woman, young or old, hunter or hunted—nothing spoke about this figure except their quest for anonymity.

Gregor opened the door at the end of the hall and stepped into the small, clean room beyond. The bed, large enough for two if they slept close, dominated the far wall beneath the window. The only other furniture consisted of a small table and two straight-backed chairs, their seat cushions worn thin from use. The sparse conditions reminded him of the monastery dorms he had grown up in and helped him feel more comfortable.

The sound of the cloak landing on the bed drew his attention back to the subject of their task and Gregor marveled again at her looks. When the Bishop had first walked into his solitary room and offered the assignment, he had expected a stunning beauty, a lady belonging in tales of knights' adventures. Arabelle Moins was no such woman. Her dull brown hair framed a round face, pleasant to look at when she offered one of her rare smiles, but it certainly remained short of beautiful. Even her figure bespoke of her farm girl upbringing—sturdy, with a few more pounds than expected on a lady of royal birth. But then she blinked and Gregor felt his gaze travel up to her eyes where their remarkable nature was revealed for all to see. Green orbs so light they threatened to blend in with the white, showing depths to lose a man in a maze of wonders. Yet, the wrinkles around those eyes and pinched lips hinted at a haunted soul. Though young in years, Arabelle had seen much and not liked most of it. Gregor had not asked for this task, this responsibility, but still he felt chills every time he thought about what he was here to do. He quickly looked away from her eyes as she turned to fully face him.

"Brother Gregor, is it still possible to get some supper before…?" Arabelle's voice trailed off from the unfinished question.

"Yes, of course, Mistress Moins. Brother Vinceni, please place our packs in the room next door and then help Brother Michel carry up some food." Gregor stared out the window for a moment, looking at the streaks of black woven through the last golden rays of the day. "Please hurry. It will be night soon."

He could barely stop from grinning.

Gregor yawned around the back of his hand, the next few words in his prayer sounding distorted and unintelligible. He needed sleep. The long day's journey had robbed him of his normal rest time and, combined with his all-night vigil, threatened to make him fall off the chair in a stupor. With the way this trip had started, he would probably doze off in the saddle during the next day and break his leg. Even so, the enthusiasm only a first assignment could deliver coursed through his exhausted body. A glance to his left showed Vinceni sitting straight in the other chair, his mouth moving in a soundless chant and eyes opened wide.

"Brother," Gregor whispered.

Vinceni flinched at the sound, cringing away as if threatened by a blow. His gaze whipped from the bed and flew around the room, searching for the danger that had eluded him. Gregor drew his attention by placing a hand on his companion's wrist.

"Brother," he continued. "I'm sorry to startle you."

"What is it?" Vinceni asked. "What do you hear? Is it in the room?"

"No. Everything is fine. We're only about two bells from dawn but I must stretch my legs and get something to drink or I will fall asleep with my eyes open." Gregor looked down at Arabelle sleeping peacefully on the bed, the blanket tucked under her feet and held in place by fists beneath her chin. "I'll only be gone for a few moments."

Sweat beads dotted Vinceni's forehead. "I... I can go get you some wine from downstairs," he said. "You can walk back and forth while I'm gone."

"Would you deny me a breath of fresh air?" Gregor asked, a smile creasing his face to remove the sting of rebuke. "Or would you rather I wake up Brother Michel, even though he sat in that chair the first half of the night?"

"No... no. It's just that I can't... she's sleeping... the dark...you being you..."

Gregor's amusement melted. "That's enough!" The whisper hissed between his teeth. "Don't you think I know what you and the others say about me when you don't think I can hear? Protector of the Chaste. Defender of Honor. For the love of God, why don't you just call me the Knight of the Night!" The play on words threatened to douse his anger but a smile never rose to his lips. "I'm no blessed miracle worker. My faith in God is no more righteous than yours. Your prayers hold just as much power as mine."

"Yes, of course, Brother," Vinceni said, his eyes not quite making contact with Gregor's. "But so much is at stake. Mistress Moins' protection and the prophecy... I'd just feel better if you were in the room with her."

Gregor sighed, the weight of the other clergy's faith in him acting as heavy hands on his shoulders, a weight he normally relished but not when he was this tired.

"Continue your prayers while I'm gone. Let the light of our God shine through you and protect this lady from the demons of the night." He hoped the blessing would give the other man more courage.

Gregor rose and walked to the door, pausing only long enough to hear Vinceni's chant begin, each word spoken with fear-driven reverence.

The common room was deserted but Gregor noticed light shining through the cracks around the kitchen door. He swung it open and nearly startled a young girl into dropping the bag of flour she carried.

"Please forgive me," he said as he stepped into the light. "I couldn't sleep and I wondered if I might find something to drink."

"Can't give you no liquor," an older woman said after waving the maid back to her duties. "Not allowed to sell liquor after third bell until luncheon. Wine or cider is the best you can do, Priest."

"Cider would be fine. Thank you."

Gregor watched the woman draw a mug of cider while barking out orders to the maid. Preparations for the breakfast crowd had started and this woman bore the manner of a queen in her realm.

"Here's your cider, Priest." Some of the golden liquid slopped over the side when she slapped the tankard into his hand.

"Thank you, Madam Cook," he said but his words were drowned out by the next string of orders she shouted at her young helper. Part of him wondered if she acted as she did because he was a priest, because of his halting French, or if she treated everyone that way. Another couple of moments watching her with the other help convinced him everyone received the same treatment—king or pauper alike.

Gregor smiled as he walked across the darkened common room and headed for the front door. He supposed everyone wanted to have at least one area of their life where they felt in control, felt the power of the cook in charge of her kitchen. The grin faded when he wondered if he would ever have any of that control for himself.

A breeze caressed his cheek while he stood in the doorway and stared at the deserted street. Gregor felt comfort in the solitude, reminding him of the days spent alone in the monastery, cloistered away from even his fellow clergy. When he was a child, the long stares from the priests had made him feel uneasy, the meat hanging from a hook in the butcher's window for all to see. As he grew older, he recognized the nervousness echoed in their eyes—nervousness that was often only a thin veil over fear.

Gregor scuffed his heel in frustration. He had grown up dreaming of blending into the Church, proving his piety with prayer and good works, and eventually emerging as an accepted priest with a congregation of his own to minister. Those hopes had disappeared the moment the Bishop gave him this task but he felt no regret. He had finally found his calling, discovered what God had put him on Earth to do for his glory.

Fingers aching, Gregor realized he held the knife hanging from his belt in a death grip. He released the hilt and shook his hand, the fingers remaining white in the light of the moon before the blood flowed back. His thoughts stayed on the weapon at his waist, however—the weapon and the power of its purpose. He wondered if he had finally gained a small bit of control over his life when the Bishop pressed the hilt into his hand or if the power had been present the day the priests discovered the prophecies. No, more likely his destiny had been decided the day he had been conceived, an abomination to some, to others a savior born to combat evil cast from God's grace. In the words of the Pope, Gregor was "fire to fight fire."

What was that? He held onto the faint hope the scream was just a traveler in the middle of a bad dream. The thump of a body hitting the floorboards above him told him it was his nightmare, however.

The steps groaned beneath his feet as he flew up the stairs, the creaks proclaiming his rush. Now was not the time to worry about sneaking up on the beast. In fact, now that the time had arrived to battle it face to face, part of Gregor hoped the creature would hear the clamor and flee while the rest wished he could run faster before it escaped. He ran toward the door at the end of the hall, his legs flying. Yet, the closer he moved the more muffled his footsteps rang in his ears. The pounding of his feet against the floor should have echoed off the bare walls. Instead, the sounds grew softer, absorbed as if a woolen blanket was wrapped around his head. By the time he threw open the door, its banging against the stop was only a far-off thunderclap, a rumble in the back of his mind.

Gregor took in the scene with one glance. A beast lay on top of Arabelle, its skin glowing pale against hers. The blanket was bunched on the floor and her shift was ripped opened with her legs thrown wide. The incubus stopped his thrusting long enough to turn his hideous face toward Gregor, mouth opening to reveal yellowed fangs dripping with spittle. He looked surprised to see the clergy awake until he sniffed the air and nodded, the mystery solved.

You're too late, half-breed, a voice said in Gregor's head, though no sound reached his ears. *You should have given me more of a challenge than the weakling.* The beast nodded his head at Vinceni, lying where he had fallen, eyes open but never to see again.

"Leave her alone," Gregor said, ignoring the taunt. "Why do you continue to haunt her?"

"You know why," this time the sound reached his ears, "probably better than any of the others. She is my chance to regain my life, to take back the power that was stolen from me. What happened to your power? You were born with the ability to rule these people... or crush them."

Gregor ignored the question, his hand falling to the hilt of the knife. "How do you hope to find your grace again? God has already thrown you down because of your failing, the lust filling your thoughts. You lived in the light of his being, yet you tossed it away."

The beast's wings, folded against his back, vibrated with warning.

"Tossed it away or had it ripped from me!? Punished for what? For how he made me? What about you, cambion? Half of you is like me. Don't you see this woman? Can't you feel her body calling to you, offering itself up for your pleasure? I can see the lust in your eyes. How does the temptation sit with your priests and their vows of celibacy?" The beast leaned forward and trailed his tongue up Arabelle's chest.

Gregor felt the heat rise in his cheeks. Except for the first brief glance at Arabelle, he had kept his gaze locked on the beast's yellow teeth, the pock-marked skin, or the bone-white horns rising from his forehead. His gaze now wandered and he saw her green eyes in the dim lamplight, staring at her violator yet seeing nothing. He felt drawn to look at her naked skin, raw and red from rubbing against the beast's belly scales. The shape of a breast half-covered by torn material, the line of her thigh against the bed—Gregor's tongue swept out of his mouth and licked eagerly at his lips.

"No!" he said, ripping his gaze back to the demon, beating down the thoughts of lust in his mind. "You know what will happen from your union. You can't be so far removed from God that you want the destruction to rain down on mankind."

"Destruction! Ha, ha! What do I care about the destruction of these people? Mankind may not survive the child that comes from this woman but I will—as will all the others like me. As will you, half-breed. We will survive and in the doing we will have control over our lives again. No being will sit in judgment over me, over my actions… over my feelings. Never again!" The incubus took a moment to thrust into Arabelle several times, stopping only when Gregor took a step forward, his gaze falling to the boy's hand on the knife hilt. "Don't be a fool. You know steel can't harm me. Embrace the side of you that was your father, the side of yourself like me. You have no choice, cambion. This vessel will have my baby and the child will bring destruction to man no matter what you deceivers do. Ha, ha! I have the power!" The beast withdrew himself from Arabelle and leaped upon the sill of the open window, its claws gripping into the wooden frame until shavings drifted onto the bed.

"You're wrong," whispered Gregor. "I can stop this."

He leaped across the few paces separating him from the window, the snick of the drawing knife only a murmur in his ears. The white edge glowed into a blurred bar when he slashed at the beast's belly, the incubus bone blade ripping through the scales into the flesh below. A soundless scream reverberated in Gregor's head and, for a moment, he shared the suffering, felt the shock of the pain. The incubus leaped backward into the night and hung there, his wings beating at the black.

A moan escaped from Arabelle and sobs shook her body as the beast's hold on her evaporated. One hand pulled the flimsy pieces of cloth together across her nakedness while the other clutched at her stomach, despair at what was now inside her written in each white-knuckled finger. Gregor stared at her in silence until she finally looked up at him, red lines running trails around the lovely green.

"You let this happen," she said between sobs. "I trusted you could protect me, protect us all. Now what will happen?"

The answer stuck in Gregor's throat. Words of comfort, words of false hope, words that cursed the day this poor woman was drawn into his world without a choice. Yet, the entire time he stared at her, all he saw was an imagined vision of his mother—dead from birthing a half-incubus, half-human child: a cambion. The same fate Arabelle would share.

And mankind would still have the child to deal with—the child of the prophecy.

"Do you know what will happen to you when it is born?" Gregor asked, waiting for the woman's nod. "Then you know this is a mercy." He hesitated, questioning in his mind whether the mercy was for Arabelle or the world. "May God's light shine on your being."

Gregor raised the knife and plunged the blade into Arabelle's chest. Her eyes flew wide and she clawed at his wrist, her fingers scratching his skin and leaving trails of blood while the incubus's scream filled his head again. The beast flew closer to the window, the claws on its arms grasping as if to pick up Arabelle and hold her close. Gregor yanked the blade out of the dying woman's breast and slashed again at the beast, her blood splattering across the wall in an arc.

"Damn you, cambion! Damn you and your accursed priests! This is not the end." The incubus turned and melted into the darkness, his wings beating the air in his fury. "This is not the end!"

Gregor let his gaze fall down to the bed, Arabelle's body blurry beneath his tears. This was not how the adventure was supposed to end. He had imagined the end in celebration, in the acclaim always awarded to a hero.

His breath grew short as responsibilities' full reality fell on his shoulders, a crushing weight compared to the pressure he had felt before. He reached for the blanket to cover Arabelle's nakedness, some dignity in death, and noticed her blood on his hand, mingling with the trails from the scratches on his wrist. Accusation flowed in the stain and he wondered if his skin would ever wash clean again.

"Dreams of ivory and gold," Gregor said, pulling the cover over Arabelle's unseeing eyes, the green fading even further into the white. "False dreams and true, the pathways of our fate."

"What happened, Brother? Did you kill the beast?" Michel asked as he ran into the room, the rest of his questions choked off when he saw Vinceni's body.

Gregor turned to look at the other priest, hating himself for taking the power of choice from his companion.

"I failed, Brother, and Mistress Moins and Vinceni paid the price. You will not be returning to the monastery anytime soon. We must hunt down the beast before another takes her place."

CHAPTER 11

NEW YORK, EARLY SATURDAY MORNING

Shadows played along the wall, gliding down its length when headlights passed the end of the alley. Morgan's heart beat against her ribs and sweat trailed down her face, stinging her eyes and making it even harder to tell what waited for her in the dark. The sounds of rustling trash floated out of the black followed by the tinkling of a bottle rolling across the pavement. She jumped at each noise, her finger twitching against the gun's trigger.

A face leaped out of the night, screaming obscenities. Morgan turned and fired, the flash illuminating a teenage boy before the force of the bullet threw his body back out of sight. The face appeared again, this time from the side, and she yanked the trigger back to the grip, lead and flash leaping out in response. Like some poorly made movie, she fired again and again and again until she had shot the boy back into the shadows three or four times what the magazine could hold in rounds.

And still the face came.

The sweat was a river now, mingling with the spray of the boy's blood as he appeared faster and faster. Was tonight the night she ran out bullets? What would happen if he actually made it close enough to touch her? The thought made her drenched clothes turn to ice.

Swearing. Silent. Leering. Expressionless. The boy attacked over and over until, with no warning, the small amount of light in the alley disappeared and thrust Morgan into a black maw. Her heart pounded but the rush of blood through her ears softened, muffled, as if the darkness flowed into her and drowned out the sound, stealing another of her senses. Only then did she realize the wall was gone from behind her, the crumbling brick no longer offering its protection.

Movement swept by her—unseen, unheard, untouched—yet she knew something circled around her with the drive of a shark closing in for the kill. She tensed, waiting for the rush.

The streetlights reappeared and this time the boy rushing out of the night was the gang-banger she had seen in the morgue. Morgan hesitated, distracted by more movement in the shadows behind the attack. Though it was the dead teenager's fingers grasping greedily for her throat, she sensed the real danger was the unseen predator hiding in the gloom.

She pulled the trigger, the boy shuddering with the impact of each bullet, but still he advanced, the sneer on his face growing until it filled her whole vision.

Morgan bolted up in bed, not sure if she was fully awake yet. Her gaze leaped along the far wall, still searching the shadows for the movement she had sensed in her nightmare. On the verge of falling back against the pillow, her eyes froze on a pool of black in the corner of the bedroom. Moonlight shone through the doors to the balcony, casting its pale gleam on the opposite wall, and should have lit the corner as well. Instead, a shadow huddled down, unmoving, staring back, a formless predator watching over its prey.

She reached out slowly with her right hand, her fingers searching across the top of the nightstand for her gun. The grip spun from her touch and her gaze flew to the table before snapping back to the corner, the sights on her gun lined up with her arm.

Moonlight lit the empty corner.

Roger blinked his eyes several times and tried to focus on the ceiling. Another knock sounded at the door, this one more forceful than the last, and made the priest lurch off his bed.

"Coming! I'm coming!" he said, stumbling as he tried to walk and put on his slippers at the same time. *What time is it?*

Roger opened the door and threw a hand up to cover the yawn splitting his face. When he was able to focus on the person standing in the doorway, his cheeks grew hot in embarrassment.

"I'm sorry to wake you, Father Greene," Cardinal Atchison said, the hint of a smile playing at his mouth. "I need to leave for the airport in about an hour and I wanted to talk to you before I left. May I come in?"

"Yes sir, yes, of course." Roger stepped out of the way and hurriedly pulled his robe closer around his body. "If you give me a minute, I'll get dressed..."

Atchison threw up his hand to silence the priest. "No, please. I'll only be a few minutes and then you can go back to sleep. I understand you and Mr. Novara did not return from your night out until seven o'clock this morning." He laughed. "You may be able to get by but I know I can't function on only three hours of sleep at my age."

So it was only about ten in the morning. No wonder he was so tired. Roger felt another yawn building.

"I came down here to tell Father Ian how sorry I was I am going to miss Sunday's mass. This will be his first time leading and I so wanted to be there."

"I'm sure he understands, sir."

The Cardinal shook his head. "How can he? I'm not sure I understand, so how can I expect him to?" He took a step closer. "How about you, Roger? After spending the night with Mr. Novara, do you understand any more than you did before? When you talked, did what he say sound any less... unusual... than the conversation in the library?"

Roger knew the word the Cardinal really had wanted to use was "crazy." He gestured toward the chairs and both men sat down. "We really didn't talk all that much about him, sir. We spent most of our time discussing my upbringing and my interest in church history and prophecy."

Atchison leaned back and set his lips in a firm line while he furrowed his forehead. Roger had seen him use the same look on him and other priests when he was disappointed in what he heard.

"Well then, what did you do for all that time?" the Cardinal asked.

"We walked. And walked and walked and walked." Roger felt his calves throb as he thought about the previous night. "We walked all over the west side, sometimes doubling back on where we had already been and sometimes circling blocks two or three times before moving onto the next. The whole time felt like all we were doing was just wandering around."

Atchison smiled. "You were born and raised here in the city, weren't you?" He waited for Roger to nod before he continued.

"When I was attending Notre Dame, every fall a group of us would drive down to southern Indiana, near Evansville, and go pheasant hunting. From what you just described to me, if Mr. Novara was a hunting dog, I'd say he was on the cast."

"I don't understand."

"He was searching for the scent, somehow hunting your prey."

Roger felt sweat break out on his upper lip at the idea. The entire night he had thought the two of them had just been walking in circles and talking without anything actually happening. He wondered what else he had misunderstood. "I don't think I'm the right person for this job, sir."

Cardinal Atchison chuckled. "Whether you or I think you are the right person doesn't matter. At this point, Mr. Novara does and he has the blessing of the Vatican so that, as they say, is that." He shook his head while his eyes reflected his amazement. "He has the audacity to debate with the Pope, Roger! Can you imagine? There is more here than we can even begin to guess at." All the humor fled from his face as he suddenly leaned forward on the edge of the chair, drawing Roger closer with the resolve in his eyes. "You must find out as much as you can from our guest. Trick it out of him or ask him outright—do whatever you must to get information." He paused. "What did it feel like out there?" His eyes glistened like a little boy's, shining in anticipation of Christmas. "What did it feel like to be out there working side by side with a hand-picked soldier of the Pope?"

"It was exciting... for a while," Roger answered, his thoughts returning to the previous night. "I think I can remember every step we took the first couple of hours but then the night just sort of dragged out and it all melts together now. If I had known what we were really doing, hunting like you said, I would've paid more attention."

The Cardinal nodded before standing and walking to the door. "I fear for your safety, Roger. Maybe something in what you pry out of Novara will keep you safe. But, despite that, despite the danger, part of me wishes I was the one staying and you were the one going to the Vatican." He opened the door but stopped just in the hallway. "I'll light a candle for you before I leave." The Cardinal closed the door softly.

Roger knew he would never get back to sleep now.

CHAPTER 12

NEW YORK, SATURDAY AFTERNOON

Morgan slung the dry cleaning bag over her shoulder and peered into the shop window, wondering how anyone who actually worked for a living could afford the dress draped over the mannequin. A better question was how a woman could wear anything that low cut and skimpy without dying of embarrassment. She laughed as she turned away, wondering what her mother would say if she wore something similar in public. The chuckle stopped when her cell phone sang its familiar tune. "Detective Kelly."

"Ma'am, it's Detective Mason."

"Hi, Frank. I doubt you missed me so much you felt the need to call me on our day off. What's up?"

"We've got another body."

The smile evaporated. "Where are you, Frank?"

"I'm driving my wife home and then I'll come to your apartment. It's on the way to the crime scene."

"Okay, I'm ten minutes away. I'll be waiting out front."

Morgan stepped around the officer standing watch over the apartment door and gasped. The foyer opened up into a great room that probably contained more square footage than the house she had grown up in with her parents and brothers. Paintings—real paints, not prints—looked down on gilded furniture and sculptures from a wall at least two stories high. A glance at Frank showed he was just as taken aback by the display of opulence.

"Detectives," a uniformed officer said from a hallway on the other side of the room. "The body is down here."

Smaller rooms branched off from the hall before opening into a bedroom dominated by a huge bed. The satin sheets draped over the mattress would never be used again, however, as pools of blood from the corpse lying in the middle had stained through. Morgan shook her head in disbelief at the mirror attached to the ceiling above it all.

"Hi, Frank. Morgan." Detective Anderson greeted them both with a nod of his head and a tight smile. "Artie and I started to process this one but the crime tech insisted we call you as soon as he looked at the body. He thinks it has a connection to your vic from yesterday."

Tech Overholt crawled off the bed and stood as the three detectives approached, carefully removing the one-piece lab suit he was wearing before placing it in an evidence bag.

"What've we got?" Frank asked. Not one to be overly talkative on any given day, he had not said a dozen words since picking up Morgan.

He's probably just pissed about working on a Saturday. Morgan hated to admit it did not bother her at all.

"At first glance, we've got the same M.O. as the coed from yesterday," Overholt answered. "Her body has been ripped apart from the shoulders to the pelvis using the same sort of slashing cuts we saw before. She had sex with someone but it was consensual and she died in the early-morning hours—probably three or four." He hesitated and glanced around to make sure none of the uniformed officers were close enough to overhear. "Her uterus has been removed, the same as the last time. I won't know for sure until I get her back to the lab and look for other similarities but my gut reaction is we are looking at the same killer."

Anderson puffed his cheeks, letting out the air slowly while Frank paled. Morgan did not blame them; she felt a little light-headed herself at the idea of a serial killer.

"You guys caught the first one," Anderson said. "How do you want to play it?"

"I've never worked a multiple at separate scenes," Frank said.

"I have." All three men stared at Morgan. She knew the investigation was her call. "Until we hear different from the lieutenant or the captain, or the lab says they're not, let's consider them linked. Jim, you and Artie stay on the scene just in case Overholt finds something to discount a connection." She turned to the technician. "We'll need to know what you've got ASAP."

"I'll take the body back and process her immediately. Just let me get someone else out here to finish the scene." He pulled a cell phone out of the holder on his belt and made a call. Thirty seconds later he hung up and nodded his head.

"Okay," Morgan continued. "How'd we find her? And don't tell me a couple of uniforms were just driving by."

"No, not this time," Anderson said as he pulled out his notebook. "Vic's name is Elizabeth Brookins, twenty-eight, single, and lives in this humble abode alone. She was found by her boss, a… hmm… ah, Mrs. Marie Stegman." He flipped shut the book and replaced it in his jacket pocket. "Artie was finishing the interview with her while I called you two."

Morgan nodded. "Let's go have a word with Mrs. Stegman." She stopped, digging into the memories of the past cases she had worked. "Nothing official to the press about the two murders until we know for sure they are linked. Even then, let's hold back the lack of metal fragments and the uterus removals as our bona fides. A serial rapist is bad enough but one that kills his victims after he's done will bring out all the kooks to claim the kills as their own. We'll need something to use as proof if anyone comes forward." The three men nodded in agreement. "Call us as soon as you're done, Overholt," she said before walking out of the bedroom with the other two detectives in tow.

They entered the great room and Morgan shook her head again at the elegant excess. After looking around more closely at the people in the room, she noticed the luxury was reflected in the woman sitting on one of the couches. What appeared to be just a well-tailored suit from a distance revealed intricate embroidery through the shine of a silk jacket up close. Pearls and multiple-carat diamond rings completed the ensemble. The style sat comfortably on the woman who appeared to be in her late thirties but Morgan suspected was older by at least ten years.

"Mrs. Stegman," Detective Anderson said, "these are detectives Mason and Kelly. They need to ask you some questions."

"I'm sure some of these you've already answered with Detective Dixon," Morgan said, "but please bear with us. Miss Brookins was your employee?" She waited for the nod. "What led you to find her today?"

Dreams of Ivory & Gold

"We were supposed to have lunch. When she did not meet me at the restaurant and I could not reach her on the telephone, I became worried and came to the apartment."

Morgan noted the woman's even voice, no trace of horror at the gory scene or distress at the loss of an employee given away with a quivering lip and tears. She could just as easily been describing the loss of her goldfish—right after flushing it down the toilet.

"How did you get in the apartment?" Frank asked.

"I have a key. The lease is in my name."

Morgan suddenly realized where this was leading. "Mrs. Stegman, what kind of business do you run?"

Just the barest hint of a twitch tweaked the woman's right eye. "I own a discreet escort business for an exclusive high-end clientele."

The detectives looked at each other before Frank continued with a shake of his head. "Okay, who was her john last night?"

"She didn't work last night."

"Why not?"

"All my girls get one week a month off, Detective."

Morgan almost burst into laughter at the red blooms on her partner's cheeks. She held it back, however, deciding to save him more embarrassment.

"How about threats from past dates? A boyfriend who wanted her to quit?" Morgan asked.

"Her latest beau doesn't know about her side job," Mrs. Stegman replied, smoothing a crease in her skirt as she spoke. "Beth graduated from NYU with a degree in drama. She's been in a few off-Broadway plays but stage acting was not enough to pay the bills, so she worked for me on the side. Besides, he wasn't even in New York last night."

"How do you know that?" Frank had regained his composure.

"Because I watched him giving a speech on C-Span from the Congressional floor."

Glances were exchanged again between the detectives. Morgan wondered which would provide a bigger media circus: A congressman for a suspect in a murder investigation or a serial killer.

"Okay. What about creeps that became too attached? Someone who wanted her all to himself?" Morgan heard herself asking the questions but in her mind she had already linked the murders. Even so, procedure required them to finish the interview.

Mrs. Stegman stared at a piece of artwork in the corner, a twisting piece of metal that vaguely reminded Morgan of a shiny card table stretched, mutilated, and left standing on its side. The detective watched the older woman for a few silent moments, wondering what thoughts were parading behind the flawlessly made-up face.

"The kind of men who can afford my business services are not accustomed to hearing the word 'no.' Being all-powerful in business and politics will sometimes try to surface in the bedroom as well." She turned and faced the three detectives. "A few well-shot photos is usually enough to discourage further activity. If I even remotely suspected one of Beth's former dates had something to do with this, you would have his name today and the tabloids would have the digital memory sticks tomorrow."

Morgan felt herself blink in surprise at the intensity in the older woman's eyes. "Thank you, Mrs. Stegman. Please let us know if any names come to mind."

CHAPTER 13

NEW YORK, LATE SATURDAY NIGHT

Roger sipped his coffee, the plastic lid doing a good job of holding in the heat. The emissary had insisted on buying them each a cup at the specialty coffee house and ordered an Italian blend with a hint of vanilla and a spice Roger could not quite place. It must have tasted as it should. Novara had gulped his down without any regard for the scalding liquid and had only sighed with contentment after throwing the empty cup into the nearest trashcan. Roger had trouble enjoying any drink that cost as much as the visitor paid for these two cups.

Careful, your working class roots are showing. He smiled at the thought, knowing exactly what his father would have said about the cost of the coffee.

The night was still considered early for a New York weekend crowd. The priest's gaze hopped from face to face as the two of them strolled down the sidewalk, his head snapping back and forth as he tried not to miss looking at any passerby. He did not want to admit to himself he still had no clue what he was looking for but he hoped he would recognize a clue when he saw it.

Music and an undulating wave of voices mixed with taxi cab horns to form a concert of real world noise, moving to a disjointed beat. At times the cacophony rose to a crescendo, usually in front of a dance club with some no-neck behemoth jealously guarding the doorway to the pleasures promised on the other side. At others, the noise dropped to the level of a television in the next room. He could hear the show and might even be able to follow the conversation if he was quiet and concentrated but more likely it remained a distraction, only white noise in the distance.

The sounds were not so loud they would have stopped

conversation between the two men, but, except for the few minutes at the coffee shop, they had not spoken. The emissary seemed perfectly content to wander through the night in silence, a solitary figure in a crowd.

Roger, on the other hand, was a victim of his conversation with Cardinal Atchison. Though his attention seemed to be entirely focused on the surrounding people, he remained aware on this night of his companion's pace, his demeanor—even his breathing—and a few things had caught the priest's attention.

Novara rarely made eye contact with men and never with women. Though he would not look directly at them, he brushed against almost everyone who passed, a fleeting touch, the barest hint of contact, and then moved on in a desperately neurotic attempt to feel a part of the other people's lives. Or at least that was how his actions appeared.

The emissary often cocked his head to one side, appearing not to listen to what was right beside him but straining to catch a faint whisper in the distance over the street noise. His tongue licked his lips—often—for what reason, Roger would not even venture a guess.

And he sniffed. Novara smelled the air like a little boy walking into a kitchen with fresh cookies on the counter. But when the priest tried to breathe in as deeply, all he smelled was the stench of the city—gas fumes mixed with people and rotting garbage.

Finally, Roger understood a little more about what the Cardinal meant by being "on the cast." The duo would walk for five or six blocks in a straight line before suddenly circling, heading off down a side street or rambling in a zigzag pattern on a diagonal from the direction they had started. An experienced cabbie would have had trouble duplicating the apparently meandering journey the two had taken, but Novara seemed unaware of how haphazard a course they walked. In fact, by his confident stride and purposeful set of his shoulders, the emissary appeared to know exactly where he was going.

"Mr. Novara," Roger asked, his raw nerves finally giving enough ground to curiosity to risk disturbing the other man's search. "When we spoke in the Cardinal's library, you mentioned the nabi before we were interrupted. Was there a point you were trying to make or were you just passing the time until the Camerlengo returned your call?"

"Both."

Nearly an entire block passed by in silence. Roger had just decided conversation was forbidden on a hunt like this when Novara surprised him by continuing. "The Bible is full of words of wisdom from God's prophets, touting what tomorrow will bring. But did you ever wonder what it would be like to be a part of a prophecy, be chained into its path with no hope of escape, no chance of choosing your own life? People throughout history have wanted to sing the praises of the heroes in those stories. Glorify the predestined ending."

Roger watched the emissary grimace and bite his lip, fighting back a pain only he knew. After a few strides, Novara began talking again. "What if the nabi had foreseen a dark path he was tied to, a trail that did not lead to the fairytale ending? Not everyone gets a 'happily ever after' in every story."

"But those types of prophesies are warnings," Roger answered, "telling us to return to God's path or evil tidings will be paid in retribution—the prophecies of denunciation you heard me describing to my catechism class. Even Sodom and Gomorrah were given warnings. If anything, the Bible tells us all can be saved, that no past sin is unforgivable."

Novara winced at the priest's final words before a cold chuckle escaped his lips. "What of the prophesies that are not in the Bible?"

Now Roger walked in silence. He felt he was being driven into a trap, part of a herd of wild mustangs led to their capture by the trained Judas-mare. However, if he wanted more information about what was really going on with the emissary—like the Cardinal had warned him—he needed to keep Novara talking, even if that meant trotting alongside the other horses and ignoring when his instincts told him to bolt in the other direction.

"You are speaking, of course, of the three prophesies of Fatima. The first two were made public decades ago and part of the third was released in 2000. But even the part still kept from the world has been known by all the popes since 1957, including his Eminence, Pope Francis. But God's grace only shined on the three shepherd children less than one hundred years ago. A new canonization…"

Novara shook his head, a smile touching his lips but never quite reaching his eyes. His gaze continued on with their serious task, darting from face to face, but Roger could tell they also watched a scene from the man's past—a scene that held no pleasure.

"No, not Sister Marto's portents." Novara finally did release a laugh, the sound tinkling in the air with the promise of a mountain brook turning into a snow-melt torrent. If the emissary ever let loose with a heartfelt belly laugh, Roger wondered if the whole world would smile along as well.

"Lucia," the older man continued. "I tell you, Father, for someone who abided by the vow of silence as an adult, we couldn't shut her up as a child. She could talk the ears off a deaf man Pius always said. Sweet girl, though." The smile faded away and now his mouth matched the emotions haunting his eyes. "And she believed every word she spoke with all her heart."

Silence dropped between the two men again, a bubble of quiet moving through the late-night bustle. Novara appeared lost in some part of his past but Roger hardly noticed, his attention focused on remembering the succession of popes. He stumbled when he realized the emissary had just casually referred to intimate discussions with Pope Pius XI, the man who had led the church eighty years earlier. *I must have misunderstood what he said.*

The two men turned at the next intersection, alternating left and right turns for a half-dozen blocks until they walked down quiet sidewalks lined with upscale brownstones. The hush between them was more pronounced when coupled with the stillness of the neighborhood.

"You remind me a lot of her, Father," Novara said, startling Roger with the sudden renewal of the conversation. "You are also the rock of the true believer, not the slightest tremor showing in your unshaken faith. Tell me," he asked as he turned his head, seizing the priest's gaze with his eyes and sending bolts of ice down the younger man's spine, "have you ever had reason to question your faith in God? A whisper of doubt? A feeling of helplessness when tragedy strikes the innocent? I'm not talking about some little bump in the road. I'm asking if you ever screamed into your pillow late at night, tears wetting the case while your hands ripped at the sheets—all while your mind silently screamed: Why? Why? Why?"

Roger understood this was no idle question. The words had been asked with too much fervor, too much hinted accusation, to be anything but a question asked from experience.

Just that quickly, he recognized the look lurking in the corners of the emissary's eyes: despair. Pure, no-hope-for-tomorrow despair. An echo of the Jews marching to the gas chambers played in there alongside the Christians in the Coliseum or the passengers in the Titanic as it sank beneath their feet. Death was the only expectation of someone with that look and Roger did not know whether to weep for Novara or run away, screaming in terror.

"Of course, we all have our tests," he replied, a slight waver making his voice crack. "But God does not give us a bigger challenge than we can…"

"You are untempered steel," Novara interrupted. The despair disappeared from his eyes and now they narrowed in anger, tiny lines at the corners standing out now that he squinted. He turned back to look at the streets as disdain dripped from the end of each clipped word. "Untempered steel can be made into the most beautiful of swords, polished and gleaming in the light. Like your faith. Your parishioners come to you to confess their sins, pit their failures against their temptations, and they see someone to aspire to become, a bright beacon leading them safely through dangerous waters.

"But what they don't understand is you have never swam in the waters yourself. You are the prohibitionist ordering the alcoholic not to drink, the virgin condemning the nymphomaniac. You have never looked true temptation in the eye—the devil, evil, whatever—and so you have never been tested.

"And like a sword made from untempered steel, your unwavering rigidity becomes your bane, shattering the blade into little pieces with the first stroke in battle."

"How dare you!" Spit flew from the priest's lips as he spoke and, for the first time since he was just little Roger from the neighborhood, he felt the urge to punch someone in the nose. "Who are you to question my faith? You barely know me."

"I know exactly who you are because when I look at you, I see myself a long time ago."

Roger's anger slipped a little, chased back by the emissary's confession. "What happened to you?" he asked, but the whisper was so faint he doubted the other man heard them. "But you told me you were not a priest," he said more loudly. "That you only worked for the Vatican."

"I am not a priest now," Novara said. "I failed my own tests."

Roger's tongue clamped to the roof of his mouth, begging to be let loose by the thousand questions in his mind. Instead, the only sounds were the steady cadence of their footsteps, tapping a beat as a background to his whirling thoughts.

He was working with someone who had quit the priesthood? Turned his back on the call from God to serve? Worse yet, what if the man had been defrocked, forced to resign? Why did the Vatican still deal with him?

"Mr. Novara..." The rest of his question died on his tongue. Roger suddenly stood alone, watching the emissary raise his feet into a sprint.

The priest followed as quickly as he could but within two blocks he knew he would never catch the older man. His breath rasped through an open mouth and a bonfire smoldered in his lungs. A half a block ahead, Novara veered down a side street and Roger followed a few moments later, lurching into the turn like a third-rate thoroughbred on his last legs at the track.

Tall, thin houses on each side of the street leaned over him like taskmasters, berating his lack of physical condition with black windows for eyes and unsmiling lines of stone for silent mouths. He tried to offer up a prayer of thanks when he saw Novara stop at the corner of the next block, but a rattling, lung-clearing cough was all that came out of his open mouth.

A scream without sound pierced Roger's thoughts, promises of horrors threaded through its wordless cry. He fell to his knees and flung an arm above his head to ward off a presence that he felt was on top of his quivering body. His heart stopped—no longer connected to a body he had once controlled, fleeing from the dizzying depths of emotions and threatened to flatten him. Time hiccupped, paused, and left Roger drowning in a sea of terror.

Then it disappeared.

The priest sensed the bird, the being, the shadow of filth—whatever had flown over his head—was gone, still winging silently away into the night, spreading the darkness in its wake. Roger sighed and he ran a hand over his face, the palm coming away covered with sweat. Only then did he notice he lay flat on his back, not remembering when he fell the rest of the way onto the cold concrete.

"Are you all right?" Novara asked, the pounding of his shoes on the sidewalk announcing his approach. "Father Greene… Roger! Can you hear me?"

"Yes, yes. I'm okay." Roger turned his head to the side and looked at the emissary. As he did, he thought he saw something flash in the man's hand, a blink of white that stayed in his sight like the remains of a spotlight on a moonless night. The hand disappeared behind the man's back and when it returned, it was empty and offering to help the priest up.

Roger groaned as he regained his feet. His head pounded a beat, sweat on his forehead cool against the night. He glanced down and realized he must have hit the pavement hard to cause his pants to rip at the knee. Hopefully there was not a matching cut underneath, but from the ache already starting, he doubted he would be that lucky.

"I don't know what happened. I must have gotten light-headed from all the running."

Novara nodded and kept a hand on the priest's elbow but he was already staring down the street. "Tell yourself what you must," he said, "but we need to move even more quickly now." Novara pulled Roger into a trot in the direction from where the thing had appeared.

Or at least as close as Roger could come to a trot. His lungs still burned and straightening his right leg sent jolts of pain shooting down his shuffling skip. The two men kept up the pace for a block, turned down the next street, and continued on for two more. Before they reached the last intersection, however, Roger saw the twirling reflections of red and blue lights shining from around the corner of the buildings. Novara slowed their pace to a walk, allowing them to sidle up to the rear of a small crowd already gathered in front of an apartment complex.

"What…" Roger started, but quickly stifled the question when the emissary turned the gentle hold on his elbow into a grip of steel.

"Shhh. We will find out all we must know but we cannot be noticed," Novara whispered. "Not yet."

The duo eased farther into the gathering of gawkers, the big-city equivalent of vultures circling a carcass in the desert. Snippets of surrounding conversations began to tell the story.

"I think he did something in advertising... or a writer..."

"... she used to bring cookies down to the laundry room..."

"... husband surprised the attacker..."

"Nice couple. He helped my Steve carry up some boxes."

"... one paramedic threw up..."

"... the door was wide open..."

"The neighbor across the hall found them, you know, the widower in 3G."

"... blood everywhere..."

"... she was a teacher..."

"The one cop said she was almost cut in two."

"...say he might live. I don't know. Looked like a damn lotta blood on that gurney when they wheeled him out."

"She never had a chance..."

"Mm, hmm. Dead before they even called for the ambulance."

Roger glanced over at the emissary and Novara motioned with his head to leave. They walked for nearly fifteen minutes until they reached a busy street, ambling now with no rush, before the silence was broken.

"We had better hail a taxi," Novara said. "Your knee will need looked after or tomorrow will hold a long evening for you."

"Who we're looking for killed that couple tonight, didn't they?" Roger knew his question sounded more like a statement. He also knew he was right before the emissary nodded in agreement.

"Yes. We were too slow this evening but he is not done yet. We will have more chances."

"That thing... how is he connected to that... that thing that flew..." Roger found it difficult to finish, the memory of his terror gripping his heart again and threatening to make him faint.

Novara whistled and waved his arm at a cab parked about half a block away. While they waited for the car to cross traffic, he stepped back up onto the curb beside the priest, his lips moving in quiet conversation.

"We have to move faster... might still have time... Did it feel me?... faster..."

Roger listened to Novara mumbling his way through a one-sided discussion. The talking continued until the cab stopped in front of them.

"Tomorrow, after you have awakened from a much-deserved nap after Mass, I want you to find out everything you can about the daughters of Philip the Evangelist and St. Hildegard. Then we can continue our conversation on our evening walk." Novara reached down and grabbed the handle but then paused before opening the door.

"And Father Greene… Roger, make no mistake about tonight. The creature that flew over us was the butcher that murdered those people. *It* is the enemy which we seek."

CHAPTER 14

NEW ORLEANS, 1858

Gregor grinned as he walked along the edge of the street, stepping lightly around horse droppings and refuse while his priest's black raiment fluttered with his motion. A light tune, barely remembered from his childhood, escaped through his lips and threatened to force his feet into what could pass for a dance.

I've won. I've done what none of my teachers thought possible. Thank God there'll be no more killing this time.

His hand trailed down elaborate wrought-iron fencing, some highlighted with gold paint to give the illusion of gilding. New Orleans was growing fast and like a little girl who played dress-up in her mother's clothes and jewelry, the display was often pretentious and gaudy. Dauphine Street was in an affluent section of town and while the houses were large and beautiful, the people could not be bothered with small items like street cleaning or decorum.

This last thought drew a grimace to his face—a reminder of why he had been summoned to this country that had so much potential but was still too young to exude any maturity. The land was raw, too raw to allow itself to be tamed by anyone but the roughest of people. Less than a day's ride could still bury a man in the dankest of swamps or the darkest of woods. The type of men and women needed to drop the wilds to its knees were driven by the biggest of egos and most fantastical of dreams. Those people also carried the deepest of hungers—for food, for sex, and for power. It took no great stretch of the imagination to see why his prey had chosen this place to seek its own desires.

The house he watched for loomed out of the morning mist. Red-gold light peeked around the clouds and shone through the iron fence, casting sticks of shadow against the brick façade. Even here, what should have been a stately home was ruined by an overabundance of scroll trim and bright red curtains pulled tight against the outside light.

At least the garish shielding held a purpose besides decoration. Gregor knew from his time here the velvet hangings cast some of the rooms into deep night broken only by the flicker of a candle or two. Other areas rivaled the outdoors, light blazing from the new gas fixtures placed in every corner of the rooms. A contrast in light and dark, the house existed on the extreme border between eternal midnight and forever day. Gregor knew this because he had lived within its walls for five long and arduous months.

But not last night. Last night had been spent in the best of what this city offered by way of hotels. The servants had been quick and courteous and the bed soft—not that a hard slab would have mattered to Gregor. After so many weeks of little-to-no sleep, he could have snored his way through a cannon battle and not have twitched an eye. A smile bloomed across his face as he wondered if the newlyweds could boast of the same restful night. This would not be the first time he would eat the traditional morning-after-the-wedding breakfast with only the friends and family while the bride and groom made a late appearance—if they appeared at all.

Gregor's footsteps suddenly faltered. The front steps of the house were empty for the first time since the day he had presented himself to Sultan Terim. The two soft-spoken, muscular young men who served as guards with their strangely curved swords were nowhere to be seen.

The priest fought down the panic that threatened to stop him in his tracks, the joy of his apparent victory from the day before vanishing in the golden morning. He trotted the rest of the way to the gate. Gregor's resolve did waver now, his gaze traveling from the open iron entry to the heavy chain and padlock still looped around the gate. He felt his gaze pulled slowly up the walkway until he saw the pool of blood that had formed on the top step.

The strength left his body. Gregor sagged against the iron gatepost and his head swam for a moment. His hand moved of its own accord to the small of his back where he felt the reassuring bulge of the knife beneath his coat. The touch of the blade, even through his clothing, gave him the courage to pull himself up to the top of the head-high fence and drop over to the inside.

The priest did not look down at the blackened pool by his feet, but he made sure not to step in the blood when he reached for the door. It opened silently on oiled hinges, the silence only making it easier to hear his gagging. Death floated on the air flowing from the house, the smell of blood mixing with sickly sweet smoke. The priest offered a silent prayer before stepping inside the doorway.

Blood coated the floor of the foyer in blackening pathways, the walls discolored where it had splashed on their surfaces. Gregor stepped over the slippery mess. He stared through the opening into the sitting room on the right, the gas lights easily showing the carnage that continued in there. What appeared to be the remains of a muscular arm lay over the side of a scrolled settee and the lower part of a torso and legs stuck out from underneath the heavy curtains. The syrupy odor was stronger here, the long hair of one of the guards still smoldering where his decapitated head lay in the embers of the fire.

Gregor continued his search but each room revealed more death and defilement, total disdain for the bodies that had once hosted souls. He caught himself chanting a prayer under his breath, a prayer old before this land had been discovered. The icy ball in his stomach melted as he said the words and his resolve stiffened. He reached underneath his coat and withdrew the knife in his belt, its white blade dancing in the rooms with gas lights and glowing in the rooms where candles should have been lit.

A sigh of relief escaped from the priest's lips as he finished his search of the first floor. *Aysel's not here. She must be safe.*

Even as Gregor felt elation flooding his body, his gaze was drawn toward the grand staircase leading to the second floor. Blood had flowed down the wood at one point, a river of crimson laid out like a carpet for a demon's feet. However, the pouring must have been hours ago because now the liquid had set into a dark mat for anyone to walk on. The ball of dread reappeared.

Every moment of the last few months—every sleepless night, every decision, every second of hope—each one paraded in his mind in a blur, stopping only when he remembered the joy of the wedding the previous night. He climbed the stairs while the faces from yesterday gave way to a procession of others from his past.

All of them wore a mask of pain and horror, accusations of betrayal imprinted upon their eyes. All except Aysel. At least he could remember her with a glowing smile upon her lips.

The double doors to the master suite stood open and Gregor watched the room come into view as he breached the top of the stairs. Tears rolled down his cheeks. Feathers and bed-stuffing lay strewn across the floor, sodden and discolored from the blood that stained them. Aysel lay across what remained of the mattress.

He prayed to be able to blush at her nudeness but so much skin had been removed from her body she could have been any piece of meat hanging at the butcher's shop. One leg hung over the side of the bed, still clinging to the rest of her body by only a small amount of sinew. Her arms had been clawed into ribbons of flesh and bone. Almost nothing remained of her from the tops of her shoulders to her hips. Gregor glimpsed part of the white bone of her back through the gelled blood and bits of internals left lying in her middle.

But it was her face that demanded his attention. Her cocoa-colored eyes were gone, ripped from their almond-shaped sockets. Claws had left deep furrows across her smooth cheeks. Her full, red-tinged lips were missing and Gregor thought he saw teeth marks in what was left of the surrounding skin.

There would be no more smiles for Aysel. This would be the face Gregor remembered now.

He grabbed the bedpost for support as he doubled over, bile shooting from his mouth until only dry heaves wracked his body. The priest staggered away from the bed, his feet moving faster with every step. By the time he reached the bottom of the stairs, Gregor was moving too fast, slipping on the blood-covered boards and falling into the gory mess. He scrambled back to his feet with speed born of panic and disgust. Hands covered with crimson left paths of red across black clothes and his pants clung to his leg, soaked through with the blood of the victims.

His feet sliding out to the side, Gregor half-ran, half-skidded down the hallway toward the back of the house. Trails of red spread across the walls where he reached out for balance. Tears clouded his eyes when he staggered around the blood surrounding a serving girl, her arm still outstretched toward the door leading to the back yard.

Cool air swept across the priest's face and he stumbled down the steps. Gregor glanced back over his shoulder as he trotted across the grass, his gaze drawn back for one last look at the house. Suddenly, his right foot refused to move forward and he stifled a yell as he fell to his knees with a grunt.

The ground had been turned over where he tripped and at first he thought someone from the household had started a new flowerbed. The hand reaching up out of the dirt told him his mistake. There would be no need to dig up the body. The royal signet ring with the enormous ruby identified the corpse as Sultan Terim.

The tears continued to flow down Gregor's cheeks. He cursed. The words tasted bitter on his tongue but he did not care.

It was all a lie. I never won. Gregor shook his head as he stood up on quivering legs, his shoulders slumping. *No one ever wins this game.*

CHAPTER 15

NEW YORK, LATE SUNDAY MORNING

Morgan's fingers danced through her hair, fluffing and primping tresses that luckily fell back into place despite the unneeded attention. The red locks were given a brief rest while her hands flattened imaginary wrinkles on her slacks and jacket before falling in an intertwined lump in her lap. Out of the corner of her eye she noticed the cabbie glancing into the rearview mirror and smiling.

"Boyfriend or family?" he asked, a guttural-tinged accent making the question sound more like a demand for information.

"Excuse me?" Not for the first time, she wondered why her mother had insisted on her taking a cab to the house instead of driving her own car.

"Are you going to your boyfriend's house or your family's?"

"Oh, it's Sunday dinner at the folks."

"Ah," the man said, waving his hand like he was shooing away a fly. A reassuring grin split his face and revealed tobacco-stained teeth. "Then all will be well, Miss. Sometimes we nervous when we go to boyfriend's or girlfriend's house, things don't work out. But family is family and nothin' so bad you can't go home."

Morgan smiled and nodded as the cabbie prattled on about one of his cousins not going home for years—she thought the reason had something to do with a lost hat but she was not listening closely enough to be sure—meanwhile she wondered how warm a reception she would receive. She had not returned to her parents' house since the last Sunday lunch several months earlier when she had stormed out the front door, fists clenched by her sides and tears streaming down her cheeks.

The streets changed from concrete paths with towering high-rises blocking out much of the sky to two- and three-story buildings, neighborhood delis and markets that switched their make-ups with the changes of the surrounding ethnicities. Eventually even the shops gave way to cookie-cutter middle-class houses that were only different by brick or siding, porch or stoop. Sure, a few of the blocks had started to deteriorate, houses with shutters hanging from one hinge or a dilapidated couch laying on its back in the yard, but Morgan only noticed a couple of houses that appeared to have been deserted and one probably on its way to becoming the local drug mart. She was happy the neighborhood had not fallen completely apart, not because of any nostalgia she might feel for her old haunts, but because her mother and father would be too stubborn to leave their house of forty years even if a war zone opened up around it.

"So you see, Miss," the cabbie said as he turned into the driveway of a house that, save for the color of the paint on the shutters and the choice of flowers in the gardens beneath the windows, was a carbon copy of the homes flanking it. "Just like cousin Dmitri, you will find out, too, all is always hokey-dokey with family. Smile."

"Thank you. I hope so." Morgan did flash the man a smile and handed enough money through the seat window to leave a generous tip. A minute later he backed out of the driveway and she walked up the sidewalk. She was still a few steps away from the stoop, and trying to decide whether to walk straight in or ring the doorbell, when the door flew open and out rushed two of her nieces and one nephew. At least someone had been anxious enough for her visit to watch from the front window.

"Aunt Morgan, we've been waiting…"

"Grandma promised you were coming this week…"

"After lunch, Aunt Morgan, can we throw the baseball in the…"

"…lunch is almost ready…"

"…you can use Dad's glove…"

"…we really missed you…"

"…we've already put the plates on the tables…"

"…Cindy's got a boyfriend and they kissed…"

"I did not! Aunt Morgan, tell him…"

"…I hope you're going to come around more again."

"I hope I can too, honey," Morgan said, wondering how she could have ever let a stupid argument keep her away this long. She smiled at each of the kids as they continued to race on with their conversations, nodding at the appropriate spots and gathering months' worth of hugs even while they somehow managed to move en masse through the front door. All the time, however, a small part of her thoughts reminded her these were her brothers' children, not her own, and a bit of the joy evaporated.

"All right, kids," her brother, Sean, said. "Let 'er breathe. She'll be here for a while. Ain't that right, Sis?"

"Yeah. I'll stick around today."

Morgan sat back in her chair and took another sip of wine, reluctant to drink too much in case she had to play a game of catch later with her nephews. Her family was a hardcore boilermaker crowd, a beer and a shot of whiskey, but her mother never allowed liquor under her roof on a Sunday or Christmas. Wine, however, was a different story. Anything that was okay for the priests to drink on the Sabbath was good enough for the family her mother had decided decades ago.

The children had already escaped into the back yard and the relative silence left in their wake made the adults' conversations seem subdued despite her brothers arguing over Ellsbury's contract and the Yankees' relief pitching. Rangers, Giants, or Yankees—it never took long to figure out what sport was in season. All anyone had to do was listen to her brothers and father for a few minutes.

Morgan leaned forward and brushed the crumbs from a half-eaten dinner roll onto the plate beside her. She always sat by the kids at family gatherings, probably for more reasons than she wanted to admit to anyone—including herself. The long table started in the dining room, every extension put in to lengthen its reach, before changing to a series of card tables that varied in height. They rose and fell beneath the tablecloths like a haphazard series of steps, trailing through the French doors into the living room.

When she and David had been married, he had sat in the dining room with the rest of the men while she enjoyed her self-imposed exile with the children at the other end of the tables. She did not want to think she should have read the arrangement as an omen to the fights they would have later.

"Morg, come on down and join the grown-ups," Patrick's wife, Peggy, said as she patted the seat of the chair beside her. She was the oldest of the sisters-in-law and had always treated Morgan like she was her own little sister, someone that needed to be watched over.

Morgan smiled as she gathered up her glass and crab-walked between the end of the couch and the tables. She eased onto the folding chair beside her sisters-in-law and shook her head when Mary jiggled a wine bottle as an offer for a refill. Sean's wife did take the opportunity to fill her own goblet before topping off Julie's without asking. If Mary was drinking alcohol, at least she was not pregnant again. Of course, after six kids you never knew when Mary and Sean might surprise the family with another "big announcement."

"You've changed your hair," Julie said, interrupting Morgan's thoughts.

"Yes, I wanted something easier to throw together in the mornings now that I'm back on duty."

"I don't know I even have hair until I've got all the kids packed off to school," Mary said with a laugh.

"Well, I like it," said Julie, the youngest sister-in-law. "It makes you look happy and carefree."

Morgan eyed the small, dark-eyed woman that had married her youngest brother, Casey. Born and raised in a small northwest Ohio town, she had met him when they both went to Bowling Green State University. Casey had earned a hockey scholarship and gone off to the flatlands of the Midwest with the hope of becoming an architect. But he had injured his knee and the surgery and recovery left him chewing on painkillers like they were aspirin. About then, Julie become pregnant so they both dropped out of school, married, and moved back to New York City where Casey had cleaned himself up and fallen into a public service career like all the Flaherty children.

"You're not fooling me. It's not her hair putting some spring in her step," Peggy said with a shake of her head. "It's because she's working again."

Mary laughed. "Good God. I can't believe you miss all that blood and guts." She took another drink of wine. "And working with all those men. You must need to swim through the testosterone to get to your desk every day. Do they let you judge the pissing contests?" Peggy and Mary laughed until tears formed in their eyes.

"Leave her alone," Julie snapped. "She's lucky enough to be able to do what she loves."

Morgan forced a laugh, hoping to cut through the wall of tension that flared up between the other women. She really did not want to participate in another argument about whether women should stay at home and take care of the children or work outside of the house. She could still be married if she wanted that fight.

"Most days you're right. I keep waiting for the cavemen to go out and kill a dinosaur to bring back. My new partner's not like that, though. Frank's such an old-fashioned guy he won't even call me by my first name."

"I don't think I could stand for that," Peggy said. "Patrick being paired up with a woman. I don't know how you sit still for a woman being in the same firehouse as Sean."

"I just make sure he's taken care of before he goes in for his shift," Mary answered while raising her glass in a self-deprecating salute. "It's a lousy job but someone has to do it."

The women laughed loudly enough the men stopped talking at their end of the table for a few seconds. Morgan chuckled even harder when they merely shrugged and returned to their heated discussion over the left-handed pitcher who had just been called up from AAA, already assuming one of them had been the butt-end of a joke but not caring enough to ask.

"You don't seem to mind too much with all the kids you've got running around," Julie said, not ready to give up on holding a serious conversation yet. "Come on, Morgan. Are you working on anything interesting?"

Visions of the disemboweled women leaped through Morgan's mind. She was so wrapped up in her memories, she barely noticed her mother hurriedly rise and go through the swinging door into the kitchen. A glance down at the phone on her belt told her Frank had not called and she still had a good signal. She did not know whether to be happy the nightly killings seemed to have stopped or to be worried the pattern was changing.

"Nothing I can talk about yet. It's a bad one, though."

Julie started on a rant about the crazy people living in a big city and why living in a small town was much better for children. Peggy and Mary took turns arguing for the city life. Morgan did not listen; she did not need to join in to know where this conversation was headed. She had heard it all many times before. Julie would argue with the other two, beating her head against a wall by trying to explain where she had been raised to two women whose idea of wide-open spaces was the vacant lot between two buildings. In the end, the young woman would simply grow quiet and stare out the window in between quick glances at Casey. And the next time Morgan saw her sister-in-law, she would appear a little more haggard, reflect a little more of a caged-animal look in her eyes.

But Morgan's thoughts were far from the misery Julie carried.

Had the killer broken his pattern? Were they really searching for one serial killer or had there just been a horrible set of coincidences? Was there really more than one person who could cause that sort of pain and destruction?

Morgan had gone to bed the night before so convinced she would receive a call in the wee hours of the morning she had laid out clothes she could easily slip into and be on the way to a murder scene in no time. In a twisted way, she was almost disappointed not to hear Frank's voice giving her an address. Of course, she had awoken once again with the thought someone was in her apartment but a search revealed no one.

"Tell her, Morg," Peggy snapped, pulling her out of her private thoughts. "Tell her you think the city is a great place to raise kids as long as you keep your eye on them."

"I think," Morgan said as she stood and grabbed a couple of dirty plates, "I think it's time I helped Mom clean up."

She pushed open the door with her elbow and walked into the kitchen. Her mother stood at the sink, water hissing from the hand hose and beating a rhythm on a plate as Morgan let the door swing shut behind her.

"Why don't you let Dad buy you a dishwasher?" She put the plates down on the other dirty dishes and grabbed a towel from the drawer to wipe dry the clean ones. "You know he'd do it."

"We don't really need one. It's only the two of us through the week and the girls are here to help on Sundays. Besides, most of the time I just let the dishes air dry now."

Morgan laughed. "Well, you'd never have let us get away with that when we were growing up."

"Of course not. You have to keep kids busy or they start finding ways to get into trouble. You'll know what I'm talking about..." Her mother hesitated a moment, shadows of inner thoughts flashing across her face. "Someday. You'll understand someday when you have kids of your own."

The kitchen was quiet for the next few minutes, the silence broken only by the splash of water and the clink of plates as Morgan placed clean dishes into the cupboards. She did not know which was worse: her mother obviously full of questions and remaining silent or being grilled for answers with all the deception of a cop on a murder case. At least she knew where she had inherited her interrogation skills. This was the part of her return she had dreaded the most and now she found herself hoping the cabbie had been right about family.

"You look tired. Are you getting enough sleep?"

The indirect route. She must be going to circle around and try to trap me from the backside. Just keep dodging; Peggy and the others will be out to help at any minute. "I'm all right. I've just had to get up the last few nights for a case." *There's no way I'm telling you I woke up in the middle of the night last night without a phone call, grabbing my gun because I was sure someone was in the apartment with me, watching my every move from the shadows.*

"Is it bad? Are people dying?"

"They're all bad, Mom. But yeah, this one is worse than most."

"It's not boys... not gangs again, is it?"

Morgan suddenly realized she had been maneuvered perfectly, played into this private conversation by a master manipulator. Peggy was in on it and probably Mary, too, but somehow they must have even convinced Julie to help. Of course, she could just as easily been an unwitting pawn, goaded into the argument that drove Morgan into the kitchen.

"No, it doesn't look like gang activity. Just your normal, everyday, sicko."

"I don't see how you can act so easygoing about the whole thing. Look at the people you have to deal with on a daily basis. It would be enough to drive anyone over the edge."

"Oh, come on, Mom! Do Sean and Casey take fewer risks when they go running into a building to put out a fire? How about Patrick when he's out walking his beat?"

Morgan watched her mother continue to wash dishes, her prune-skinned fingers never faltering as they scrubbed each one clean. She wondered if her mother had said too much, allowing some of her true feelings to surface.

"Did they give you a good partner?"

God, she is good. When faced with an answer or a situation that is unexpected, a good interrogator returns to the script and allows themselves time to re-evaluate what has happened.

"Yes. Frank's a good guy. I think he and Dad would hit it off. They're about the same age and he's old military. You know, everything in its place."

"You could learn a thing or two there if you keep your desk anything like you used to pick up your room."

The allotted time must have elapsed as both of them cocked their heads to listen to Peggy's voice as it grew louder through the door. Morgan let out a silent sigh. She had survived the inquisition and nobody's feelings had been crushed. Bruised, but not crushed.

"I'm glad you came home today, honey. You know you're always welcome to come back and eat anytime… or talk. There's other people you can talk to, too."

The other three women pushed through the swinging door—Peggy and Mary grinning broadly. Only Julie felt guilty enough to look sheepish about her role in the set-up.

"I know, Mom. I know."

CHAPTER 16

NEW YORK, SUNDAY AFTERNOON

Roger leaned back in his chair and rubbed his eyes until little white spots floated in his vision. A yawn started deep within his body, crept through his throat and stretched his mouth wide. When he was done, he sat up straighter in his chair and began reading again from the book lying open on the table in front of him.

The priest sat still for the next twenty minutes, the scanning of his eyes and the flipping of pages his only movements. His right hand hung in the air above a notebook, a pen wedged loosely between his fingers. Only a few lines were written on the white paper and he did not add any more. After turning one last page, he sighed and tossed the pen onto the middle of the table.

This is ridiculous. There's nothing here that's important to the emissary. This was just a wild goose chase to give me something to do and stay out of his way.

Roger picked up the pad and glanced at his scant few notes, wondering again what was supposed to be here that the emissary would want to discuss.

St. Hildegard—family name unknown (1098-1179)
Mother Superior of Diocese of Speyer
Horrible health, starting in childhood, barely able to walk, sometimes lost sight
learned to read psalms but never learned to write
had visions of future events starting in childhood
credited with several miracles
with the help of a local monk wrote Scivias —trilogy of books of her

visions
first book—6 prophesies
second—7
third—13

Roger's information on Philip the Evangelist was even skimpier.

Philip the Evangelist
not the apostle
one of first 7 deacons of the church, appointed to look after the
 apostles' widows and the needy
converted Simon the Magician
told by an angel to take ministry to Ethiopia
converted one of Queen Candace's eunuchs, led to the formation
 of the Christian church in the country

Roger studied the lines again. He repeated each word, jumping from Hildegard to Philip and back, searching for some connection between icons of the early Church that had lived a thousand years apart.

Nothing. There's nothing here!

He slammed the tablet down on the table and rose from his chair in a flurry of frustration, his bandaged knee protesting while he paced the library floor. He might as well get used to the pain; he would be walking all over the city again in a few hours.

Another yawn stopped him in his tracks. Roger knew he should have slept more this morning but he had really wanted to be at Ian's first Mass to provide moral support. Then he had needed to cut short his nap after lunch so he could attend to his "homework." A glance at his watch showed him he still had time before the third reason arrived for his early rise.

There must be something here. Novara is not the kind of man to waste time, including mine. What am I missing? I've checked every reference work here. If only Cardinal Atchison... that's it!

Roger walked over to the Cardinal's desk and fingered through the Rolodex. A few moments later he listened to the clicks as the connection left the country and moved halfway around the world. At last the call rang through and a man picked up on the other end.

"Buonasera. Posso t'aiutare?"

"Ah, yes. This is Father Roger Greene of St. Patrick's Cathedral in New York. Can I…"

"Americano? Mi scusi."

Roger heard the distinct click of being put on hold. He had not thought about the language barrier and now that he had placed the call to the Vatican, he wondered if it really was a good idea to talk to the Cardinal or just a fanciful thought fueled by his fatigue. Luckily, he did not need to wait long enough to decide whether or not to hang up.

"Good evening. This is Father Baston. May I help you?"

The voice was decidedly British with a touch of another accent Roger could not quite place. But the man was pleasant enough, even with a little boredom tossed in for good measure.

"Hello, Father Baston. This is Father Roger Greene from St. Patrick's Cathedral in New York. Would it be possible to speak to Cardinal Atchison?"

"Is it an emergency? The Cardinal only arrived a few hours ago and it is almost midnight. I am certain he is asleep by now. Perhaps his assistant can help?"

Argh! The time zone difference! Is there anything else I didn't think of? I really must be tired. "Oh no, please don't disturb the Cardinal. What I was calling about is not that important. It was just something that Emissary Novara said…."

"Excuse me, Father. You are working with Mr. Novara?"

"Yes." Roger had heard the waver in the other man's voice and a chill raced down his spine, wondering what could cause fear in a man half a world away.

"Just a moment, please."

Now Roger had plenty of time to consider whether he had made the correct choice by phoning the Vatican. If he had not given his name to his fellow priest, he probably would have hung up and allowed them to think he was only a crank caller. Several long minutes of silence passed, broken only by the periodic click denoting an international call. A lump sat in his stomach, spinning and bouncing with the thought Father Baston was off waking up Cardinal Atchison. Roger could not even imagine how six time zones of jet lag would punish a person's body. When a voice finally spoke, however, it was not the Cardinal on the other end of the line.

"Hello? This is Camerlengo Nowaski. Am I speaking with Father Greene? Is Novara okay? Is he hurt?" The deep bass voice echoed with a thick Polish accent around what could only have been a yawn.

Roger was so stunned he could barely speak. They had awoken the Pope's right-hand man for his call.

"Yes... I mean no, Camerlengo Nowaski. Emissary Novara is fine. This is Father Greene. I am terribly sorry to have disturbed you at such a late hour." Though the voice still sounded young and vibrant, the man was in his mid-eighties and he surely would have much rather had an undisturbed night's sleep.

"Nonsense. You are working on an important project for the good of the whole Church. Anytime you need something, do not hesitate to call me." The man cleared his throat and coughed, a clear indication the pleasantries portion of the conversation was over. "What can I do to help you with Mr. Novara?"

Roger noticed the Camerlengo had split the two of them apart, pitted them against each other, almost as though he could not believe they could be working together in tandem. *I can barely imagine it myself.*

"Camerlengo, every time I try to question Emissary Novara about exactly what we are doing, he somehow leads our conversation back to biblical prophecy. He could be a politician with the way he can talk without actually saying anything."

"How much as he told you about... I mean, have you seen it?"

Roger began sweating when he thought about the shadow flying above him on the street. "Yes." He wondered if the priest on the other end had even heard the strained whisper. "Yes, we were close enough that it flew over us in its escape last night." Anger flushed heat into his cheeks and chased away his fear. "But what is it!? Even when I asked him directly, Novara would only tell me to look up all I could on two more people from early Christian history."

"It flew over you? So close... so close." The Camerlengo's voiced trailed off, the man obviously lost in his own thoughts for a few moments. "I'm sorry, Father Greene. I suppose in his own way, Novara is trying to protect you, shield you from what must be done. Tell me, did you find the information you went looking for?"

"No. That's why I called. I have exhausted all my reference material here, but nothing connects any dots. I'm still just as lost now as I was earlier today."

Nowaski grunted. "Who did he tell you to research?"

"St. Hildegard and Philip the Evangelist. Should I tell you what I have found? It won't take very long."

Nowaski grunted again. Greene was beginning to think the grunt was the Camerlengo's version of Novara's humorless chuckle.

"No, I can imagine what you found. I probably edited some of the passages myself. And besides, Gregor most likely meant the four daughters of Philip the Evangelist. They were the prophets." There were several long moments of silence and Father Greene began to worry the call had been disconnected or the elderly priest had fallen asleep. But then he heard the Camerlengo clear his throat. "I will fax you the information Gregor wanted you to see. I must stress that no one else—no one!—is to see what I am sending to you. Destroy the documents when you are done reading them."

"Yes, Camerlengo Nowaski. Right away." Roger really regretted making the telephone call now. "Thank you for all your help, sir."

"Cardinal Atchison spoke very highly of you this evening, Father Greene. He called you an island of faith." Roger flinched at the identical description Novara had used the previous evening, this time as a compliment.

"Hang onto that faith, my son. Grip it in your heart and with all your soul and I believe you will see the other side of this trial. Know that I and everyone who works for me will be saying prayers for your safe deliverance. His Eminence is personally aware of your danger and has offered you his blessing."

"Thank you." Roger nearly passed out at the thought the Pope was praying specifically for him. "I'm sure Mr. Novara will not let anything happen to me in this hunt."

"Don't depend on that hope." The reply was delivered quickly and matter-of-factly, as if Nowaski had long ago known the answer to that statement, and with enough cold emotion to freeze the air in Roger's lungs. "Novara has his own objectives, his own set of rules. He's not like the rest of us in the Church; he's not like anyone else period. He has lost so much of whatever there was of himself along this path God chose for him, I believe he has even lost his faith—at least in his own way—and yet he continues on. He has come so close to completely losing himself but he has always found a way to move along the path. I don't know if my greatest fear is he will not complete his task or that he will not be able to stop once it is finished.

"Remember, Father Greene, the Church and God will forgive you anything you must do to complete this mission. Anything. You read what I am sending to you and much, much more will become clear.

"Please, no matter what happens or if you need help of any kind, give me a call." One last grunt. "You can even call me if something happens to that bastard Novara."

With that parting shot, Roger listened to dial tone.

The first page was barely out of the fax and lying on the sheet holder before Roger snatched it up and started to read. His gaze raced along the page, devouring two or three handwritten sentences then leaping back to the beginning to read the passage again. Each time he read a little bit farther before returning to stare at words that should have changed to make some sort of sense instead of remaining the same.

This is nonsense! It has to be. This is just somebody's idea of a bad joke.

But even as Roger tried to talk himself out of believing what was coming out of the fax machine, somehow he knew it was too crazy not to be true. Now he understood what Novara had meant by questioning his unwavering faith. It was not his faith in God the emissary had doubted. It was the question of whether or not Roger could bend his ideas of what he thought he knew about the Church. Novara had manipulated him, knew he would ask for and receive this information from the Vatican, and now the emissary would be able to judge the strength of the young priest. Roger wondered if he was being tempered.

A hand touched his shoulder and he half-leaped, half-fell from the chair while stray papers fluttered off his legs to the floor.

"I'm sorry to startle you, Roger, but you have visitors in the sanctuary. I've been calling your name for the past two minutes but you acted like you were a million miles away."

Roger glanced up at Ian but quickly returned his attention to gathering the loose papers scattered across the floor. Once he clutched them all back to his chest, he accepted the younger priest's hand and stood on his feet.

"It's not your fault, Ian. I was concentrating so hard... I mean, all of this is so unbelievable... did you say my appointment has arrived?"

"Yes," Ian said around a laugh. "They're here, but I would hurry if I was you. They don't look very happy. Just give me your papers and I will put them back into order for you."

Roger started to hand over the fax papers from the Vatican before suddenly remembering the Camerlengo's instructions. He snatched them back to his body and made the other priest jump in surprise.

"No, I can't. I'm sorry but I can't let you or anyone else see these papers." Roger hesitated, considering a lie before deciding the truth with an omission would better serve his purpose. "Ian, this fax is from the Vatican."

"Oh, Roger, why didn't you say it was official business for the Cardinal? Did he have a good flight?"

"Cardinal Atchison arrived with no problems." Roger stole a glance at the clock beside the mantle. The whir of the fax machine announced another sheet of paper and reminded him he had two responsibilities to perform at the same time. "I need you to do me a favor, Ian. I have to go out and counsel the Flahertys, but more of the fax is still coming through. I don't know how long it will take to finish. Will you stay here and make sure that no one looks at it while I'm gone?"

"Sure, no problem. I'll just sit here and work on my notes for catechism class."

Roger smiled his thanks and put the wrinkled papers in his hands down on the corner of the desk before walking to the door of the library. He stopped and turned with his hand still on the doorknob.

"That 'no one' includes you too, Ian. And one more thing—you did a terrific job today during the service."

Roger left the young priest beaming while wild thoughts about the portion of the fax he had read dropped a scowl over his face.

"Cathleen, you make me think I should still be stealing cookies off your countertop when you aren't looking." Roger gave her a quick hug before extending a hand to the silent hulk behind her. "Mr. Flaherty, you're looking well, sir." It may have been twenty years or more since the time when neighborhood parents took it upon themselves to discipline each others' kids—and he had felt his ears boxed by Morgan's father more times than he wanted to remember—but he still could not imagine himself calling this man by his first name, John.

"So what can I do for you two? All you said on the phone, Cathleen, was you wanted to talk. Don't tell me you're finally going to let me baptize one of your grandchildren. Are Casey and Julie going to have another one?"

Cathleen shifted her feet and cleared her throat a couple of times but did not say anything. John remained as still as a statue behind her, his gaze fixed beyond the priest's head on the altar. Roger realized this was not going to be a happy reunion meeting.

"Perhaps it would be best if we found a quiet corner where we can talk," he said. "Then you can tell me what is troubling you so much you came all the way into the city to talk to me."

"They want you to talk to me, Roger."

He had ignored the woman sitting a few feet away in the last pew in his haste to greet his old friends. But now he took a closer look at the red-haired woman with the green eyes riding above a freckled nose. She was as pretty now as she had been cute back when they were both kids. "Morg, is that you? You look great. What could you possibly need to talk to me about?"

"Call the station house. I was kidnapped and brought here against my will. I thought I had just been invited out for Sunday lunch. Now I think I may need to ask for sanctuary."

Roger thought the smile she offered was almost a grimace and, for a moment, she reminded him of Novara and his humorless laugh.

"Tell him!" Cathleen blurted out, not waiting on her daughter to become serious. "Tell him about your nightmares, about not being able to sleep. God knows you won't talk to anyone else in the family about it." The woman finally lost her composure and turned to hide her face against the stone-still body of her husband.

"We're going home now," John said, the rock of Mount Rushmore breaking free enough to allow lips to move. "Will we see you next Sunday, Morgan?"

"I don't know, Pop. Probably. I… I don't know. Goodbye, Mom."

Roger's gaze darted back and forth between Morgan and the retreating figures of her parents, moving with the sloth-like speed only weariness and worry for a child can cause. Once they disappeared into the sunlight beyond the doors of the cathedral, he half-sat, half-leaned against the end of the pew across the aisle from his childhood friend. "Is David working or has your father finally scared him away from the Flaherty Sunday buffet because he's a Red Sox fan?"

"David and I are divorced. Almost four years now."

So much for a humorous remark to break the ice. "I'm sorry, Morg. I hadn't heard about it. Was it your jobs?"

She shrugged. "Partly. I was ready for kids and David said he was too but he didn't want me to keep working once they were born. He said kids shouldn't have to wonder if they were going to lose both parents to a criminal's bullet. You can guess how I felt about that." Morgan laughed. "Those were some fights to write home about. It's a wonder the neighbors didn't call the precinct with all the yelling."

"Well, I'm truly sorry to hear about it. I thought if anyone could make it, it would have been you two." Roger walked across the aisle and sat in the row in front of her, turning sideways so he could look over the back of the pew and face Morgan. "But somehow, I don't think those fights and a four-year-old divorce are what worked your mother up enough to drag you in here to see me."

Morgan sighed. "No. Mom was pretty mad about the divorce but she understood the reasons why. At least she said she did."

She paused for a moment and pressed her slacks flat against her legs with her palms. Roger remembered this sign of nervousness from their childhood and it almost made him smile.

"Does it have to do with the shooting a few months ago?"

Morgan nodded her head. "Detective Kelly, hero of the war against gangs. It's a funny thing about being a hero. No one ever tells you that once the television cameras go away and all the newspaper articles have been written, all you're left with late at night is yourself and the memories of what you've done." She leaned back against the pew but still gave the impression of a wound spring, ready to leap away at a moment's notice.

"I read all the stories about it. That gang member would've

killed the girl and you know it. You had to shoot him to save her. He would've killed you, too, if you'd given him a chance."

"I know, Roger. I know. But you didn't see how young he looked once they took off his bandana and covered his tattoos. And going through the shooting once was bad enough. Do I have to go through it every night when I dream? When I can sleep enough to dream? When is the whole damn thing just over?"

Roger reached over and gave his friend's hand a squeeze. He was surprised by the strength with which she returned his grip. "Have you talked with anyone else? I mean a professional?"

"Oh, yes," Morgan said and chuckled dryly. "Department regulations dictated I meet with a shrink. He only let me back on full duty this week. Trust me—I've talked about the shooting until I'm blue in the face."

"The sessions didn't help?"

Morgan shrugged. "Yeah, a little. I guess. I used to see the banger I shot every time I saw a teenage boy's face. Then I saw him every night in my dreams."

"Maybe your mind is still working through the whole ordeal. It must be getting better."

"It is, it is."

Roger watched Morgan look off into the shadows down the sides of the sanctuary, peering intently into the nooks and crannies seemingly in search of something.

"Ever since I've gone back on cases," she continued, "my nightmares have changed. I used to see Manuel so clearly. Now he's a blur, like a faded old Polaroid picture that's losing its color and getting hard to see. Sometimes it's even hard for me to bring his face up in my mind. But then I wake up in the middle of the night and it feels like someone is there in my apartment, in my bedroom, hiding in the shadows, watching me and waiting for my next move. Deep down I know I'm alone, but it all feels so real."

Novara entered the sanctuary from one of the side hallways and Greene immediately spotted the man. He watched the emissary search the cathedral with his eyes, leaping from spot to spot with the same intensity he used every night on the hunt. Greene thought the man looked upset, the set of his jaw giving the appearance of anger. Or perhaps it was the way he stood with both hands behind his back under his coat. Novara looked like the captain of a warship surveying his enemies sailing on the horizon. *Blast him for being angry. He can wait. I have other duties of the Church to attend to besides him. It's not time to start tonight's hunt anyway.*

"You know, Morg, we're never really alone as long as we still have our faith with us."

"Ha, ha." Morgan's laugh reached out and echoed back from the walls, the noise sounding off-kilter in a place much more accustomed to solemn reflection. "I suppose I expected something like that from you, Roger. At least you didn't lecture me about my divorce."

The laughter drew the notice of several people either touring the artworks or searching for forgiveness in the pews and most paused to stare at the priest and the red-headed beauty. But, none of them attracted Father Greene's attention as much as the emissary. Novara's head had snapped around at the sound and now he continued to stare at the back of Morgan's head with unguarded intensity.

"There must be at least some small portion of yourself that still holds onto your faith. Despite your views about the Church, you would not have allowed yourself to be brought here even with your joke about being kidnapped. Remember, I know what it's like to try and change your mind after you've decided on something."

Roger was relieved to see a real smile cross Morgan's face. His own froze on his lips, however, when he glanced up and noticed Novara had disappeared. He couldn't help but look down at his watch to check the time while his thoughts jumped back to the fax in the library.

"Well, I'm sure you have more important things to do besides reminisce with an old friend and remind her what a terrible temper she has," Morgan said as she picked her purse off the pew.

"Yes... I mean no, of course not!"

This time Morgan's laughter sounded right, full of merriment with just a touch of teasing around the edges, and he quickly joined in with his own chuckles.

"Oh, Roger. You always were a silver-tongued devil."

"I'm so sorry, Morg. I do have something else I need to see to but I want to help if you'll let me. Promise me you'll come back tomorrow night after you get off work. We can talk about anything you want."

"I think I'd like that." They both stood up and began walking towards the doors leading outside. "Don't be surprised if I need to cancel at the last minute, though. I told you before I'm back on a case and it's a bad one."

Roger noticed her half-close her eyes as she spoke, wondering if that somehow helped to fight off the memories.

"It's so bad, in fact, last night was the first time since Thursday I haven't been called in the middle of the night because of it."

"That's okay," Roger said as he pushed open the door and they both stepped out into the fading light. "Just give me a call if you can't make it. Please try though, Morg. I think it will help."

"I will, Roger."

He watched her walk out to the curb and get into one of the waiting taxis. A few seconds later she was waving goodbye as they sped away from the cathedral.

Only then did he notice Novara standing off to one side. The emissary stared after the departing cab, his eyes fixed on the car weaving through the stop-and-go traffic. Once it was several blocks away, the man turned and walked briskly back into the cathedral, his lips moving in silent conversation with himself.

What an odd man. But the observation was all the time Roger allowed for the other man's peculiar behavior. Instead, his mind was already returning to the Vatican's fax and how much he could learn about Novara's mission before the evening's hunt.

CHAPTER 17

LONDON, 1888

Hawkers yelled about the qualities of their wares, screaming for attention with their voices but just as willing to grab a timid walker by the elbow and drag them closer to their stand.

The best meats! The finest breads! Women's fashions straight from Paris!

But both buyer and seller knew the meat was what the butchers across town could not sell last week, the bread was stale and hard enough to be used as a club, and no lady would ever drape what passed for a dress here over her shoulders.

Music, of a sort, broke up the sounds of the merchants' tales and the undulating noise of the crowds. Singers sang tales of lost loves while poets told of adventures. The paradox of the place was reflected in these performers: The more garish and ridiculous the costume, the more horrific the talent. One man in a bright red jacket with worn green lapels carried out his song by waving his arms, stamping his feet, and throwing winks at the listening women when his lyrics suggested a double entendre. Meanwhile he only occasionally hit the correct note—and even then almost by accident.

A few more paces down the block stood a woman who had to be younger than the worn-out expression on her face. Wisps of hair escaped from her bun and floated across dirt-smudged cheeks. Her blouse was so worn at the elbows the color of her skin was visible through the fabric and her skirt held stains so old and deep no amount of time spent on the wash rack would ever clean it again.

Yet her voice was that of an angel, sent down as a gift from above to bring tears of joy to all who heard her. Those who could afford the gift, reached into their pockets to dig out coins to toss at her feet and those who could not, cursed the fact they did not have even a shilling for just one more chorus.

The day sat just after dusk but on High Street the flickering light from the lamps made it appear earlier. Gregor walked through the display of light and sounds, a brooding shadow with a clenched jaw and steady pace. No merchants tried to lure him closer to their booth, no musician attempted to entice him with a song. In this section of Whitechapel where too long a glance at the wrong person or an argument over a farthing could buy the unwary a knife in the ribs, the survivors of the streets recognized the look of someone not to be trifled with and let him pass untouched.

Tonight he moved off the main road and turned his attention down Commercial Street, the smaller cousin of the thoroughfare winding off to the east. Here, other entertaining diversions could be found, diversions of a more basic nature.

Raucous laughter spilled out into the street along with a path of light from an open tavern door. A hulk of a man tossed some poor bastard out into the roadway, chasing him with one last curse. Too deep into his cups to notice the blood streaming from his broken nose, the sot lurched to his feet and staggered off in search of one more drink.

Sweet, sickly smoke drifted out of doorways where only the glowing embers in opium pipes lit the rooms beyond. A hacking cough and the rustle of clothes were the other scant clues of the people who sought anonymity in the pursuit of that evil.

The street lamps here were not as bright as on High Street, scattered farther apart and lending only sporadic pools of light. Standing beneath these dim moons were women. These were the prostitutes of middling fare, still retaining some of what nature had provided them in their youth but now birthdays past what even the most generous would call young. Most stood in loose groups around one or two men, their low-cut dresses pale colors beside the bright makeup touching their cheeks and lips. These ladies-of-the-good-times smiled and made small talk before whispering of their talents in the ears of passing men.

Then there were the solitary figures standing alone on the edge of the light. These women wore their makeup for a different reason—to hide the blooming purples and yellows of a two-day-old black eye. Perhaps they did not smile as much because their swollen lips hurt too badly to move or to hide the chipped teeth caused by a fist. These women were the outcasts, once members of the groups beneath the lights but now working without a manager, without the watchful eye of a man wielding a blackjack for their protection. They were walking down the path of their profession, picking up speed on an ever-increasing slope. In a few months they would not be afforded the comfort of even the edge of the light and would need to survive in the darkness of the alleys.

Past them all walked Gregor. His pace quickened and slowed, changing its rhythm like a drunkard trying to match the tempo of a song playing only in his head.

This was where the hunt held for the moment. Gregor caught flashes of his prey in his thoughts while he moved—the red brick corner of a building, the yawning black of a desolate side street, the laughter of many women at once.

The images drew clearer as the evening turned to night and then passed into a new day with the tolling of twelve bells. By now he had walked nearly to Hanbury Street and turned back, the siren call of the hunt urging him along the path he had already walked.

One woman, alone from the group that had been her greatest protection.

Gregor turned down the black trail between two buildings—too wide to be an alley but too dark and cluttered to be considered a street. Here was where the lowest forms of human existence eked out some sort of survival. Drunks passed out in the urine and filth in the gutter while barely two steps away a woman gave a man what he paid for, standing, with only the rough stone of the building behind her to act as a vertical bed. The deed done, she scurried away, a few coins in her hand to buy either the drink or the pipe to help her forget her part in the world.

Gregor's footsteps faltered at the thought of the woman rustling away into the night. He wondered what it would be like to worry only about his own needs, his own pleasures, and not be saddled with the responsibilities of so many other souls. He slumped beneath the weight on his shoulders, leaving him with the doubt he would ever find the promised light at the end of the trip or if the lantern had been snuffed out, the promise rescinded.

The smell of soap and water.

He turned again, this time traveling only a short distance before emerging from the man-made valley of shadows in front of the George Yard buildings. Gregor knew where he was now and lifted his feet into a trot, feeling his search nearing its end. He hesitated for a moment when he reached the corner of the nearest structure, his attention caught by the voice of a man. It went on and on—rising and softening, quickening and dropping—until at last it stopped, applause and laughter of a small group of women signaling the end of the performance.

Milky white skin, pale enough to rival the purest pearls.

Gregor lurched forward with this new vision, so real in his mind as to leave the salty taste of the woman's skin on his tongue, smell the alcohol on her breath and the stale smoke clinging to her clothes. He could not have stopped his hunt now, turned in yellow retreat, even if he found the will to try.

A dog barked in one of the dark labyrinths of paths and a curse followed on its heels. His fingers felt raw against the surface of rough brick. Gregor told himself he only used the wall as a guide for his footsteps in the dark, not admitting the touch kept him grounded, the scratching focusing his thoughts on his prey.

The corner of the building loomed out of the night. A sliver of light escaped through the crack between two buildings and shone on an irregular angle, distorting his perception. It was the same light he had seen in his vision.

A moan, almost a growl, escaped from an open window a few paces away. The sound was not the faked call a few coppers could buy. Ecstasy rode on its wings, rising and falling with a woman's gasps for breath.

Gregor stared boldly over the sash. Memories of New Orleans flashed through his thoughts. He would not wait. The memory of the stench of drying blood and death rose up in his mind along with bile in his throat. He could not wait.

The wood creaked beneath his hands as he swung his leg up and over, ducking his head under the upper panes before standing inside the room. The rhythmic swaying of the bed never slowed, but Gregor saw the beast looking over its scaled shoulder at him, the low light of the dampened lantern gleaming in its eyes.

"Good evening, half-breed," the incubus said, its voicing soothing with offers of unspoken pleasures. "It's been a long time.

Tell me, did you enjoy my gift the last time? The dark-skinned one?"

Gregor shuddered at the memory of Aysel's mutilated body. He reached under his coat and gripped the hilt of the white knife. The beast watched every movement with unblinking eyes, the rhythm faltering for only a count before continuing.

"Let's finish this. It's time the chase was over."

The incubus shook his head, a smile mocking him with jagged teeth behind slavering lips. "Not so fast, cambion. There's still time to savor the sweetness of this world. Join me in a taste of this one's flesh." He ran a scaly, four-fingered claw over the girl's bare thigh and left a red scratch in its trail. "Tell me you can smell her skin, drink in the lines of her breasts." The incubus looked down at the girl's face, wings quivering against his back where they lay folded. "Wake, child. Tell him your name."

The women's eyes fluttered open, losing the glaze of ecstasy and for a moment revealing only terror. The beast murmured something too soft for Gregor to make out and the fear poured away from the woman's face in a rush of emotion. Passion replaced the void.

"Mar… uhh… tha… uhh," she said in rhythm with the thrusts.

"Come to her, priest. Come to Martha." Every word reeked of lust. Razored claws sliced easily through the partially open bodice, naked breasts and stomach suddenly filling Gregor's sight. "Take her, cambion. Fill your soul with her passion and let it feed you throughout the centuries. Feel the power you've locked away behind your faith in the deceiver. Answer your desires, your needs."

Gregor suddenly realized he stood several paces closer to the bed than he remembered only a few moments earlier. He yanked the white knife from its sheath beneath his coat, searching for the courage to beat down his nature.

The incubus hissed at the sight of the weapon, anger and the memory of pain riding on the sound. The blade gleamed in the room, a beacon of hope or harbinger of despair, the answer lay in the eye of the viewer.

"So anxious are you to end our game of cat-and-mouse? Every step you take brings you closer to me, brings you closer to the side of you that belongs to me."

"I am nothing like you!" Yet even as Gregor denied the accusation, he felt his gaze drawn to Martha's breasts, dart down to where she and the beast joined.

"Look at him, child. Show him what he could be."

Martha turned her head toward Gregor. Her eyes fluttered open, fighting against the pull to close them in delight. He read the pleading call in their depths, heard the beckoning in her moans. She raised her hand toward him and he watched it sway as the incubus thrust again, fingers reaching to grab and yank him close.

In that moment he understood the unguarded look between two lovers, basked in the glow of adulation between worshipper and god.

Something flew open in Gregor's mind. A door only he knew existed slammed against its stop. He took another halting step forward but his mind and body told him to rush to Martha's side and push the beast out of his way. He ached for what he could take from the woman, roll in the nourishment of her emotions. Whatever tenuous grip his human half still held on his body stopped him at that one step, his head shaking in reply.

"No? You don't want a taste? Well, since I've had my fill," the incubus said as he withdrew from Martha and crouched above her still body on the bed, "and she's only tonight's meal..."

The incubus punched downward with his hands, driving his talons into her flesh with a sickening, wet plop. As Gregor watched in horror, the beast struck again and again, blood pouring from the wounds and splattering on the wall and floor. He finally remembered the knife in his hand and lunged forward, raising the world's redemption above his head for the final blow.

The incubus leaped upward and glided on silent wings even as the knife dived down, missing its mark and plunging into Martha's chest. At last her eyes flew open, the incubus's hold broken, fully aware of the pain wracking her body. Gregor's face was only scant inches from hers, close enough to smell the copper of her blood and powder on her cheeks. Crimson flowed between her lips and she gurgled "Why?" before her body went limp for the last time.

Gregor pulled back, staring at the blood on his hands and jacket sleeve where it had fallen across what was left of her stomach. He turned toward the window when he heard the beast laugh.

"More's the pity, half-breed. Martha was not the one for my dreams, but now I must hunt her, alone, until you decide to give in to what you really are."

The incubus leaped through the window and disappeared, powerful wings carrying him off into the darkness.

Gregor walked down the street, his tired steps leading him east on Whitechapel Road. He had been ready to turn in and call it a night when a vision of his prey had formed in his thoughts. Three and a half fruitless weeks had passed since the night of Martha Tabram's death, nights without even a hint of where the beast hunted, but the chance to end his frustrations added speed to his steps.

He turned to look over his shoulder as he moved, an uneasiness playing at the back of his neck, telling him someone followed in the dark despite his eyes declaring there was only a deserted street. His hand drifted into the pocket of his coat, gripping the letter he had received just three days earlier. Something in his last report to the Vatican had upset them, upset them to the point they pleaded with him to ask for help from the priests at St. Mary and St. Michael Cathedral. Even if he had wanted the help, the priests would have been too busy tonight with the feast of St. Raymond to come along on the hunt. Of course, that was only if they believed his story at all.

This time he thought he caught a glimpse of someone slipping off into the shadows when he turned a corner and looked back. He quickly forgot about the feeling when the vision of a woman leaped into his mind.

Gregor's pace lifted into a trot and he reached for the knife in his belt. There would be no conversation with the creature tonight. Tonight his hell ended. Tonight he would attack as soon as he found his quarry, take away the chance to be influenced by lies and temptations.

Temptations. Gregor did not want to admit to himself how much he had thought and dreamed about Martha since the night with the beast. Her smell. Her skin. Her beckoning gesture. The look of adoration in her eyes still made his breath come short and form sweat on his lip. The memory was enough to make the centuries-long hunt endurable.

Buck's Row rose from the street in front of him. He had searched this way before, the home of a number of prostitutes, but he had never felt the draw he felt now. Gregor slowed to a walk as he passed the line of pitiful buildings that served as houses. Leaking roofs and broken windows were minor inconveniences when compared to the filth in the streets and the rats scavenging the garbage with little regard for nearby people. An open door and a lit candle served to make one of the indistinguishable hovels different from the rest. Gregor crept through the doorway, the white blade leading the way.

His attempt at stealth did not matter. When he walked into the one-room shack, the incubus leaped out a broken window at the rear.

"Is Polly the one, cambion? Is she the one I searched for?" it asked before winging away between the houses.

Gregor walked to the side of the bed and stared down at the naked woman just beginning to wake up. This time he did not feel the want of desire, feel the pull of lust after her flesh. No. He saw only red, felt only rage.

Why must it be me? Why do they all need to die? Why does the Pope keep my mission a secret so I'm forced to live out this nightmare alone?

But Gregor knew the answers. He knew he was the only chance of saving the world. He had become the right hand of God—judge, jury, and executioner—the very manifestation of God's will. He would not and could not fail no matter what the price.

His left hand held the poor woman's throat as his right rose up and down, slicing and hacking at the womb that might carry the incubus's seed. The job finished, performed with only the remorse a butcher displayed for a side of beef, he wiped the gory mess off the blade on the corner of the bed sheet and left.

Gregor was three blocks away from Buck's Row when he realized someone else walked on the other side of the street, matching him stride for stride. Fear struck at his heart.

Is it a bobbie? Was I seen? Will I be stopped before God's mission—my mission—

is completed?

Gregor held his breath as he continued to walk, stealing furtive glances at his dark companion. Then the shadow walked under a street lamp and the pent-up breath escaped from him in a rush. The figure was no policeman. He recognized him as one of the poor street poets—Thompson was his name—who cited verses for money on High Street. Gregor also believed the man to be insane since he was often seen wearing a leather apron and calling it "bedding for the weary."

He nodded to the other man as he passed a public house on the corner, its windows darkened by the late hour, the folded letter still in his pocket. Gregor would continue on his mission alone. The Vatican did not understand. God's right hand needed no help.

His chin bobbed down and bounced against his chest. Eyelids sprang open and his head shot up, wakefulness gaining ground for the next few minutes.

Gregor was tired. Not just physically but mentally as well, his thoughts slowing as every minute of every night had become one long nightmare of constantly staying alert, always on the lookout for the slightest hint of his prey.

Prey. What he really wanted to do was pray. He longed to lose himself in a chant that would rest his soul as much as it rested his body. He needed the cleansing of confession.

But Gregor knew both sides of the sword. The prayer and sleep would rejuvenate his body and the confession would cleanse his soul but they would block him from sensing the incubus the same way he would be sheltered from the beast. Now was not the time to lose track of his quarry. Not when he felt so close to finally finishing his mission.

Gregor readjusted his weight and leaned against the building again while his gaze stayed fixed across the street.

29 Hanbury Street

Since his first glance at the home earlier in the evening, he had not sensed the incubus. That had been the pattern the last few evenings—a brief glimpse and then a trail gone cold. Minutes turned into an hour which took the night one step closer to dawn.

White skin against a gray blanket

Gregor sprinted across the street and leaped at the closed door like a madman. The jamb gave way with a wooden crunch and he tumbled across the floor beyond, clawing and scrambling on all fours until he gained his feet again.

Clenched eyes and a soft moan

He burst into the bedroom and threw himself at the pair of bodies writhing together. The incubus hissed in surprise and flashed his claws, but Gregor paid no attention to the danger. He struck and the knife dug deep into the woman's flesh, almost before the beast had withdrawn. Over and over he raked the blade through skin and organs. Blood covered his hands and splattered up on his face but still he struck.

"Not the one, half-breed. But now I'm still hungry." The incubus half-waddled, half-hopped through the broken doorway, as awkward on the ground as he was powerful in flight.

What happened? Why did I kill the woman first when I had a chance to strike at the evil?

Gregor pulled a handkerchief from his coat pocket, hands still shaking from his rage. He watched an envelope drift toward the floor at his feet. The letter from the Vatican had burned in his little stove a few nights earlier and now he found he did not care what he left behind. The moment of infernal fire gone, the rest of the world now paled until its concerns and its inhabitants were only reflections of what was important.

Leaden feet carried him back out of the house over the broken door. The gift of life from the hunt and kill drifted away on the night breeze. Now his weariness settled back over his body like a tattered old coat, worn and comfortable in all the places that mattered.

"Top of the evening, Jack. Been rippin' about town have you?"

Gregor's hand found the hilt of his knife and started to pull, revealing two fingers worth of the white blade before he realized it was only the crazy poet who had spoken.

"My name's not Jack, Mr. Thompson."

"Sure, Father. Whatever you say. Been out holdin' St. Adrian's hand this evening? You know, I…"

Gregor shook his head in disgust and walked away from the rambling lunatic, his mind already turning to the next night's hunt, wondering who would be next to fall before his judgment.

Tears should be running down my cheeks.

Gregor knew he should be weeping with the souls of the eternally damned, walking through a hell that bloomed around him, weeds and thistles choking out all the good for as far as he could he see.

Instead, he was laughing at some idiotic verse Thompson was performing. Pale street lamps shone dully on the leather apron hanging around the poet's neck, making it appear as if the light was muted, as if nothing could hold back the black in this wretched place.

Gregor did not even attempt to ease away from the crowd anymore. Oh, he had tried more times than he could remember but Thompson always appeared in the street around him eventually. For nearly a month, Gregor had not been alone for the hunt, dogged by the questions and insane soliloquies of the other man.

Three nights earlier the entire fiasco had come to a head. Visions of flesh had swirled in his mind, baiting him, leading him to the next woman. He had tracked her down in time to see the beast winging away as he ran toward the judgment, Thompson hot on his heels.

Gregor sliced the woman open, spraying the wall with gore and blood even as she tried to awaken from the creature's spell. The poet had stood in the open doorway, watched him standing over the body, the white blade gleaming through a crimson cover.

But before any word could be said between the two men, more images had leaped forward. A red shawl, lipstick-covered lips and the curve of a neck. A flash of thigh and the groan of a bed. Gregor had trotted through the streets in search of the other woman, Thompson beside him step for step. Together they had burst upon the incubus with his next victim. The poet stumbled out of fear of the sight and the effect of the beast's voice, falling down with his eyes staring off into a dreamless void, his own little knife a forgotten object in his hand.

Gregor had driven off the incubus by himself and let his knife hold judgment on the woman's womb—the beast had referred to her as Sweet Catherine—before collapsing in a sobbing heap beside Thompson.

But that had taken place three nights earlier and now Gregor sat on the edge of a crowd listening to song and poetry while munching on an apple pasty. He should have been crying from the absurdity.

"So, what do you think, Jack? Goin' to be a light evening?" Thompson grinned, pieces of greasy crust hanging from his lips.

"It's about time we started hunting," Gregor replied, brushing crumbs off his lap before leaning closer and lowering his voice. "I've been thinking. What if the beast has been with two women before the other night? I thought that was something new but now... I'm not so certain. I can't afford to be thrown off the trail."

"That's the God's truth, Jack. Where do we start?"

"He's been content so far to hunt the ladies on the side streets. Let's begin there. Perhaps I'll see someone who sticks out."

Long hours passed beneath the moon and the pale lamps. Every step, every painted face, every beckoning gesture, all served to darken Gregor's mood as the night marched on. Thompson prattled for a while but eventually he shut up, trudging along in silence beside the brooding hunter.

They passed through certain sections of Whitechapel more than once. Some of the women had gone to service paying gentlemen while new faces appeared, come around for another shift of work.

Gregor's hand slipped inside his coat every few steps, his fingers caressing the hilt of the knife. He found no reassurance in its touch this night, no certainty of the righteousness of his work as God's envoy. Desperation settled over his thoughts, fog threatening to turn him into a hunter lost in the wilderness, his prey vanished in the trees, searching for the path home. He eagerly stared at the women now, lingering on their hidden curves and the line of their necks.

His gaze locked with the soft brown eyes of a woman still young enough to be new to the side streets of her profession. They stood several paces apart, each barely within the circle outlined by the lamp above their heads, but he felt the damp of the October night on her skin, smelled the remnants of cheap perfume over smoke, and tasted life on her breath. A fire smoldered within the woman's eyes, waiting for only the slightest urging to be stoked into a blaze.

Gregor wanted her. Not for bait for the beast nor for his judgment and punishment under the knife. He needed her for himself. To touch, to taste, to feed his soul—he wanted her.

Click. The door opened.

Thompson staggered against his back and slumped to the street. The two men standing closest to the street light, the small slick-haired one and the larger hulk with scarred knuckles and crooked nose, reached for the post while they also fell, half-closed eyes seeing nothing but their dreams. The other four women lay in a pile, probably the first restful night's sleep they had seen in years.

Only Gregor and the woman with brown eyes still stood,

nothing disturbing the connection between them. He gestured and she led the way through a twisting maze of unlit alleys and dark streets. He had no idea where they were, his attention leaving her face just long enough to avoid a drunk passed out in his path, a pile of garbage overflowing its bin.

When finally he could stop the urges no more, he spun her and pinned her in a doorway. Her body screamed a siren call for his ears alone. She gave herself with the lust no farthing could buy and he took all she gave and wanted more. His soul sang with the touch of her life, feeding an empty chamber that had rang hollow but now felt nourishment filling every crack.

Her pale skin glowed in his eyes. His tongue licked, teeth bit, and fingers clawed at it with the desperation of a condemned man at his last meal, savoring every morsel.

Gregor exploded inside her while she howled like an animal at the moon, giving her life to grow within her even while she gave back life he had not known existed. They panted in each others' ears. His knees trembled but held them both up, her legs wrapped around his waist and arms clinging over his shoulders. She purred words into his ear and he smiled in the dark, not understanding what she said, his need sated.

She climbed down and rearranged her clothing before running a hand gently across his cheek, a parting gesture between intertwined souls. Gregor returned the smile and for a moment the fire built within the woman again. He turned away to dress himself and the moment passed.

She walked into the darkness and he watched her go out of sight before he realized what had just happened. Horror gripped his heart. His breath froze in his lungs at the thought of his seed in a woman's womb. God's righteous weapon turned into the creator of doom.

He leaped into the night, the lover turned back into hunter. She heard his approach and started to turn, but the knife in her throat cut off the cry she tried to unleash. The white blade flashed forward countless times, biting deep enough to shatter bone, driven with the strength of terrified fervor. The woman had long since quit moving, a motionless hunk of meat before the onslaught of a mad butcher. He tossed her head in one direction while hands, arms and legs went in others. Gregor held the trunk of the woman to his chest, clutching the part of her that contained part of him. He ran, some part of his addled mind telling him what remained of her body needed holy ground to be made right.

An iron fence loomed up out of the night. Revulsion and the need to retch forced him to toss the bloody remains over the spiked top and out of his worries. God would see to her now just as Gregor had seen to mete out her judgment on earth.

"We've never been down here before, Jack."

Gregor only grunted in reply. The wind whipped down the street, tossing stray papers into the pale light. Dancing ghosts on marionette's strings, they dipped and rose like drunken birds before vanishing back into the voids between posts.

His life existed in the black spots, the areas sent from hell. The light was only a memory, a remembrance of a promise echoing hollowly with screams from what was left of his soul. His God-divined mission was all that kept him on his feet, all that made him eat and wake each day. Yet the mission was also the reason he endured a hell-on-earth. His tongue tasted nothing but blood with each drink, he smelled only fear, and he saw only death around him.

"You're ready, Thompson? You remember what you're to do?"

"Yes, Jack." The man blew on his hands and pulled his threadbare jacket closer to his body. "Do you see 'im?"

"No, but it has to be soon." Gregor tilted his head away from the November wind and looked at his companion. "It's never gone on this long before without him leading me to his chosen."

"Why here? Why tonight?"

"You heard Mrs. Lyon down at the Queen's Head Pub. This Mary Kelly girl has been going on and on about not being able to sleep. Says she wakes up after all sorts of dreams."

"Well, if it's 'er, let's just go on and rip 'er belly. God's will be done, Jack."

Gregor wondered if the chill racing down his spine was from the weather. "No. This may be my last chance this time to put an end to the evil. If I miss... years of waiting, wondering if I missed one of his victims, praying the abomination will rear its head again. Do you understand? I would have to pray for years I will go through this hell again!" Gregor reached out and grabbed Thompson by the elbow. His fingers ached with the strength in the grip. "You must not fall under his spell! We have to hope you remaining awake will be enough of a distraction to the beast to allow me to finish it."

"And then we can kill the girl, Jack?"

The shudder again. "Yes. If the beast has already lain with her, yes, then we can kill the girl, too." Gregor pulled his knife from the sheath beneath his coat. Grimy fingers squeezed the hilt while the blade stood out white against his dark shadow. "Let's go."

The two men crossed Dorsett Street and ducked into the darkness defining the stoop. Thompson watched the street while Gregor checked the door. It was locked but one of the two panes was broken and only an old blanket hung across the opening to keep out the night. He reached inside, pulled the bolt and eased open the door.

Rusty hinges whined in protest. Gregor winced at the sound but still he stepped into the room beyond, his blade leading and Thompson following close on his heels.

He paused for a moment for his eyes to adjust. As dark as the street had been, the black was even deeper in this cave of a room. Finally, the pale light passing through the doorway and around his shadow revealed a white apron slung across the back of a chair. Thompson drew his attention to the bed in the opposite corner and the pale-skinned woman asleep on it.

"She's alone. Do we kill her or go?" he whispered into Gregor's ear, rancid breath and the slightest hint of whiskey carrying to his nose.

Gregor did not move. Everything about the peaceful scene told him the right thing to do was to leave. But the hunter's breathless urging in the back of his thoughts screamed to him something was wrong. The woman lying quietly on her bed, the pale white of her stomach...

The woman was naked.

She was still soundly asleep, despite the racket of the bolt and hinges.

"Start your chant. Thompson. The beast is here."

Gregor ignored the sing-song murmuring behind him as his

gaze darted around the room. Shadows upon shadows, blacks deepening further into night—long moments passed but still nothing moved in the room except for his eyes and his companion's lips.

There! Hell's night hung in the corner above the table. Light cowered before the beast clinging to the wall near the ceiling, no longer able to touch the dark where a soul had once lived.

Thompson's mumbling slowed and a yawn fought its way around his tongue.

"Keep praying, man!" Gregor urged. "Your life depends upon it."

He lurched forward as a hiss shattered the stillness. Wings beat the air and white talons flashed out of the darkness, the claws attached to grasping fingers that sought to rip Gregor to bloody ribbons.

The priest leaped high and slashed. The blade found a wing and bit through, changing the hiss to an echoing scream. The beast fell out of its flight and tumbled across the floor, knocking into Thompson and frightening the mad poet into forgetting the chant for a moment. As soon as he stopped mumbling, he slumped to the ground, asleep.

"Why, cambion? Why do you persist in trying to stop me when you come so close to grasping your potential?"

"There is nothing you can offer me but death and chaos."

"Chaos?" The incubus laughed but the sound left his throat more like a rough blade running over a whetstone than any chuckle. "Tell me, did the one you took in the alley taste like chaos? I wanted her, too, but I left her for you. Did you feed on her like chaos? Or are you upset because *you* chose death as her final tale?"

Gregor grasped the chair with his free hand, tears stinging his eyes at the memory of the girl in the alley. "You must die." The words were barely loud enough to leave his lips. "The world needs you to die."

"The world, half-breed? Or you?"

Gregor moaned, low and guttural. The sound threatened to shake the walls of the room with despair, peeling back the paint and plaster to reveal the ribs of a gigantic monster and its shriveling heart. He turned and drove his knife into the girl lying motionless on the bed, only his grip keeping the blade from diving through her body with the force.

"Sssssssss!"

The click of talons on the wood floor gave Gregor all the warning he needed. He whirled and slashed wildly, the blade a bar of white through the darkness. The tip caught the side of the incubus's face. Puss oozed from the wound and dropped in green, smoking globs onto the stone hearth. The beast leaped to the side before Gregor could strike again.

"It's over for now, cambion. But I only need to succeed once. You can never let down or I win. And I have time and the ages on my side. Until the next time…"

The beast waddled past Thompson out onto the stoop and jumped up into the night. By the time Gregor reached the doorway, the sky held only a few wan stars and wisps of clouds.

Rage and agony at his failure whipped him back to the bed where he hacked and stabbed what had once been a pretty young woman, turning her into a pile of bloody meat. No rationale directed his actions—his responsibility had been completed when the blade dove through her heart the first time—but still he mutilated what was left, his soul weeping with the despondent thought he would need to travel through this hell again. Another place, another time, but still the same hell.

A moan from Thompson brought Gregor back to the present. He ran from the building and continued running until he reached the corner with High Street. The lamps were strong enough here to make their light dance and glisten on the blood on his hands. Revulsion coaxed bile into his throat but he swallowed it down, swallowed it like he had with every moral and righteous thought in his mind.

Bloody fingers grasped the priest collar and tore it from his neck. He stared at it for a moment, blood mixing with the grime to form a paste that reminded him of the beast's wound, before flinging it as far into the night as his strength would allow.

"Goodbye," he whispered to the throngs of people wandering beneath the lights. "May the souls of Whitechapel hope to God I never need return."

CHAPTER 18

Her breathing breaks the silence, surrounding us. Hair flows across her pillow like crimson rivers, moving with the tide over the rocks hidden below.

She, too, is danger. I feel the foreboding crawl across my skin, wriggling into the pockmarks and over the scars left by the half-breed.

I must ignore the warning.

It reminds me of before the fall, when fear and pain were only words spoken in a language so foreign the translation held no meaning. The light sheltered me from those words, kept me safe in its bosom…

No!

The light betrayed me and left me like this—misshapen, horrid and hungry. Oh, so very hungry. Just the thought of what I need to survive makes me look down again at my chosen. I feel the spittle flowing out of my mouth, running off my chin and dropping onto the pillow beside her hair. She does not awaken.

I must have my revenge against the light!

And that is the danger I smell on her, the glow still burning beneath her surface. The light could flare at any time and send me scurrying away, leaving the cambion with another victory. Yet, I cannot leave here despite the danger.

I only need to win once.

Sniff, sniff.

It is almost her time. Then I must move quickly to beat the bastard to her. He has come close. I smell it on the night and hear his footsteps on the breeze.

But he has not found her yet.

And she is so close.

But not tonight.

Tonight, I feed.

CHAPTER 19

NEW YORK, LATE SUNDAY EVENING

"Are you sure you wouldn't like a cup of coffee, Father?" Roger glanced at Novara before turning back to stare at the people walking by on the sidewalk. "No, thanks."

He wanted to say more—wanted to joke about not owning a house to take out a second mortgage on to afford another cup of the expensive brew, wanted to beg Novara to call off the night's adventure so he could go back to his little room and get some sleep, wanted to scream to the night the fax from the Camerlengo had only posed more questions rather than offering answers—instead, he simply shut his mouth and continued watching.

"Ah, too anxious to begin our walk this evening?" Novara paid the coffee cart vendor. "Grazie. Okay then, Father. Let's start out on our mission."

The two men moved down the sidewalk. Roger's knee grumbled for a while, each step changing the dull ache to a sharp stab. He tried to forget about the pain, tried to think of the best way to receive answers from Novara for all the questions swirling in his head. Instead, he merely plodded along silently beside the emissary.

"You are very quiet this evening," Novara said. "I'm sorry if you are tired but I couldn't let you sleep any longer and still come on the hunt this evening. As it is, we have started much later than I wanted to."

Roger felt heat rise in his cheeks, a mixture of embarrassment and anger fueling the fire. After Morgan had left the Cathedral, he had returned to the library to finish reading the Camerlengo's fax and fallen asleep in the chair with the papers spread all over his lap. He had woke up to Novara gently shaking his shoulder. "Why?" he asked.

"I wanted to hunt farther to the east tonight and…"

"No, no," Greene interrupted, slicing at the air with his hand. His anger had won the battle. "Why here? Why now?" He paused. "Why me?"

"Ah, that 'why.' You have obviously studied on the questions I gave you. What have you learned?"

Roger glanced at Novara, expecting to see the smirk of someone who had all the answers—the older brother who knew an answer the little brother did not or the smile of a professor standing in front of a class of freshman.

But there was no grin, no hint of egotistical superiority. Instead, the emissary continued to search the faces of the men and women streaming by them, his jaw set and gaze darting back and forth with the same emotionless mask he always wore.

"St. Hildegard was the Mother Superior of the Diocese of Speyer. Credited with several miracles, including healing. Her most significant work appears to have been writing the 'Scivas,' a series of books filled with prophetic visions. All Church reference books say there were only three books containing six, seven, and thirteen prophecies respectively." Greene paused before taking the plunge into a darkness that promised no light. He was too mad to care. "That belief is a lie, however. There were seven visions in the first book. The Church hid away the missing portion."

The words tasted like poison in Roger's mouth, rolling around his tongue like vicious bile until he wanted to throw up on the expensive shoes of the people walking past them. *The Church has lied to its followers for centuries!* His only satisfaction came from the sharp glance from Novara, revealing the emissary's surprise.

"You've had help I see. I thought I recognized Lolek's letterhead on your lap when I woke you. Have you read the visions, Father?"

Roger gave a quick shake of his head. Now that he was on the verge of learning more about Novara and his mission, he was more scared than he could ever remember. "Only a summary of the original visions." There was a squeak in his voice he cared not to think about.

Novara walked the next half a block in silence before finally nodding, accepting the outcome of whatever discussion had just taken place in his thoughts.

"The introduction to the books paints a picture of God at the top of the Holy Mountain while mankind represents the boulders at the base. What the popes and cardinals found as the easiest way to explain these first visions to the illiterate peasants of the time was to show God held all the power at the top of the mountain while man was just a subservient beast, inconsequential rubble at his feet. Nothing in the known six visions contradicts that teaching."

Roger suspected now was the time to throw his hands over his ears and run away screaming. He had wanted answers, demanded them, but now the words were unlocking a doorway into a nightmare he had never knew existed before today.

"St. Hildegard's seventh and final vision of the first book shows she meant something entirely different," continued Novara. "She had described how she was shown the condition of mankind, its fall and redemption and the struggles of man's soul with free will.

"But the seventh vision also spoke of the beings that comprised the slopes of the Holy Mountain—the angels. Most of the time they are invisible when mankind looks up and they exist in the light of God shining down. But halfway between heaven and earth, the angels were given both some of the power of God and the free will to answer to the weaknesses of mankind.

"Now the power of the Holy Mountain appears entirely different. Now it is not God's power holding down man under his weight. It is man and his faith, along with the angels, which holds everything up and gives God his power."

Roger's head still spun with the ramifications of the ideas the vision posed, just as it had this afternoon when he read the fax the first time. "Ideas like that during the time of St. Hildegard would have had to have been considered blasphemous," he said. "I'm shocked she wasn't burned at the stake."

"I'm told it was discussed."

Roger blinked at the matter-of-fact tone Novara used to describe a hellspawn's death for the woman who was later recognized later by the Church as a saint. He watched the emissary for a few strides while the man continued his intense study of the passersby.

"St. Hildegard did not have an army at hand like Joan," Novara said, "thousands of soldiers willing to die for her visions. Luckily for her she had… what is the term in your television police shows?

Corroborating testimony."

"What does the seventh vision say?" Roger asked.

Novara raised an eyebrow at the question. "Your helper? My friend?" The emissary's last word was clipped and spoken through clenched teeth. "He did not tell you what the prophecy said? No? Hmmm."

Roger grabbed Novara by the arm and pulled the man to a stop, spinning him face-to-face. Even so, there remained something odd, a little off-kilter about how the emissary returned his stare. "Tell me. Tell me now."

"Father, we must keep moving. Our hunt is too important and we dare not be late…"

That was the final straw. Roger suddenly realized why talking to Novara was so tough. The man rarely looked him in the eye. He came close—a cheek, an ear, his hair—but only a couple of times had he returned his look eye-to-eye. Roger heard his father's voice screaming in the back of his mind, telling him he should never trust a man who would not look him in the eye. "I have a right to know," he said. "It's my butt out here with you every night."

The comment made Novara's lips curl in just the barest hint of a smile before he nodded. "Yes, of course. It is your butt, too. But please, Father, we must continue to walk as we talk." The two men began moving again before Novara spoke. "The seventh vision spoke of an angel falling from God's grace and being banished from Heaven. Not Lucifer, she speaks of him later in one of her Wiesbaden essays. This unnamed angel performed an important service for God but in the process was ensnared by the temptations of man. For that sin, he was pushed from God's sight for all eternity."

The two men walked silently for the next twenty minutes. Roger was lost deep in thoughts about what he had learned, the passing faces no longer in his mind. When he finally noticed his surroundings again, he saw they were in a residential district, this time surrounded by apartment buildings of all heights. "It was Philip's daughters, wasn't it?" he asked. "They were the corroborating testimony."

"Hmmm? What?" If possible, Novara's gaze darted around even more quickly than usual, leaping from windows to doors to rooftops. His pace quickened as well and every dozen or so strides, Roger felt the need to jog for a few paces to keep up. "Uh, yes. Philip's four virgin daughters all were given the gift of prophecy. They foretold a fallen angel would try to bring down God, not to rule over him like Lucifer, but to drag him down so all creatures were on the same level—God, angels, and man. He wanted God to battle with earthly temptations, test him like he tested man and the angels sent here to do his bidding. The fallen angel wanted God to struggle and fail like he had. Now please, Father, come along and keep up!"

Roger trotted around a corner behind Novara and then across a street in mid-block. He no longer felt the stabbing pain in his knee because the pain traveled up and down both of his legs, gnawing at his hamstrings and calves. His breath came in short gulps and a small fire kindled deep in his chest. He was so engrossed with how awful his body felt, he almost ran into Novara's back. The emissary had stopped cold in one stride, his head swiveling back and forth while his gaze swept the night sky.

A faint scream floated on the breeze. The sweat on Roger's face grew cold and clammy while his body gave an involuntary twitch from the chill in his spine. His hands started to fly up to ward off an attack before they stopped halfway, his paralyzing fear an emotion remembered from the previous night.

"Damn it!" Novara growled, his voice rumbling more like an animal's than a human's. He whirled on Roger. "And damn you, too, priest! The beast is gone and another life is lost because you needed to sleep and then you needed to stop to talk. Damn you and your weakness!"

"Now just a minute," Roger said, his own temper flaring. "I'm trying to figure out exactly what we are doing and why we are out here every night. Why…"

"Why!? And while you discover all the answers to the mysteries of the universe, someone else pays for your lessons with their own blood."

Roger took a step back. He could not remember seeing a face so filled with rage. Novara wore a mask blanched white except for red spots high on his cheeks. His lips snarled like an animal's and his eyes slanted nearly shut. It was the mask of a lunatic, a deranged killer. "Now relax, Mr. Novara," he said with all the calm he could muster. "Maybe you're wrong. Maybe it was scared away before it killed again."

Novara stepped close enough his breath carried the smell of expensive coffee to Roger's nose.

"Read the newspapers tomorrow and then tell me I'm wrong." He stepped around Roger and took a few strides back the way they had come. "I can do this task alone. But there should be two of us to make sure the mission is completed and nothing else… nothing else goes wrong." Novara half-turned and jabbed a long, slender finger at Greene. "Make no mistake, I will see this hunt to its end, by myself if need be. And if you can't keep up, then I will leave your body for the beast and the police, Father."

CHAPTER 20

NEW YORK, MONDAY MORNING

Morgan's head lolled to the side, swaying with the turn of the car. She jerked back awake in an instant, her eyes flying wide, but not before her head banged into the window.

She noticed Frank glance at her before returning his attention to the early-morning traffic. In another half-hour, the streets would be a tangled snarl of cars but, for the moment, he was able to weave back and forth through the gaps and make good time.

"I'm sorry for the rough ride, Miss. I don't want to get caught in a jam before we get to the scene."

"Frank, I'm going to call your wife as soon as we get back to the station." This comment drew another, longer, glance before her partner looked back at the street in time to veer left around a cab. "I want to ask her where I can shoot you that she won't mind. It's pretty damn obvious my asking you to call me by first name hasn't gotten through that thick cap you call a skull. Maybe she can give me a suggestion or two." She paused. "Don't worry about bouncing me around. The ride is the only thing keeping me awake. I guess I was hoping we'd get another night off."

Frank grunted and slapped the wheel before whipping into the right-hand lane, accelerating past a tinted-window limousine. "This is the strangest case I've ever worked," he said. "It's so damn frustrating, waiting for something to happen, feeling like we're one step behind and waiting for the suspect to make his move. Was it like this for you the first time?"

"Worse. All of us working the case had started calling the guy 'The Werewolf' because he only killed on a full moon. Think about that one, Frank. Think about how frustrating it was to go over all the evidence, realize we still didn't have what we needed to catch him and we needed to wait another month for our next chance. That's the dictionary definition of frustrating." Morgan sighed at the memory.

"How'd you finally break it?"

"I didn't. One of the other officers finally saw the pattern. Besides the full moon, the bastard was picking his victims off an Internet chat room for dog owners. We set a trap for him with a woman officer and we nailed him. But not before seven long-ass months went by." She stifled a yawn behind a hand. "Turned out the guy was looney-tunes… thought he was some kind of half-dog, half-man thing and he was passing out justice on the people who were keeping his dog-kin as pets. A real nut job." Morgan started laughing. "Even tried to call PETA for his lawyer."

Frank whipped around another corner and slowed down. The flashing lights of other police cars and an ambulance were only a block away. "You said someone else saw the pattern. I thought you were the one who got the guy."

"Oh, I got him. Shot him in the leg as he went after the officer who was the bait. Whined and barked like an injured mutt but still tried to crawl after her.

"Yes, I stopped him but we might still be looking for the guy without the other officer seeing the pattern. You'd have liked him, Frank. A damn good cop and a guy who stood up for what he believed in."

The car rolled to a stop and the two of them quickly got out and walked up to the policemen establishing a perimeter to hold out the small but growing crowd of morbid sightseers. They both flashed their badges and walked under the tape. Another detective was waiting for them inside the foyer of the apartment building.

"Detectives." He shook both of their hands. "I'm Pinelli from the one-eight. Can you tell me what the hell is going on? My partner and I caught the call this morning and started processing the scene. The next thing I know, the techie from the chop-shop says we've got to stop everything and call you. Before I can even call my louie, three more of the white-lab-coat types show up and they're drooling around the vic like a damn tub of ice cream at a fat farm."

"We're running a string," Morgan said. "If the techs wanted you to call us, they must think this one is connected."

"Well, fuck me. Really? A serial killer?" Pinelli shook his head in disbelief. "If you're looking for a nut job, this guy's it. Damnedest slice-and-dice I ever saw."

"Who are they?" Frank motioned toward a handful of people sitting in chairs on the other side of the foyer.

"They're the people living in the rest of the apartments on the same floor. We were treating this like a one-off murder and didn't know if it was one of them or if the killer was still in the building, so we have uniforms going room to room while we're doing interviews down here."

"Okay. We'd better head upstairs then," Morgan said.

"Apartment 908. I'm going to stay down here and help with the questioning in case the murders aren't connected." Pinelli hesitated and Morgan thought he turned a little green around the edges. "I don't need to see that room again... I don't need to see anything like that ever again. Ever. I hope it's your mess now." He pointed toward the elevators before walking over to the residents.

Morgan was deep in thought when she and Frank stepped into the elevator. Was Overholt already here? Was this related to the other deaths? If so, why did they have a night when no one was killed? What was the pattern? She was so engrossed in her train of thought, she jumped when Frank spoke.

"What happened to him?"

"Shit, Frank! Huh? What happened to who?"

"I'm sorry, Miss. What happened to the other officer in The Werewolf murders?"

"Oh. He was just finishing his master's in psychology. The FBI snatched him up and off he went to Quantico. Became a profiler and got almost everything he wanted."

"Sounds like a guy that'd be interesting to meet. Maybe someday," Frank said. "Sounds like you knew him pretty good."

The elevator doors slid open and revealed a hallway bustling with activity. Uniformed and plainclothes police scurried back and forth between open doors like lab mice looking for the way through the maze to the cheese at the center.

"I did," Morgan said as she stepped toward the doorway about halfway down the hall where crime scene technician Overholt and a woman officer were standing. "He was my partner before he went Fed on me."

"That must have hurt a little." The pair had almost reached the others.

"Not nearly as much as the rest," Morgan said quietly, a dry chuckle escaping her mouth.

"Good morning, Detectives," Overholt said as they approached.

Good God. He's as excited as a fourteen-year-old boy with the Sports Illustrated Swimsuit Edition. Morgan turned to the other officer, an older woman with gray hair and piercing blue eyes. "I'm Detective Kelly and this is Detective Mason. You must be Pinelli's partner."

"That's fuckin' right. Detective Bev Patterson. Now what kind of happy horseshit brings you two into a case in my fuckin' precinct?"

The older woman had a thick Brooklyn accent and the mouth of a dock worker. Morgan had no doubt she was as tough as one. Every woman on the force knew Patterson's name. She had made detective thirty years earlier when women were usually desk jockeys or meter maids and almost never allowed to walk a beat, let alone work a homicide. Patterson had needed to be tough against both the bad guys and the good guys and the stories sounded like it had been rough to tell them apart at times. She was the first to break through, taking all the rotten pranks and lousy jokes that made it possible for Morgan and others like her to follow in her footsteps. There was even a story about how she had been suspended for beating the crap out of her first partner when he told her to stay in the car while he made a collar because the perp was too dangerous. She made the arrest by herself and then drove her partner to the emergency room. But no one ever told her to stay in the car again.

"Two other cases in the last three days," Morgan said. "Both with the same style of killing and weapon. If he's asked for us," she motioned to Overholt, "then he must believe your case is a part of it."

"I know your rep, Kelly," Patterson said, a smile widening her mouth. She put up her thumb and forefinger and shot a pretend gun like a little kid. "You'll do what you need to do to make sure the fuckin' suspect pays. You're no pretty girl pussy. You've got balls and I like that. If the bastard who did this is your boy, I want in on it."

I'll bet she never had to make a visit to the precinct shrink. All Morgan could do was nod, the crassness of the other woman stunning her into silence.

"Whatcha got for us, Overholt?" Frank asked.

"It sure looks the same at first blush, detectives. T.O.D. about 3 a.m. She's cut open from her rib cage past the pelvic region. If there was sex, it was consensual." He stopped for a moment and glanced at Patterson before looking back at Morgan. After she nodded, he continued but lowered his voice. "Like the others, the uterus has been cut from the body and is gone. I ran a quick scan with a wand and did not find any metal fragments. I'll do a more thorough examination back in the lab."

"Is that what you're holding back when you go public?" Patterson asked.

"Yes," Morgan answered. "We'll have every nut job in the city coming out of the woodwork when we make a statement on these cases. We needed something to make sure who we talk to is for real."

"I can keep my goddamn mouth shut. Who else knows?"

"Frank and I, our lieutenant, Overholt here, two more detectives from our precinct. Who on your side?" she asked the tech.

"Just my boss," Overholt answered. "The other people in my department were only told to look for the mutilation before they call me."

"Okay, let's keep this a small party for as long as possible." Morgan waved toward the apartment. "Let's go take a look."

The apartment was a stark contrast to the previous murder scene. Where the high-priced prostitute had lived in a world of ostentatious wealth, this home revealed the reserved taste of a middle-class upbringing. Prints and family photographs adorned the walls above used and sensible furniture. The bedroom was just as straight-laced and mundane as the rest of the apartment. The place could have been Morgan's except for the splashes of crimson on the walls and the mutilated body on the bed.

"She's black," Morgan said with a shake of the head. They could not seem to catch a break on the pattern. "That's new. You'd better give us the rundown."

Patterson pulled out her notebook and flipped a few pages before starting. "Tamela Lynn Robinson, twenty-eight. A corporate attorney downtown at Bernstein, Bernstein and Benjamin. Originally from Macon, Georgia, went to school at Grambling and then Georgetown Law."

"She doesn't live like a bigwig lawyer."

"Super says she was moving out next month at the end of her lease. She was sending money back home to put her kid sister through college but she was graduating and Robinson could afford to move on up to something more like you'd expect."

One of the other technicians called out to Overholt and he walked over to the window to talk to her.

"Boyfriends?" Morgan asked.

"Some, but nobody regular and nobody recent," Patterson answered. "Looks like a good old, down home girl made good. Most of the people in this building are young couples and families. She babysat every once in a while for one mother down the hall. This wasn't some fuckin' slut partying it up."

"How'd we find out about it so soon if she was alone?" Frank asked.

"The mother. Seems she called yesterday and again this morning from Georgia to talk to her about a visit and when she didn't answer her cell or house phone, she panicked and called the super. He keyed in, found the mess and called us."

"Has anyone told the mother yet?" Morgan hoped the phone call would not be her next duty.

"Yeah. I finished that shit-ass job right before you two showed up. She's gonna come up and claim the body in a couple of days."

"We'd better call her back and tell her to hold off. Overholt probably won't be done with the body by then if anything new shows up."

"Detectives," Overholt called out. "You should come look at this."

The three of them walked over to the window. Morgan watched the woman tech snap off another half-dozen photos before moving out of the way so they could see what was so interesting. Light sheers fluttered in the breeze blowing through the open window. On the sill were two bloody smears.

"You think these are from the killer?" Frank asked.

"It's a good bet," Overholt said. "We'll need to check with the building superintendent and make sure he didn't touch some blood, get sick, and regurgitate out the window, but barring that, yes, I think these prints are from the killer."

"So the rotten bastard took the time after the job was done to lean out the window and get some fresh air before he left? That's one cold son-of-a-bitch right there." Patterson spit out the words.

"Yes, but it could also be his downfall," Morgan said. "Someone in that building across the street might have seen him looking out. We'll need to get some uniforms over there to start asking questions and it will have to be fast before people start leaving for work."

"I'm on it," Patterson said as she pulled her phone out of the clip on her belt. "I'll have the lou send over some more men." She started to dial and moved away from the group.

Morgan leaned out the window to check the line of sight and to make sure there was not a fire escape within reach. Satisfied no one left the apartment by this route, she started to pull back inside when she noticed the wood on the outside of the sill was scratched and splintered.

"Overholt, what could have caused this?" she asked, gesturing to the marks and then moving back.

The crime scene technician leaned out the window for several minutes before pulling back in and calling over one of his colleagues. After another few minutes of fast-talking discussion between them, he turned back to Morgan and Frank. "I don't know what caused those marks but did you notice how the scratches line up with the blood smears? It looks as if," he took his hands and mimicked gripping down on the wood but was careful not to touch the jamb, "the killer grabbed here and left the marks with his hands."

"Some kind of knives on the end of his fingers?" asked Morgan. "*A Nightmare on Elm Street*, Freddy Krueger sort of thing?"

"Maybe, but not metal. I looked for traces and did not see any shining in the sun. I'll check with the wand in a minute but I'll remove the whole jamb and take it back to the lab, also. Looks like my people are going to need to go back to the other sites and look for similar marks."

"Okay, the lou is assigning some uniforms but he was pretty pissed about the whole jurisdiction thing," Patterson said as she moved back to join them. "I didn't tell him about the other killings but he knows a dead fuckin' mackerel when he smells it. He worked the street so he knows something is up. He's probably calling your louie right now to give him an earful of shit."

"In the meantime," Morgan said, "we'd better get back downstairs and help Pinelli interview the residents from this floor while we're waiting on a report from Overholt." It was turning out to be one hell of a day.

CHAPTER 21

NEW YORK, MONDAY AFTERNOON

Morgan sighed before walking through the secure entrance of the precinct house—the entrance with Frank holding open the door—and into the chaos beyond. Now the feelings of frustration with her partner changed, sluicing away and leaving behind only the contentment of someone who had been away for a long time but was now coming home. The incessant tones of the computer telephone system, the frenzied rise and fall of voices spiked with the occasional yell, swear words used as nouns, verbs and adjectives—and the assurance the person at the next desk would be watching your back when bullets started flying. She did not need to question why she would never leave the force; the answer was in front of her face.

She stopped at the restroom to make sure she was not wearing any more of her lunch than normal and ended up staring at herself in the mirror. Morgan tried to ignore the little crow's feet deepening at the corner of the eyes staring back from the glass. They were easier to turn away from than the dark circles underneath advertising how long it had been since her last good night's sleep.

The door opened and another female officer walked into the restroom, a younger officer with a lot of bounce in her step, encompassed by the din outside. Morgan quickly gathered her things from the sink top and headed out to the detectives' department.

She was still several steps away from where her desk and Frank's butted up against one another when she noticed her partner was not sitting in his chair. Morgan looked around the area where all the homicide detectives called home. She wondered for a moment what could keep Frank from poring over his notes from this morning's scene, going step by step in his methodical, almost military march toward solving the case.

Morgan's last couple of steps quickened as her phone rang, adding its voice to the noise. She moved some loose papers off the handset and pushed the flashing red button. "Homicide, Kelly."

"I want in, sweet cheeks."

"Detective Patterson? Is that you?"

"One of those goddamned murders happened in my precinct which means you'll need a go-between. And I've spent too many fucking years hoofin' through cases that didn't mean shit to miss out on a good one. Botched robberies. Street punks. Domestics. Bullshit cases any Nancy-fucking-Drew could have solved. I ain't no goddamn rookie."

"Whoa, whoa, Patterson," Morgan said when the other woman paused for a breath. "I've got no idea what you're talking about."

"Don't fuck with me, honey. You're probably supposed to keep it under your hat but my louie just told me they've flown in some fed help and they're formin' a damn task force for your slash-and-dash. Word is you're going to be in charge."

Morgan glanced toward her lieutenant's office and could see through the glass it was empty. She stood and looked around, searching between the bustle of the other officers, witnesses, suspects—and what appeared to be the water jug guy—and neither her boss nor Frank were in sight.

"I don't know what to tell you, Bev." Morgan said. "I just code sevened. My partner's not at his desk, my lou is nowhere to be seen, and nobody has told me a thing. Are you at your precinct house?"

"Pinelli and I are getting ready to go out and follow up the damn questioning of people from the building next door. Call the desk jockey and have her transfer you to my cell." She paused. "Don't leave me twisting on this one, huh, kid?"

"I won't. As soon as I know something, you'll know it too." Morgan saw Frank walking out of a hallway from the rear of the station and she could tell from thirty feet away his gaze was fixed on her. "My partner just came back. I've got to go."

Morgan turned around to hang up the telephone before looking to find where Frank had gone. She did not need to look very hard; he must have stepped out quickly because he was almost within arm's reach. "Frank, I just had the damnedest call from…"

"No time for that, Miss," he interrupted. An awkward moment stretched out as he reached for her elbow but stopped before actually touching her. Instead, he settled for waving toward the back of the station house. "They need you in bullpen two. The captain, the super… Christ, the Deputy Commish is in there. And they all want to see you."

Morgan nodded her head and they began weaving their way through the desks to the relative quiet of the far hall. "So Patterson was right about them making a task force. She said something about the FBI coming in too. Has a profiler arrived?"

"There's a suit in the room that I didn't recognize. He spent the whole time I was in there talking with the D.C." Frank reached out as Morgan put her hand on the doorknob to the meeting room, this time actually grabbing her elbow. She was so stunned she froze, only her head whipping around to stare at Frank.

"I think the two of them have been arguing about something. The captain told me to hoof it and find you fast." For the first time since she had met Frank, he looked unsure, his breathing fast and his body tense.

"It'll be okay, Frank. Everyone just wants to find this son-of-a-bitch."

She turned the knob and walked into the room with Frank trailing behind her like an obedient dog—an overweight menacing dog with a bad bite—but her dog nonetheless. Their captain and the chief of detectives, Super Chief by NYPD rank, nearly ran over to greet her.

"Thanks for finding her, Frank," the captain said. "We've only got a couple of seconds, Morgan," he continued, his voice dropping to little more than a loud whisper. "You don't have to do anything more than you want to… than you feel you can do. No one says a word if you walk away from this one."

"That's right, Detective," the chief chimed in. "I won't put the well-being of one of my men or women officers above a case. No matter how bad it is. That damned pencil-pusher has never walked a beat. He's a political appointee." He moved in and Morgan suddenly realized she was surrounded, very closely, by her two superiors to the front and Frank behind her.

"Captain Baker tells me this is the first case you've caught since psych signed off. There's not a damn thing wrong with saying you're not all the way back yet."

"Besides, Morgan," Baker said, "there are other issues here that..."

"Ah, Detective Kelly. It is so good to finally have a chance to meet you."

The captain and chief of detectives parted and allowed a man a couple of inches taller than the others approach. His silk suit shimmered in the harsh glare of the florescent lights and his face wore a broad smile that meant nothing, sitting like an accessory below two eyes devoid of emotion. When Morgan shook his offered hand, his grip was firm, perhaps a little more firm than was necessary.

"I'm First Deputy Timmons and I am here to tell you firsthand Police Chief Wilson and I have the utmost faith this killer will be caught and brought to justice. We are sure your experience will prove invaluable. You just tell me what you need to do the job and I will get it for you."

"They're forming a special task force," the chief of detectives said, "and Deputy Vincenne's office has chosen you to lead it."

Morgan tried to slow the racing of her heart while hoping her face remained calm. Even with the warning from Patterson, the formal announcement was a lot to take in all at once. She flicked a few loose hairs back while nodding her head slowly. "I'll need some uniforms assigned for canvassing. Having the same men asking questions will make it easier to find consistencies."

"Done," said Timmons.

"I'll need a temporary rank of lieutenant to command them."

Timmons looked at the chief of detectives with a cocked eyebrow.

"Even though a rank of Detective Investigator is technically higher than a uniformed patrolman, she has no authority over them," answered the chief to the unspoken question. Morgan thought she heard just a touch of disgust in his voice at needing to explain the NYPD ranks to his boss. "A sergeant has more say in that case than she does."

"Okay, done. What else do you need, Detective Kelly?"

"I want Investigator Overholt's CSU people tasked to the case. He knows more about the evidence and what we're looking for than anyone else in the lab. Also, this case has already crossed precinct lines. I will need a couple of temporary reassignments so I have liaisons with those departments."

"Done."

Morgan hesitated a moment before taking the final plunge. *What the hell, it's only my career.* "Your office chose me, sir? No one else knew about it?"

If it was physically possible, the man's smile grew even wider. "That's correct, Detective. I chose you myself because I thought you were the most qualified to find the killer."

"If that's the case, then I'll need to report directly to Chief Wilson. You see, I'd already received a phone call from another precinct telling me I was chosen to lead this task force before you called me in here. You have a leak in your office and until it is found, we can't afford to have information get out to the press. That would make our jobs a helluva lot harder and might even torpedo the case."

The smile only wavered for a moment, drooping into a scowl before Timmons regained control. "Yes, of course, Detective. Your suggestion would only be prudent. I will let you know when we have found out who that person was and is punished." He glanced down at his watch. "I must be going now. I'll let you gentlemen make the introductions. Good luck, Detective."

This time Morgan was sure Timmons gripped her hand extra tight in the handshake. After the man had left, she turned to the others.

"Introductions? What…"

"That's just like you to want it all, Morgan," said the man facing out the window on the far side of the room.

She had completely forgotten the First Deputy had been talking to a man when she entered. His voice, however, made a shudder race down her back. She felt like Cybil for a moment, two people living in one body. Part of her wanted to laugh with joy while the rest of her wanted to pull out her piece and empty the clip at the man's back.

"Well, how nice of the FBI to send someone who doesn't need to ask where the restrooms are," she said as the man turned around. "Or did you volunteer for this duty, David? Are the Red Sox in town this week?"

"It sounded like an interesting case on the telephone. But I'll admit I can't find a decent slice of pie in Virginia." He walked across the room. "And no, the Sox are not in town. I'm afraid I don't know everyone here. Is this your new partner?" David stuck out his hand to Frank.

"Agent," said Captain Baker. "This is Kelly's partner, Detective Mason." The man was sweating as he talked, something Morgan could not remember him ever doing in the precinct house except for that week in July two years earlier when the air conditioning broke.

"Call me, David."

"Frank."

Okay, that's enough of this happy horseshit. Frank is my partner and refuses to call me by my first name but thirty seconds into an introduction, he and David are old buddies. I can stop this. The part of her that wanted to pull her gun and start firing had won, at least for now.

"There you go, Frank," she said. "You got your wish." Her partner turned quizzically toward Morgan before looking at the other men. The chief of detectives was suddenly very interested in his watch while Baker looked like he may have swallowed a whole lemon. Only David was smiling with a twinkle of mischief in his eye. That same damned twinkle. "Yeah, Frank. You said you wanted to meet the man who cracked The Werewolf case. Here he is. David is my former partner." She waited until Frank turned to him with a smile on his face before she let him have it with both barrels. "And my ex-husband. He served me with the papers the day he was accepted at Quantico."

"Now dammit! That's not fair, Morgan," David said, the twinkle replaced by sparks of anger. "Don't drag him into…"

"Detective Kelly!" Baker said, each syllable clipped and pronounced with precision. The growl was the voice he used when an overzealous rookie was tempted to cut a corner to build a case. The only time Morgan could ever remember him using it on her was when he had ordered her to see the police shrink. "Detective Kelly, can you or can you not work with the representative the FBI has graciously allowed us to have for this case? Because, if not, then Timmons can go screw himself and I'll make some personnel changes. And after your last little statement to him, he will probably go along with my suggestions." Baker's voice softened. "No matter how right you were to say it."

The chief of detectives was nodding his head, his lips pursed in thoughtful agreement, or he was trying not to laugh, Morgan was not sure which. The thought of not working this case made her sick to her stomach. Even worse—and the part she really did not want to admit—the thought of working with David again had chased away her gun-pulling, evil side and left the half that wanted to smile and reach a hand up to touch his cheek.

"No, sir. I mean, yes, sir. I can work with Agent Kelly to solve this case. With this bastard on the loose, I'm sure it will take a team effort to bring him. I'm willing to make the sacrifice." Apparently the shooter had not completely disappeared.

"Excellent!" the chief of detectives said while rubbing his hands together. "I'm sure everything will be just fine. Baker, forward the paperwork for Kelly's temporary promotion directly to my office and I'll see it's processed immediately. Send along the names of any detectives from the other precinct she wants. Anyone in mind, Detective?"

"Patterson and Pinelli from the one-eight to start with. Anderson and Dixon, too."

"Bev Patterson? Hmm. Ever work with her before?"

"No, sir. But they caught this morning's victim so they are already familiar with that part of the case."

"I'll bet she was your warning phone call, too." He raised his hand. "No, don't tell me. I don't want to know. She's an A-number-one, royal-pain-in-the-ass but she'll stay on your back no matter how bad it gets. Baker, work up a list of about twenty uniforms and I'll pull some from the surrounding precincts to help out. Overtime is approved on this one. Run some extra phone lines in here and make this room the command post. Now, let's go and let them get started."

The two men paused at the door and the chief turned around.

"Let's make this one work, people. Get this bastard before we've got a panic on our hands. David, it was good to see you again."

David remained silent until the door shut behind the two men. "Dad always said he was a good guy to work with."

"David's father was a detective, too," Morgan explained to Frank. "He and the Super were partners back in the day."

"Yeah, he was one of the guys who came over to the house for a while to make sure we were okay after Dad was shot." David sighed. "Okay, hey, I've got a pretty big pile of reports to go through before I can even begin to formulate an analysis. Have you two written up anything on this morning yet?"

"No," Morgan answered. "Frank, could you please start on a report? I need to call Patterson ASAP and let her know what is going on."

"Give me a few hours and I'll probably be through enough of the information to be able to ask some intelligent questions. Early evening? Maybe over some food? All three of us, of course, and probably your lab guy, too," he added with a rush. "Your mom says you're probably not eating very well."

"My mother?" Morgan's voice was quiet, barely above a whisper but she noticed Frank take a step back at the question. The gun-puller had returned in full force.

"Yes, I talk with her at least once a week."

"Once a week. David, you talk to my mother once a week? Every week? For almost four years since the divorce?" Frank took another step back.

"Hmmm… uh…. yeah. Every week." David was now sweating almost as much as the captain had been earlier.

"No," Morgan said. "I can't have dinner with you tonight. I'm meeting a friend."

She turned quickly on her heel and walked out of the room, barely noticing Frank had moved enough that his back was now flat against the wall.

CHAPTER 22

NEW YORK, MONDAY EVENING

"I really wish we'd gone somewhere else to eat."

"I could always break into the sacramental wine," Roger said. "Red or white?"

Morgan's laugh bounced off the walls of the kitchen, the echoes wending their way back to where the two old friends sat. The chairs were made of the formed, poly sort of plastic that made you think of a cheap fast food restaurant and the table wanted to wobble on one shorter leg but to her, the room seemed to fit the situation.

"I can't believe you have a kitchen in the church. What do you use it for?"

"To cook with, silly. Do you think the Church pays its priests so much money we can afford to eat out every night? Besides, there's always something going on—pizza night for the catechism class, church meetings, bible studies, visiting dignitaries—this part of the annex built in the Seventies gets used a lot." Roger took another bite of his sandwich and washed it down with a gulp of coffee. "So, you had a bad day?"

"It's that obvious? Yeah, kinda."

"Is it the case you talked about yesterday?"

Morgan nodded her head. "Frank and I... oh, Frank's my new partner. Nice guy and a good cop. Anyway, Frank and I got the call early this morning on a fresh victim."

"Is it bad? Like Manuel?"

"Bad? Oh yeah, it's bad." She shut her eyes for a moment and Roger watched her flinch her head to one side, fighting off a sight only in her mind. "But not like Manuel," she said after a few seconds. "No kids or gangs involved... at least not that we've seen so far. It's just..."

Roger waited for her to start again. Long seconds of silence turned into one, two minutes. He had seen this scene many times over the years when he had counseled people. Morgan had walked up to the abyss and was peering over its edge. In a moment she would take a step of faith and talk about what was troubling her or she would back away and probably take a while to get back to this point again. Possibly never. But the worst thing he could do would be to attempt to push her over the side.

"Are you on the clock, Roger?"

Good. She had already decided to take the step and was now only looking for affirmation she had made the right decision. "Of course, Morg. We can be as formal or informal as you want, but either way, friend or priest, what you say to me goes no further."

Morgan nodded her head. "This case is a bad one. As bad as I've seen since... I don't know if I've ever seen one worse. The psycho that thought he was a werewolf gnawed on his victims a little. Thought it would turn them into werewolves, too, like in the movies. But this guy, this bastard is ripping these women apart, Rog."

"How many so far?"

"Three. Well, three for sure."

"But you think there's more."

"Yeah, maybe. I don't know. We had two on back-to-back nights, then nothing for a night, and then another one last night. Breaking a pattern is unusual for these kinds of guys. You can't believe how the victims look when we find them. It's nothing like I've ever seen before. Sliced and diced open, their insides ripped out until they look like an empty rag doll with all the stuffing gone. They've formed a task force, a special unit to catch this guy."

"Is that why it's so bad? Are you not in the group and you want to be?"

Morgan laughed, dry and husky, the chuckle bordering on an insane cackle. Roger held back a wince. "No, I'm on it. In fact, I've been given a temporary bump to louie so I can head it." She fiddled with her cup while she talked, staring at the coffee swirling in the bottom while rolling the Styrofoam back and forth between her palms. "It's funny in a way. No one ever wants this kind of crap to happen. Good cops don't wish it on anybody. But when some sicko gets loose and it does go down, when there's a real hairball case like this, your blood starts pumping faster, you find yourself looking forward to the phone calls in the middle of the night. I suppose it's like being a surgeon. They don't want their patients to be sick. But when they get that really big challenge, that once-in-a-lifetime surgery, they get jazzed."

"There's no reason to feel guilty about loving your job, Morg," Roger said. "That's only natural."

Morgan waved her hand, swatting away his words while her other hand brought her sandwich up for a quick bite. "Oh, no," she said while chewing. "I made my peace with the feeling a long time ago. Well, mostly anyway. No, today was so rough because we called in the FBI for help and they sent up a profiler from Quantico."

"That should help," offered Roger. "I'm sure they'll have lots of ideas and maybe a fresh perspective." He stopped when he finally noticed the grimace on his friend's face. As realization slowly crept into his thoughts, he felt his mouth opening wider and wider until he imagined he looked like one of those carnival games where you needed to throw a bean bag through the hole of the painted clown's face to win the prize. "Oh, no," he said. "They didn't. They couldn't. They wouldn't dare send him back to New York to you and this case!"

"Oh, yes. Oh, yes. And oh, yes. The FB freakin' I sent David to be the profiler to help catch this psycho."

"Who's David?"

Morgan and Roger whirled in surprise at the question. Novara stood in the doorway to the kitchen, leaning casually against the frame with his arms crossed.

"Please, forgive me," he said after a moment. "I didn't mean to startle you. I smelled the coffee and, well, you know how I am about coffee, Father Greene. Oh, did I interrupt Church business?"

Roger blinked as if awakening from an afternoon nap. He glanced over at Morgan. She stared intently at her cup again but he could see red spots on her cheeks, probably blushing from embarrassment over what she had been about to say. *Damn the man for interrupting.* "No," Roger said. "Just two old friends rehashing our youth."

"Ah, you won't mind if I join you then." Novara crossed the room, grabbed a cup and poured himself some coffee. Roger was stunned by the brashness of the emissary. "Well, Father," Novara said after he sat down on the chair beside Roger and began stirring cream into his coffee. "Will you make the introductions or shall I?"

Roger could not help but stare at the man beside him. In the few days he had known him, he had never seen the emissary look so relaxed, a pearly white grin splitting his face with joy. At best the man's personality could usually be described as aloof or driven, but not right now. There was something else out of place about his manner as well but Roger couldn't quite put his finger on it.

"Emissary, this is Morgan Kelly. Morgan this is Emissary Novara of the Vatican. He is staying with us for a little while he works... while he works on a special project for his Holiness."

"Oh, so formal," Novara said with a laugh. "Please, call me Greg."

Morgan glanced up long enough to shake the visitor's hand before her gaze, which had never risen any higher than where their hands met, snapped back down to her cup.

"Tell me, Miss Kelly, was Father Greene always so serious when he was a boy as well? Tell me that at least he used to run around and play ball and scrape his knees."

Morgan giggled at the question and the sound reminded Roger of a teenage girl laughing at a cute boy's bad joke. "Oh, he tried to play basketball and football, even hockey. But you're right, he usually went home limping at the end of the day."

"Now wait a minute," Roger said. "I think I held my own."

"Really?" Morgan asked. Now she did look up and this time she stared her friend in the face, a twinkle in her eye spelling out trouble for Roger.

"Do you remember the time Sean hit you so hard on the opening face-off of the neighborhood hockey game he knocked you out? No, of course not. You were unconscious."

"Completely out on the opening play?" Novara asked.

"Oh, it's worse," continued Morgan. "We didn't realize the check also unclasped his suspenders so when we were carrying him home his pants started to fall off. We delivered him to his front door with his pants down at his knees and his underwear showing."

The two shared a laugh, but as soon as Morgan turned to look at Novara, Roger saw her immediately drop her gaze away from his face.

"If you don't mind my saying so, Miss Kelly, you look tired," said the emissary. "Are you getting enough sleep?"

"No, I'm not. I've got this case I've been working on…. one that has me up late at night a lot, but even when I do get a chance to lay down, I can't seem to sleep through the night without waking up."

Roger felt his mouth opening in shock again. It had taken him, a life-long friend, almost an hour of chit-chat to get Morgan to begin to open up. Novara, a total stranger, had achieved the same thing in less than ten minutes. No matter what else the man was, the Church had lost a gifted counselor when he left the priesthood.

"I'll bet you feel like there is someone there in the room with you, just out of sight," said Novara.

Morgan nodded. "Yes. It feels like something is right there, right there lurking in the shadows. But I know it's not true because there's never anything there when I wake up."

"Do you mean like a dream?" asked Roger. "Like a dream about Manuel?"

"No, not like that at all." Morgan sighed and the noise sounded like the air being pushed out of a stepped-on balloon. "I knew when I woke up with the bad dreams, that was all they were—bad dreams. This feels real. It feels like someone is physically in my bedroom." She sat back and crossed her arms over her chest.

"Perhaps I can be of assistance," said Novara. "I've seen this type of affliction before."

Morgan's head snapped up at the offer and for the briefest of moments, Roger thought her gaze rose up enough for her to make eye contact with Novara. But then, just as quickly, she looked back down at her watch and then reached for her purse. "I, uh, I have to meet someone, uh, back at the station. It was very nice to meet you, Mr. Novara." She stood and walked quickly toward the kitchen door. "I'll call you tomorrow, Roger. Good night. I can show myself out."

Then she was gone.

Roger turned to speak to Novara, to yell at him about pressuring his friend but also to ask how he had opened her up so quickly. He never got the chance. The unsmiling emissary had returned, the cloak of relaxation cast off this man's shoulders.

"We will leave an hour later than normal tonight," Novara said.

"I will meet you on the sidewalk in front of the Cathedral."

The puzzle piece slid into place for Roger. Now he knew what he could not put his finger on earlier. The emissary was staring at his ear, looking at his forehead, staring past him to the wall behind—anywhere but at Roger's eyes.

But Novara had been trying to catch Morgan's glance, trying to get her to stare him in the eyes.

Roger wondered what that meant.

CHAPTER 23

POLAND, 1944

"I need twenty volunteers for a special work detail inside the camp."

Gregor hesitated long enough to allow a handful of other men a chance to move forward before he took a step away from the line to join them. He had been trying to figure out a way to get inside the walls of the camp for two weeks with no success, but now he did not want to appear too eager.

After the count reached twenty, the Italian officer turned and spoke in halting German to the two soldiers behind him, both wearing all-black uniforms with the Totenkopf insignia—a human skull. Gregor walked toward the three men when his commanding officer motioned for him to join them.

"The corporal tells me you speak some German," said the officer on the right, the bespectacled commandant of the camp everyone referred to as The Doctor. Gregor did not know and did not care if he was a real physician. "Is this true?"

Gregor almost burst out laughing. The man was trying to trick him by asking him in German if he spoke German. The deception was typical of some of the malicious and petty behavior he had seen since he had arrived at the Polish railroad station at Treblinka.

But he did not laugh, did not even crack the barest hint of a smile because this Schutzstaffel officer could have him shot whenever the whim grabbed hold. "Ja, Herr Kapitan," answered Gregor. "Enough at least for conversation. I also speak some Polish and a little Hebrew." This last bit of information made all three of the other men's heads snap up and drew raised eyebrows from the German officers. The revelation also drew a gasp from his fellow Italian.

"Mein, Kapitan," stammered Lieutenant Calavara. "I had no idea! I would never have…"

Sweat poured down the man's olive-skinned face as the commandant raised a hand to stop his rambling excuse. It was impossible to tell if Calavara was sweating from the early August heat or from fear for his life. Gregor decided the answer was probably a little of both.

"How is it that you know the language of the Jews?"

This time the question came from the larger officer on the left, the one Gregor had not seen before yesterday when the man stepped from a private railway car. He had not noticed the officer give an order, yet every one of the German SS soldiers appeared to keep an eye on him at all times, like someone would keep watching a strange dog on the edge of a yard, not quite sure if it would leap out and bite. This vigilance included the commandant.

"Before the war, I was part of the Vatican security. I was sometimes assigned to travel with priests when they went on trips to foreign lands. I spent almost six months in Jerusalem and over a year in Warsaw." The lies flowed so easily from Gregor's lips now. "Mein… ?"

"This is Inspector Glucks," said the commandant. "I am Dr. Eberl. If you are a soldier, why aren't you fighting for your beloved Benito?"

"He was deemed too old for frontline duty," Calavara said quickly, anxious to show he did know something about his men.

"How has he performed at the station?" asked Eberl.

Gregor felt the men were looking him over like a piece of meat that may have spoiled while hanging in the market for too long but he kept his anger in check.

"He has done everything he has been ordered to do," answered Calavara. "In fact, he is one of my most forceful men. If the situation calls for a push to keep the swine moving, he is not against using a rifle butt to do the job—especially with the women. But since you don't care what kind of shape they're in when they arrive at camp, I don't stop him."

The two German officers continued to stare at Gregor. Dr. Eberl still looked him over with black, unblinking eyes, but Glucks suddenly appeared amused by the whole situation.

"We can always use men who know how to get things done," Glucks said after a few moments. "Doctor, why don't you put him in charge of the Italian crew and the Jewish prisoners on clean up. At least he will be able to speak to them without an interpreter."

"Jah," Eberl said with a nod. "Novara, take the other men into T-II, that's we call the camp, and find the nurse. All of you will need to be checked out by her on a regular schedule. My aide, Obersturmfuhrer Kroeger, will find you later to assign you a barracks and tell you about your responsibilities."

"Jah, Dr. Eberl. Heil Hitler."

"Your Polish is good, Sierzant Novara. You were in Poland before the war?"

Gregor nodded his head once but kept his jaws clenched together. He had spent the last two hours with the camp nurse, translating her orders as the other Italian soldiers came into her office in groups of four and five. In that time he had made up his mind about her.

She was a whore like most women.

In her piled black hair, red lipstick and white uniform, Gregor saw the same whore he had seen over and over again in Whitechapel. Even her perfume was so overpowering the odor threatened to make his eyes water. Who could get lipstick and perfume during a war? Only an uncaring whore, Gregor decided. She was probably the mistress of half the German officers in the camp.

The nurse certainly did not have the decency to blush when she had his men pull down their pants so she could check for hernias. She had simply reached out like a common whore and grabbed them—his youngest men looking away in red-faced embarrassment while the older ones looked her right back in the eye and smiled.

"Not very talkative today, Sierzant?" she asked. "As you wish. You've probably just been away from home for a while and are feeling shy... your ears are fine. Let's check your heart... sounds good. Has it been a while since you've seen your wife? I'll wager you have a houseful of children waiting at home. Let's have a look at your eyes."

The woman's incessant chattering had nearly lulled Gregor to sleep. Before he could step back, the nurse leaned in front of his face with a little light. He tried to look away but there she was, inches from him, her dark eyes staring into his own. She gasped and raised her hand to caress his cheek.

Whore. Gregor let the door open in his thoughts and the nurse's hand dropped to her side, her eyelids blinking slowly shut before snapping open about halfway.

"I'm sorry, Sierzant. We are going to need to finish your examination later," she said as she staggered over to her desk and slumped into the chair. A yawn split her lips before she could go on. "I can't seem to keep my eyes open."

Gregor did not even acknowledge she had spoken as he slipped his uniform blouse on and buttoned up. After he reached the door, he glanced back at the nurse who was now slumped over with her forehead resting on the backs of her hands on the desktop like a child in school. Disgust filled him as he shook his head. He had not tried to capture her, had not tried to look her in the eye, but still she had fallen completely for him.

Just another whore.

His new responsibility was the type of work that threatened to send men over the edge into insanity. Gregor had seen the middle of the process before but now he had a clear idea of the end of the program as well.

The Jews were herded up in the ghettos of Warsaw and loaded into boxcars. They were easy to find in the slums because it was where the Germans had forced them to move after Poland had fallen to their blitzkrieg. Living behind the barbed wire and brick walls, they were stuffed into the railway cars so tightly at least a handful died every time on the forty-two mile journey to the Treblinka station where they would slump to the ground after being held up by the press of the other living bodies.

The trains ran night and day. Once they arrived at the station, SS soldiers along with Gregor's fellow Italians pushed, prodded and beat the Jews out of the cars and down the road to T-II. Crying mingled with the sounds of shuffling feet along the stone path. They smelled of unwashed bodies and disease; they smelled of death. Gregor barely noticed. His thoughts had been reserved for making sure no one escaped on his watch and ruined his chances for getting inside the camp.

Now Gregor had witnessed the final steps.

Almost all of the Jews were stripped and maneuvered into metal vaults after they walked down the quiet, tree-lined road to Treblinka II. Gregor and others who spoke Polish and Hebrew told them the vaults were for cleaning and de-licing. Like mindless cattle they staggered into the deathtraps without so much as a whimper. A few might become alarmed when the soldiers continued to stuff and beat them in, shoving so many into the confined areas some were forced to crawl on top of the shoulders and heads of others.

It was a simple formula really—the less air space remaining in the chambers, the less gas needing to be pumped through the vents in the walls to kill them.

Once the screams and coughing stopped, the gases were flushed and the men under Gregor's supervision took over. His nineteen men were supplemented by nearly 1,300 Polish Jews, men who had escaped the grasp of death for a short time because of strong hands and backs. Gregor wondered if they still considered themselves lucky to be alive after they performed their tasks on their countrymen. There were also several hundred Ukrainian prisoners the Germans referred to—and treated—as sub-humans. Gregor did not speak their language so a handful of SS soldiers who did led them.

The sealed metal doors swung open and the bodies toppled out like stacked blocks pushed over by a child's hand. They plopped against the cement with the sound of wet fish against a wooden deck while the stench—no, there was no odor. Gregor had been surprised to find after a few days his nose could no longer smell the bodies and death in the air. The first time he entered the chambers he had gagged to the point of retching on his boots but now, nothing.

The bodies were loaded by the thousands upon pushcarts, stopping the line of dead only long enough to wrench open mouths to search for gold teeth or fillings. The soldiers all carried heavy pliers to rip teeth out of their jaws and drop them without a second glance into buckets so the precious metal could be removed later. Only a little force was needed to remove them since so many of the Jews were malnourished.

Finally, the carts were taken down a hill to long, deep trenches in the farthest clearings. Gregor was told the first bodies had been cremated before disposal but now the fuel was needed for tanks and airplanes so mass graves became the disposal system. He had been touched at first by the careful way the bodies were placed down in the holes—he supposed for some dignity at last in death. He was wrong. Later he learned they were placed so carefully because more could be fit into the graves if they were stacked neatly in rows by hand instead of using a bulldozer to push them haphazardly into their final resting place. German efficiency at work.

It was backbreaking—and heartbreaking—work. In addition to almost losing one man who became violently ill after a chamber did not completely vent its gasses, two of his Italian soldiers had requested to return to the railway station work. Gregor suspected the SS had them killed because the replacements who came into the camp did not report seeing the two men return to the docks. Even for his soldiers, Treblinka threatened to be their end as well. Gregor did not care, about any of them or himself, so long as he killed the beast.

He did not know why he had been called to this place, this time, to find the incubus. He no longer even questioned how he knew where to be when the creature reappeared. Now the sense was just a part of his damned life, damned by his responsibility, damned by his being alive.

But the whole ordeal made him question whether the long centuries he had spent with his duty were worth the effort. If this genocide was what the world could do to itself, was mankind worth saving? Would the hell the incubus was trying to unleash upon the world be any worse than the war that had sucked so many countries into the fighting? Gregor often wondered if he had already lost, that somehow Hitler and men like Eberl were the beast's progeny of prophecy.

Gregor stood in the dark. On the other side of the blanket serving as a door, a spotlight illuminated the side of the flimsy wood structure, thin bars of light peeking around the edges of the wool like fingers tentatively reaching into the night.

The light was just enough to see by as he walked between the rows of mats lining the walls on both sides of him. The remains of the day's heat swam through the stench of unwashed men. Here he did not have the blessing of not being able to smell and the smell made his eyes water. Mingling with the breaths of the exhausted were sobs and the mumbling of prayers. Despite his misgivings of mankind's worth, Gregor knew if his quarry escaped him, this was a scene that would play out around the world.

He moved aside the blanket and stepped out into the spotlight. Blinking in the sudden glare, he held his arms out wide and looked straight up at the guard tower, waiting for a couple of moments until he heard "Angehen," the order to continue on his way.

The crunch of stone beneath his boots hung in the still air. Even at this late hour, in the night's last gasp before dawn, the whimpers and sobs of damned souls broke the silence. But he heard nothing this night. This night the camp sat on the edge of a precipice, looking warily down into the dark below before taking the plunge.

Gregor spun on his heels, reversing his direction, and headed toward the low barracks serving as shelter for the female prisoners. With every step he picked up speed, reaching a sprint when noticed the German soldier in one tower slumped over, asleep on the rail.

Just as he reached the blanket hanging over the doorway, screams shattered the night's silence. He felt more than saw his prey escape into the black sky, a shadowy blot of death, passing before the twinkling of stars.

Gregor burst through into the black hole beyond, the blanket torn from its nails and crumpling to the ground in his wake. Polish curses mixed with Hebrew prayers, weaving its panicked lamentation around his head while he brutally shoved horrified women out of his way until at last he burst into an open area. He stared at the remains of something that had once been human.

More noise and cursing rose as other soldiers appeared at both doorways and someone turned on the string of lights hanging from the rafters. Blood and gore glistened on the floor with the yellow glow the bulbs provided. Gregor wondered if the whore had enjoyed the beast's pleasure before she was killed.

A sigh escaped his lips. It spoke of fear—and of relief.

There would be no more waiting.

The hunt had begun again.

After the first night, Eberl had been more interested in the mutilation of the woman than who had killed her, assuming the murderer was one of the soldiers who had some fun with a piece of chattel doomed to die anyway.

Instead, he had been so fascinated by the gashes in her skin, Eberl held an impromptu lecture and autopsy for some of the officers and guards, concentrating mainly on the wounds and the inferior organs and build of the Jewish corpse. Glucks stayed for the show before shaking the doctor's hand and then leaving in his special railroad coach.

The next day, when the second body was found, Eberl was a little less curious, a little less amused. He ordered a guard posted at each end of the women's barracks.

On the third morning, the discovery of the next woman sent Eberl into a curse-laden fit. He had the two guards shot for falling asleep on duty and posted a squad at each door the next night.

Now, on the fourth morning, Eberl glared at the thickening blood on the floor with pieces of skin and entrails winding through it. The two squads who had been assigned guard duty the night before stood off to one side, sweat darkening their black uniforms even more.

"Dr. Eberl?" asked Gregor. He knew now was his time to take a chance. "May I make a suggestion, sir?"

Only one curt nod showed he had been heard.

"All of the killings have happened inside the barracks," Gregor said. "But all of the soldiers have been posted outside."

Eberl finally looked up, his brow furrowed with concentration—and a touch of anger.

"I need someone inside," he said. "You speak the women's language, Novara. I can't put a German soldier inside. They would find the order beneath the post of a Waffen Schutzstaffel. But you, feldwebel, will stay inside the barracks tonight. For your sake, I hope you have better luck."

For the first time since Gregor met the man, the doctor smiled. Thin lips pulled back, showing his teeth while his nose scrunched up and tilted his glasses forward. It was the face of a man who would never care about others, the face of a killer. It was the face of a wolf on the hunt.

And now Gregor was the shepherd watching over the sheep.

His plan was simple. Now that he had access to what the demon wanted, he would take the whores away until the beast was driven to a mistake. He did not know how he did it—did not really care—but he knew he could keep the women away from his prey. He had kept the beast away from Arabelle, kept it away from Aysel. His failing to the women had been in his diligence, not the power of his prayers. Though why God still listened to them when Gregor had lost so much faith was beyond understanding. They might have even worked in Whitechapel, but Whitechapel…

Gregor's shoulders slumped and he cringed to ward off an unseen blow. Whitechapel was better left forgotten.

"Sierzant! Sierzant!" The nurse's voice cut through his memories and he opened his eyes. "Sierzant, please ask him to breathe deep."

Gregor repeated the request in Italian and he watched one of his men go through the rest of his exam. Two hours later, all of the Italian soldiers had been through the little room, poked, prodded, and sent on their way.

"Now, Sierzant, let's begin with you. Take off your shirt and pants please."

A few minutes later Gregor was standing in only his underwear when the door behind the nurse's desk swung open. A little girl of five or six years peeked around the edge with her mouth cracked open in a yawn. He flushed with embarrassment and quickly grabbed his pants off the chair to cover himself. The abrupt movement caused the nurse to look up from her chart and see what had happened.

"Julka! You know you are never to come into the office," the nurse exclaimed.

"I had a bad dream, Matka," the little girl said. "It was about Tato."

"Hush, Julka!"

Gregor saw the nurse look back and forth from the girl to him out of the corner of his eye. He was busy trying to find a way to put on his pants without exposing himself again but he noticed she appeared nervous, her voice shaking when she spoke.

"Julka, go back to our room. I'll be inside in a few minutes."

Gregor saw the door swing shut at the same time he looked up from fastening his pants.

"Children," the nurse said, her laugh high and tinny before it ended abruptly. "They never listen at that age. I'm sure yours are much better behaved, Sierzant."

Gregor looked at the sheen of sweat across the nurse's forehead that had not been there a few moments earlier, saw the way she gripped the stethoscope until her knuckles were white with tension. Her perfume, the awful overpoweringly sweet scent, mixed with something he could only think was fear.

"I wouldn't know," he said as he reached for his shirt. "I don't have any children."

"Really? I would've sworn... I mean, the way you look at them..." She paused and took a deep breath. "I'm sorry. I've seen you before when you look at the children who are, who are processed, I assumed you had children of your own. I'm sorry." She laughed again but this time it sounded as if she meant it. "We never seem to be able to complete your exams, Sierzant. I need to put Julka back down for her nap." She stifled a yawn before continuing. "I haven't been sleeping very well lately so I might as well lay down with her. Perhaps tomorrow?"

"Yes, tomorrow."

Gregor straightened his hat and walked out into the main yard, his mind already off the whore and onto the night's business.

He sat in the dark, his lips moving in whispered prayer. Gregor did not have a gun with him, his pistol and rifle stored safely in his barracks. It did not matter; they would be useless against his prey anyway. Instead, his hand gripped the hilt of the knife sticking out the top of his pants, its white blade out of view.

His concentration wavered at times during the long hours of the night but never completely faltered. Most of the time his thoughts were deep in the bottom of a pit, shining brightly enough to keep the black at bay. Other times the power ebbed and the night moved closer in his thoughts. That was then he heard the sobs and prayers of the Jewish women around him in the dark. That was when he sensed a shadow moving just out of the light in the pit, felt the intrusion of a vigilant figure standing out of sight.

The beast was here.

Gregor could reach out and point at his prey—first here, then there. One time he twisted on the creaking old chair and raised the blade a little, the presence just out of reach behind him.

The beast was searching.

His prey wandered through the small hours of the morning, casting back and forth, sniffing for a trail just out of range. Gregor found no amusement in the search that became more frantic as the night passed. Their battle had been going on for too long. He had given up far too much, sinking to depths he never imagined existed. No, he would not smile at the demon's confusion; he would plunge the knife into its throat instead.

The beast was gone.

Slowly, Gregor became aware the women were moving around him. The cracks around the blanket revealed the first light of a new day, not the glare of a guard tower spotlight. He stood up and stretched, careful to cover the hilt of his knife before walking toward the doorway. The Jewish prisoners parted for him like water before the prow of a boat. Tentative hands reached out, not quite touching his uniform as he passed, but he felt them nonetheless. Some women whispered their gratitude while others, voices shaking with fear at being beaten for the blasphemy, asked for the blessings of Yahweh on his head. They thought he had saved their lives.

Gregor grimaced as he exited the barracks and waited for the guard detail to clear him. He breathed the fresh air deep, clearing away the stench and the despair. He had not saved them. The Jews were cattle for the kill, sheep to the slaughter. He would keep them safe like a butcher watched over a flock for his shop. Tomorrow night the beast would be even more desperate, even more confused. Then Gregor would step back and the women would be exposed as the bait in his trap.

He had not saved them. In Treblinka, they were already dead.

Two more nights passed and Gregor kept the incubus at bay. The second night had been like the first. The demon searched for the women until almost dawn, probing, picking, pushing at Gregor but never finding his way through to the barracks. He had felt the beast's anxiety grow.

The third night had been different.

Gregor felt the beast early in the evening but the search had been fainter and less desperate. He had needed to concentrate to feel the incubus casting back and forth. The change made him smile to think of meeting a weakened incubus, but then the search stopped long before the sun peeked over the forest. The absence worried him. It was time to act.

Now, as the fourth night fell, Gregor took a final look at the top of the sun as the orb slid behind the trees. The shadows, which had long before started their march across the main yard, reached the barracks and cast the building into the dark. He nodded to one of the German soldiers on guard duty and pushed aside the blanket over the doorway.

The Jewish women lined both sides of the aisle down the center of the building, the light from the bulbs overhead casting drawn cheeks and eyes into shadowed skulls. The barracks were silent with only his steps on the floor and the breathing of the women to let him know he had not gone deaf.

Gregor reached the chair where he would spend the night. On its bare seat sat a piece of cloth. He reached down and picked it up, letting the material unfold between his hands.

The gift was only a small, rectangular piece of what had once been white fabric. From each of the grimy corners hung crude tassels, probably torn from clothing. He did not know the religious significance of the cloth, but he recognized the tassels as tzitzits, Jewish reminders of the mitzvoth, the hundreds of commandments the Jews were told by their God to follow. But since he was a goy, a gentile, the tzitzits were reminders of good deeds. He looked up and every woman in the barracks stared back at him.

"Dziekuje," he said, thanking them in Polish.

The women shuffled to their mats and lay down. A moment later a guard reached in under the blanket and turned off the light.

Gregor stared into the dark, silently blinking away tears. He hated the incubus for what he was about to do.

He hated God almost as much.

Gregor stopped praying. Barely two hours into his nightly vigil, he had not yet sensed the beast. He pulled the knife from inside his shirt.

The trap was set.

But soon the minutes stretched into an hour, the hour into two, and then three. The night dragged on, and with each moment he did not feel the demon's presence, Gregor's thoughts grew darker.

Was the beast gone? Had he missed his chance?

More time passed and his thoughts fell further into despair.

Was he now the prey? Had the incubus found a way around his prayers?

Another hour trudged by and Gregor's thoughts were of Whitechapel and all the women sleeping around him.

Had the beast been with one of the women in here and hidden his action by killing another? Would Gregor need to kill them all himself to be sure, making Whitechapel's insanity feel like a cloudy day compared to a hurricane? Could he even kill every woman in the barracks?

But not every woman in the camp was in the barracks, Gregor suddenly realized. There was another.

Another who need not worry about surviving the gas chambers.

Another who was having trouble sleeping.

Gregor leaped to his feet, the chair banging against the wall. His fear grew as he sprinted down the aisle, none of the women waking at the eruption.

His fear grew to terror when he burst through the blanket and fell over a sleeping guard who never woke. Gregor rolled and crawled on his hands and knees until finally gaining his feet again and sprinted across the open yard, his feet given wings made of panic.

His terror changed to rage when he raced past a dead German soldier, the man's neck broken when he fell, asleep, over the guard tower rail.

Gregor's breaths were ragged gasps as he burst into the nurse's office, his shoulder aching from the force that ripped the door off one hinge, leaving it hanging at an impossible angle. He staggered toward the opening where he had seen the little girl a few days earlier. He jerked the handle and…

There was the beast.

Its wings were tight against its back while its horns glistened in the moonlight streaming through the open window beside it. The nurse lay off to one side, sobbing, the tattered remains of her clothes strewn across the floor.

The incubus captured his attention, crouching with one taloned foot resting lightly on the throat of Julka. The child was asleep, a smile of innocence on her lips.

"I've been waiting for you, cambion," said the beast. "You were so busy hiding the others, I thought I might need to leave before you joined us."

"Sierzant, my baby. Help me, please," pleaded the nurse.

"It is your baby we're going to discuss," the incubus said, more of his fangs showing when he grinned. "But not the one you mean."

"Let the child go," Gregor said, his fingers gripping the knife's hilt. "I'll just kill the woman and we will start all over again next time."

"Yes, the same as before. Except this time, if you kill the mother, I kill the daughter. This little one's blood will be on your hands. Just like the ones who did not need to die in Whitechapel."

Gregor almost fell over. It was one thing to kill the whores down through the centuries, but it was another to cause the death of one so young, so innocent.

"I propose a truce," continued the incubus. "The mother lives and I take the girl with me to ensure you walk away.

Was that even possible? No one, not the priests, not scholars, not even he knew after all these centuries where the beast went in between his hunts on earth. "No," Gregor said. "I can't. Too many others will die by letting her live." He took a step toward the nurse.

The incubus hissed and drew a single talon slowly across Julka's throat. A red line appeared in its wake, just deep enough to draw a few drops of blood.

"No!" screamed the nurse. "She's so little."

"But if you live," Gregor said, "the child he put inside your womb will unleash hell on earth. Millions upon millions will die. Enough to make your Fuhrer's plans look like child's play!"

The nurse cried louder and crawled toward a chair.

"So what do we do, cambion?" The incubus drew a breath through a clenched mouth, each word a cold hiss. "You decide who lives and dies."

Gregor's head was light. Nothing in the long years of his duty had prepared him for the question.

"No," the nurse said from the corner, her voice suddenly

calm and strong. "I decide." Her hand flew to her mouth and she swallowed something.

The incubus screeched loud enough to make the walls shake as he leaped forward, Julka forgotten on the floor.

Gregor moved just as fast. His arm slashed downward as he ran around a chair, the white blade slicing through the beast's skin on one haunch. Another scream, this one of pain, threatened to bring down the building. The incubus wheeled and lashed out with an unfurled wing.

Gregor met the attack with the knife, the blade cutting through, but the blow made him stumble backwards. Now a foot-long gash in the beast's wing matched the slice on its leg. Blood dripped from the wounds, thick and black in the moonlight. The stench of the incubus made Gregor gag. Evil rode in the odor, the smell of stolen souls in its drops. The blood hissed on the floor and the wood smoked where green flames popped up.

The incubus fought back, one claw grazing Gregor's left arm and sending pain through his body. He ignored the hurt and stabbed at his prey's arm, the knife biting deep into flesh again.

Gregor watched the beast waddle backwards. Both of them were panting; the battle something they had anticipated for a long time. The incubus glanced down at the woman lying on the floor, unmoving, then tried to look around Gregor at the little girl.

"It's not over, half-breed. I'll come back. I'll always come back." With the final curse spoken, the incubus jumped twice, the second carrying him through the window and into the night beyond, one last scream a sign of the pain it its wing.

Gregor walked to the nurse and knelt by her side. White foam trailed out of one corner of her mouth, blood striping it red. Whatever poison she had taken was killing her quickly. Her eyes fluttered open. "Julka?"

"She's fine. Still sleeping."

The nurse nodded. "I knew you were not what you seemed, Sierzant. Knew it from the first time I saw you." She coughed and more blood mixed with the foam. "We're Jewish but nobody knew. My husband died when the Germans came over the border. We changed our names and moved to Warsaw. Everything I did, everything, I did to keep Julka safe." She coughed again and again, each one a little weaker than the last. "Take her away. Take her away from all this death. She…" The nurse's voice trailed off and her eyes stared at the ceiling.

Gregor rocked back until he landed on his butt with a thump. He blinked slowly as he stared at the nearly naked woman.

Not a whore.

What deceit and lies he had sensed when he met the woman were not born of base desires or the greed of someone who wanted only for themselves. The dishonesty had been the deceit of a mother, the lies told to protect the one she loved more than anyone—more than herself.

Not a whore.

A mother.

Gregor crawled over to Julka, pulled her close and staggered to his feet, his left arm on fire where the beast had cut him. He would need to move fast if he was going to be gone before the camp woke. But even as he ignored the pain and trotted across the yard toward a car, his steps were light with purpose.

A mother's love was worth fighting the beast.

CHAPTER 24

*T*his body traps me, a painful prison made of bone and skin. Before the fall, time was a whispered thought, the sentence on those the Light sent down in the bodies of his beloved creations.

Time.

Time laughs at me with rasping chuckles, echoing in my head and leaving me with the realization it is my enemy as well. All while his creatures—his mankind—trudge through the blandness of their lives, unaware of the pleasures he has allowed only them, all while time kills them.

But the bastard knows. He knows what time holds dear. He knows his time will run out and that frightens him. That fear has pushed him to the edge of darkness before, driving him before it like a deer before the pack, the wolves howling and nipping at his heels. He has cracked before.

This time he will break.

The edge. I must drive him to the edge again. With a whisper and a thought, I will whip him toward the abyss in blind haste. If he cracks again, he will never heal. He will break like a dried, dead limb against the wind. In his madness, he will join me and not even know it.

I must drive the cambion mad.

CHAPTER 25

NEW YORK, EARLY TUESDAY MORNING

Roger stumbled as his toe caught an uneven slab of concrete, the streets in this section of the city already in decline. The neighborhood hung on the edge of being chic with must-have loft apartments or starting a downward spiral into run-down housing and unsafe streets. All it would take was a couple of artists or musicians making it big and the people with too much money and too little to spend it on would swoop in and grab the cheap real estate and return the buildings to their former glory, making it "the" place to live for a while. Or just as easily, a few too many robberies or fights between gangs trying to claim the street for their own and the area would disintegrate, driving away anyone with the choice to live somewhere else.

He felt a kinship with the neighborhood. Roger also felt he stared at two paths, wondering which one to step down. In the past few days he had felt awe in the emissary's presence. He had also felt anger and more fear than he had known existed. But right now, he just felt his lungs burning as he attempted to keep pace with Novara.

"Do you know where you're going?" Roger asked.

Novara did not answer for so long the priest was afraid he had not been heard. On the verge of asking the question again, the other man finally spoke.

"It taunts me, Father. Leading, leading, leading me." His voice was strained and tight as if he struggled to move a great weight. "But not there, no, not there where she…" Novara stopped and glanced toward Roger. "No, not there where I would have thought we'd go. This is too easy."

Roger felt his stomach drop. The fear he knew on the night the shadow flew over them still lingered in his mind and now it came forward.

"A trap?" Roger did not know which answer he dreaded more, yes or no.

"A trap?" Novara laughed, a cold rasp that did nothing to quell Greene's fear. "Of course, it's a trap. But not for you. Besides, you have your unquestioned faith to keep you safe, Father."

Anger flashed hot and for a moment the priest forgot his terror.

"I've had enough of your belittling my faith, Mr. Novara," Roger said. He felt his voice rising but he could not find the will to put it down. "I do not need to put up with insults. Is that what happened to you? Did the Vatican cast you out because your faith was found lacking?"

The emissary chuckled again. Roger knew where he had heard the laugh before. He heard the same sound when he visited Saint Vincent's Hospital to minister to the psychiatric patients. It was a laugh claiming the patients were not the insane ones. The rest of the world just did not understand what they saw, what they did. Roger's fear returned.

"When I left the Church, they sent a thousand men looking for me." Novara paused and cocked his head to one side. Though Roger heard nothing but the normal sounds of the city, the other man acted as though he listened to a whisper on the breeze. A moment later he was off again, picking up the pace and crossing at the next intersection in front of a cab, the car horn blaring in protest. The priest ran to catch up, but Novara had already restarted his conversation before he was back within hearing range.

"… hid in the darkness. So dark there, so easy to get lost. They did not follow me there, could not follow me. And when I came out of the darkness, there was Julia. Sweet, sweet little Julia. Karol was so proper when I took her to him at Krakow. He insisted on calling her Julka. Insisted. But he was the one who protected her after I left, so it was his right. He got her to safety with some of the other Jews he saved."

Roger choked. The man had just referred to Pope John Paul II by his given name again. More than that, he had referenced the former pope's work while he was still in seminary during World War II when he helped escaping Jews. Madness! That would make Novara at least eighty-five years old!

"Why did you try to look into Morgan's eyes?"

Novara stumbled, the rhythm of his footsteps stuttering before regaining their beat. "Her problem is very real," the man replied after they had traveled another half-block. "More real than she knows. More real than you know, although you have seen enough to begin to guess—if you open your eyes."

"Dreams," Roger said. "She can't sleep. I know her mind can make her believe what she dreams is real, but you shouldn't feed that..." He stopped talking and broke into a run as Novara veered again, this time across the street to the left.

The priest gasped for breath, his lungs threatening to go from a low heat into a full-fledged fire. There was no way an eighty-plus-year-old man was running him into the ground. The emissary was either mad or talking about another Karol.

"We shouldn't feed her neurosis," Roger panted. "It won't help her in the long run."

"I have seen many women with her... affliction," Novara said.

"Is that your excuse for barging in when I was counseling her? I was just making progress and then, bam, there you are with twenty questions. What if she had clammed up? What if all my progress had just gone poof?" Even as Roger said the words, he knew his anger was more jealousy talking than concern for his friend. He just found it so hard to admit the emissary had accomplished more in the first ten minutes of talking to her than a lifetime of friendship had done for him. The realization hurt.

"I must help her or she'll be gone."

"No," said Roger. "She will not give in to the dreams. We'll get her help..."

He was talking to himself. Roger watched as Novara picked up the pace into a sprint before turning sharply down an alley. He willed himself into a run and he lurched into the alley, careening off one wall and nearly hitting head-on with a dumpster.

The priest weaved back into the center of the dark canyon. He had the impression of darker shadows on each side of him as he ran along, frightening him into a burst of speed he did not know he had left. The smell of urine and stale booze told him some of the shadows were men, or at least the shells that had once been men before the bottle or life brought them here. A cat howled and hissed while a dark figure yelled something unintelligible.

Roger ran through the paths of hell, his lungs burning with the retribution of God's fallen angels. The street lamp on the next block hovered into view and what had seemed dim and unassuming before shone out like a spotlight now. The gauntlet of shadows he raced between changed, morphing into stacked boxes or garbage cans. The smells of the wretched fell behind, staying in the darkness where they hid themselves from the world. He lurched around the corner and stumbled, his legs reaching their final strength.

Roger never quite got his head up to see what he ran into, but he hit someone hard enough to move both of them. His eyes swam from the stench crawling inside his nose, rotting eggs and meat mixed with sulfur, assaulting his body with the force of a punch. He pushed blindly away from whatever he half-lay across. His palms met bone-hard ridges and slimy leather.

A scream filled his ears with hatred, anger and pain—but mostly hatred. Suddenly another yell was there as well, this one the sounds of shouted words. Novara's face, blurred and skewed through the tears in Roger's eyes, swam into view and he felt himself jerked violently toward the emissary. Pain followed, not in his shoulders where he had been grabbed, but from behind, on the calf of his leg. The priest screamed.

Novara tossed him to one side and he lay where he landed, the sidewalk cool against his cheek. He gritted his teeth against the inferno in his leg, against the flames in his lungs—against being alive. He willed his eyes open and he saw Novara, crouching with something brilliant white in his hand. The emissary stood between him and the alley, facing the shadows they had run out of, his mouth moving silently, although Roger was not sure of this since he was not certain if he had been struck deaf. Then the man stared up, watching something dart into the sky.

Roger closed his eyes again, only for a moment, then Novara jerked him to his feet, dragging him into a shuffling, pain-filled trot.

"You must move, Father," Novara said in his ear. "Your screams surely woke the neighbors and we can't let the police find us with the bodies. We have to be gone when they arrive."

"Bodies?"

"Shhh!" Novara pushed Roger into another alley and a few seconds later a police car roared by with its lights flashing. As soon as the patrol car was gone, the emissary pulled him into motion again, this time getting them a handful of blocks down the street before they ducked into the shadows to hide from an ambulance as well as more police.

"You said bodies. What bodies?" Roger asked.

"You fool," Novara answered. This time the man's strong hands did not pull Roger into a walk but instead lifted him until he stood on his toes, his back pinned against the building. "I had it. Our prey was cornered, nowhere to go with the fire escape above it. And you come stumbling out and land on top of the beast. I should have let it kill you. The loss would have been worth the sacrifice to end the hunt."

"What are you talking about?"

"I saved the one, I think. The other, may God have mercy on her soul. But the beast just kept talking, taunting me…"

"What are you talking about? What was taunting you?"

Roger never saw the hand. All he knew was one moment he was standing up trying to understand what Novara was saying and the next he was on the ground, his cheek numb and eye throbbing.

"Do not get in my way again, priest, or I will let it kill you. Is that what you want, to die along with your friend? If you can't do this, I will hunt alone."

Roger watched Novara stomp away, wondering if he had served enough penance for whatever sin caused God to assign him this task.

CHAPTER 26

NEW YORK, EARLY TUESDAY MORNING

Morgan hit the alarm again but the incessant noise would not stop. She leaned up on an elbow and only then realized the clamor was not her alarm but her telephone ringing.

"Yeah." One word was all she could muster around her yawn.

"Lieutenant? It's Frank."

Damn the man. He had almost started calling her by her first name and then she had received the bump in rank. "Yeah, Frank. What's up?"

"I'm on my way to you. Two vics this time and we might have caught a break. A witness looked out her window and saw something. Maybe even more."

Morgan's feet hit the floor and any thought of more sleep was gone. "Let's get Overholt…"

"Already on his way, Lieutenant."

She did not hear him use her rank this time. "I'll be downstairs when you get here."

Morgan burst out the front door of her apartment building just as Frank's Ford roared round the corner, the cherry spinning on top of his unmarked car and throwing shafts of red against the apartments. She did not give him a chance to even think about opening the door for her. Instead, she jerked on the handle while the car was still rolling to a stop. A quick hop on one foot and she plopped onto the seat beside him while the car continued to move forward. Frank looked horrified. "Let's go."

The car leaped away from the curb as Frank buried the accelerator. Morgan's thoughts raced along with the speeding car. This was a frustrating time—knowing there was a possible break at the scene and she was not there.

"Any idea how reliable the witness is, Frank?"

"No. Sounded like a woman's cat woke her up because of a ruckus below her apartment. She looked out the window and saw something, but the uniform on the scene didn't say what."

Morgan nodded her head. They would ask their own questions anyway so whatever she had told the first patrolman probably would not matter. "Did you say there might be more?"

Frank smiled. It was the grin of a little boy who had just put over a joke on his mother. "Yeah, Lieutenant. One of the vics was still alive when the first car arrived on scene."

Morgan's heart stopped for a moment. Every major case had a point when something clicked, a puzzle piece falling into place to make a nice, neat little present. A piece of scrap paper left at a scene, half a license plate number, someone looking out their window at just the right time—but almost never was the break a victim who escaped from a serial killer. That solution was too easy, too Hollywood.

"That's too good to be true. What's the catch, Frank?"

"She may not live. She was cut up pretty good."

Another couple of minutes and they saw familiar lights playing off the buildings before they rounded the corner. Frank stomped on the brake and slid the car to a stop. Morgan immediately picked out a dark suit with a white shirt and red tie underneath the glare of the portable investigation lights. David had beaten them here and was dressed in the FBI uniform of the day. Frank must have noticed him, too.

"Lieutenant?" Frank asked as they both got out of the car and began walking the last part of the block to the crime scene.

"Yeah."

"I was confused about something so I asked my wife about it."

"About the case? That's okay, Frank, as long as she keeps her mouth shut. Everyone needs to have someone to bounce ideas off. What'd you ask her?"

"I asked her if we like Agent Kelly."

Morgan's head snapped around but her partner was staring straight forward. "What did your wife say?"

Frank wiped his hand across his forehead and then stretched

his neck. He was sweating a lot for a cool night. "She said that it was up to you."

"I need to meet you wife, Frank. She may be the smartest woman I'll ever know." Morgan turned to look forward again. David had spotted them and was waving them forward. "Yeah, Frank, we like him." Her voice dropped to a whisper. "Probably too much."

David stood on the edge of a pool of light and gestured at the roof of his car. "I picked up a couple of coffees on the way. Plenty of sugar for you, Morg. I didn't know how you took yours, Frank, so there is cream up there, too."

"Thank you, Agent Kelly."

David tossed Morgan a puzzled look. She grimaced in reply.

"If you can figure out how to get him to use your first name, let me know. I have already threatened to shoot him and he hasn't stopped."

The lights of the investigation team were easily bright enough to show the red climb into Frank's cheeks. "I'll get the coffees," he said.

Morgan stepped over to where Overholt was squatting beside the remains of a twenty-something blonde with dark purple streaks in her hair. That was about the only part of her not covered in blood. "What've we got?"

"Hey, Lieutenant. Congratulations on the promotion. Uh, looks like the same guy. We've got the slashes with the weapon going in both directions like before. Preliminary look says there was penetration and a little tearing, although I need to get her back to the shop before I will say that for sure." He stopped and made sure only Morgan, David and Frank, who had just walked up, were close enough to hear. "Her uterus is gone like the other ones, too."

David bent down and stared at the girl's insides as Morgan took a coffee from Frank.

"Any further indication of the weapon?" David asked.

"No, Agent Kelly. Still no initial signs of metal fragments and there are some pretty deep gouges on her pelvic bone here and here. I'll look all of them over myself for slivers, but I'll bet my next paycheck it's the same guy."

"The first call said there were two vics," Frank said.

"Yeah, over here." Overholt stood up and led the trio about ten feet away where a pool of blood was congealing into a red-black goo. "They found her lying up against this wall, but I think the attack happened back over there by the other girl."

"What makes you say that?" Morgan asked.

Overholt pointed at little plastic placards with numbers on them on the ground. "We have a blood-splatter trail here. We are checking the blood but I think it is the live victim's." Overholt stopped and gestured down at the blood by his feet. "But this is a lot of blood so she was really bleeding fast." He paused and looked back up. "I think she was thrown from there to here. There would've been more splatter and it would be closer together if she staggered over here after an attack. Besides, look how it has tear-dropped, like the vic was moving really fast."

Frank let out a low whistle while David cupped his chin in his hand and looked back and forth between the two spots.

"That's a long way," Morgan said. "Could she have been running away, trying to escape?"

"I don't think so," said Overholt. "Her abdominal muscles were all slashed up, so it would be hard for her to move at all, and even then there would be a lot of pain."

"If?" Morgan asked. "You mean you haven't seen the victim?"

"No, they were so worried about keeping her alive, the paramedics took her to the hospital right away. The first bus arrived on the scene almost immediately after the 9-1-1 call. I've got one of my best people at the hospital and I will go there myself just as soon as we finish with the primary scene."

"Okay, get back to it. We'll all get together back at the station as soon as you have a preliminary report."

"Okay, Lieutenant."

Morgan turned to look at the two men. "Frank, you look like you played football. Could you throw someone, even a woman, that far?"

"Wrestler. Too slow for the football team. And, boy, I don't know. I suppose if she was really small... it's a long ways."

"David? What do you think?"

"No, I don't think so," he smiled though as he talked and gestured toward Overholt with his coffee. "Your man looks like he knows what he's doing and he will give you a hypothesis. I admire that because most people in his shoes don't want to take the chance of being wrong. But... no, I want to wait until we get the blood work back before we try to figure out how she got over here. There's just too much speculation otherwise."

Morgan paused for a moment. She had forgotten how calmly analytical David could be on a case. Emotional detachment was a great trait for the job but not so much at home. But, damn, it was hard not to like the man.

"You're right. Let's wait until we see what the evidence tells us. Have you spoken with the witness yet or gotten the rundown on the vics?"

"No," David answered. "I figured there was no sense doing it twice."

Morgan looked around and saw a young patrolman standing beneath one of the portable light stands. He had his hat off and he kept rubbing a hand through his hair. She smiled. *That's got to be the first man on the scene.* "Patrolman, I'm Lieutenant Kelly. Give me the rundown."

He fumbled with his hat as he tried to keep it in his hand and open his notebook at the same time. His nervousness finally won out and he dropped the hat by his feet. Morgan bent down and picked it up before the stunned patrolman could move.

"It's okay, Hatcher," she said, reading his nameplate. "First murder scene?"

"Yes, ma'am. It's a lot of blood."

"Don't worry. This is one of the worst ones you'll ever see. You make it through this night and you'll never have to worry about being nervous at a scene again. Okay? Now, tell me what you've got."

"Yes, Lieutenant." He looked down at his notes. "The deceased is named April Mooney, twenty-six. She's an artist and lives in this building," he gestured over his shoulder, "in 3A. The live victim is Elizabeth Klinger, thirty-one, though she apparently goes by the name 'Liza.' She works as a scheduler at a marketing firm, uh, Marko and Davis down off the Avenue of the Americas. She also lives in 3A. Only Klinger had a purse, still had cash and cards inside. Oh, uh, Mooney's ID was found in what was left of her jacket pocket along with a credit card."

"Has their apartment been searched yet?" Frank asked.

"Yes, sir. Nothing appeared to be out of place although the patrolmen said it was kind of messy. The next-door neighbor said he thought he heard them talking about going to an opening tonight. He figured it was an art thing. There is another officer waiting upstairs for you and the techs in their apartment."

"What about the witness?" Morgan asked as she looked around.

The patrolman began shuffling back and forth on his feet. "The witness's name is Gladys Tumbleson. She is a widow who lives in 3G, uh," Hatcher pointed toward a window. "That one right there to the left of the fire escape."

"Well, where is she?"

"She's in her apartment," Hatcher said. "She said she didn't care who died, she wasn't standing outside in her nightie for nobody. There is a patrolman at her door and a female officer inside the apartment with her. She's pretty old."

Morgan, David and Frank looked at each other for a moment before Morgan and David started laughing. Even Frank smiled—a little.

"It's okay, Hatcher," Morgan finally said. "Sometimes witnesses are like that. You made sure she was secure and that's what matters. Good report. Make sure we get copies of your notes." She handed him his hat. "You survived."

The trio walked around to the front of the building and past the two patrolmen stationed there. Morgan was still chuckling. "An old walk-up. You gonna be able to make it, Frank? David will start complaining about the second floor."

"I'm not waiting that long," David said. "It's the twenty-first century. You'd think some of these New York landlords would have heard of elevators."

"Where do you want to go first?" Frank asked. He was already grimacing and they had not yet reached the first landing.

"I think we should see the old lady first," David said. "It's really late and she probably wants to go back to bed."

Morgan nodded in agreement. The next few minutes passed in silence—silent except for the sounds of their shoes on the worn wooden stairway and Frank's grunts as he labored up the steps. She dropped back beside him as David moved ahead. "You okay, Frank?

I was just kidding earlier."

"It's just my knees, Lieutenant. I'm fine walking where it's flat but steps are killers. Don't worry, I'll make it."

Morgan patted him on the shoulder and matched his pace. A minute later they broached the third floor and headed down the hallway to where David was talking with a patrolman standing outside an apartment door. He just nodded and opened the door when they moved close.

Morgan spotted the witness, Mrs. Gladys Tumbleson, asleep in a rocker recliner with what appeared to be a forty-pound tabby on her lap. It was hard to tell which one was snoring loudest. A female officer approached the trio from the other side of the room where she had been watching the door and windows.

"She fell asleep a little while ago, Lieutenant. The night was so late I just left her be, figured we could always wake her up when you got here." She started to go back to her spot by the window. "Better be careful of the cat. I thought it was going to tear me apart when I walked over to her one time."

"Well, that's great," David said. "Who wants to risk getting clawed to wake her up?"

"Maybe we can just yell at her from here," Morgan suggested.

Morgan and David chuckled together but she stopped when she noticed Frank walking slowly toward the chair. She heard him making a deep, humming sound with some sort of a trill interlaced through the noise, rising and falling with his breathing. The cat slowly raised one eyelid and then both before lifting his head to stare at the approaching detective. Morgan was about to warn her partner to be careful when the cat began purring and then rolled over on his back, exposing his belly to be rubbed. Frank scratched under the cat's chin for a few seconds and then scooped the tabby up, its legs and belly draped over his arm while he continued to stroke the cat.

"Mary and I never had any kids," he said. "But she always had her cats. We've got three right now."

"You're lucky Mr. Buttons likes you." Mrs. Tumbleson's voice was old—weathered and cracked like a building that had stood against the elements for a long time. But there was still strength in the words. "He damn near tore a finger off one of those punk kids down the hall who thought they were going to pick him up one day. Go ahead and hold onto him for a little bit. He's so fat now he puts my legs to sleep."

Frank only nodded as he sat down on the couch and began making the odd noise again. The cat fell back asleep as soon as he was comfortable.

"Mrs. Tumbleson, I'm Lieutenant Kelly and this is Special Agent Kelly of the FBI. We need to ask you a few questions about what you saw earlier tonight."

"Both named Kelly? You must be married. Good for you. You two look good together."

Morgan blushed but she felt a warm feeling go through her when she noticed David was smiling—not laughing, not waving off the comment—just smiling.

"Ma'am, what happened tonight?" Morgan asked.

"Well, I had stayed up and watched the beginning of the news on Channel 5, you know, the one that tells you the next day's weather up front. I can't abide listening to all the bad stuff that they call news these days. As soon as I knew it was not going to rain tomorrow, I turned off the TV and Mr. Buttons and I went to bed. Sometime in the middle of the night, he jumped off. Wakes me up every damn time he does that. Shakes the bed something fierce.

"Anyway, he trots over and jumps up on the window sill where I can see him against the street lights outside and he starts hissin' and the hairs raise right up on his back. You wouldn't have been able to pick him up then, sonny." She gave Frank a wink and a yellow-toothed grin. "Anyway, I went over to the window to see what had him so riled up. That's when I saw them."

"So you were able to see the two women?" Morgan asked. "They were both still… standing when you looked out?"

"Oh no, I only saw one of them girls. They live together, those two. I think they're, you know." She clasped both hands together in front of her. "Anyways, I could only see the one little one, the painter, uh, April. I didn't know the tall one that dresses so ritzy was even on the sidewalk until the policeman took me downstairs."

"Well, then, Mrs. Tumbleson," David asked. "Who did you see?"

"At first I only saw one guy. Never got a good look at his face. His back was to the light down there. He was looking straight underneath my window. Looked like he was having an argument with someone. Then all the sudden he jumps forward and grabs this guy I couldn't see before and throws him back toward the street."

"Did they fight or continue arguing at that point?" Morgan was trying to picture the scene in her mind even as the old lady was describing it.

"No. The first man did the damnedest thing and went back to looking underneath my window. Then, poof, he looks straight up at the sky and I ducked behind the curtain. When I peeked back out, they was both gone so I called 9-1-1. I could see that poor girl down there was bleedin' and she needed help. God may send both of 'em to hell for how they was livin' but they was always nice to me. Helped me carry my groceries up a couple times."

"Thank you, Mrs. Tumbleson," Morgan said. "Will you excuse us for a minute?"

Morgan and David walked over by the couch so Frank could hear. "What do you think, David?"

"She's a little touched in the head and way out of step with the times, but I think she's a good witness. We need to get her with a sketch artist ASAP and see if we can come up with some kind of composite."

"There's something else, too." Morgan looked over at the window before turning back. "One of them saw her. Or at least, we can't take a chance they didn't see her in the window. We've got to move her and put her into protection. Except for that girl they took to the hospital, right now Mrs. Tumbleson's our only living lead."

"I agree. Do you want to use a federal house?"

"I may. Let me check when we get back to the precinct and see what's available in our department." Morgan walked over to the elderly woman.

"Mrs. Tumbleson, we think it would be best if we leave a couple of officers with you the rest of the night. Then tomorrow, we will take you some place safer for a while."

"You think he saw me? Ha! Let 'im come." She reached down between the side of her chair and the cushion and brought out an ancient Lugar pistol. Morgan flinched when Tumbleson brought it right up and pointed it at her. "My Bill brought this back from the war. Said he took it off some German officer he killed. I suppose it will still do its job if it has to."

Morgan slowly reached out and took the gun from the elderly lady's hand.

"Mrs. Tumbleson, we would feel a lot better if you would let us handle the guns right now. Besides, consider it a vacation on the government's dime. No cooking, no cleaning and no worries."

"Mr. Buttons needs to go, too."

"Of course. Mr. Buttons will go along as well."

Morgan popped out the magazine, which stuck a little as it cleared, and placed the two parts on the mantle. Frank laid the monster cat off to one side on the couch before he joined the other two walking toward the door.

Just as Morgan was reaching for the door handle, Tumbleson's voice rang out again.

"Hey! I almost forgot. You need to know about the second guy."

The trio turned.

"Yes, Mrs. Tumbleson, was there something unusual about him?" Morgan asked.

"I'll say. He was a priest. I saw his collar when he was lying on the sidewalk."

CHAPTER 27

NEW YORK, EARLY TUESDAY AFTERNOON

Roger stretched across his bed, right leg propped up on the wooden chair he usually sat in at his desk. He tried not to move, not to breathe—not even to blink. Every twitch made pain shoot up his leg until just the thought of moving made him flinch.

But the throbbing did not stop his mind from whirling like a top. Ever since the previous night's adventure, every moment he had spent with Novara rolled around his thoughts, for a while playing like a DVD caught in a loop, each scene beginning again and again. Then his thoughts leaped forward or backward, disjointed and out of sequence, with minutes of one moment melding into the seconds of others. He had lain on his bed since his return in the wee hours of the morning with only bits of nightmare-filled sleep but still none of his time with the emissary made any sense. He needed to talk with someone.

Roger gritted his teeth and sat up, settling his feet on the floor before he could change his mind and then lurching to his feet. The pain spiked in his leg and then receded into something he could tolerate as he shuffled to his desk.

At least I can move if I need to. He rifled through the lap drawer, taking only a moment to find the slip of paper he was looking for and then grab his phone. The return steps were less painful than the previous ones, but he still stopped long enough to tilt his calf up while he glanced down. The six-inch scratch had bled very little but it had the appearance of an angry brand down his leg. He hoped the wound was not infected because then he would need to explain the injury and have the parish official tell him when he had his last tetanus shot. Even if he wanted to, he was not sure he could explain how he had been hurt.

Roger shook his head as he resumed his position on the bed. Across the world, it was late at night at the Vatican, but not too late to keep him from calling.

Click. Click. Ring.

The first time he had telephoned, Roger thought the overseas connection had taken a long time to complete. This time, he felt like the call was answered right away. He wondered for a moment if that was because he really did not want the answers to his many questions.

"Buonasera. Posso t'aiutare?"

"This is Father Roger Greene of St. Patrick's Cathedral in New York in the United States. I need to speak to Cardinal Atchison as quickly as possible."

No "please," no "if possible," no "when he has the time" —the sentence had been the next thing to a demand.

Part of Roger hoped the man on the other end of the line would be insulted by the tone of his voice. Part of him wondered if being cursed at in Italian and hearing the receiver slam down half a world away would be the easy way out of this situation.

If so, he had to settle for being disappointed by the man's reaction.

"Yes, right away, Father Greene. I am made known your mission for his Eminence and we have been waiting for your call. I will find Cardinal Atchison at once. Would that I get Camerlengo Nowaski as well?"

Roger hesitated for a moment, unsure if he really had any say in the matter.

"No, just Cardinal Atchison, please."

Now the time dragged. Roger flexed his foot back and forth, testing the limits of where the pain began and ended in his leg. The sharp flame only reminded him he would be back out on the streets in a few hours, searching with Novara for whatever had wounded him. He winced again and stopped moving.

The hum on the overseas line crawled through his ear and settled in his head, filling the nooks and crannies and muffling out the rest of the world. His thoughts drifted...

"Roger! Roger, are you all right?"

The Cardinal's voice was loud and he sounded out of breath.

Worse than that, the words had startled Roger out of the beginnings of sleep.

I must have dozed off. Tonight is going to be a long night. "Yes, Cardinal. I'm okay. I was hurt a little last night but I'll live."

"Praise be to God. I've been very worried about you. So has his Eminence and Camerlengo Nowaski." Cardinal Atchison paused before going on, his voice dropping to little more than a heavy whisper. "This is so much bigger than we could have ever thought, Roger. Now tell me, really, how are you?"

Roger barely hesitated. "Scared out of my mind... and completely confused."

The hum sat on the line between the two men, spanning two continents and somehow drawing them together.

"How much has Novara told you?"

"Not as much as I would like, probably not as much as I need to know. I'm scared, sir."

Again a pause highlighted the white noise on the line but the break was not as long as the first time.

"Scared of what you hunt?" Atchison asked. "Or scared of Novara?"

Roger bit his lip. The answer he wanted to give—the safe answer—was to tell the Cardinal of his terror when the thing had flown over him on the street. The answer should be to tell him of the gut-wrenching nausea when he stumbled over their prey, the pain he had felt in his leg when he was hurt, and the fear that had echoed in his head when it screamed. That was his easy answer.

And it would be a lie.

"Both," Roger said. "What scares me the most is I must depend on Novara to stay alive according the Camerlengo. I know this. I understand this. But part of me is screaming there is something seriously wrong with him, something I'd be better off far away from. He might be insane, sir."

"There is so much I would like to tell you, Roger. He is a chosen weapon of God. Some of the things I have seen here, some of the stories about his life... just a minute."

A long moment passed but this time Roger could hear two men talking. Suddenly the sound from the phone turned into a slight echo and the voices sounded farther away. He realized he had been put on speaker phone.

"The Camerlengo has joined us, Roger. He wants to know why you are frightened by Novara."

"He threatened to kill me." He could not believe how the statement sounded coming out of his mouth. *I have an appointment after lunch. Yes, it is hot today. A Vatican emissary has threatened my life.* He was surprised he was not curled up into a ball on the floor, laughing hysterically or crying himself into a sobbing mess. He waited for the reassurance he had nothing to worry about.

It did not come.

"Why did he threaten you?" the Camerlengo asked, his accent clipping the words precisely.

"He says I'm holding him up," answered Roger. "He also thinks I don't fully understand how important this job is." He sat up suddenly, the springs of his bed creaking. "And he's right! How can I know how important this job is when no one will tell me anything? I feel like I'm blind."

He realized his voice had grown into a shout. His chest heaved in and out and his skin was clammy with sweat. He sensed if his hand was not holding the phone tight to his ear, it would have been shaking.

He was little Roger from down the block and he was so mad he could barely move.

He also realized, now that he had stopped shouting, his bedroom and the room on the other end of the line were painfully quiet.

"You hold us all in the palm of your hand, Father Greene," Camerlengo Nowaski said. "You and him. The world rests in your hands, waiting to see if you are its savior or its last failure."

"Roger," Cardinal Atchison started but then paused long enough that for a moment the priest thought the line had gone dead. But in his mind, he could see the Cardinal silently asking for permission to continue, asking the man who could not say Novara's name to relent, to allow some fraction of information to be set free. Nowaski must have blinked.

"Roger, there is a prophecy, one that has never been made public," Atchison continued. "It is part of the Scivas, but the early Church hid it away."

Roger's thoughts leaped back to his second night walking with Novara.

"Yes, I know. St. Hildebrand's books. The Camerlengo and the emissary told me there were actually seven prophecies instead of six. Novara told me a little about it, but they never actually told me what the missing prophecy was."

"It describes the birth of a man, a man who will bring hell to earth. The destruction foretold by St. Hildebrand under this man made me cry to read it. You can not imagine."

"The anti-Christ?" Roger asked, his head spinning. "Are we talking about the anti-Christ?" He hoped he had been able to keep the incredulity out of his voice.

"Yes," Nowaski quickly answered, apparently deciding the Cardinal had said enough and he needed to take control of the situation again. "And no. Not in the way you mean it. Not in the way John meant it in Revelation. But in every real way this person would be the opposite of everything Christ had been. Bringing pain instead of healing, hate instead of love, deception instead of truth.

"In the Book of Revelation, the anti-Christ is a man—an evil, malevolent man—but just a man. He gathers his forces together after years of pain and suffering. The forces of good are joined as well. The two great armies prepare to meet on the field of Armageddon and then, the battle is over. God's army wins. It is a foregone conclusion by John in Revelation that God wins. There is no description of the battle because it does not matter. God wins."

"The battle's outcome is not a certainty, Roger," Atchison interrupted. "That is where John had the end times wrong. St. Hildebrand came along centuries later to correct the mistake in the prophecy. But the early Church hid the prophecy away, frightened by what it meant and what its discovery would do to the faith of the followers."

This time the pause stretched past uncomfortable and became unbearable. Roger's head swirled with what he had just been told—a tale that from anyone besides the Camerlengo and the Cardinal would have left him laughing in disbelief. He still might laugh, but first he would probably puke on his shoes. "So what do I do?"

"Help him. Stay with him. Do exactly what he says." Every

word fell out of the Camerlengo's mouth, pushed out of the way by the one behind it.

Roger shifted his weight on the bed again, the pain in his leg now just an annoying fly buzzing in the background. "Tell me he knows what he is doing, sir," he said. "Tell me I can trust him."

One, two three, four... Roger was not sure if he was more afraid of the answers he was receiving or the lengthening pauses after his questions.

"He's been doing this a long time," Cardinal Atchison finally answered. "A long time. He is the chosen champion of the Vatican, Roger. He is…"

"He is what we have," Nowaski interrupted. "We have put all our hopes and dreams on his success. We have put the fate of the world on his shoulders and now yours. Trust him? I can not tell you to do that. But he is what we have to fight the evil with."

"I am praying for you, Roger," Atchison said.

The line went dead.

CHAPTER 28

NEW YORK, TUESDAY AFTERNOON

She hesitated, her hand hanging in the air with the tip of the marker not quite touching the grease board. There was no turning back once she started writing—or at least that was how the situation felt.

Morgan moved her hand forward, the squeak of the felt tip covering up the sounds of movement on chairs and shuffling feet. She caught the smell of the—ink? Is that what they called it?—as she continued to write. Chalk dust had always sent her into sneezing fits as a kid, something her brothers had never let her forget. Sean had once put three full erasers under her blanket and the nuns in elementary school had not found the allergy amusing, either. At least there would be no sneezing today and no chance for white smudges on her pant suit.

She stepped back and looked at what she had written. The board was no piece of artwork but at least it was legible, if you squinted and did not look too close. Morgan tried to put the cap back on the marker as she read and suddenly realized she had missed, the tip sliding across the skin of her left hand and leaving a black trail.

Dammit! How long will that be there? She looked to the right and there stood David, the barest of smiles tugging at the corners of his mouth. He did not say a word, however, only giving a quick wink. The desire to shoot him was becoming harder and harder to drudge up.

Morgan took one last deep breath and turned to face the room. Twenty-four faces stared back at her and she took the time to look at each one. Rosie and Pinelli were there, a challenging glare lighting the other woman's eyes. But as soon as Morgan looked at her, Rosie smiled and nodded her head with reassurance, only to have the glare return a moment later. Apparently that was her default look.

Anderson and Dixon were there as well, chosen because they had caught the call for the expensive hooker's murder. They had been there on the scene, witnessed the blood and gore and destruction.

Frank stood beside David, no, not quite beside but behind by just a few inches. She suspected it was his military experience, the non-com showing deference to the officer. But that assumption would imply Frank felt David was a superior and that would not do. She would need to talk to him about it later.

The other twenty officers were beat cops, accustomed to spending day after day on the streets where these murders took place. They knew the people, knew the stinking alleys and dark side streets as well as the junkies and sewer rats. They knew where to go, who to talk to, and what did not feel right in the neighborhoods.

All except for two. The only women in the room besides her and Rosie, Morgan had requested them from another precinct. Only a couple of years out of the academy, they were both in their mid-twenties, slim, and pretty.

They were the bait.

Morgan knew at some point she may need to draw the killer out, force him to make a mistake, and she did not want to bring in anyone new who did not know what was going on with the case. Until that point, the two women would help man the hotlines and stay out of the public eye.

This was her task force.

"You've all heard the rumors," Morgan said. "Most of them are not true. But we do have a killer on our hands. A sick, sadistic bastard of a killer." She let it sink in before she continued. "And he's got a real taste for women. Frank, pass 'em out."

Her partner grabbed three stacks of loose-leaf binder reports and distributed them. Inside each one were crime scene notes from each of the murders, interviews, and photos. Morgan saw two of the officers go pale, another turn so green she was sure he was going to lose his lunch on the officer in front of him, and Rosie, somehow, looked even more pissed off than before.

"You have all been assigned to me," she continued. "You are the task force and this room will be our command center. Study those reports. Memorize them. They are everything we have to use to find the killer. And if we don't find him, more women will die."

She paused for effect and to glance around at her officers again. This time she saw anger, she saw resolve, and in a couple, she saw fear. Morgan made a mental note of who those men were. Fear was acceptable if they were able to channel the emotion into action. But if fear grabbed hold of them and they froze, they or other officers could be killed.

Morgan remembered she had been scared when she was on The Werewolf case. But she had been more afraid she would fail and someone else would pay for her mistake, maybe even her partner, David. But when that barking, howling loon had come after her and the policewoman bait, she had not hesitated to pull the trigger.

"So let's find him," she said with a nod. "Here to help us with the case is Special Agent David Kelly from the FBI's Behavioral Analysis Unit. For those of you who watch too much television, he's a profiler. Agent Kelly, tell us what we're looking for."

David took off his jacket in one smooth motion as he walked toward the center of the board, tossing it over the back of a nearby chair as he moved. He smiled while he rolled up his sleeves, an effortless grin that said he knew what it was like to walk a beat and he was your friend. Morgan had seen him charm confessions out of multiple-time felons and about five minutes into his first meeting with her mother—long before their relationship was anything more than professional—Mrs. Flaherty had been ready to marry her off on the spot. The fact the marriage had actually taken place was her mother's crowning achievement, and biggest disappointment when they divorced.

"Ted Bundy. John Wayne Gacy. Ed Gein. Albert Fish. Coral Eugene Watts." David paused. "Motives, methods, desires—all different. The one thing all these famous serial killers had in common was they had a total disregard for human life. Only their own needs mattered to them." David turned to the board and wrote down the numbers one through five before facing the group again. "But there are some generalities we can assume as we piece together more of what makes this guy tick. First, just what I said: a guy. Serial killers are almost always male and the presence of sexual activity in each of these cases makes it even more certain this time.

"Two, the violent nature of these murders suggest someone

younger—say, someone in their twenties or thirties and in good physical condition.

"Three, because there has been no indication of a snatch-and-hold where he keeps someone a prisoner for days, he may have a semi-regular girlfriend or even a wife that may have no idea what is going on. No children, however. He probably can't, either, maybe because of infertility. This is what makes him angry, angry enough to kill the victim, some unlucky Joe who happens to walk by at the wrong time, or you. Keep that in your mind when you're on the street.

"Four, our man is ambidextrous. A killer with either hand."

David stopped. He glanced at the board where he had been writing down the characteristics as he spoke. Morgan recognized that look—the slight squint, the lips tugged over to one side of his mouth, the deep breath and release. He was frustrated. So frustrated he had felt the need to step back for a minute and think about each individual word he was about to say. She had seen the look on tough cases when they were partners. She had seen the look when he was faced with bureaucratic nonsense. She had seen the look used on her the night she had suggested they separate.

David carefully wrote the word "Pattern" and then followed it with a big question mark. "There is a pattern here with the killings but we have not found it yet," he said, turning to face the group again. "There is always a pattern. Always. The victims have something in common, the times of the murders, hair color, jobs, the places of the attacks—there is always a pattern. It's never random. Now we need to find that pattern to find our killer.

"Oh, and one more thing before I give you back to Lieutenant Kelly. This killer has an area of comfort, someplace where he feels very much in control. It may center around the location of his house, his job. For many other serial killers, the area centered around highways because the bodies were easy to dispose of and easy to display as the killer became bolder. That does not appear to be the case this time but keep it in mind. There is a pattern." He stepped back and nodded to Morgan.

"Everyone check the duty roster," she said as she walked to the front of the group again. "You'll notice there are twice as many of you on the overnight as during the first two shifts of the day. This bastard kills at night and we need to be ready when he strikes. Study every last detail in your folders. Know that one of those crazy, minute details might be the one to reveal the pattern Agent Kelly was talking about. Okay, let's get to work."

The room was quiet except for the turning of pages and the occasional mumbled words. Morgan listened the best she could, straining to understand if fear kept down the conversations or anxiousness. What she wanted to hear was determination.

"I want all of you to pay special attention to the sketch in your packet." Papers ruffled all over the room as she posted a copy to a cork strip at the top of the grease board. "This man was at the last scene. He may or may not be our killer—we don't know. You'll also notice in the report that a second man, someone wearing a priest collar, was spotted with him." Morgan still could not come to grips with the fact a priest may be involved. "We don't know what the connection is between the two men; we don't know if they only stumbled onto the murder scene. But we need to talk with them."

There was a knock on the door and a uniformed officer walked in and handed Morgan a note. She read it through twice before looking back up at the task force. "And just to drive this home to all of you one last time about how dangerous and vital this is, besides these two men, only two other people have been at the murder scenes and lived to tell about it. One was in the ICU and she died about forty-five minutes ago. The other is a feisty old woman with enough guts to give this description to our sketch artist." She gestured at the group to go back to work.

"That's too bad about the Klinger woman," David said as she walked close. "So what do you want to do now?"

Morgan turned to look at David. Frank was still there, off to one side and one step behind. She straightened her blouse. "Talk to the only people worse than the serial killers," she answered. "I'm going downstairs to release some information in a press conference. You'd better grab your jacket and come along."

CHAPTER 29

NEW YORK, EARLY TUESDAY EVENING

"What happened?"

Morgan winced and took a sip of her dirty martini. She wondered if the regular bartender, Jack, had seen something in her eyes when she ordered her drink because there was so much olive brine in the glass she could barely taste the gin.

"I couldn't help it," she answered. "That pretty little Miss Bitch wouldn't be able to protect herself from this guy if her life depended on it. And it would. I wasn't going to…"

"No, no, no," David interrupted with a laugh and a wave of his hand. "Not her."

During the question portion of the press conference, a reporter from one of the major evening newscasts asked if Morgan had been made the head of the task force so the city would save the cost of a trial, insinuating she would kill the suspect when they found him. Morgan had been about to fire back—verbally—when David saved her by stepping up to the microphone and fielding the next question. "What do you mean then?"

David's smile slipped away. "What happened with Manuel? Not the shooting. After. What happened to you?"

Morgan stared down at her drink, the cloudy mixture changing briefly into the night in the alley. She felt the gun kick in her hand, saw the flash from the muzzle. There was no sound, however. At least not right away. Not until later when the night crashed back down on her. She gulped the last of the martini and waved the empty glass at Jack.

"I don't know, David. It was a good shoot. I know it was. He had a gun. There were civilians. He pointed the gun at me instead of dropping it." She stopped talking while Jack sat a fresh drink in front of her and then ate one of the olives before continuing. "I know it was a good shoot. But you didn't see him, David. Even as I squeezed off the round, I could see he was scared. Just a damn kid that was scared to death."

"There have been lots of funerals where dead cops have been killed by scared criminals," David said. "You know that. I checked the report. Everyone said it was him or you." Morgan looked up and stared at David. He stared right back. "Yeah, so I checked up on you when I found out what happened," he continued. "So sue me. I would have done it for Ted or Jimmy or any of the partners I rode with before you. Wouldn't you do it for Frank?"

Morgan dropped her gaze back to her glass and nodded. Yes, of course she would have checked up on a previous partner and, in fact, had done it once or twice. But there was more to him checking on her and she knew it; they both knew it. The partner part of the reason was a lie. But it was a lie with good intentions, so she let it go.

"It wasn't just that," she said. "Manuel never had a chance. No father. Two older brothers that had both been in the same gang. The next oldest had already done time in juvey. He never had a chance. His life was headed for that alley the day he was born." She swallowed half her drink.

"And you think you were going to change his life when he had a gun pointed at you?" David asked while Morgan shrugged. "But the shoot wasn't why they kept you off duty. What happened next?"

"I couldn't sleep. Every time I closed my eyes, there he was. I would walk down the street, there he was in the shadows. I would walk into a store, bingo. He was with me everywhere I looked." She waved the empty glass at Jack again. "I must have looked like hell because they never let me come back off of administrative leave from the shooting. Cap sent me straight to the doc for some tell-me-your-problems time."

"Did it work?"

She wanted to say yes. She meant to tell him everything had gotten better right away. But she could not. Morgan knew she had never been able to lie to David about anything—at least not anything important. "Not for a while. After a few weeks, I stopped seeing him on street corners with the other teenagers. Then I started to sleep through the whole night here and there without nightmares."

"So when was the last time you dreamed about him?"

Morgan opened her mouth to answer and then stopped before tilting her head to the side. "I... I haven't dreamed about him since the night before this all started. I've had other bad dreams, sure, but it's been several days for Manuel."

"All it took was a serial killer," David said.

"Can I quote you on that?" asked a voice from behind them.

Morgan turned on her barstool to look at the man standing beside her and immediately realized two things: In a cop bar only two blocks from the precinct house, this guy stood out like a cat in a dog kennel. Oh, and the third martini had gone straight to her head. She should have eaten something.

"Excuse me?" she asked. Even though the room was spinning a little, Morgan was aware this man dressed in khaki pants, polo shirt, and a light jacket was holding something in the pocket of his coat. She also noticed the three off-duty patrolmen sitting behind the stranger had also noticed the man's hand in his pocket and stopped their conversation.

"I asked if it would be okay for me to use the term 'serial killer.' You never said that today at the news conference."

"I'm sorry, sir. Have we met before?" David asked.

"No, not you and I," the man answered. "But Detective Kelly and I have."

The man pulled his hand out of his pocket and shoved something small and metallic toward Morgan's face. She immediately reached for her gun and leaped sideways off her stool.

But she had forgotten about the three martinis.

Morgan was still flipping open the strap on her holster when her shoe caught on the bar stool stretcher and sent her staggering sideways. Just as she was about to crash into the table to her right, she heard a man cry out behind her and the sound of something heavy hitting the floor.

Morgan gave up trying to pull her gun, barely missing the table as she landed on the linoleum. One of the patrolmen was beside her half a count later to help her to her feet and she turned to see what had happened.

The stranger was face down on the floor and David held the man's wrist with both hands and a knee shoved into his armpit. The arm was bent backward at a nearly impossible angle while another patrolman lay across the man's legs. The third was quickly moving chairs out of the way and searching the floor.

"Wait, here it is," the officer yelled and then reached under another table. A few seconds later he stood up with a disgusted scowl on his face. "I think it's what's left of a voice recorder."

"Of course it's a recorder," the man said. "I'm a reporter."

Morgan watched David close his eyes and shake his head before gently lowering the man's arm back down to the floor and climbing to his feet. "I'm sorry for the confusion, sir," he said. The official FBI voice did not mix with the untucked shirt and the skewed tie. "The department will, of course, replace your recorder."

"I'm more worried about if I will get the feeling back in my arm again," the man whined as he remained seated on the floor.

"I recognize you now," Morgan said. "You live in the same apartment building as one of the girls who were killed. You are?"

"Probably going to sue," the man said as he lurched to his feet, refusing David's offer of a helping hand. "Peters. Roy Peters. I write for the *Post*."

Morgan tried not to wince while she attempted to remember if she and David had said anything that might hurt their case. The "serial killer" slip would be embarrassing and might cause a bit of a panic, but would not be devastating. She hoped.

"Well, Mr. Peters, we are certainly sorry for the misunderstanding," Morgan said. "Was there a reason you came to see us? Did you remember something that might be helpful in the case?"

"No, but I told my editor after that lawyer was killed in my building something was wrong. I could just tell from the way you cops were acting."

"The murder scene was pretty gruesome, Mr. Peters. You were probably just sensing their reaction to how bad it was."

"How bad it was?" He perked up at the thought. "Was she dismembered? Cut up? Tortured before she was killed?"

Morgan opened her mouth to answer but quickly slammed it shut. She could not believe she had almost told facts about the case they had decided to withhold. To a reporter! Damn that third martini! "Was there something you wanted, Mr. Peters?" she asked after a moment.

A smile played around the corners of his mouth. "That's why Alison did it, you know. Saying those things about you shooting the suspect. Everyone knows they can get under your skin, make you say things you didn't mean to."

Morgan felt the heat rising in her cheeks. Before she could respond, however, David stepped in between the two of them, signaling to the off-duty officers for help. "I think it's time you left, Mr. Peters," he said. "You might have hit your head in the fall to the floor." He and the other three men herded him toward the door.

"You said they were gruesome murders," Peters yelled at Morgan. "How many of them are there actually? Did you tell us about all of them today? What kind of woman does he like? Is he really a serial killer?!"

The front door of the bar shut behind the five men, but David returned a few seconds later. "Let's get you out the back door before he comes back in," he said as he tossed some cash on the bar for Jack. "Make sure the three patrolmen get a round on me when they come back."

"David, I may not need another drink, but I think I damn well want one."

He looked at her for a few seconds before he nodded. "Okay, but we are going someplace where no one will bother you."

CHAPTER 30

NEW YORK, EARLY WEDNESDAY MORNING

Adele's "Rolling in the Deep" shattered the silence of the bedroom. The singer belted out most of the refrain before Morgan rolled over and grabbed her cell phone. "Hello."

"I'm sorry to wake you, Lieutenant, but we have another one," Frank said. "I'll be at your apartment in about twenty minutes."

Before she could answer, another phone started going off. David quickly rolled out of bed, grabbing his phone on the move, and answered it as he walked out into the hallway.

"Don't do that, Frank."

"It's okay, Lieutenant. The scene isn't very far from your apartment. The command center is calling Agent Kelly right now."

"I'm not at my apartment."

Three. Four. Five. Six. Seven seconds of silence passed before Frank spoke again. "Okay, Lieutenant. I'll meet you at the scene. Here's the address…"

David walked back into the room, waving a piece of paper. "I've already got it, Frank. I'll see you there." She hung up before he could respond. "I think I just caused Frank to have a brain hemorrhage," she said.

"We better get going," David said. "This is a long way."

Morgan nodded and threw back the covers. A split second later she was clutching for the blanket and yanking it back up to her chest. She was naked.

"David, oh my God. Did we…?"

He laughed. "You weren't so bashful a few hours ago." He hooked a thumb in the waistband of his shorts. "No, we didn't. I decided to do the thinking for both of us. Besides, if it happens, I want you to remember it." He turned to leave the room again.

"David."

He looked back from the doorway, the smile still on his lips. Not mocking, not laughing at her—just a smile between friends. She knew what she wanted to say, knew what she should say, but she could not say it. Not now, not yet.

"Was that Dokken on your phone? Are you still living through your hair metal days?"

His smile morphed into a full grin. He knew she wanted to say more but he did not press the issue.

"I'll have you know that Dokken's 'It's Not Love' is timeless. Last week I had a Ratt song as my ringtone." He turned and walked down the hallway out of sight. "Hurry up," he yelled back over his shoulder. "We've got to get moving."

An ambulance pulled away as David turned into a spot beside a marked police car. Morgan hopped out before he turned off the engine and she glanced around to see how the task force had responded.

On the way to the scene, she had given instructions for uniformed officers to be in charge of crowd control, but two of her task force members were to be dressed in street clothes, circulating outside the tape lines with the artist drawing of the man seen at the previous murder. Many serial killers liked to revisit their crime scenes and see the reaction to their work. The show was an extra thrill, a display of their courage. As they grew bolder, they might even flaunt their power over the situation by reappearing when the police were still present. She relaxed a moment later when she spotted two of her men moving through the growing crowd, glancing down at the composite and then comparing the drawing to the people.

She turned her attention to the building where the murder had taken place. Unlike the neighborhood from the night before which still teetered on reliving its glory and falling into the abyss, this area had already taken several steps toward ruin. Broken shutters and iron bars over once-beautiful windows, missing trim, and crumbling brick all told the story of a proud and beautiful woman who had fallen on hard times, now doing whatever she could to slow the slide and survive.

"It was probably really something to see back in its day," Morgan said, gesturing at the building.

"Damn rent control," David answered. "If you keep rent artificially low, then there's no reason for landlords to fix up the properties."

The two of them went inside and headed toward the second floor, the crime scene area if the amount of noise drifting down the staircase was any indication. They carefully stepped around where a broken step had been marked off with yellow tape and then continued to the landing.

About thirty feet down the hallway, two civilians were with members of her task force. The one standing, a man in his late twenties with pale skin and the blotched complexion of someone who spent too much time in front of a computer monitor and not nearly enough time in sunlight, looked like he might puke at any moment. Judging from his shoes, he already had at least once. The other man was older, maybe early forties with slicked hair and an expensive-looking suit. The suit would have looked even better if not for what appeared to be blood drenching the left side of his body. He appeared to be sitting because his wobbly legs would not hold him up any longer.

Frank looked up and then walked over from the group. "Lieutenant. Agent Kelly."

"What's going on, Frank? We saw an ambulance pull out as we drove up. Do we have a live one?" Morgan kept her gaze glued to her partner's face, searching for some hint of accusation? Disgust? Curiosity? She decided she was glad she had not played poker with him yet because she could not read anything in his eyes.

"No, she's dead. Janawitz broke through the stairway and they were afraid he might have busted his ankle. They took him to the hospital for an X-ray."

"What about these two?" David asked.

Frank looked down at his notes. "Anthony Arelli," he said, gesturing to the seated man, "came to see his business associate, Aleesa Hopkins, twenty-seven, who lived in that apartment. When he let himself in, he found Hopkins already dead. He either passed out from the sight or slipped on the blood and knocked himself out—he's a little fuzzy on the details. When Colton Jensen," Frank pointed at the standing man, "came home—he shared the apartment with Hopkins—he found Arelli lying in a pool of blood and Hopkins still dead. He was the one who called for us."

Morgan simply nodded, slipped on a pair of booties from a box by the door, and walked around the small group into the apartment. It was no wonder Arelli had fainted. Blood was everywhere. Some parts of the walls were coated with the drying, viscous mess. She, David, and Frank stayed by the doorway.

"Sir, I think I have some scratch marks," said a technician who was leaning with a powerful flashlight out an open window. "It's hard to be sure, though. There's not much paint left, but these marks look fresh."

Overholt looked up from where he was crouched over the remains of a woman's body. He noticed the trio by the door.

"Okay, Devon. Make sure you photograph everything and then remove the sill so we can take it back to the lab. Tammy? Tammy, have you processed the carpet over here?" He pointed to a section of rug to one side of the body.

A technician near the couch stopped collecting samples long enough to glance up.

"Yeah. Digital, fibers—it's already bagged and tagged. But not the chair."

"Good," Overholt said as he faced the door again. "Lieutenant, if you stay close to the wall and circle around the chair, be sure not to touch it, then you can stand here and see the victim."

A minute later, the trio was staring at Hopkins' body, or at least what was left of it. Overholt crouched on the other side.

"How about it?" Morgan asked.

"Definitely our guy," he answered. "Left- and right-handed slash marks here and here. Uterus, gone. No noticeable metal fragments. Possible marks on an open window and I was told the door was locked when she was found. Anyone want to bet if she had sex tonight? Personally, I wouldn't go against those odds."

"Is there anything different from the previous murders?" David asked as he bent over for a closer look. "Anything at all?"

"No, not yet. I'll go over her with everything I've got when I get back to the lab, though."

"It doesn't make sense," David said as he stood back up. "Gacy changed. Dahmer became better at cleaning the bones. They all evolve at least a little." He turned to Morgan. "We're missing something."

"Lieutenant?"

She turned to look at the officer in the doorway. "Yes."

"We have a sheet on the deceased."

"Go ahead. Give me the highlights."

"Misdemeanor fraud, check kiting, theft, ID theft...."

"She's a con artist," Frank said.

"Yeah, and I'll bet the two in the hallway have matching sheets," Morgan said. "Check them out, too. Make sure there's nothing violent and no outstanding warrants." She glanced at David who merely raised an eyebrow in response. "I know, but we have to cover the bases."

"A college girl, a prostitute, a lawyer, a PR person, an artist, and a grafter—what do they have in common?" David asked.

"I'm inclined to leave out the Klinger woman because she didn't have sex according to Overholt's report." The tech nodded in affirmation to Morgan so she continued. "Just a case of being in the wrong place at the really wrong time."

"Okay," David said. "Where do you want to start?"

Morgan paused. "Frank, let's get somebody digging into the lawyer's work. I know she was doing the corporate bigwig stuff but maybe she started out in the D.A.'s office or doing some pro bono. See if she had a connection to the others."

"Okay, Lieutenant." He skirted his way near the wall and out the door.

Morgan turned to talk to Overholt...

... and she was floating on a sea of black. Somewhere, far off in the distance, she heard shouting. Even farther away were screams. But she did not care, not as long as she was floating in a black sky that had never known the sun or stars.

Slowly, or quickly, nothing mattered since time was a wisp and a memory here, she became aware she was not alone. She could not see through her blindness, could not hear through deaf ears, but something was there, stalking her in the black. She wanted to scream, tried to scream, but she was on her own. Floating...

...and then it was gone. The black melted away, replaced by soothing peace. Morgan suddenly realized she was draped over

David's arm at a severe angle and Overholt had his hands up, trying to help keep her from landing on the victim's body.

"Morgan! Morgan!" David yelled. "Wake up, Morgan!"

She leaned back into him. "What happened?"

"I don't know," David answered. "One second you were talking and the next you almost took a header into the vic. Are you okay?"

"Yeah, I think so." Morgan stared over by the couch and saw Tammy sitting on the floor while Devon helped keep her upright. "Only the women?" Morgan asked.

"As if this case couldn't get any weirder, yes, only the women just fainted," answered David.

Morgan stood up under her own power and took a deep breath. "You've got to find it, Overholt," she said. "You've got to find what's different. Or what's alike. Find what we've missed and what we need so we can nail this bastard."

"We'll do it. If I need to pull them all back out of storage and start over, I'll do it."

Morgan could not see the tech's whole face with most of it hidden by a cloth mask, but his eyes were all she needed to see to know how much he wanted to find the link. "David, help me outside. Maybe some air will clear my head."

She was still leaning on his arm when they walked out the front of the building. There was a lot of commotion on the sidewalk where some women were still lying or sitting on the concrete. Morgan looked up at David but he did not notice. His attention was fixed on a spot across the street. She followed his gaze and then she saw it, too.

It was the shadow of a man standing in an alleyway, slightly down the street. He did not move, either, just stood on the edge of the black, motionless.

The three of them stared at each other for several long seconds before he simply backed into the gloom and out of sight.

"Who…"

Morgan did not finish her question. A voice screamed her name in the night, screamed it from the rooftops and whispered it in her ear. It was the voice from the black. It spoke of pain and pleasure. Hatred and love. It spoke of death.

Morgan let out a cry of her own. She threw an arm above her

head to protect herself from what she knew would be an attack from above. From what, she did not know, but the danger was there, somewhere above her and death followed. Her death.

A bright light flashed and the voice was gone.

Morgan stared into the front row of the gawkers on the sidewalk and there stood Peters. The reporter did not wait for his camera to "accidentally" break like his recorder. As soon as he realized he had been spotted, he turned and pushed his way back into the crowd.

But not before giving her a smile.

CHAPTER 31

NEW YORK, WEDNESDAY MORNING

Roger had no idea what to think now.

After the disaster on Monday night when he hurt his leg and Novara threatened to kill him, he had steeled himself for another long, miserable night walking up one street and down another. But what happened was like no other night he had spent with the emissary.

Novara had, of course, made a stop along the way for coffee and Roger had joined him. Partly, the cup was to see if sharing in the ritual would put the other man in a better mood, which did not happen. However, drinking the coffee was also an attempt to settle his stomach. Roger had swallowed more aspirin than he had ever taken at one time in his life in an effort to dull the pain in his calf. That try, at least, had worked marginally better.

But the shared drink was where the familiarity ended. Once their nightly adventure had truly begun, Novara walked straight to a spot on one street and stopped. He had not wandered about, going on the cast, or doubled back. Along the way he had mumbled repeatedly about babies killing their mothers, ran through a rambling list of women's names, and went on and on about the streets of London. The whole speech sounded like it should have been heard in a ward for the insane.

Once they arrived at their destination, however, the two men stood in the shadows between two buildings and stared for hours at the parts of the two apartment buildings they could see through the opening on the other side of the street.

They had not just watched, however. Novara began a rhythmic prayer and kept the chant up for hours. Roger recognized most of the words, in Latin, but not the prayer itself. It sounded old, forgotten over the centuries only to be resurrected for a single purpose.

But the prayer held power. Roger was surprised to later discover just how long they had been in the one spot. He had not felt frustration at the lack of action or conversation, had not felt anger at the lack of answers. In fact, during the time the other man was chanting, he could not even remember the questions.

What Roger had felt was an enveloping peace. And safety. There was definitely a blanket of safety that had descended over the pair, leaving him the most secure he had felt since the day Novara arrived on the cathedral's steps.

But then sometime around two in the morning, the visitor abruptly stopped his chant and turned to stare at an angle farther into the alley. He glared as if he were looking through the brick wall of the building, watching events unfold far off in the distance.

After standing perfectly still for several minutes, Novara had simply motioned for Roger to follow him back out to the street where he flagged down a cab and put the priest inside, saying only that he would return to the cathedral as quickly as possible. They were the only words Novara had spoken all night except to order the coffee, ramble, and chant. In hindsight, Roger thought the night was more disturbing than when his faith had been challenged. Well, almost.

"There's just no pleasing some people," Roger mumbled as he spread jam on a piece of toast.

"Excuse me?"

Roger turned to see one of the younger priest's pulling a mug out of the cupboard to pour himself some coffee. "I'm sorry, Tim. I didn't hear you come in. Don't mind me, just talking to myself." He looked the young man over. "You look tired. Didn't you sleep well?"

Tim started to smile before a yawn turned his face into more of a grimace. "Last night was my turn to volunteer on the suicide prevention line. I no more than made my way back here and crawled into bed than our visitor appeared at the side door, pounding to be let in. You didn't have to go out with him last night?" All of the other priests and the staff were aware of the two men's nightly excursions, but not the reason.

"He sent me home early. What time did you let him in?"

"A little before six."

"I'm sorry, Tim. I hope my assignment is not becoming a burden on the rest of you."

"No, we understand," the younger man said with a laugh. "We just wish you could tell us more about your adventures. The not knowing is the hardest part."

"For me, too. Maybe I can tell you someday."

Tim glanced at his watch. "Well, I'd better get this coffee in me or I won't be awake enough to help with eleven o'clock confession."

Suddenly, the idea of just being able to perform his normal priestly duties sounded like the greatest thing in the world to Roger. "Tell you what," he said. "Give me the coffee and you go back to bed. I'll cover confession."

"Are you sure?"

"Go on and get some sleep. Remember? I was home early last night. I'll have just enough time to leaf through the newspaper and eat a little breakfast before I need to be ready."

Tim thanked him on the way out the door. Roger remained seated at the table and began flipping through the newspapers stacked on its top. A few were a couple of days old and he shuffled through for a minute to find the Wednesday editions. He did not really have time to get caught up in anything lengthy so he just skimmed the headlines and glanced at the interesting photos. He had just shoved the final bite of toast into his mouth when he froze, his eyes blinking in surprise.

POLICE TERRIFIED OF SERIAL KILLER

The headline on A1 of the *Post* was in bold print and at least a fifty-point font. Underneath was a photo of Morgan, cringing in terror with her arm thrown above her head. The spread stretched from one side of the page to the other and even extended beneath the fold of the newspaper. In fact, the accompanying article was the only one on the front page.

"Oh my God," breathed Roger.

CHAPTER 32

NEW YORK, WEDNESDAY AFTERNOON

Morgan sipped her coffee while she hunched over the notes of the previous four murder scenes. She wanted everything to be at her fingertips when Overholt's preliminary report on the latest victim arrived. Plus, she had the interview of the two men from earlier that morning, the rap sheets of all three con artists, and the crime scene reports from the two officers who had canvassed the crowd.

The case stack was growing from a hill into a small mountain of paperwork on her desk inside the command center. She could not stop clawing through the piles and files, however. The answer—the key to finding the killer—was in those reams of paper somewhere. She just had to find it.

She heard a chair sliding across the floor and looked up in time to see Captain Baker on the other side of the desk. "Hey, Cap."

"You know, if you stare at those reports for too long, they all run together like some bad TV show where the characters are all the same," he said.

Morgan leaned back and rubbed her eyes. "I know. But I had to do something while I was waiting on the write-up from last night's bloodbath."

"I heard it was bad, worse than the other ones."

"They've all been pretty damn gruesome, Cap. But yeah, it was pretty bad. A couple of the guys got sick."

"You?"

Morgan shook her head. "No, I'd seen it before."

"You look tired. Are you getting enough sleep?"

"It never feels like enough when you keep getting the call in the middle of the night. A nap would sure…" Morgan stopped and looked up. The captain had just asked her three questions in a row about her physical and mental condition. He was a good leader and had always cared about the officers under his command but this was going overboard. "What's up, Cap?"

He wiped his hand across his face before he tilted his head toward the door. "He showed up here a little while ago."

Morgan did not need to see the man's face. She instantly recognized the salmon-colored polo shirt, light blue pullover sweater vest, and the khaki pants. She had no doubt there were a pair of docksides on his feet as well, even though they were hidden by the chairs between them. The police psychologist, Dr. Shaffer, was standing in her command center.

But Morgan was not really looking at the doctor. She was staring at David because she recognized the look on his face. The slight squint of his left eye, the drawing back of the right corner of his mouth from grinding his teeth. Worst of all, the bloom of red on his neck above his white shirt. She knew the look because she had been on the receiving end of that stare when they were married. David was one hundred percent, through-and-through, pissed.

"What's he want?" she asked.

"You… off the case," answered Captain Baker.

She hurt her hip a little when she walked through the first line of chairs. But, she did not break stride through the second, and by the time Morgan was at the third row, she was grabbing a chair with each hand and half-pushing, half-throwing them out of her way. Dr. Shaffer must have heard her coming because he turned to look at her before backing up with an odd look on his face.

"What is this unauthorized person doing in my command center?" Morgan asked without looking away from the psychiatrist.

"Detective Kelly, you've obviously had a relapse," he said, waving what appeared to be a rolled-up newspaper under her nose. "But no one will tell me who your commanding officer is so I can rescind my previous diagnosis and have you relieved of duty. I've…"

Morgan reached out and grabbed the man by the throat, shoving him hard against the wall and pinning him there. Out of the corner of her eye she saw David take a step forward but then he stopped.

"First of all, Doctor, it is Lieutenant Kelly," Morgan said between clenched teeth. "Second, this is the command center for a special task force for which you have no jurisdiction." She increased the pressure on the man's neck in an upward direction so he was now standing on his toes. He dropped whatever had been in his hands and clutched at her wrist.

"And third," she continued, "you can't find my commanding officer because I report directly to the commissioner's office. I'm the officer in charge here."

Morgan let go of Shaffer and he bent over at the waist, coughing.

"I'll have you institutionalized for that attack," he said once he regained his breath. "You're a menace to...."

"What attack?" interrupted David, drawing a quick look from the doctor. "I watched the lieutenant restrain unauthorized personnel who entered a restricted area."

"That's what I saw, too," Frank said.

"You can bet your sweet fucking ass that's what I saw," Rosie said from a few feet away. "And you can be damned sure I wouldn't have treated you as nice if I had my hands around your neck."

"Also, as the FBI behavioral consultant on this case, my report shows the killer we are looking for may have had general medical training. Since you broke into this command center, Doctor, I suggest we hold you while we thoroughly search your background for abnormalities related to this case. That would include any of your private practice complaints as well. And if we find anything, it might take weeks to conduct interviews with former patients and colleagues."

The whites showed all the way around Dr. Shaffer's eyes as he looked from person to person. "You... you can't," he stammered. "That would ruin me. Just the allegations... I'll never be able to practice again."

"Having the lieutenant removed from command of a special task force for a psych eval wouldn't blow up the rest of her career, you goddamn prick?" Rosie asked.

"But you don't understand," the doctor pleaded. "She needs my help. She's sick. I've seen that look before."

"Read him his rights and stick him in an interview room while I evaluate the FBI report," Morgan said. "If he causes a fuss, put him in lock-up with the general population."

Two uniformed members of the task force dragged the struggling psychiatrist away.

"No! You can't!" he yelled. "I've seen that look in her eyes before! That's how she looked when she first came to me! I've seen it before!"

"This won't be any fun to explain to the commissioner's office," Captain Baker said.

Morgan did not answer but bent down to pick up what Shaffer had dropped. David also stooped and reached for it as well, but she beat him to the newspaper. She glanced at him as they stood up and she noticed the red bloom was gone. Now his anger had been replaced by a frown.

"We've got more important things to worry about than him, Cap," she said. "Where is that damn Overholt with his report? We've only got a few more hours…"

Morgan stopped talking. She almost stopped breathing. Everything she had been thinking was forgotten. Her whole world tilted, swirled, then narrowed to the photo plastered across the top of the front page of the *Post*.

The photo was of her, taken outside the murder scene early that morning. She was cringing as she glanced up and for a moment the memory of the terror on display in the newspaper touched her thoughts again.

But Dr. Shaffer had been right. Her eyes were the most disturbing part of the photograph. Even in newsprint they looked haunted—or hunted. She barely even noticed the blaring headline. The story and the photo were by Peters.

"I'm so sorry, Morg," David said in a quiet voice. "I was going to tell you later."

"You knew?" she asked when she finally looked back up.

David just stared back. At least Frank had the decency to blush.

"You all knew about this?!"

Morgan threw the newspaper in David's face before storming from the room.

CHAPTER 33

NEW YORK, WEDNESDAY AFTERNOON

Morgan looked at the spires of St. Patrick's Cathedral. She had not had any idea where she was headed when she ran crying from the precinct house, but as soon as the cabbie asked for her destination, this was the first address that popped into her head. At least Roger would not lie to her when she asked if she had gone completely over the edge.

A good number of mid-week tourists walked around the inside the magnificent structure. Even though they spoke in hushed voices, their conversations about the beauty of the architecture echoed down the sides to form their own whispering crowds.

The middle of the cathedral drew Morgan's attention. There, scattered in small pockets, sat individuals or small groups of two or three. These people had not come to see the beauty of the building. They had arrived in search of peace, relying on their faith and the priests to find some solace. Today, they were her kindred spirits.

Within a few minutes, Morgan was wondering if she would receive any of that peace today. Roger was nowhere in sight and every priest she did see appeared to be too busy to bother to ask where he was at. She turned to leave.

"Hello, Miss Kelly," said a voice from her side. "I'm sorry. Lieutenant Kelly. Are you searching for Father Greene?"

She turned to see the man she had met the last time she visited Roger. "Yes, Mr. Novara, I am. Have you seen him?"

"I'm sorry, but he is helping with confession right now and may not be finished for at least another hour. Perhaps I can help. I am always ready for a cup of coffee and some good conversation."

Morgan looked at the man standing casually with both hands in his pockets. Tenseness lay beneath the relaxed attitude, a hint of energy just waiting to be let loose. She had seen the look before in members of the tactical units of the force. Those men and women could leap from calm to full alert in the blink of an eye. She wondered what Novara was capable of—good or bad—but she did not look into his eyes for answers.

"I don't think so, Mr. Novara. But thank you."

"Please, call me Greg. I am a good listener. Father Greene and I walk and talk every evening, sometimes for hours."

She hesitated for a two-count before answering. "No. I really need to be getting back to the station. Maybe the next time." She turned toward the exit and took a step before he spoke again.

"You are not crazy, Miss Kelly."

Morgan literally stopped with one foot hanging in the air before it slapped back down. She whirled to face him. "What did you say?"

"I said you are not crazy. You really do have a reason to be frightened."

"You've seen the newspaper."

"Yes," he replied with a nod. "I've seen the newspaper and read all the sordid details, but the Vatican did not send me here to this place because of any police investigation." He took a step closer and let his voice drop to a whisper. "I am here because of the voice you heard on the wind."

Morgan gasped and staggered backward until she was brought up short by the last row of pews. "I haven't told... how did you know?"

Novara gestured to the pew and she walked around the end, scooting in so they could sit beside each other.

"I have traveled around the world helping women just like you who heard that voice." He held up a hand to stop Morgan, even before she realized she was about to ask the obvious question. "No," he continued. "You are not crazy. That voice and the being on the other end are very real."

"Who is it?"

"To understand the who, you must first understand the what and how and I am not sure you are quite ready for that yet. But understand this, the Vatican and the Pope have always believed in evil, real evil, here on earth. Let me ask you something, Miss Kelly, and I mean no disrespect. Do you consider yourself a faithful Catholic?"

"We can always improve our practice and I have certainly done things in the past that the Church would not like," she answered. "But yes, I have always considered myself a faithful Catholic."

"You believe in the Trinity and that the Virgin Mary gave birth to Jesus Christ, God's own son, here on earth?"

"Yes."

"And that the angels described in the Bible were here on earth as well, performing miracles?"

"Yes."

"So why is it so hard for people to believe evil can come to the earthly plane as well? In your work, you've seen people do horrible, horrendously evil acts to each other. I am just saying you need to take that little leap of faith about evil. If angels can appear to perform miracles at the bidding of God, why can't the other side have representatives here, too?"

Morgan opened and closed her mouth twice without saying anything. She wanted to protest, ask the man if he was feeling okay. But he was right. If she had faith in God's existence, she had to believe in evil as well. Besides, she had seen firsthand the monstrous acts people could perform. Her tongue felt like an old rag drying on a clothes line, stiff and like cardboard. After several attempts, she finally swallowed and spoke.

"You want me to believe I heard Satan speaking?"

Novara laughed quietly. "No, no," he said. "*That* would be crazy. No, I am only asking you to believe evil's forces can take many different forms on earth. Just like the angels in the Bible you said you believe in."

Morgan suddenly realized the paradox she had backed herself into. When she looked into her heart, she really did believe Christ was God's son, that he had walked on water, cured the leper, changed water into wine, and risen from the tomb. She also believed in angels and they had come to earth as well. So why was it so hard for her to imagine evil coming here, too? She had seen evil; she had hunted evil. But each time those had been people doing evil things.

"And there is one more thing, Miss Kelly," Novara said. "It is hunting you."

Morgan's head did snap up at that comment. "What!?"

"Tell me you haven't been waking up in the middle of the night, certain someone else was in the bedroom with you, positive you were being watched from the shadows. Tell me you didn't hear your name in that call last night. Deny it and we will have a cup of coffee and talk about other, happier things."

Morgan felt sweat on her upper lip and wiped it away with the back of her hand. She wanted to tell Novara no. She knew she should. But she would never forget waking up in the night and staring at black voids across her bedroom. She remembered pulling her gun on a shadow. She remembered too much to deny any of what he said. "What can I do?"

"Look at me."

Morgan looked him in the eyes. She stared into their depths and felt herself falling into them. A sing-song chant weaved in and out of her thoughts, laying out a path of peace where nothing could harm her. For the first time in as long as she could remember—maybe since the days when she had not understood danger as a child—she was completely, utterly safe.

She blinked. The feeling evaporated and Novara had looked away. Instead, he faced the front of the cathedral. Morgan felt her cell phone vibrating on her hip.

"Kelly," she answered.

"Morg, it's David. Don't get mad and hear me out. Overholt is here at the command center and he said he found something."

"Okay, I'm on my way back right now." Morgan hung up before she realized she had not been the least bit angry to hear David's voice.

"Mr. Novara, I need to go back to the station house right away," she said as she stood. "I do want to thank you, though. You've given me a lot to think about."

"Please, take this," he said, holding out a card with a phone number on it. "I bought one of those disposable cell phones to use while I am in the United States. If you hear the voice or have the feeling of being watched again, call me. Any time or any place, I will come at once. You felt what I just did. I can protect you."

Morgan nodded as she took the card.

"And Lieutenant, you don't have a lot of time left."

CHAPTER 34

NEW YORK, EARLY WEDNESDAY EVENING

Morgan walked into the command center and David and Frank immediately moved to meet her. Neither appeared to be very happy and both looked like they were setting their shoulders to weather an oncoming storm.

"Morg, we're sorry," David started. "We should…"

She stopped him with a raised hand. "Frank, you're my partner and we're supposed to watch each other's back. You did what you thought was best to protect me. We're good." She turned to face David. "You and I, however, will talk later." Then Morgan did something she could never have imagined a couple of hours earlier. She gave him a quick wink. David's mouth dropped open. "Okay, people. Before we start with Overholt, what's the situation with the doc?"

David grinned at the question. "He's gone."

"You had to let him go?" Morgan asked. "Damn. Okay, we'll deal with that problem when it comes up again later."

"No," David said, the smile growing even larger. "He's gone. A quick check showed no credible complaints against him but since I 'slipped up' and let him know we might be looking for a killer with a medical background, we placed him into protective custody. He's on his way to a safe house in Philadelphia."

"I'll bet he didn't like that idea," Morgan said.

"Not at first," Frank agreed. "But we showed him some of the photos from the crime scenes and after he got over being sick, he practically begged to be taken away from the case."

Morgan laughed. "You two make a pretty good team. Remind me not to make you both mad at me at the same time. Okay, what's Overholt got?"

"He only told me enough to let me know it was very important," David answered. "I called in everyone, including the officers on the phones. Cap assigned some uniforms to help during the briefing."

Morgan walked to the front and stood by Overholt. He quickly looked up from where he was working on a laptop. A large stack of reports was also on the desk.

"Are you ready?" she asked.

"Yes," he answered. "And for what it's worth, I feel like an idiot."

"Don't worry about it. As long as you found something to catch this bastard, we'll be good." Morgan turned to the members of the task force in their seats. She waited until she was sure everyone in the room was paying attention. "Okay, let's give Tech Overholt our attention and see what the lab has uncovered."

"What I am passing around first," he gestured to two of the officers and they began dispersing a stack of papers, "is the report on last night's victim. Except for what seemed like an excessive amount of splatter, there is really not anything new. Uterus removed, apparent scratch marks on the window sill, et cetera, et cetera. Just a small escalation in the violence it appears." He paused for a minute while the two officers finished. He then picked up a much smaller stack and began passing them out himself.

"However, we discovered two new links for the cases. First, we have found bone fragments in the bodies of all the victims. Until now, we were only testing them to ensure they were human and not metal. Now we have the DNA results back from the FBI and I found out today some traces are inconsistent; they do not match the victims. They were able to discover, however, the inconsistent fragments were old. Much, much older."

"How old?" Morgan asked.

"Perhaps a little more than two thousand years old."

Whispers swept through the room before a voice rose above the rest.

"A bone knife," said one of the officers in the seats. "I remember hearing about someone in South America, the Aztecs or the Incas maybe. They used to sacrifice people using knives made from bone."

"That's what we think now," Overholt said.

"A good start," David said, "but not just there. Africa, Australia, the Far East, even some Native American tribes—almost every culture has used weapons made of bone at some point."

"Okay," Morgan said. "We can ask for help from a couple of local anthropologists the department has on retainer and I am sure the FBI has resources we can bring to bear, as well." She paused to look at David but all he did was nod as he continued to send a text message to someone. She turned her attention back to Overholt. "Anything that old should be registered with a museum or collector and should be easier to find. What was the second link?"

Overholt wiped a hand across his face. "They couldn't get pregnant. None of the victims could get pregnant. The college girl was on the pill. The prostitute was on the pill and menstruating. The lawyer was on the shot. The artist had already had her ovaries removed because of a tumor when she was younger and last night's victim had her tubes tied. None of them could become pregnant, even without the killer ripping out their uteri."

"Oh, my God," Rosie said.

"The odds would be huge…"

"He's got to have access to medical information…"

"Pharmacies."

"Hospitals."

Morgan could barely be heard above the rising din. "Okay, people, okay!" she yelled. "Quiet down!" She waited until the voices died out. "Okay, let's work the problem. Rosie, pull together the information on all the victims—ob-gyns, where they bought their birth control, what hospitals they had procedures in, what health insurance coverage they had. Take whoever you need and I will look for more help if we need it. And Rosie, we don't have time for any HIPAA bullshit. Break down doors if you have to. We will work the bone knife angle with the FBI."

She paused before continuing.

"People, don't forget. We only have a few hours until it's dark again."

CHAPTER 35

NEW YORK, EARLY WEDNESDAY EVENING

Roger did not bother to knock before bursting into Novara's room. "You talked to her!"

The emissary looked up from where he sat at the small table along the wall. Slowly, almost deliberately, he took the white-bladed knife he had been holding in his hands and placed it inside the case in the center of the table.

As soon as Novara shut the lid, Roger let loose with a sigh. He had not realized he had stopped breathing until the latches snapped closed. For a moment, he had a vision, a memory, of a blinding white light in the darkness. He knew the light was real and somehow tied to the man sitting at the table. But beyond that, Roger felt he was grasping for sunshine streaming through a window.

"I assume you are talking about your friend, police officer Kelly," Novara answered. "Yes, she and I spoke this afternoon."

Roger shook his head in disbelief. "What... I mean, why did she talk with you?"

"You were busy taking confession and she was about to leave without speaking to anyone. I saw her and thought she looked like she could really use a good conversation. Remember, Father Greene, I received my training in counseling from the Vatican long before you were wearing that collar."

Roger collapsed more than sat in the chair across from Novara. "What did you... can you tell me what you talked about?"

Novara let loose one of his humorless smiles, the kind that either creeped Roger out or made him mad. Somehow, this time, the grin did both. "Yes, I believe I can without breaking any vow of confidentiality. She was coming to see you anyway and we did not talk about anything private." He leaned back in his chair. "There was a photo of her in today's newspaper. She was afraid it would reflect poorly on her position and it might make people think she was losing her grip on her sanity."

"What did you tell her?"

"I told her she was not crazy. She deals with pain and violence and evil on a daily basis with her job. Especially now. I told her there was a reason for being frightened. You remember that reason, Father. You remember the night you fell and cut your knee."

Roger found himself calmly nodding but his thoughts were racing. *My God, was that only a few nights ago?* He did remember the shadow that flew over his head and left him a quivering mess on the sidewalk. He also remembered he had been more scared than at any point in his life—up until that moment anyway. Now the memory had competition for the Most Scary title.

"But that was... we were looking for..."

"Yes, Father. The prey we have been seeking is stalking your friend." He paused. "It is also the evil she has been trying to find."

The room tilted to one side and sweat ran down Roger's forehead into his eyes. He placed his hands on the tabletop to steady himself. "I don't know what we've been searching for, but what you just said is insane," Roger blurted after a moment. "You didn't tell her that, did you?"

Novara shook his head, a sneer on his lips. However, Roger thought he saw a hint of disappointment in the slump of the man's shoulders as well.

"How could I do that? You have been out with me every night for nearly a week. You have been frightened to the point of paralysis. Vatican officials, including the Camerlengo, have told you what I am doing is of the utmost importance, that what I have been hunting down through the years must be destroyed. Yet, you still do not believe. How could I ask the woman who is so important to my time here, someone who is also frightened out of her mind and searching for answers—how could I tell her the truth? She is not ready to make that connection yet, just like you. She is not ready, although her life depends upon a leap of faith." Novara paused and looked down at his hands. "You have wondered why the Vatican continues to use my services, Father Greene, even though I gave up the priesthood long, long ago. I do not fit your idea of someone the Pope would choose and you know I am no favorite of the Camerlengo."

"Yes," Roger answered, even though he realized the man's words had been more a statement than question. "I have."

"It is because I understand the evil better than anyone else ever could. I have hunted it for so long, so very long, it is now all that I am. My hopes are gone. My dreams are just bitter memories. I have become a part of the evil that must be destroyed."

"Who are you?" Roger barely heard the whisper as it left his lips. Part of him hoped the question had not reached Novara. He did not need to worry. There was no answer offered.

"My time here on this hunt is growing short," the emissary said after a few seconds. "Because of your lack of faith, I will understand if you no longer want to go with me at night."

Roger's first thought was to tell the man he never wanted to see him again, let alone walk miles of lonely streets in the middle of the night with a bruised knee and cut calf. But then he remembered the phone call with Cardinal Atchison and Camerlengo Nowaski. They had not given him any more answers than the man seated across the table, but they had begged him to stay with Novara, to be his shadow.

"I'll be ready to go tonight."

CHAPTER 36

NEW YORK, WEDNESDAY EVENING

Morgan looked at the row of windows set in the wall near the ceiling. Although their height from the floor meant no one but a professional mountain climber could look into the room from outside—or shoot in, either—neither could someone on the inside have a good look at what was going on outside the building. They did, however, allow some natural light into the room. What the dwindling light told Morgan was the sun was setting.

Damn, not much time left. She turned back to stare at the map hanging on a sliding cork board. With the new information provided by Overholt, all afternoon the task force had been pouring over the previous reports, trying to look at everything with fresh eyes. So far, nothing else had surfaced.

On the map were two sets of push pins. The blue pins indicated the home address of each of the victims while a set of red pins showed where each of the murders had taken place. Each pin had a little flag attached to it, indicating the victim's name, date of the murder and the appropriate address. The process was all very neat and tidy but so far the map had not led them to anything new, either.

"Okay, let's start over," David said as he pulled all the pins from the board and sorted them on a table. "Home address first."

"College girl, prostitute, lawyer, artist, scammer." Morgan read off the list, pausing after each one so David could find and place the pin.

The trio stared for a few minutes before David sighed. "I don't see anything," he said.

"It's the college girl," agreed Morgan. "Her off-campus apartment is way off to one side of the map."

"Let's try the murder scenes," David suggested.

"Okay, but this time just the murder scenes," Morgan said.

David shrugged and pulled out the blue pins again. "Okay, read 'em off."

"College girl, prostitute, lawyer, artist, scam artist."

"I've never noticed that before," Frank said.

Two heads snapped around to face him.

"What? What did you see, Frank?" Morgan asked.

"It's easier to see without the blue pins in the way. Plus, you were looking down at the list, Lieutenant, and David was looking at the addresses on the pins. Watch the order of the murders."

Frank walked to the board and slid the cork over about three feet so he could draw on the grease board behind it. He picked up a marker and drew a dot in the same position as each of the murder sites then drew lines from each point in order. He stepped back when he was done.

"Oh, never mind," he said. "When David was going back and forth, it reminded me of how they used to teach you in school to draw a star. You know, go side to side until you end up where you started. But this is nothing." He picked up an eraser.

"Stop!" David said, loud enough for the other officers in the room to look their way.

"That's because it's not a star," David continued. He took the eraser from Frank but only removed the lines. Then he drew lines from the college girl to the prostitute and then one from the two artists in the alleyway to the scam artist earlier that morning. Only the dot representing the lawyer was untouched.

"Okay, because some of these murders happened before midnight and some after, let's just go by what night they occurred. First night, second night," he continued, pointing to the college girl and the prostitute. "Fifth night, sixth night. We have the lawyer on the third night but what has always been the one anomaly? The fourth night, Saturday night or Sunday morning, when we did not have a body. But what if there was a murder that night?" He put a point exactly opposite the lawyer's murder site then drew a line connecting them. The new mark intersected with the other two lines exactly in the middle of the murder sites.

"Shit!" Morgan said. "We're missing a victim! Where is that on the map?"

"This will be a little rough on the estimate," David answered. He used the edge of one of the reports to draw straight lines on the map. When he was done, he drew a circle. "If I'm right, there should be a murder right in here that fits our guy."

"Oh, no," Morgan said as she leaned in close. "That's the four-two. Another damn precinct!"

She quickly walked over to the phone on her desk, opened up a guide, and then dialed a number.

"Homicide, Detective Johnson."

"Detective Johnson, this is Lieutenant Kelly. I need to know if you have an unsolved murder on your board from late Saturday night, early Sunday morning. You'll know this one. A real nasty one with lots of blood and the vic all cut up."

"Yeah, we've got one. Made a couple of guys toss their cookies at the scene. But it won't be on the board for long. They've got the husband in a room and they're sweatin' him. They think he's about ready to confess."

"What's the address on the murder?" She repeated it to David and he placed a pin on the map. It was directly in the middle of the circle he had drawn.

"Detective, I need to speak to your captain immediately."

"He's still here but he's watching the confession from behind the glass. He's not going to want to leave."

"Detective, you tell him if he's not on the phone in less than a minute, the next phone call will be from the commissioner's office."

"Yes, ma'am."

It took more than a minute, but not much longer, before the phone was picked up again.

"Captain Barnes, and this better be damned important."

"Captain, this is Lieutenant Kelly of the commissioner's special task force."

"From the *Post* today?"

Morgan winced but she kept going. "Yes, not exactly my best side. Captain, you've got the wrong man on this murder."

"Hamler? You bothered me for that? You're wrong, Lieutenant. The husband is good for this. Found in the apartment, middle of the night, covered in blood, no forced entry. He's our guy."

"No, you're wrong, Captain. Your vic was split from her neck to her pelvic area and gutted like a fish. Her uterus was removed. The autopsy said the murder was by an ambidextrous person using a blade in each hand but no metal fragments were recovered. Also, there was an open window in the bedroom with scratch marks on the sill."

"I don't know about the window and any scratch marks but how did you know about all the rest?" Barnes asked. "We didn't release any of that information."

"Because I've got five more just like it," Morgan answered. "That murder is one of mine which means I've got a murder six nights in a row from the same guy. And Captain, it's getting dark outside right now."

Barnes gave a low whistle. "What do you need, Lieutenant?"

Morgan leaned back in her chair. The convincing was over. "Starting now, your detectives that caught the case are assigned to my task force until this is over. I'll have one of my men coming to you right now to help pack up everything you have to bring it back with the detectives." She pointed to Frank. He simply nodded, grabbed his coat, and headed for the door. "Captain," she continued, "do you still have the body?"

"Yes. We didn't release it to the next of kin for obvious reasons."

"Okay, our lead forensic on this is a tech named Overholt. He'll make arrangements immediately to pick up the body." She did not need to gesture to David. He was already dialing one of the other phones.

"One last thing, Captain. All these things I just told you about the murder scenes have not been given to the press by our task force, either. I'd appreciate it if you kept a lid on it from your end."

"Will do. Lieutenant, get this bastard."

"We intend to, Captain."

CHAPTER 37

*M*y time is leaking away. The night, the black, the hell in between will soon keep me from escaping to feed.

Yes, my time is close but she is closer. The half-breed hides her from me at times and at others she shines like a beacon in the night, leading me to the end of my dreams, my hopes.

But he is there as well. The cambion is always there on the edge, watching, watching and waiting. He plays a game, trying to lure me in, knowing I must get to her before the night overcomes me.

He has not fallen. I felt the wall giving way, cracking and crumbling beneath my fingers but still he stands.

And he waits.

I will wait no more. In this time, in this place, it ends. This time when I leave to sleep, my task will be completed and he will be gone.

I will send the cambion to the permanent night.

I will kill him.

CHAPTER 38

NEW YORK, WEDNESDAY EVENING

"I'm not seeing anything new," David said. "Just a reaffirmation of what we found in the other cases."

Morgan leaned back from the desk and rubbed her eyes. "Overholt may find something on the body or from the apartment." She sighed. "But yeah, I think you're right. It's one of ours, but I don't think we're going to learn anything we don't already know."

"That's not entirely true," David said as he stood and walked over to the map. He drew two invisible circles with his fingertip. "Now we can see the pattern. But we have open spots. If our guy sticks with it, then he will be in one of these two areas tonight."

Morgan walked over beside him. "But which one? Even with the two new guys," she tilted her head toward the side of the room where Frank was bringing the two detectives from the 42nd precinct up to speed on the other murders, "we don't have enough manpower to canvas both areas at once."

They both stared at the map in silence for a couple of minutes.

"What do you want to do?" David finally asked.

Before Morgan could answer, Rosie walked up beside them.

"Hey, Lou. It's too early to call it for sure but we're drawing a big fat fucking zero right now on connections between the vics. Near as we can tell, the lawyer never had any of the others for clients, not even the whore or the con, none of them shared a doc, and there are three different health insurance companies so far. We just got started on the new vic from the four-two, but I'll bet you a beer to a shot of whiskey we don't find nothing there either."

"All right," Morgan said. "Your people can pick the loose ends up again tomorrow." She gestured toward the map. "There's an elementary school just down the street from my apartment. That's pretty close to the mid-point between the two areas where we think he might hit tonight. I'll ask the captain to put on extra patrols in those areas and we will stage at the school. That way we'll be close to both of them."

Rosie whistled. "We're just going to sacrifice one?"

Morgan's head snapped around. "Not if I can help it. I hope we will be close enough to get to the scene and catch the bastard before anyone else dies."

"What time do you want to be at the school?" David asked. His voice was so quiet she had trouble hearing him.

"Let's have everyone there at eleven o'clock in full tactical. We'll only leave the people manning the phones."

"Okay, I'll spread the word," Rosie said before she walked away.

"You don't approve of my plan?" Morgan asked after a few more seconds of silence.

"No, I'm not thinking of that," answered David. "You don't have much of a choice with the number of officers we have on the task force." He turned and leaned against the wall so he could look at her as he crossed his arms over his chest. "We figured out his geographic pattern; we know what kind of woman he wants. What's bothering me is we still have no idea how he is finding them.

"And here's the million-dollar question: What happens if we don't catch him in the next two nights? His grid will be complete. Will he just disappear into the city? He wouldn't be the first serial killer to take time off in between sprees."

"He also wouldn't be the first to just reappear somewhere else in the country," Morgan said.

"I think we have to consider we have a potential time factor on this case as well," David finished.

Morgan rubbed her eyes before nodding in agreement. "Okay, I'm going to go talk to Cap about the extra patrols then I'm going to go home and get some sleep and fresh clothes."

"Do you want some help with that?" David asked.

"Not tonight," she answered. "I really do want to get a nap." She smiled. "But keep asking."

CHAPTER 39

NEW YORK, EARLY THURSDAY MORNING

Roger was slightly behind Novara in the same alley they had been in the night before. They had stood there long enough on this evening that their coffee was long gone, the empty cups tossed into an overflowing trash bin.

So many things about this night's adventure had been different than any other night. First, after taking care of Novara's caffeine fix, they had ridden in a taxi to only two blocks away before walking to their vantage spot. Roger had been stunned when the other man actually made a joke about the ride, smiling when he said the priest was in danger of wearing out one shoe if he continued to limp on it each night.

They also were not chanting as they had the night before when they spent hours staring at the same apartment building. The two men had not been completely silent, however. In fact, they held what Roger considered a perfectly pleasant conversation about Church news—the naming of a new Cardinal in Spain and a recent speech by his Holiness against the Planned Parenthood program—but now they stood quietly, wrapped in silence just as the shadows cloaked them in black.

Roger wondered how differently he would feel about Novara if all the other nights had been like this one. He still did not know the answers to any of his one thousand questions, so he was no better off than before, but somehow he felt closer to the other man than at any time since his arrival.

"Tell me, Father Greene," Novara said, breaking the quiet. "Do you feel the weight of your responsibilities with the Church?"

Roger watched the man's dark outline turn to look over his shoulder.

Dreams of Ivory & Gold

"It is a straightforward question. I know I have accused you of certain things in past conversations but this is not one of those times."

Roger paused. Novara's voice had been a mixture of melancholy and resignation. If the emissary had followed up his question with a sigh from the depths of his soul, the sound would not have been out of place. The priest decided to take him at his word.

"Yes, I constantly feel the pressure of my position. I feel it every time I take confession. I feel it when I must give last rites. I feel it every time I preside over communion or lead the sermon. I think all of us who are called feel the weight to varying degrees."

Long minutes passed again in silence except for the occasional passing car in the street.

"Does it ever feel like too much? Like the responsibility will crush you?"

"Yes, I have felt that way before, too. I remember one time when I was counseling a young couple that had lost their baby. I could not find the words to comfort the mother. I was afraid I was going to lose her and more importantly, that she would lose herself. But once I remembered I did not need to find the words, that God already knew the words and all I had to do was to let him speak them through me, the burden lightened. I had to let God lift some of the weight and carry it for me."

The pause was not as long this time.

"What if God thinks of you as an abomination? What if there has been too much pain? Been too much death?"

Roger felt his chest tighten as he listened to Novara call himself what the Camerlengo had already labeled him.

"If this goes badly," the man continued, "you have the strength to go on. Your strength is why I chose you to be my helper. There will be things required of you by the Church. Do what you will, I cannot tell you what to decide. But for me, remember this, I want to return to my home in Italy. See that I make it there, not back to the Vatican to be packed away by the Camerlengo as one of his trophies."

Before Roger could respond, a plain four-door sedan pulled up in front of the apartment building and stopped. Inside sat two men. A few seconds later, the building's main door swung open and out walked a woman.

Roger recognized her red hair at once. It was Morgan. He watched his friend hop in the car and take off down the street.

"This is Morgan's apartment," he whispered loudly. "We've been sneaking around, spying on my friend!"

"Spying?" Novara asked, his old tone of disdain returning. "Did I not tell you what we hunt is evil? Did I not tell you it hunts your friend? Did I not tell you she was in danger? Every time I think you are getting close to understanding, you find a way to show that your faith, your belief, is blind."

Roger opened his mouth to respond but even as he did, Novara pushed him hard against the alley wall. The priest could see the other man outlined against the opening to the street. He had expected the man to be glaring at him, threatening him as he had before, but instead, the emissary had turned his face toward the night sky.

"What are you…"

"Quiet!" Novara hissed. "Do you remember the chant I taught you? Do you!?"

"Yes."

"Good. When I tell you, start chanting. No matter what happens, no matter what you see or feel, keep chanting."

For a few moments, everything stopped in the alley. Roger heard the sounds of the city in the distance, like noise from a radio playing down the block on a summer day. He felt a trickle of sweat rolling down the side of his head, just missing the corner of his eye, and then moving over his cheek. The world did not exist, not really. This alley was all that mattered.

Novara suddenly whirled, pulling something from beneath his jacket even as he turned. "Now, Father!"

Roger began to chant as a huge shadow winged through the alley. The shadow had substance, however, as his hair and clothes felt the wake in its passing.

A scream shook the night, threatening to stop Roger's heart after the next beat. The call was the same one that sent him cowering to the sidewalk a few nights earlier. He nearly stopped chanting in his fear, faltering for a few beats, and a wave of exhaustion blanketed him while his head bobbed in sleep. But in the next instant he picked up the sing-song again and managed to keep his eyes open.

Every time the shadow dove through the alley, Roger watched Novara stand to meet the attack with the white object in his hand. Once, the man staggered beneath a blow, stumbling backward into the trash bin and making the metal echo from the hit. The shadow screamed again, calling out in the night. But as long as Roger chanted, the call remained muted, still frightening but no longer threatening to steal his life on the spot.

Novara gathered himself and stepped away from the walls. This time when the shadow dove, he leaped, slashing at the black with the white in his hand. He paid for the attempt by tumbling head over heels for nearly twenty feet down the alley.

But he had hit his mark. This time the scream was not one of anger or victory. This time the call echoed with the sound of pain. Something dropped from the shadow, burning brightly with a green flame as it arched through the air and rolled behind Novara.

Whatever the object was continued to burn and allowed Roger to see the emissary clearly, lying on his side in the middle of the alley. He was helpless.

Roger limped from his spot along the wall, still chanting as he moved, afraid the attacker would reappear before he could reach Novara.

But the shadow was gone. The priest searched the sky for a few moments before he let his gaze drop. A huge, crooked bone continued to burn green a few feet away and allowed him to see what Novara still clutched in his hand.

It was the knife—the knife with the whitest blade he had ever seen.

Novara groaned as he moved, slowly at first before suddenly sitting up with a jerk.

"It's gone," Roger said, trying not to remind himself he still had no idea what *it* was.

"You did well, Father. Not everyone can keep up the chant through an attack without failing." The man slipped the knife back into a sheath in his belt. "Now, if you would be kind enough to help an old man to his feet."

Roger helped him stand, Novara grabbing for his ribs with a grunt.

"I don't suppose I can convince you to go to a hospital," the priest said.

"No," Novara agreed. "You can not. We will be going straight back to the cathedral. First, however…"

He walked a few steps and reached down slowly, picking up the still-burning bone, the green light dancing across his hand. Novara shook the object up and down for several seconds and flame dripped off, almost as if the fire was liquid. When the blaze burned out, he slipped the bone into his inner jacket pocket.

"You never know when that might be useful. Now, let's find a taxi. This time for both of us."

CHAPTER 40

NEW YORK, EARLY THURSDAY MORNING

The car screeched to a stop and Morgan was out and moving while the sound still rolled down the street. She paid little attention to the two uniformed officers in the alley opening—one so pale he could be seen in the dark and the other still puking up whatever was left of his supper. Her interest was trained upon the figure that lay half in the light of an open doorway and half out of sight in the shadows.

Well, at least what was left of her body.

Morgan had covered a homicide in a meat packing plant early in her career and the smell in the alley took her back to that time. The odor of blood was so thick, if she breathed deeply, she could taste the bitter iron on her tongue. The victim's blood was fresh enough to still flow like a river of crimson, not a dark and thick Jell-O. This was a recent kill.

"Did anyone come out since you found her?" she yelled at the patrolmen. "Have you seen anyone?"

"No," the pale one answered. "No one has come in or out since we found her and we can see both doors from here."

"Frank, let's get all of our people out in pairs going door to door. He couldn't have gone far."

David stepped up beside her. "He may not have gone anywhere," he said, tilting his head toward the open doorway.

"I know," Morgan said before holding up a hand to Overholt and two of his techs who were moving toward the body. "Overholt, we're not secure here yet."

The trio immediately stopped and began backing up slowly.

"Get on the front of the building," she yelled down the alleyway at the two patrolmen, the pale-faced one dragging his sick partner out of sight down the sidewalk. Morgan turned her attention back to David and she pulled her gun out of her holster. "Think we can jump over the blood through the doorway?"

David leaned over to look inside. "The lights are still on, let me go first. There is a desk on the other side of the room. I think if I do a shoulder roll, I can come up behind it. It doesn't look like a very big room."

"Okay," Morgan said before a short pause. "Be careful, David."

He backed up two steps, took a deep breath, and ran toward the door. Morgan slid to her left as he moved, trying to give him as much cover as possible through the opening.

His landing would not have scored a "10" from the judges in the Olympics—his grunt from the impact echoing out into the night—but his momentum carried him on over onto his back and then to his knees. He rose up about a foot short of being completely covered by the desk, but even as he moved the rest of the way behind it, he was already scanning the room, his gun tracking with his eyes.

This was the worst time for any partner, even without the feelings that had resurfaced with David's appearance, and Morgan hated the churning of her stomach now. They possibly had a killer cornered, her partner was in a dangerous spot on point, and her cover position gave her a very limited field of vision to help.

David's movements slowed to a stop. Seconds turned into a minute. Morgan blinked to clear her sight and felt a hair brush against her cheek. David finally removed his left hand from his gun and signaled for her to enter.

She gathered herself for the run and leap over the transom. There would be no need for a shoulder roll but she still needed to miss the blood so Overholt could do his work after they cleared the building.

In her mind, Morgan was already on "two" of "one-two-three-go!" when she abruptly spun around and dropped to one knee. Her eyes trained up her right arm and through the Glock's sight as she swept back and forth along the roof line above her. She heard someone swear softly from her left, possibly Overholt, and then something landed hard on the ground. But that was not what she was looking for.

For a moment, she had felt she was being watched, felt it as solidly as if someone had dropped a hand on her shoulder. The feeling still lingered, kicking around in the corners of her mind, but the sense was already fading, moving off into the distance like the whistle of a departing train.

"What do you see, Lieutenant?" Frank asked. Morgan had not heard him come back into the alley but he sounded like he was only a few feet away.

"Nothing," she answered. "There was nothing there. Just a feeling was all." Morgan turned to look at her partner. "Are we deployed?"

"Yes. In pairs, two blocks out. The captain heard the radio call and ordered extra patrols into a four-block circle."

"Are those two uniforms on the front door?"

Frank nodded. "With the two new guys from the four-two."

For the first time, Morgan noticed Overholt lying face down on the ground behind Frank. She smiled. "Did you do that?"

He shrugged and if there had been more light in the alley, she was sure she would have seen red rising in his cheeks. "He was just standing there like a big target in his white suit."

"Can I get up now?" Overholt asked, his voice muffled because he was still facing down. "I'm going to need to change before I can begin the examination. This suit is contaminated."

"Yes, go," Morgan said with a chuckle, but then her thoughts turned back to the task at hand and the smile melted. "I'm going in with David. You've got the door, Frank." She turned to the doorway. "Comin' in."

With that she stood and ran, leaping over the red pool and what was left of their victim. She cleared the girl's dark hair with about six inches to spare and skidded down into a crouch beside David.

"What happened?" he asked. "I saw you looking up at the other building."

"I would have bet good money someone was up there watching us," Morgan whispered. "It was like I could reach up and point right at him. But there was nobody there." She looked around a room that was only fifteen feet by fifteen feet. "What took you so long to decide there was no one in here?"

"I'll show you later," he said. "Let's clear the building."

They moved around the desk to the closed door leading into

the main shop. The area was not very large, including the little loft that served as a stock room, but the search still took about twenty minutes for them to weave their way in and around the clothing racks and display cases. The shop was one of those businesses that charged three times too much for jeans that hung too low on the butt, blouses that left nothing to the imagination, and accessories that twenty years earlier would have only been worn by hookers—cheap ones. The walk through made Morgan feel old.

"I think we're good," David said.

"Yeah," Morgan agreed as she holstered her weapon. "Let's get Overholt to work on the body."

They walked back into the little office but stayed away from the open door to the alley.

"Frank," Morgan yelled.

"Yes, Lieutenant," he answered from the darkness.

"We're all clear. Tell Overholt he can get to work. Oh, and let the officers out front know we are going to be coming out the door in a few minutes."

"Will do."

Morgan turned to David. "So what did you want to show me?"

"Look over here," he said as he walked to the far wall. "It's hard to see. I was only able to catch glimpses of it when I was crouched down."

Morgan stared at the wall where he was pointing. At first, she saw nothing but then she began to stoop down to get in the same sight line David had earlier. There! A slight glistening as if wet paint was almost dry.

"Is that writing?" she asked.

"Maybe," David answered. "And now that I am closer, I think that and that, and maybe even there, are scratch marks."

Morgan walked immediately to the door to the alley. The area outside was already brighter as the portable lights were in the process of being set up. She saw Overholt approaching the victim's body.

"We think we have writing on a wall."

The words had been spoken without emotion but her heart was racing in her chest. Overholt looked at her and blinked, twice, then turned quickly to talk to someone out of view.

"You start processing the body," he turned his head again, "and you start in on the alley around the scene." He looked over his shoulder at Morgan. "Can I get in the front door?"

"We'll unlock it right now." She turned to David but he was already disappearing from view into the shop area. By the time she turned back to Overholt, he was also out of sight but she could still hear him yelling orders for someone to "grab a light stand" and "bring the camera now!"

Morgan was so excited she could feel her hands shaking. Contact from the killer might provide clues to his location, his reasons for doing what he was doing, or in this case, how he was choosing his victims.

Within minutes the little room began to fill with people and equipment. Although the temperature was already starting to climb, she was certain the mercury went up another ten degrees the second the portable lights were switched on.

"We're losing it," Overholt said immediately. "Take as many photos as you can!"

The room was silent for the next few minutes except for the sounds of shuffling feet and the camera whirring through photo after photo. The tech with the camera finally stepped back.

"You can see where it is soaking into this old wallpaper," Overholt said, gesturing to the wall. "We're starting to lose the shape and pretty soon it's going to look like a badly pixilated photo, indistinct and blurry."

"What's the ink?" David asked.

"I won't know for sure until after the tests, but best guess is the victim's blood." "What does it say?" Morgan asked. "Is it code? Is it even a language?"

"Oh, it's a language," answered Overholt. "In fact, I think it's…"

His voice trailed off as he turned to the laptop he had placed on the desk and he plugged in the camera. He flipped through several photos before dragging one into a graphics program and then highlighted the markings with yellow lines. Then he saved it to the desktop and attached it to an email. A second later he pulled out his cell phone and made a call.

"Deena? Deena, it's Sam. I'm sorry for waking you up, baby, but it's important. I just sent you an email with a photo. No, not one of those. I'm at a crime scene and I need you to help me. You got it? Great. Honey, is that Hebrew? I know, that's why I highlighted it. It is? Okay. One more thing, Deena. Can you read it? I know it's been a while, you can't exactly take the goy to synagogue, but try. Can you spell it for me? Thank you, Honey. I owe you a big dinner for this. I'll call you tomorrow. Bye."

Morgan had no idea what she looked like but if her expression matched the ones on David's and Frank's faces, they might as well have all three been standing there with their mouths open.

"What?" Overholt asked. "You think I only know dead people? Deena's father is a rabbi and he doesn't like me because I'm not Jewish. She said she thinks the writing is the Hebrew word, 'toldot.'"

"So what does toldot mean?" Morgan asked.

"She couldn't remember all of it. Deena said toldot had something to do with bloodlines. You know, family trees. It is a big deal, though, because the word is spelled differently in different parts of the Hebrew Bible. Kind of a scandal. But that's all she remembered."

"Who do we know that's an expert on that?" Frank asked.

"Looks like it's my turn to wake someone up," Morgan said as she pulled out her phone. "My conversation won't be nearly as lively, though." She smiled at the blushing tech.

"Roger, it's Morgan. Did I wake you? That's good. No, not good that you can't sleep, you know what I mean. No, I'm not mad that you couldn't talk to me yesterday. You were taking confession. It's your job. Roger, Roger, I'm not mad but you need to listen. I have a question and it has to do with the case I'm on. Yes, the bad one. Roger, can you tell me the religious context of the Hebrew word toldot? Uh, just give me the summary on the phone. Uh-huh… uh-huh…. so you mean like a direct descendent? Okay. Looks like seven. Uh-huh…. uh-huh. Okay, this is what we were looking for. Can you write down the detailed version? As soon as possible. Tomorrow's, well, today, is great. Yes, just email it to me or drop it by the precinct. Either myself, David, or my partner, Frank. Thanks, Roger.

"Good catch, Overholt," she said once she disconnected. "You call that girl today like you promised and take her to dinner. Expense it and I'll sign for it." She turned to the others. "Father Greene said the toldot is still a little controversial in some corners of the Jewish faith.

In Genesis, or the Torah for Jews, the word refers to God creating all the generations of heaven and earth. At that point, toldot is spelled in Hebrew one way. But, after Adam and Eve are kicked out of Eden, the Torah spells it a different way. The—I think Roger called it the vav—is missing so the Hebrew Bible is spelling the term wrong.

"The spelling stays that way until the Book of Ruth. When describing the descendants of Perez, son of Judah, the vav is back and the word is spelled correctly, but just in that one part."

"I'm sorry, Lieutenant," Frank said. "But what does a misspelled word in the Bible have to do with us?"

"In Ruth, they are tracing the genealogy of Perez because they are showing the family tree of King David. Now both Judaism and Christianity believe the Messiah will be born from the line of King David. For Christians, that was Jesus Christ."

"But for Jews," David interrupted, "the messiah has not arrived yet. So what we've got is a word referring to a line of ancestry and a bunch of sexually assaulted dead girls who can't become pregnant with all their reproductive organs ripped out of their bodies."

"So is he trying to end the line?" Overholt asked.

"No, I don't think so," Morgan answered. "Some of the women could never have children so those lines were already ended. But, I don't know. Anybody?"

David shuffled back and forth on his feet and stared at his hands. Morgan had seen that look hundreds of times before. He had an idea but he had not had time to run the thought through his head, look for the loopholes, and process it.

"Go on, David," she said. "We understand this is a theory made on new evidence at the scene of the crime. It's your best off-the-cuff guess. No one is going to hold you to anything if it turns out not to be right."

He nodded. "The other girls could be—could be—the symbols of the broken lines. There is sex, but no baby. Remember how we talked about the pattern? If there is another murder tomorrow night where we think it will occur, it will close another gap. What if these women, these symbols, are representing what has already happened? What if his real purpose is to restart the line of Perez?"

"Oh, my God," Morgan gasped. "He thinks he is going to father the Messiah."

"The Jewish Messiah," corrected David. "For this theory to work, our killer was either born Jewish or converted."

"And converts are usually much more fanatical," Morgan said.

"Uh, Lieutenant?"

Morgan turned to look at the two uniformed officers who were the first to arrive at the scene. They were standing just inside the doorway to the shop. One of them appeared to still be sick.

"Yes."

"Excuse me, but everyone else is a part of your task force and have their assignments. Did you want us to go back to the station house and type up our report right away, help with the canvassing…?"

"Just talk to me for a minute and then you can go back to do a full report. How did you find her?"

"We had the notice from the captain about watching extra close so we were running our light up the alleys. Officer Hallett thought he saw a little light down this one and then with the spot he could see part of her body. We both exited the patrol car, drew our weapons, and proceeded into the alley. We were approximately fifteen feet into it when something big went over our heads and scared the sh… scared me pretty bad. And then it screamed, that's the only way I can describe it, above us and I dropped to one knee. I almost squeezed off a round. We continued down the alley after a few seconds with Officer Hallett in the lead. That's when we saw what had happened to the girl. We called it in and positioned ourselves where you found us, where we could see both doors in case the suspect was still inside."

Morgan looked at the others who merely shook their heads.

"Okay, good report," she told the patrolmen. "Go back to the precinct and type it up." She waited until they left. "Frank, we need people on those roofs. They saw something up there and I felt it. David, do you want to go back to the precinct with the patrolmen and start working on that theory while we finish here?"

"Yes, I think that's a good idea."

"You better hustle to catch up with them. Let's go people. We may only have one more night to catch this bastard before he disappears on us."

CHAPTER 41

MANNHEIM, GERMANY 1973

Greg heard the DJ prattling on about the Rolling Stones playing "Sweet Virginia" at their concert in Mannheim the night before, but he let the noise wash around him and fade away without paying any attention. His ears were focused on what was happening on the other side of the half-open door in front of him.

The rhythmic squeak of bedsprings were echoed by grunts and moans. Greg gripped the knife tightly in his right hand as he slipped through the opening and took in the room in a glance.

The beast was on top of the girl on the bed along the far wall—exactly where he had helped Sohndra move it a few hours ago. He slammed the door shut.

The incubus whirled and pulled its legs up underneath its body, its claws holding his body up on the edge of the bed. Wings quivered in anger and a hiss escaped through yellow teeth.

"So half-breed, you have finally appeared. It took you a long enough to find me this time. I half-thought something had happened to you, that you had given up on our game. But now I assume you will kill her after I am gone and we will start all over again in another time, another place."

"You're right. I will need to kill the girl after you are no longer here. But you are wrong about taking a long time to find you." Greg reached over and locked the bedroom door, putting the key in his pocket when he was done. The incubus hissed again and glanced at the open window in the opposite corner of the room.

"I found Sohndra almost the moment I arrived in Mannheim," he continued. "We have been waiting for you." He turned to face the window. "Helmutt!"

Greg's shout still echoed off the walls as the window slammed shut and a sheet of wood closed off the night sky. Hammers pounded at nails, answering the yell with echoes of their own.

The incubus stared at the window for several long seconds and the hammers lost their cadence, the rhythm falling off and nearly dying before a solo beat picked up the previous pace and continued.

Helmutt. I knew he could do it.

The beast screamed. Greg felt the anger roll over him like waves in the surf, pushing and then pulling his emotions.

"Scream all you want," Greg said as he stepped toward the middle of the room. "It still will not help you get out of this room alive."

"But if I can go nowhere, then neither can you," came the reply, spittle flying from the incubus's mouth. "Maybe I will be the one to fly away and she will live after I leave."

Greg shook his head. "No. Even if what you described comes true, you will still lose. Sohndra was preparing to enter the sisterhood. She is ready to take her own life if I am killed and the Pope has agreed to grant her absolution for the mortal sin. No, we have been waiting for you." He paused. "And I have been waiting for this moment for a very long time."

The incubus screamed a challenge as Greg moved forward. When the man was still a few feet away, the beast did the one thing the former priest had not been prepared for—it reached down with one razor-clawed hand and threw Sohndra at him.

With the knife in his right hand, Greg tried to brace himself and catch her with his left. He might as well have tried to stop a charging bull with tissue paper. Her body slammed into him with enough force to make them both tumble into the far wall. Greg felt a flash of pain with every breath that promised at least one broken rib, maybe more.

He struggled to stand and then leaned against the wall. The beast still squatted on the edge of the bed, its claws digging through the mattress while its slowly beating wings roiled up small clouds of dust.

"I begin to tire of you, half-breed," the incubus said. "After all these years, I begin to think you really would rather kill me than join in ruling over these pitiful humans."

Greg stumbled forward, his anger fighting down the pain. This time he ducked the wooden chair the beast threw at him. He heard the furniture hit the floor and skid before slamming into the wall. But he did not slow down to watch the chair. Nor did he stop for the little table that had served as a night stand. Greg was already leaping forward and slashing at his enemy, fulfilling his centuries-old responsibility that had kept him from a normal life.

He scored a slice against the creature's right wing and leg before he was knocked off his feet by a blow from the left wing. His short flight through the room ended against the window and board.

Greg missed the frame by a few inches, probably saving himself a broken back to go along with the rib. Even so, the crack echoed in the little room and scared him for a moment until he realized the sound came from the wood giving way, not his body.

The beast attacked while Greg still struggled for his second breath. He fought back blindly through tears of pain, slashing and stabbing as fast as he could move. Most of the time the swings were a wasted effort, his white blade cutting only air. But two slashes hit the incubus sufficiently to make the blade slow and a stab poked deep enough into the gnarled hide to draw another scream.

The beast hopped backward. Every time some of its blood hit the floor, green flame burst out, charring the wood. Eventually, the incubus reached the bed again.

The cambion and the creature stared at each other. Two warriors—battered, bruised, and bleeding—they gathered themselves like two prize fighters entering the final round with the championship title on the line.

Only this time the title was life.

The beast grabbed the bed with both hands, spun like an Olympic discus thrower, and heaved the frame at Greg. He dove to his right but he was still clipped by the missile. The plaster gave way when he hit the wall but he did not hear the snap or his own coughing in the dust. All he heard was the sound of wood shattering into kindling. Cool wind swept into the room and kept Greg conscious.

"So, this is not the end after all, cambion," the incubus said, sitting on his haunches in the window opening. "Not the end I dreamed for and not the one you so carefully planned. We will meet again in another time, another place." Then, the beast was gone.

Greg lay in the corner for a few moments before he gripped the knife tightly in his hand and crawled the few feet to where Sohndra lay against the wall. He saw at once he would not need to finish the deed, her head already bent back at an awkward angle. The chair that missed him had snapped her neck as she still slept under the incubus's spell.

Only Helmutt was left. Greg used the wall to lever himself into a standing position. Two of the small green fires had grown into real flames and he knew he did not have much time now. He limped to the window. "Helmutt?" he called.

But the boy who had been so helpful during Greg's time in Germany was not on the little balcony. He and the two others, Helmutt's friends, lay still on the stone street three stories below the window. Greg turned and hobbled toward the bedroom door, digging for the key in his pocket as he moved. He was alone, again.

Now he would wait for the next beginning, wait for the next time the beast found the line of King David.

CHAPTER 42

NEW YORK, THURSDAY MORNING

"I just received an email from Overholt." Morgan leaned back from her computer. The command center was quiet with only three other members of the task force in the room updating evidence books.

"That was pretty quick to have finished processing this morning's victim," David said from near the map. "Did he find something new?"

"Not new. Old. Victim number seven, Miss Theresa Marlune could not get pregnant. She had received the shot." Morgan swiveled her chair around to face David. "That keeps alive your theory about the victims being symbols of the broken line." She stood up and walked over to stand next to him. "Have you thought through it anymore?"

David let out a breath of disgust. "I don't know. It could be dead on or it could be a piece of crap theory, and I don't know because the idea has asked more questions than it answered." He turned his back to the wall and leaned against it so he and Morgan were looking at each other. "Let's assume for a minute the theory is correct and our killer is using his victims to mimic the broken toldot. How is he choosing the women? Are they only chosen because they cannot have children, and if so, how does he know? Why does he have sex with them before he kills them? Is that also a symbol?"

Morgan nodded her head. "The theory does raise a lot of questions."

David ran his hand through his hair in response. "That's only the beginning, Morg. You said it last night, this morning. What if this guy thinks he is going to father the Jewish Messiah? After tonight, when he most likely closes up this pattern," he tapped his knuckle on the board beside the map, "does he continue to kill? Does he start a new box in a different part of the city? Or, does he reappear in a few months or a few years in another state?"

"Or does he try to consummate a pregnancy and father the Mashiach himself?"

Morgan and David both turned to see Roger standing beside Frank a few feet away. The priest had offered the final question.

"Roger!" exclaimed Morgan. "It's about damn time. Do you have that report?" She ignored Frank wincing at her language.

David saved the situation, however, shaking the priest's hand and smiling. "What your childhood friend is trying to say, Father Greene, is we could really use your help."

"Yes, yes," she agreed, red blooming over a smile. "I'm sorry, Father. We are very thankful for your help."

Roger finished shaking David's hand and then gave Morgan a quick hug. "Nothing to be sorry about," he said. "I know as well as anyone how you can be a bull in a china shop when you get something in your head." He handed over a stack papers in a clear-cased cover. "But I don't know how much help this is going to be."

"You might be surprised," Morgan replied. "But first, why did you ask that question?"

"Because it fits with the questions you asked me last night and the report you wanted. It's also the logical next step. The toldot is all about lineage and broken family lines." Roger went to the board and picked up a marker. He wrote six symbols on one line and five symbols directly below them.

"These are both the word toldot written in Hebrew. The top one is found early in the Book of Genesis in reference to the generations of the heaven and earth, basically creation. That usage stops after the fall of Adam and Eve and their exile from Eden." He underlined the word with five Hebrew letters. "From then on, toldot is spelled this way, with a missing vav. The only other time the word appears spelled the original way is in the fourth chapter of Ruth when toldot refers to the 'generations of Perez.'"

"And from the Perez family line comes King David?" Morgan asked.

Roger turned back to the board and began writing. "The name Perez comes from the Hebrew word, 'paratz.' Paratz means 'to break through.' So the Perez name means God is going to break through the fall of the families of man and restore the original intent of the creation. Yes, from the descendants of Perez rose the family of King David."

"And from King David came the Messiah," David said.

"Or Mashiach, if the believer is Jewish," Roger said with a nod.

"But then why haven't all the victims been Jewish?" Frank asked. "Only two were and one of the women was an African-American Southern Baptist."

Roger shrugged. "You have to remember Christianity is a pretty new religion compared to Judaism and others on the world stage. Our family lines have all descended from other religions, many of them Jewish if you go back far enough."

"So we could be looking at anyone as a potential victim," Morgan said with a sigh.

"Not necessarily," Roger replied. "How was toldot spelled last night?"

David walked over to the desk and flipped open the evidence folder from the last victim. He took only a few seconds to find the photos of the wall with the writing. "Toldot is missing the vav."

"I thought it might be," Roger said. He pointed to the second spelling. "So your victims are part of the broken lines, the sinners cast from Eden."

"Hang on there, that gives me an idea," David said. He walked over to the phone, made a call, and spoke to the person on the other end of the line for about a minute before returning to the group.

"So our victims could be anybody," Morgan said to Roger. "But you've got an idea beyond that. I recognize your little smile from when we were kids and you thought you knew something we didn't." She hoped they would find an end to this maze so her head would stop spinning.

"I don't know if what I have is an idea or a theory or too much late night TV," the priest said. "And even if I am right, I don't know if it helps you. Let's say the victims are the broken toldots and the bad guy really believes he is either ushering in the path for the Mashiach or he is going to father the Mashiach." Roger tapped a finger on the board beside the top spelling of toldot. "He is going to need this. Either he is from the line of Perez or he is going to need a mother from the line of Perez."

"Can we even do that?" Frank asked. "Can we even find people from that old of a family tree?"

"David?" Morgan asked.

"I don't know, Morg," he answered after a few seconds. "We've got a lot of information in a lot of computers at Quantico, but we might be a lot better off pulling in the Census bureau. Even so, we don't really have a place to start and a search will be slow going. Plus, there's always the chance our killer's insane and only thinks he knows the Perez line."

"But you're all missing the point," Roger said. "To have the Mashiach, you need a living mother. You're going to need to have a living victim at some point."

Silence fell over the group for several seconds before the phone rang. David walked over to the desk and answered it.

Morgan barely noticed he had left the group. She was still trying to wrap her thoughts around what Roger had just told them. She knew her friend was wrong about one thing, however. Although their backgrounds could make them seem completely random, the victims' inability to become pregnant at the time of the attacks tied them all together somehow.

"That was Overholt," David said as he returned. "On a hunch I had him pull the window sashes from the lawyer's and scammer's apartments out of evidence to look at the scratch marks again. After looking them over, he believes they are crudely carved toldots. Now he is having his people go back over everything from the other scenes to see if they can find the word there."

"Tomorrow night," Morgan said, her thoughts finally snapping into place. "If our man follows his pattern, he will kill tonight in the area we have designated. Then tomorrow evening, he'll find his living victim, the mother, someplace in the pattern."

"So what do we do?" Frank asked.

"We find a way to stop him tonight," she answered.

CHAPTER 43

NEW YORK, LATE THURSDAY AFTERNOON

"David."

The word, said in an ordinary conversational tone, sounded both like a whisper and a shout. Chairs scraped across the floor and mingled with shuffling papers and closing evidence folders. There was plenty of noise in the command center to drown out the word, but since it was the only thing spoken, it grew in volume in Morgan's ears and threatened to echo off the walls.

"Hmmm?"

Morgan knew David was barely listening to her, his attention on the report and notes on the table in front of him.

"I want you to stay here tonight."

That sentence caught his full attention. David's head snapped up and he stared at her with the same expression he had used as their marriage splintered: unblinking eyes looking at her over lips held together in a straight line, his jaw moving slightly with grinding teeth. He was mad.

"Not much of a chance of that happening, Lieutenant."

Yep, he's pissed. "Now hear me out," Morgan said. "You could coordinate the efforts from here by radio and be at any scene in fifteen minutes if we find something new. But also, for the next several hours while we are cruising around, you could be working on finding the woman this guy thinks can give birth to the Mashiach. If we miss him tonight, we've probably only got until tomorrow night to find this guy. Every minute is going to count."

David opened his mouth to protest but the next voice came from her left.

"You know she's right," Frank said. "Our time is running out fast and everybody needs to be doing what they do best to catch this guy. You're the one with the experience to get into his head. That's what you need to do."

David's jaw worked even faster, but she knew they had won the argument when he dropped his stare to the desktop. "Where are we on finding a hereditary line?" Morgan asked, attempting to turn the conversation to task and allow David some space to accept what just happened.

"We have full use of the computers at the FBI but so far we haven't got much," he answered. "The Israelis have offered their full cooperation but we haven't received any information yet. Until we do, we don't have a very good starting place for the search."

"What about Israeli officials, representatives? Could one of them be from the line?"

"The U.N. delegation and consulate are in complete lockdown," David said. "By the way, their ambassador appeared to take this very seriously. Apparently this is not the first time they've had to deal with nut jobs and the end of the world."

"We may be the ones who end up looking like we're insane," Morgan said. She turned to look at the task force members leaving the room to begin their patrols. "Okay, Frank, let's get moving."

"Frank..." David's voice held more question than statement but the look on his face said everything he could not.

"I know," Frank said. "She's my partner. They have to go through me to get to her."

Morgan watched the two men exchange a look. If the stare could have been written down on paper, it would have been signed and notarized to serve as a contract. "Frank, go ahead and I'll be out in a minute. I want to talk to David before we go." Morgan waited until her partner was moving toward the door before she turned back to her ex-husband. "When this is over, I think we need to sit down and have a long talk. I mean, I think there are things we need to talk about." Now that she was finally voicing what she had been thinking for the past couple of days, Morgan was nervous. "That is, if you want to talk..."

"I've been wanting to have this talk for a long time," David interrupted. "And this time, I'll listen as well."

"Me, too."

CHAPTER 44

NEW YORK, LATE THURSDAY EVENING

Roger knocked on the door again, this time hard enough to sting his knuckles. "Mr. Novara, is everything all right?"

Silence was still the only reply. Roger checked his watch and noticed the time was just before midnight. He had not seen or spoken to the emissary all day. He had been too busy writing the report for Morgan and then he had taken a nap after supper. Now, well past time for the nightly hunt to begin, Novara was still a no-show. The emissary's absence was what had brought the priest to the man's bedroom door. He reached down and discovered the door was unlocked.

"Mr. Novara," he said as he slowly opened it. "I'm sorry to disturb you but I wanted to know if we were going out tonight."

Roger stood in the doorway and stared at the room. The bed was made with precision, crisp corners and arrow-straight folds. The chairs at the little table were pushed in tight and the curtain was all the way to the side of the closet opening, revealing only empty hangers on the metal bar. The room was deserted.

"He's gone," Roger said, stating what was so easy to see. Just to be certain he walked over and opened up two drawers in the dresser. Only bare wood looked back at him.

He could not believe it. After all the late nights, the insults, the questioning of his faith, the panicked calls to the Vatican—after all—Novara had disappeared with no trace of where he had gone and no goodbyes. As quickly as they began, Roger's days and nights of torment were over.

I don't know whether to laugh or cry. I suppose I better call the Camerlengo and let him know Novara has left.

Roger walked back to the door and reached over to flip off the light switch, making a mental note to say something to the cleaning staff about the cobweb stretching between the lampshade and the wall.

The room was dark and the door nearly shut before Roger burst back into the room. His hand shaking, he turned the light back on.

The web was so elegant in its design. The outer lines circled the rest of the pattern, holding in the straight lines and completing the outside. But it was the lines themselves he stared at, noticing how they fanned out from the center of the spider's trap, allowing the creator to sit in the middle and still know everything happening in the entire web.

The web was a miracle of nature and beautiful in its design and function.

The web was a pattern of life and death.

The web was a pattern he had seen before.

The pattern looked like the lines on the map in the task force room at the police station.

Roger sprinted down the hallway.

CHAPTER 45

NEW YORK, EARLY FRIDAY MORNING

"Dammit!" Morgan reached out for the wall, another person, anything to grab onto. She touched only air.

She went down on one knee as her foot continued to slide on blood-soaked garbage on the alley pavement. Only someone grabbing her by the collar kept her from putting her hand down into the gore and trash, or worse, falling face first onto the victim.

"I'm sorry, Lieutenant," Frank said from behind her as he helped her back to her feet. "I didn't mean to grab you anywhere… you know."

"Holy crap, Frank," she replied with a snort. "Not even your mother would complain about you touching the back of my neck. Helluva catch, though. Thanks."

"I thought you were all the way in it, that's for sure."

"Don't move!" Overholt said as he stepped over to a plastic tub. A few seconds later he was moving toward Morgan with a large evidence bag. "Give me your pants."

Morgan felt her mouth drop open. "You… you want my pants?" she stammered.

"Lieutenant, you have blood from the crime scene soaking into your pants. Not only do I need to bag-and-tag them for evidence, I don't think you want a stranger's blood up against your skin. Do you have any open cuts on your legs?"

"No, no cuts that I can think of," Morgan answered, thankful for once she had not been very diligent about shaving her legs since this case began. She was already unbuckling her belt, a touch of panic making her fingers fumble with the clasp. "What in the hell am I supposed to do? Run for the car once I'm naked?"

"No need for that," Overholt said. He turned to his assistant.

"Tammy, go get another set of coveralls and a pair of booties. I think I see blood on her shoes, too."

"Come here, Frank." He had pivoted away as soon as Morgan reached for her belt. She already had one leg out of her pants when he turned to look at her and she could see the red rising in his cheeks in the harsh light of the portable lamps. "Stand beside me and at least block the view of me from the street." He quickly moved beside her and faced toward the opening of the alley. A few moments later Tammy returned with the coveralls and the slip-on booties. Morgan dressed as quickly as possible and soon looked just like Overholt and the other technicians.

"It could have been worse," Morgan said. "David could have been here." She noticed Frank's furrowed eyebrows. "He never would have let me live this down," she explained.

"Not that, ma'am. I was wondering what you were doing so close to the body."

Morgan waved at the wall above the victim. "I thought I saw writing, but now I think it was just splatter."

Although Overholt had appeared engrossed with his examination of the victim, he immediately stood up and shined a hand-held light on the wall. "Where did you think you saw writing, Lieutenant?"

Morgan pointed at a couple of spots but they quickly decided the splotches were just that—splatters of blood from the vicious attack. Overholt, however, told his people to begin a thorough search for writing.

"What've we got, Frank?" Morgan asked, trying to take her mind off how awkward she felt in the very thin, nearly see-through tech clothes.

Frank flipped open his notebook. "The victim was Sara 'Sissy' Tutino. She was a bartender right here at the Pale Moon Saloon. Stepped outside a little before midnight for a smoke and never went back inside. The owner came out about a half-hour later and found her." Frank looked back up at Morgan. "He said he thought he saw something fly away as he came out the door."

"Lieutenant!" They both turned to look at Overholt as he walked toward them. "Thompson found it," he continued. "He found 'toldot' scratched into the door frame of the bar."

A heavy silence weaved its way around the trio, pulling them all into its tightening embrace.

"We missed him," Morgan said after a few seconds. "Dammit! We had one last chance to catch the bastard and we missed it." She sighed as she straightened up, stretching her back. "Now, if our theory is right, tomorrow we won't be looking for a body. Instead, we'll be digging through buildings and apartments in search of a kidnapping victim. That's going to be damn tough unless we get lucky on the genealogy side."

"What do you want to do, Lieutenant?"

She shrugged at Frank. He was so reliable, ready to plug forward despite the long odds. "Unless we're looking at something new here," she paused while Overholt shook his head silently, "then we might as well go back to the precinct house and see what we can come up with for tomorrow. My apartment isn't far from here, so you can drop me off, Frank. That'll give me a chance to grab a shower and change my clothes. I'll just catch a taxi then and meet you and David back in the task force room. Let's keep working the problem, guys."

CHAPTER 46

NEW YORK, EARLY FRIDAY MORNING

Roger walked quickly into the task force command center but he was not too fast for David. The FBI agent was on the telephone but he looked up immediately and waved the priest closer.

"Hello, Father," he said as he disconnected his cell phone. "That was our friends from the Israeli embassy."

"Are they going to be any help?" Roger asked.

"Oh, they're already sending us reams of information based upon the Perez ancestry, but I don't know how much help it's going to be. They've got branches of the family tree going through France, Eastern Europe, Germany, and Saudi Arabia. They even show one line through County Clare in Ireland. I think that's where Morgan's family is from originally. I'll have to ask her when she comes back."

Another piece of the puzzle fell into place for Roger, the words adding more pounds to the weight crushing his chest. He collapsed into the chair beside him, the wooden legs screeching across the floor as he struggled to gulp in a breath.

"Father, are you all right? Isn't it very late for you to be out?"

"Where is Morgan?" Roger asked, ignoring the agent's concern for his health. "You said, 'when she comes back.' Is she gone?"

"You'll know soon enough anyway. She's on the scene of another murder. We had another attack. We found the toldot, too."

Roger jerked upright. "Where? Show me where!"

David stared at the priest for several seconds, the tick of the cheap wall clock the only sound between them. When he finally moved, he walked slowly with his head slightly turned so Roger was always visible out of the corner of his eye. "Right here."

More weights were added.

Now David moved quickly. He whirled to face the priest. "You know something, Father. What is it?"

Roger wiped a hand across his forehead. His palm slid through a layer of sweat he wiped off onto his pants. "It's so obvious. For the past week, we've had a man staying with us at the cathedral. He is from the Vatican but something is… something is wrong with him." Roger paused before taking the final plunge. "For the past two nights, I have stood outside an apartment building with this man until long after midnight on orders directly from the Vatican. We were also at the place where the two girls were attacked on Monday, the apartment of the husband and wife on Sunday, and the police brought him home last Friday morning at dawn."

"You were the priest they saw at the scene of the two girls?"

Roger nodded. "Draw the line connecting the last two murders, David."

The agent turned and used a marker to draw a fourth intersecting line.

"It's been right there in front of you the whole time," Roger continued. "Where all the lines meet is the apartment building we've been watching the last two nights. He knows. Somehow, he knows what the killer wants, where he is going, who he chooses to kill. He claims—and the Vatican backs him up—he was sent here to fight evil, his words and theirs. Your killer is the so-called evil he has been chasing. It flew over us one night and scared me out of ten years of my life. I would have been surprised if County Clare was not on the list of places for a limb of the Perez family tree." Roger looked David straight in the eye. "The murder lines all intersect at Morgan's apartment building. That is where we have been the last two nights. He thinks the evil is after Morgan."

David's face contorted, mouth flying open while he blinked in rapid succession. "No, it can't. Father, it's all just a coincidence. How could he know anything? Look, where is he? We can get this all cleared up."

"He's gone. I came here because he has packed everything he had with him and left. He even took the knife."

David stood up. "Knife? What knife?"

Roger shook his head slowly. "I never got a real good look at it, mostly just glimpses. It was some sort of religious relic. The blade was curved a little and unbelievably white. I don't think it was metal. Maybe bone."

David yanked his cell phone from his pocket and thumb-flipped through his contact list. He was mumbling but the words were so soft Roger could not make out what he was saying. The agent found the number he was looking for and touched the screen.

"Zig? Ziggy, it's David. I'm in New York working a multiple. Yeah, it's bad. Listen, I need you to check TSA records for a U.S. entry and I do not have time for normal channels. Mmm, hmm. Thanks. Last Thursday into New York. His name is… hang on. Father, what's the man's name?"

"Greg Novara."

"Greg Novara. He was probably in diplomatic under a Vatican passport. I need to know everything about him and anything he brought into the country. And Zig, I've got nine dead here. I need this yesterday. Yeah, this phone. Thanks." David disconnected.

"You say he cleared out?" he asked Roger. "Do you think he'd try to leave the country? Maybe go back to Italy?"

Roger shook his head. "I don't know where he'll go when this is finished, but I can just about guarantee it will not be back to the Vatican. Why?"

"Father, our victims were all killed with what appears to be a curved bone knife. Now you tell me about a man with just such a weapon, a man that has something wrong with him, a man who is 'hunting evil,' and he has been to maybe half the murder scenes—of course I want to know where he is at. Did it ever occur to you he might be our killer?"

"He couldn't be," Roger answered. "He was with me for hours leading up to the husband and wife murder and we were blocks away when it happened. The girls were already on the ground when we found them. The last two nights he was with me at Morgan's apartment. He couldn't be the killer."

David rubbed his hand through his hair. "Well, maybe he has a partner. How else could he have known where the murders would take place? Did he talk to anyone, call anyone? Did anyone come to visit him at the cathedral? Think, Father. We've got to find him before tomorrow night when our killer goes after the mother of the Mashiach."

It was Roger's turn to gape in disbelief. "David, there's no tomorrow. Novara thought the killer was after Morgan. That makes her the mother of the Mashiach. She is the one he believes is from the Perez line and that might actually be possible with the family tree going through County Clare. Morgan is the live mother and her apartment is the center of the spider web for all these murders. And if I know Novara, he is going to Morgan, too. The final attack will happen tonight."

The two men stared at each other as the seconds ticked away. They both jumped when David's cell phone rang. "Yeah, Zig, what've you got for me? Mmm hmm, yeah, okay. What about the knife? Okay, thanks." The blood drained from David's face when he looked back up at Roger. "Novara was on a Vatican passport, the knife was listed as a holy relic, and the blade was made of bone." He reached for his phone again. "We've got to find out where Morgan is."

"I can answer that," Frank said as he walked through the doorway to the command center. "The Lieutenant got blood on her clothes at the scene and she wanted to shower and change. I just dropped her off at her apartment."

David and Roger looked at each other before they ran for the door.

CHAPTER 47

NEW YORK, EARLY FRIDAY MORNING

Morgan was halfway across her living room and reaching for the lamp switch when she saw the night move, blacker than any shadow, and she realized she was not alone. As her hand flew to the gun at her side, a hiss shattered the silence of the apartment.

The Glock never cleared its holster.

Greg slid the superintendent's key slowly into the lock, each scrape of metal on metal sounding like a thunderclap to his ears.

This was the night. Either his responsibility in this centuries-old struggle ended or started again with more years of waiting for the nightmare to continue. He felt this was the night. But now, with the chase so close to finally being over, he did not want something as stupid as a noisy lock to give the beast a warning and a chance to get away again.

The deadbolt slid smoothly and he reached for the doorknob. The latch gave a little before catching, then sliding out from the jamb.

Greg stopped when the door opened a couple of inches, unsure of whether the amount of time he had needed to take the key from the building superintendent had allowed the beast to beat him to the woman. Rhythmic grunting and the sound of furniture creaking told him he was too late. He squeezed his eyes shut for a few seconds, sorry about the inevitable outcome for the woman. The police lieutenant was no London prostitute or prospective nun volunteering to give her life for the cause. She was just a woman who had dreams of a husband and kids, a career, and a normal life. More than that, he had hoped to save her if for no other reason than the fact she was Father Greene's friend. Despite what the other man thought, he had truly enjoyed the walks and conversations with the priest.

Greg swung open the door a few more inches and stepped sideways into a tiny foyer. The next room was dark except for the lamp lying across the arm of the couch, the shade crumpled on one side and pushed at an angle into the cushion. In the shadows beyond, Greg saw the beast half-hunched over the dining table, thrusting into the woman lying on top.

He did not throw out a challenge. He did not taunt his ancient enemy. He did not cry out for the incubus to stop or plead for Morgan's life. With the beast turned away, he did not take the time to do anything but think of the centuries his fate had been tied to the evil before him. Greg took two running steps, jumped on the arm of the couch and launched himself into the air over its back.

The incubus heard his approach. But Greg was moving so fast, the beast was only able to turn slightly as the man flew toward him, the blade raised above his head for a two-handed stab.

But the small move was enough. The relic, which had been aimed for the middle of the beast's back, missed its mark when a wing beat into Greg's body, sweeping him sideways and out of reach.

The attack was not lost, however. The knife stabbed through the other wing and continued on to bite into the shoulder beneath. The blade buried itself deep, twisting from Greg's hands when he tumbled into the chairs on the other side of the incubus.

Tar-like blood oozed from the wounds, starting green fires wherever it fell onto the table or the carpet. The incubus screamed. Not a challenge or a cry of victory as so many victims had heard throughout the centuries. This was a cry of anguish and anger, fear and hatred.

"Cambion! This is the end! I try to teach you all you could be and this is how you repay the debt. I will repair the toldot again, give life to another son. But this one will not be for your deceiving light. This one is for this world and he will rule the earth as he sees fit."

Greg untangled himself from the chair but stayed crouched on one knee. "You're right," he said, the green light dancing in his eyes. "Our hunt does end tonight. And tomorrow, after both of you are dead, I will finally have the life to live that was taken from me."

Drool escaped the beast's lips as it laughed. "How, half-breed? I can still feel your father's bone sticking in my back." Greg felt his mouth open and the beast laughed again. "They did not tell you? Of course not! Those men that spread the lies of the light would never have told you all the truth. The knife you have carried for centuries was made from your father's bone. They never told you and yet you fought for them. Bah!"

Greg and the incubus stared at each other. Rising smoke swirled in the few feet separating them, thickening as the green flames spread into oranges and reds. But while the smoke danced and wound, the old enemies stayed perfectly still, two beings trapped on the edge of the world and eternity.

They leaped at the same time, the incubus with both front claws grasping for the man, Greg with his empty left hand reaching for the beast's throat.

The two met in mid-air. Two talons left gashes on the side of Greg's face and blood poured from the wounds. Another set of claws ripped through the jacket into his shoulder, sending bolts of pain down Greg's left arm and stopping his hand only inches from the beast's gnarl-skinned neck.

But Greg's right hand was no longer empty. In his hand he grasped an object—white but not gleaming like its cousin, raw and unpolished without the keen edge. But it still had a point that was sharper than any human could have made.

Greg held the beast's talon he had sliced off during the battle in the alley.

He twisted against the incubus's claws, his momentum pushing them farther into his shoulder so he could move closer. Greg used the movement and drove the talon point into the beast's chest with the strength only hate and redemption could supply.

Again a scream vibrated the room but the sound tailed off at the end, stopping with a gurgle. The incubus staggered back on its haunches, dragging Greg with him until the claws finally released his shoulder. His enemy wobbled for a moment on uncertain legs and then toppled over to the floor. Now the drops of blood became a river, oozing like molten lava into a green stream of fire.

"Cambion," the beast said, its voice weak against the growing crackle of flames. "Will you teach my son?"

Greg shook his head, unsure at first if the incubus could see him through the rising smoke. "No. I will kill him."

"Then it is over. The toldot is broken. The Light wins."

Greg walked around the body and reached through the green flames, pulling the knife from the beast's back. More blood flowed from the wound and added to the fires.

"What was that?"

Greg was startled by Morgan's voice and he looked at her trying to lever herself up onto one elbow.

"Oh my god!" she yelled. "The fires! We've got to get out of here now!" Only then did she look to see the tattered remains of the coveralls, shredded into ribbons down the front and exposing her body. "No, no!"

"It will be all right," Greg said, his voice a calm brook against the inferno raging around them. "I will help you get away from here. Look at me."

Their eyes met and joy spread over her face. He pushed her gently back onto the table top and offered her what he had given to very few of the women down through the centuries—comfort. She smiled.

He raised the knife above his head.

They saw the smoke leaking under Morgan's apartment door but the trio did not break stride. Roger had pulled Frank up the last flight of stairs and now he was several strides behind David. The FBI agent swung into a little arc, like a baseball player rounding first, before turning hard and barreling into the apartment.

The door must not have been completely latched because it burst away from the jamb, slamming into the wall of the foyer. Smoke billowed into the hallway, followed by a blast of heat, while David fell into the gray beyond.

He rose to his feet as Roger and Frank ran into the apartment. Now the gray smoke twisted with orange and green fire. Even through the gloom, Roger recognized the figure standing over Morgan, white knife raised above his head. "Novara, no!" David and Frank did not bother with shouts. They fired at the same time, two guns spouting their own flames and death into the room. Novara jerked sideways and stared at the trio for a moment before he tumbled backward over the green glow and disappeared into the flames behind it.

David and Roger ran forward. Morgan was already attempting to climb down off the table, weak kneed and unstable. David grabbed a blanket off the back of a recliner and wrapped her in it before sweeping her up into his arms and moving through the smoke toward the door.

But Roger's thoughts were already on the body on the floor. He had to know.

Novara was still out of sight beyond the flames and Roger had no idea if the man was alive or dead on the other side. But the body lying by the table transfixed him, tying him to the spot where he stood.

Bathed in green and orange flames, the corpse was the most beautiful, perfect man he had ever seen. He looked like he had once been covered in some sort of grotesque leather, pockmarked and scarred, hiding the beauty that lay beneath. Wherever the leather had burned away, only perfection showed now. Roger felt a vise tighten on his arm.

"Come on, Father!" Frank yelled. "We've got to go now!"

"No! We need to find Novara!" Roger screamed back, gesturing to the other side of the body. "He wanted to be returned to his village in Italy. I promised."

"It's too late, Father!" Frank pulled on his arm again.

Roger chanced one last look at the man and then for Novara through the flames. He turned and ran with Frank toward the door.

David and Morgan were not in sight when the two men burst out of the smoke into the street. Roger, in between coughing fits, caught himself staring back up at the building, trying to understand what had happened.

The questions were not just about the last few minutes or hours, but days. Questions about Novara, some no longer important and others that leaped out new, rolled through his mind. The more he thought, the more his stomach roiled at the secrecy of the Camerlengo and the Vatican. For a moment, he thought he might throw up on the asphalt.

Anger quickly replaced the nausea, however. Why had they thought it so important to keep him in the dark when he was doing their work? How had Novara known the man on the floor? Was the man the killer? Was he the evil? How long had the Church known? Why had Vatican officials kept those secrets, the secrets that had almost killed his friend?

He reached up and ripped the collar from his neck, staring at the band in his palm. No longer white, the ring was now stained gray from a mixture of sweat and soot with smudges ground into the material. Is this how the Camerlengo saw the world? Shades of gray with no white or black? He dropped the collar to the street as the questions continued to swirl in his mind.

"Father Greene," David said, interrupting the priest's thoughts. "They are taking Morgan to the hospital. We really need for you to tell us everything you can about Novara and the other man in the apartment."

For a moment, he just stared at the collar lying in the street. "Roger," he finally told the FBI agent. "Just call me Roger."

AFTER

NEW YORK, NINE MONTHS LATER

Roger walked into the crowded waiting room and smiled. Morgan's brothers and their wives were along one wall while her mother sat in the opposite corner, the smile on her face offset by the wringing of her hands. A gray-haired woman sat beside her and talked quietly, reaching over and patting her on the arm every once in a while. She must have been Frank's wife because he was also there, silently pacing back and forth with Morgan's father, the two of them walking an imaginary track in the middle of the room.

"Hey, Roger," Casey said. "Glad you could rip yourself away from those college girls long enough to see how your first girlfriend is doing." His wife, Julie, slapped him on the arm but then her hand returned to rest on her stomach that obviously had its own baby growing inside.

Roger laughed along with everyone else. "You're the one that should be paying attention, Casey," he said. "If that ends up being a girl, you'll be the one worried about all the boyfriends."

That set off another round of jokes from the brothers while the sisters-in-law, Julie included, stuck their heads together in a quieter conversation.

Roger nodded to Mr. Flaherty and Frank as he walked to the corner and sat down beside Morgan's mother. Her smile faltered for less than a second but the slip had been enough for him to notice. He wondered if she would ever forgive him for giving up the priesthood. "Hello, Cathleen. Mrs. Mason. Is there any news?"

Morgan's mother shook her head. "No, Fath… Roger. We haven't heard anything from David or the doctors since she arrived at the hospital."

"I'm sure everything is fine."

He was about to say more, offer words of encouragement, a bit of scripture—the process all still came so easily to him. But he no longer wore the collar, so he simply patted her on the leg and leaned back against the wall.

While he doubted Mrs. Flaherty would ever fully accept his resignation from the priesthood, his own parents had already moved on. They had always been very proud of his accomplishments as a priest, but early in the fall, as he and his father sat on the front step with the Boston College football game on in the background, his dad had mentioned it would be nice to have a grandson to take to the games someday.

In the initial moments after his soot-covered collar fell to the street on that night months earlier, Roger had felt good about his decision. Within a few hours, however, questions began to creep into his thoughts.

He had no doubt he had been called by God to the priesthood. He had loved his work within the Church from his first day. Was it right to throw away years of work and sacrifice over his frustration— no, disappointment—with the institution behind the religion?

Those questions disappeared quickly. After telling David everything he could remember about Novara, he had stumbled into his bed by late morning.

That afternoon, however, his telephone woke him from a sound sleep. On the other end was Cardinal Atchison with plenty of questions about what had happened. Still groggy, he had told the tale of the night before—the race to the apartment, the green flames, David and Frank firing at Novara, the beautiful body on the floor— but the real issue quickly became apparent when the Cardinal had almost no interest in what had happened to Novara. He asked only one question about the stranger: Had the body been recovered yet by the authorities? Atchison did not ask about Morgan's welfare, either.

The Cardinal was also in no mood to answer Roger's questions. The call had been on speakerphone at the Vatican end and Roger suspected other people had been listening the entire time. Pauses before some questions as if they had been hastily written down for Atchison to read, a muffled cough in the background, and the rustling of papers—all small clues that more than one set of ears were listening intently to what Roger had to say. But there was never an admission others were present. The deception and lack of concern for Novara and Morgan finally made Roger so mad he had hung up the phone while Atchison was still speaking.

But the next day when he stopped at the hospital to see Morgan, his decision was set in stone. David told him in the hallway outside her room that Vatican officials had done everything but disavow knowledge of Novara's existence. They finally admitted he had once been a priest from a small Italian village but he had dropped from the service many years earlier. They claimed he had been allowed to keep his diplomatic passport out of courtesy, because of a favor he had performed for the former Pope. They also grudgingly admitted he had been used as a courier once or twice but he was no longer employed in such a way. However, they were aware a holy relic knife had been missing for some time so they requested, formally through the Secretary of State, to have it returned if it was found.

The Camerlengo made no such request for Novara's body.

The Vatican officials also flatly denied they had any idea who the other body might have been in the fire. They did request, again through diplomatic channels, to examine the remains with their own doctors, however. Not that the request mattered since nothing had been recovered from the burned-out shell of the apartment building.

Of course, the kicker to the whole situation was the little information received had been very difficult to gather. Apparently, the Vatican claimed the Camerlengo did not speak a word of English and he had insisted on a translator. David told Roger this last part with a disgusted shake of his head since it was well known Nowaski had studied for his doctorate in England and had given interviews in the past—ones that could still be seen on YouTube—in fluent English.

The upshot of the whole ordeal was the Vatican did not care if Novara and Morgan were dead or alive and Roger had been tossed aside to fend for himself.

The continuing lies and secrecy told Roger his decision to quit had been correct. Even so, nearly two weeks later he was still sleeping in his little room in the priests' quarters with no idea what he was going to do with the rest of his life.

That was when he had received a telephone call from the dean of the history department at City University of New York. They had served on two panels together and discussed how religious histories still guided a large number of countries in the Middle East in modern times. The university had recently received a large endowment to be used for expanding the history department and after reading about Roger's adventures and help with the police in stopping the serial killer—somehow a reporter found out about his help in deciphering the toldot angle and wrote an article that read like he had been a lot more involved and helpful than he believed he had been in reality—the dean wondered if the former priest would be interested in turning the panel into a course. He would also have the freedom to develop a class on using religious writings as historical documents and several other ideas they discussed on the phone. The dean offered him an associate professorship and a fast track toward tenure and Roger accepted the proposal on the spot.

He was six weeks into teaching the fall semester when he discovered the CUNY president and Cardinal Atchison had been on the baseball team together at Notre Dame. Also, no one really knew who had provided the endowment, only that the contributor was a large organization wanting to remain anonymous.

But by then, Roger did not care. He loved teaching the students and his new found public notoriety led to full classes with a waiting list. On a personal note, he had also recently eaten lunch a few times with an English professor who had taught overseas in Cairo where she had grown to love their ancient writings. Certainly the meals had not been dates but they were still the first step toward his father having someone to take to BC football games. No, his only regret about quitting was not being able to preside over the ceremony when David and Morgan had remarried.

Roger sat beside Cathleen for nearly an hour before he stood up and joined Mr. Flaherty and Frank in their silent pacing. When he tired of that exercise, he sat and talked quietly with Morgan's brothers. Their loud laughs and jokes had long since died away to be replaced with the sound of tapping feet and glances at the clock. Hours had passed since Roger arrived at the hospital. Something was wrong and everyone in the room knew it.

At almost midnight, a nurse appeared in the doorway. "Is Roger here?" she asked.

Even when he was still a few feet away, he could tell she was tired by the stoop of her shoulders and the way she half-leaned against the jamb. He followed her out under the brighter lights of the hallway. Sounds swirled and flowed around them but to his ears they were muffled noises and only the nurse's voice was clear.

"Mr. Kelly wanted me to talk to you," she said. "He said you used to be a priest and would understand what to do." She stopped and pulled the surgical cap from her head, taking the time to run the back of her hand against her forehead. "It's not good."

"The baby?"

"No," she said at once with a shake of her head. "The baby is doing great. He is one strong little bugger and he's doing just fine. We just need to get him out."

"Then it's Morgan."

This time she nodded. "Yes. It seems like the closer the baby is to being born, the worse she gets. We were going to try a C-section about an hour ago but her platelets started acting funny and we were afraid she was going to bleed out so we stopped. We've given her some medication to slow down the process but this baby is going to be born and when he is, it does not look good for the mother."

"What does David want me to do?"

"Prepare them," the nurse said, tilting her head toward the waiting room. "He's afraid to leave her, just in case, but it is really only a matter of time. He apologized but he said you would know how to handle it."

Roger nodded. Yes, he knew how to handle this situation. He knew how to handle it because he had been trained by the Church and he had been in this position before. He had told mothers their sons would not be coming home from war. He had told husbands they would never hug their wives again. Yes, he had been in this situation before and he had hated the responsibility every time.

More hours passed. The crying in the waiting room had stopped after Roger explained the circumstances but the silence gripping the room now was worse than the wailing. He had gone from group to group after his talk, offering up prayers for Morgan and the baby, giving words of comfort, and talking about hope. By now, even Mr.

Flaherty and Frank had finally settled into chairs, giving up their pacing.

That left Roger alone with his thoughts of Novara and the madness he had taken part in months earlier. His initial reaction had been to try to forget the night the other man had rambled on about babies killing mothers and the evil they would become. At the time, the mutterings had been one more sign of the madness in the man, but now, Roger was not so sure. As the minutes dragged on, he wondered if there had actually been something to the insanity-laced tirade or if this was all just a coincidence.

The shadow fell across the carpet to Roger's feet before he heard anything. He looked up and saw David standing in the doorway.

"She's gone," he said between sobs. "Morgan's gone."

Mrs. Flaherty screamed and nearly fell out of her chair while her daughters-in-law rushed to her side. The men of the family were less demonstrative but no less affected. They all sat still, staring at nothing. All but Casey. He immediately walked to his wife and stood with his hand on her shoulder while she put both of her hands on her growing stomach.

Roger walked to David and gave him a hug, one the FBI agent returned with the power of a starving man holding onto a loaf of bread.

"What about the baby, David?" Roger asked. "The nurse said earlier he was doing fine but we haven't heard anything since then."

David stepped back and wiped away his tears with both hands. A smile lit up his tired face. "He's beautiful, Roger. Even the nurses said he was the most beautiful baby they'd ever seen. You should see him." The smile faded as he glanced up at the clock. "Just after six. Mom's flight does not leave until eight-thirty. I better try to reach her so she doesn't walk into this without knowing what's happened." He took a deep breath and released it with a little shudder at the end. "Go see him, Roger. They were taking him to the nursery when I came here."

Roger nodded and walked down the hallway while David went the other way in search of a telephone. After a quick stop at the nurse's station, he learned the nursery was one floor up. He pressed the button for the elevator and absentmindedly noticed one car went down past his floor as another climbed toward him. His thoughts were still on the baby, Morgan, and even Novara as he stepped inside the elevator and pushed the button for the next floor.

He heard the first scream before the doors opened. The second echoed in his ears as he stepped into the hallway, two hesitant steps that changed quickly into a sprint. Roger could already see four people lying on the floor and a fifth, a nurse, stood screaming as she pointed in horror at something he could not see from his angle.

Roger hesitated over the first person only long enough to see there were no wounds, no blood, and that they were still breathing. In fact, all four appeared to only be sleeping, smiling through a good nap. He noticed at least two doctors and several nurses running around a corner of the hall so he stepped forward to see what the nurse had been screaming at before she finally collapsed to her knees, her hands covering her eyes.

He looked through the long glass window at the rows of bassinettes filled with babies. Roger took only a moment to find the baby in the second row—a boy according to the blue blanket—the baby that would have been beautiful by any standards.

Beautiful except for the knife sticking out of its chest.

Beautiful except for the blood soaking into the blue blanket, turning it dark.

Roger did not need to check the nameplate to know this had been Morgan and David's son. He did not need to look because he recognized the stained leather on the hilt of the knife. He recognized the inch of gleaming white blade that had not been plunged into the newborn. It was the holy relic the Vatican barely acknowledged but would like to have sent back as soon as possible.

He staggered past the doctors and nurses as bile worked its way up his throat, hoping he would make the walk to the window at the end of the hall before he puked all over the floor. He missed by about four feet.

Once he was done throwing up what little was left of his supper and half-a-dozen cups of coffee, he stepped the rest of the way to the window, resting his forehead against the cool glass. After a minute, he raised his head and looked out at the new morning. Unlike the death and chaos still shaking the hospital behind him, Roger saw only the peace of an early winter morning outside. The sky had let loose with snow at some point during the night, a layer of white covering the dirt and filth of the city. The morning outside was so peaceful and so early just one person was in sight, a solitary figure walking away from the hospital, tracked by the only set of tracks disturbing the parking lot.

Roger noticed the man had stopped moving and was looking back up at the building. The long leather coat hid his body and an old-style fedora shadowed the man's face. Even so, it was easy to tell the man was staring straight at him.

Roger put his hands on the glass, his breath threatening to fog up the window. There was something familiar about the figure but he could not quite put his finger on what.

Then the man raised his right hand so he could drink out of a Styrofoam coffee cup.

Roger screamed as Novara turned and walked off into the snow.

ABOUT THE AUTHOR

Kirk Dougal has had fiction works appear in multiple anthologies and released his debut novel and the first book in the Fallen Angels trilogy, DREAMS OF IVORY AND GOLD, in May of 2014. The second novel, VALLEYS OF THE EARTH, is scheduled to publish in December of 2017 and the concluding chapter, THE DREAM OF SOLOMON, will be seen in 2018. He began his new series, The Dowland Cases, with RESET in May of 2017 and followed with QUEST CALL in October. The third book, GEMINI DIVIDED, is scheduled for a May 2018 release.

Kirk is currently working in a corporate position with a group of newspapers after serving as a group publisher and editor-in-chief. He lives in Ohio with his wife and four children. For more information on his writings or just to find out what he has been doing, you can find Kirk at his website, www.kirkdougal.com, or hanging out on Facebook and Twitter.

Curious about other Crossroad Press books?
Stop by our site:
http://store.crossroadpress.com
We offer quality writing
in digital, audio, and print formats.

Enter the code FIRSTBOOK
to get 20% off your first order from our store!
Stop by today!

Printed in Poland
by Amazon Fulfillment
Poland Sp. z o.o., Wrocław